His world's true history was lost in time, obscured by
tales of demons coming out of the sky when a red star
shone in the constellation Capricorn. The ancient stories were not myths, however; they were based on fact.
And when the red star reappeared, it was young Zorn
who had to face those terrifying legends come alive. For
though he was no warrior, he *was* heir to a long line of
"demon" fighters, honor-bound to protect his people.

DATE DUE

DEMON
MOON

BOOKS BY JACK WILLIAMSON

The Legion of Space
Darker Than You Think
The Green Girl
The Cometeers
One Against the Legion
Seetee Shock
Seetee Ship
Dragon's Island
The Legion of Time
Undersea Quest (with Frederik Pohl)
Dome Around America
Star Bridge (with James Gunn)
Undersea Fleet (with Frederik Pohl)
Undersea City (with Frederik Pohl)
The Trial of Terra
Golden Blood
The Reefs of Space (with Frederik Pohl)
Starchild (with Frederik Pohl)
The Reign of Wizardry
Bright New Universe
Trapped in Space
The Pandora Effect
Rogue Star (with Frederik Pohl)
People Machines
The Moon Children
H. G. Wells: Critic of Progress
The Farthest Star (with Frederik Pohl)
The Early Williamson
The Power of Blackness
The Best of Jack Williamson
Brother to Demons, Brother to Gods
The Alien Intelligence
The Humanoid Touch
The Birth of a New Republic (with Miles J. Breuer)
Manseed
Wall Around a Star (with Frederik Pohl)
The Queen of the Legion
Wonder's Child: My Life in Science Fiction (memoir)
Lifeburst
✱ Firechild
✱ Land's End (with Frederik Pohl)
Mazeway
The Singers of Time (with Frederik Pohl)
✱ Beachhead
✱ The Humanoids

✱ denotes a Tor book

DEMON MOON

Jack Williamson

TOR

A TOM DOHERTY ASSOCIATES BOOK NEW YORK

DEMON MOON

Copyright © 1994 by Jack Williamson

Edited by James Frenkel
Maps by Ellisa Mitchell
Design by Maura Fadden Rosenthal

A Tor Book
Published by Tom Doherty Associates, Inc.
175 Fifth Avenue
New York, N.Y. 10010

Tor ® is a registered trademark of Tom Doherty Associates, Inc.

ISBN 0-312-85718-7

Printed in the United States of America

For our Wednesday morning breakfast group:

Tracy LeCocq
Marcia Howl
Rick Hauptmann
Bob Huber

Demon Moon was invented for my own entertainment on long plane flights and long bus rides and long nights in strange hotels on a tour of China. The Dragon Mountains are the Himalayas, which we crossed on a cloudless winter day on a non-stop flight from Karachi to Beijing, and again in full moonlight on our return. I found the demons on the walls of a sandstone canyon near Beijing, carved there by Buddhist monks eight hundred years ago. A good deal of the beginning comes from my own earliest recollections, when the Mexican Revolution exiled us from my first home in a little grass-roofed rock house on a cattle ranch high in the Sierra Madre of Sonora, to a small farm in West Texas. The unicorns owe something to horses I used to know.

Contents

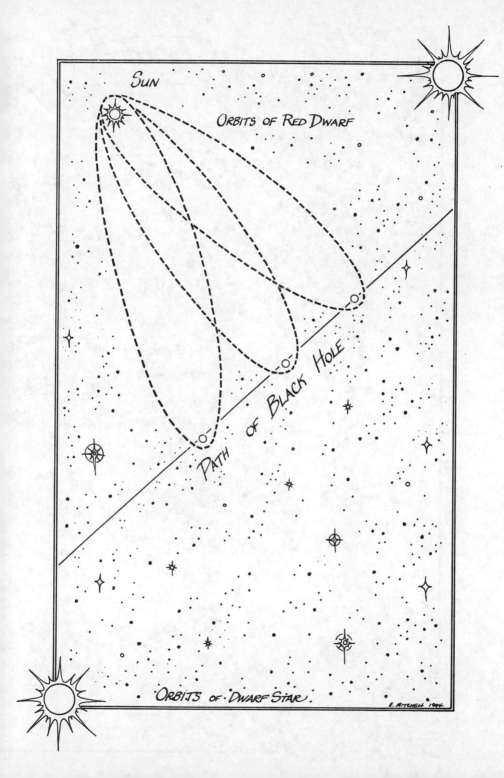

Sun

Orbits of Red Dwarf

Path of Black Hole

Orbits of Dwarf Star

E. Mitchell 1994

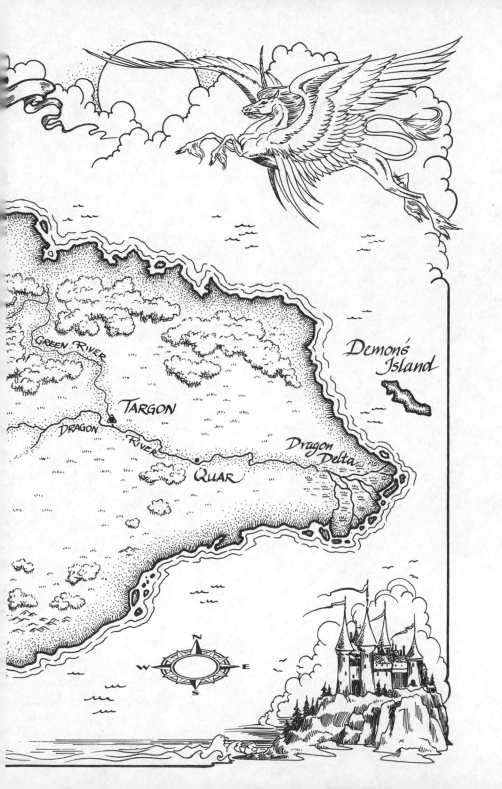

GREEN RIVER

Demon's
Island

TARGON

DRAGON
RIVER

Dragon
Delta

QUAR

N
W E
S

DEMON
MOON

Prologue:
The Wyvern Queen

"Save my husband!"

Kneeling barefoot at the earthen altar in the garden shrine on the great hall's roof, she whispered her prayer to the Three.

"Save him from the devil-god Xath. Save him from the were-wolves and wyvern and the dragons that rule them. Save him and all our world from the demons and the evil moon where they dwell."

Cupping her hands into the silver font to dip water for the hallowed soil, she bowed lower to kiss the grains of golden corn, the apple, and the rose: the sacred symbols of the Three. The sweetness of the bloom gave her courage to pull her boots on and walk out into the garden.

It was her own private place, sacred to her memories of Rendahl since they stood here for the wedding ceremony. She loved the luminous blooms, the feather-leafed ferns, the falling vines that draped the gravel oaths. It always restored her faith in the Mystic Three.

Surely they would hear her prayers.

It was nine days now since the raiding werewolves and the wyvern queen had called Rendahl away.

"Must you?" She had come with him to the flight stage that topped the castle's tallest tower. "Must you fly in this dreadful weather?"

Waiting for his answer, she snuggled close against him to escape the chill dawn wind. An angular, rangy man, he had the fair hair of the Vars. Weather had bleached his neat short beard to the color of bronze. He was already in flight leathers, and she caught the peppery unicorn scent. Silent for a moment, he shook his head and stood frowning at the cloud-banked north horizon.

"Joy Bird, you know I must." He liked to call her that, though her name was Eyna. "It's the bad winter itself that drives the creatures down out of their mountains to ravage the riding. I dreamed last night about the queen."

She shivered now, even here in the sheltered garden, remembering the moment.

"She came diving at me out of a storm." His voice was hushed, the dread of the dream still upon him. "A fearful thing, her black wings wide as the sky. Long black talons snatching at me, great fangs dripping blood.

"And I thought there was a man—"

He stopped to look down at her face, yet his blue Var eyes seemed blind to her, as if all they could see was that haunting nightmare.

"A serpent man," he whispered. "A black-robed priest of Xath, his bare head shaven and dyed the color of blood. I thought he was riding the wyvern, waving his black snake staff and yelling commands to a great pack of wolves hunting me over the snow."

He had felt her shudder.

"I'm sorry, Joy." He shrugged and gave her a suntanned grin. "The dream came out of the bad news we've had from the North and the rumors of a man with the wolves, but it was just a dream. Who believes in dreams?"

Mystics did, and she was more than half a Mystic. Rendahl was a Realist, a laughing skeptic of magic, but her father had been a professor of Mystic philosophy. She lived torn between the two beliefs, but dread felt like ice inside her as they stood waiting on the stage for the trainer to bring Zeldar, his great bay stallion.

"It hurts to leave you." His strong arms caught her closer. "More than ever now. But you know who I am and where my duty lies."

He was Rendahl ir Var, the lord of Wolver Riding and heir to all the noble generations of warrior Vars who had reconquered the rid-

ing from the wyvern and the werewolves and kept them hunted out
of it for so many centuries.

"I know," she whispered. "You warned me before we ever
married and conceived our son. The holy Three—" She had to
catch her breath. "The Three be with you!"

Too soon, the trainer brought Zeldar.

In the garden now, she remembered the feel of his lips when he
kissed her, the hot-scented wind from the unicorn's wings, the thundering hooves on the flight deck, and then her tears dissolving everything as he turned in the saddle to wave.

City-bred, she had grown up in Targon, far off in the long-settled
lowlands, and met Rendahl when he came there to school. Wolver
Riding was a stern frontier, still alien to her. Dragonrock castle had
depressed her at first, because it seemed so cruelly prisonlike. It was
all gray granite, the huge roughhewn blocks as immense as if its
builders had been actual giants. Now, however, she had learned to
see those same towering walls with a mix of awe and love. They had
Rendahl's rugged strength. She needed that strength now, since the
old midwife listened at her belly and promised her a son.

"Care for yourself." Old Nanda had scolded her for flying.
"Care for the baby! He'll be the next Var."

"I do care," she answered. "But Vars ride unicorns."

She had come out this morning ready to fly, in white kidskin and
the white fur parka that covered her dark hair when she slipped it
on. Falcon Child had been Rendahl's first gift, and she had learned
to sing the flight commands. The tawny-winged filly was spirited
enough, already well trained and gentle in the air. Soaring on her
had been pure delight. At least so long as he soared beside her.

She was turning to leave the garden when a far shout stopped
her.

Or had it been a shout? At first she wasn't sure. Craning to look
up, she saw men running along the edge of the high flight stage.
One was pointing into the narrow scrap of sky above the parapets.

Dazzled at first, she squinted and found a dark fleck against the sky.

Zeldar? Bringing Rendahl home?

Knuckles against her teeth, she stood breathless, watching till the descending unicorn was gone beyond the battlements, still too high for her to recognize. Louder shouts echoed against the walls. Shivering to the memory of that evil dream, she rushed back into the donjon and down the corridor to the elevator.

The machine was new to the ancient castle, a gift from Rendahl when she told him she was pregnant. Parts for it had been shipped on the steam trains that came as far as Dorth; freight wagons had hauled it up the rugged scarp into the highlands; and engineers had come from Targon to install a turbine in the river for power.

All that was Realist science, and not entirely welcome here. Nanda still refused to enter it, puffing and groaning as she climbed the endless stairs, whispering that electricity was dangerous magic stolen from the devils of Xath. But Eyna felt thankful now for the speed of the little cage, lifting her fast to the stage. Rendahl had recruited all the unicorns and their trainers to support his expedition, and the crew house was empty.

She darted out of it, against a gust of cold north wind. A shock of disappointment stopped her. The incoming unicorn had landed. She saw it kneeling for its rider to slide down across the folded wing. It was not the bay Zeldar, but a shining black stallion. It looked exhausted, panting heavily and flecked with white foam, its bright-horned head sagging almost to the deck.

Not Rendahl, the rider was a brown, scrawny, tiny man, his flight leathers worn and soiled and splashed with something dark as drying blood. He limped away from the wing and turned to sing to the unicorn, voicing the notes with a melodious power that surprised her. The unicorn whickered gently, lurched back to its feet, and followed him to a water trough at the end of the stage.

She waited while he unsaddled it and watched it nuzzle his face, with a soft whinny for him, before it dipped its splendid head to the basket of suncorn. She ran to meet him when he turned toward the crew house.

"Lady—" He stopped as if astonished to recognize her. "You're the Lady Rider?"

"I am," she said. "Expecting my husband."

"Sorry, Lady." She remembered him when she heard his voice and saw the face beneath the blackened blood that had oozed from a raw gash across the side of his hairless head. "I'm Scorth, the rider's trainer. I wish I brought better news."

"Is something—" A sudden lump ached in her throat. "Is something wrong?"

"Nothing good. Nothing good."

"Has something happened to him?"

"I had to leave him, Lady, if you'll forgive me." He was staring past her toward the crew house, and she saw him swaying on his feet. "In a bad spot, Lady, far out beyond the wyvern border."

She followed him back to the crew house and made him let her clean his wound. It was shallow, but she put a bandage on it.

"A sad story, Lady." Able at last to tell it, he sat on the side of a bunk and sipped a bowl of yara tea from the urn steaming on the heater. "And none of it the Lord Rider's fault. I beg you not to blame him. Or me for the news I bring."

"Is he—" she whispered. "Is he—"

Her voice was gone.

"Alive, Lady, by the grace of the sacred Three. Alive when I left him, but—" He shook his head and flinched as if it hurt. "What can I say?"

"Tell me!" she begged him. "I want to know—everything!"

"If you'll forgive my rude way of talk." Hairless as his scalp, his face was round and smooth, almost a child's. His eyes were an odd yellow color, and they blinked at her owlishly. "I speak more to unicorns than men."

"Just tell me where my husband is."

"Far west, Lady . . ." He paused to sip his tea. "In the high cold heart of the Dragon Mountains, where we followed the invaders. A dreadful wilderness of wolves and wyvern and ice that never thaws."

"What took him there?"

"Pursuit." Deliberately he chose his words. "Pursuit of that fearful werewolf pack. They'd come down across the west border, in flight from this ugly winter. Hundreds of wolves, the wyvern queen with them. Commanding them, I think. You've heard of the wyvern?"

"My husband spoke of the queen." She felt sick. "A flying monster."

"Enormous!" He spread his arms to show the creature's size. "With two of her half-grown wycks and her legion of wolves. Armed as they never were, because a human renegade was with them. A red-skulled priest of Xath; we saw him riding one of the wycks."

She shivered, remembering Rendahl's dream.

"They had weapons they never did before. They've always grown more cunning, with what they learn from the wolves who had been men, though nobody knows how much of the man lasts through the change. Now the Lord Rider thinks the serpent priests have been arming and instructing them. These had spears and powerful bows and a kind of clumsy catapult. One of their missiles hit me."

He touched the bandage gingerly.

"Somebody has taught them fire. They set grass fires to drive cattle into their traps. Shot fire arrows into straw roofs to burn helpless settlers out of their homes. And ate them in the snow."

"Dreadful!" she breathed. "But about my husband?"

"A warrior, Lady." His blood-streaked baby face tried to smile. "A noble warrior! Never doubt it."

"So what happened?"

"We flew against them." He gestured north and west. "Half a dozen of us on unicorns. We crossed fire-black deserts that had been farms and ranches. Found gnawed bones scattered over the ice. Overtook the wyvern and their wolves near Battle Bluff, the outpost town they had surrounded. We fought them there."

"My husband?" She had to prompt him. "He fought the wyvern?"

"And the werewolves, Lady. Fought them with the courage born in the Vars. He carried a rifle, a heavy three-shot weapon he brought from the lowlands. You must understand that the unicorns themselves are peaceful. They don't like killing or even the noise of guns. The rest of them carried only supplies for the men on the ground, but the great Zeldar had learned your noble husband's daring.

"He let the rider use the rifle and lead our little force to relieve the town. The wyvern queen and her wycks came to meet us, screeching in the wind. Monsters, Lady! Even the half-grown wycks looked larger than our unicorns. One of them dived to meet the rider, black talons spread and red jaws wide, bellowing to frighten us.

"I was with him, Lady, on his spare mount, Sharabok, Zeldar's fine black son. I remember the wyck's great eyes, arrow-shaped and green. Though unicorns fear the wyvern with good cause, because the wyvern kill so many of their foals, Zeldar never wavered.

"Well ahead of me, the Lord Rider fired. A great shot, Lady! He hit the wyck. Its right wing crumpled. It fell into the snow. The other dropped to help it. Their mother turned away and climbed to circle over us. The wolves ran, Lady, like the sneaking beasts they are.

"When the landing strip beside the town was clear, the others landed to unload the supplies they had carried. But not the rider, Lady. He circled above the wycks. The injured one tried to fly again and fell. The other left it dead and climbed to join the queen. They left the panicked wolves and flew together back into their forbidden wilderness.

"We pursued them."

He shook his head very slightly, as if the movement hurt, and waited again for her to refill his bowl with the steaming tea.

"I begged him, Lady! Begged him to turn back. If the winter blizzards in the high country had been too savage for the wyvern and the wolves, I though they would be too savage for us. Even in the summers, the fools that followed the wyvern too far had never come back from those high summits where the dragons den. I begged till I felt ashamed, but the Lord Rider heard nothing I said.

"I followed him, but not from courage of my own. Sharabok was following his noble father. The black queen flew fast, shrieking at her wyck when it lagged, but we kept them in sight. Through the grace of the all-forgiving Three no blizzards caught us, but the cold was cruel. Even in winter leathers, I grew numb to the bone.

"Beyond the border, the wyvern took us high. Too high for our unicorns; they had to labor hard. The sun had no warmth there above the timber line, and the whole world was blinding white. All we saw was needle peaks and dreadful black-walled canyons and glaciers in the canyons under us. Unicorns warm themselves when they fly, but I felt frozen to the saddle.

"Zeldar was stronger than Sharabok, able to climb higher in that thin and bitter air. Close upon the wyvern, he carried your noble husband across a great glacier and far into the heart of the Dragons. Though Sharabok had given all he had, we fell behind—too far behind to see much of what happened. The wyvern had dived behind a peak and out of my sight. The great Zeldar was climbing bravely to clear the crest when something struck him.

"Nothing I saw, Lady." He shrugged in apology. "Don't ask me what it was. But Zeldar was somehow stricken. His wings seemed to fail. He dropped in the air, fought to recover, and glided back to meet us before he finally fell. Down on the glacier, his wings spread and flapped and stopped. Sharabok believes he died. I'm afraid he did; unicorns have a special sense for each other."

Scorth shook his naked head, and she saw tears on his sun-browned baby cheeks.

"My husband?" she whispered. "Where is he?"

"I tried to save him. Believe me, Lady!" His eyes had narrowed, and she wondered. "He is alive, or was. I swear it, Lady. I saw him walk away from Zeldar's body, and I tried to sing Sharabok toward him. But we'd climbed too high for him, and he was far too spent to carry double.

"He tried to sing of something else that hurt him, but it was something he had never known. He had no language for it. He was shattered, Lady. Broken! Unicorns love each other, and he had loved Zeldar. Your husband looked unhurt when we saw him walk, but we had no way to help him. He knew it, Lady. He waved us to leave him."

"And you left him?"

"We had to, Lady. A deed that rankles in me, and I'm ashamed." He made a helpless shrug, yellow eyes blinking. "Ashamed to say we left him there on the ice with his dead unicorn. But at least we left him alive. Alive and well enough when I looked back. And still he had his gun. Perhaps—''

The catch of his breath was almost a sob.

"Perhaps the blessed Three will intervene to save him. He's a nobleman, Lady. Strong enough, and the bravest man I ever knew. He's in a desperate spot, down on the ice in the wyvern wilderness, among the peaks where dragons are said to den. But I saw no wolves around him, nor wyvern still in the sky. I'll pray for him, Lady. Pray that the merciful Three may let him escape."

"Why?" Her white lips were quivering. "Why did he go so far?"

"Because of what he is." Pride lit his dark-streaked face. "He's the Var, never forget. Rendahl in Var, heir to twenty noble generations. One Nuradoon ir Var took these highlands back from the wyvern and the wolves, and his heirs have held them well. Vars have died, but never yielded. Dragonrock has never fallen."

"I know," she whispered. "I love Rendahl for what he is."

"I grieve for him, Lady. I grieve for you." In the red-streaked baby face, his yellow eyes blinked with a solemn concern. "In the face of evil, we must trust the holy Three. They saved Sharabok and saved me. Brought us back off the ice alive, and down across all those bare peaks and endless fields of snow, which is itself an amazing miracle. We stopped first in a lower valley, at a warm spring where he could drink and I could bathe to thaw myself, and landed again to let him graze a suncorn field the invaders had not burned. The Three flew with us, and here we are."

She stared at him silently, eyes still dry in her tight white face.

"Forgive me, Lady, but the thing is done beyond undoing." He shrugged, blood-grimed hands spread wide. "It's true we had to leave him on the glacier where he fell, high in the wyvern wilderness, but the choice was his own. A cruel fate for him, but the good Three allowed it. We are not to judge them, Lady. They don't reveal their reasons."

I

The Red Moon

The red moon, unforecast by Realist science and unwelcome even to the archimage in holy Quar, though it had been foretold in *The Esoterica of Xath*, had been so long delayed that its terrors were almost forgotten. With no data on its orbit still surviving, astronomers at the Realist Institute had come to suspect that it was only one more myth of the mages.

It did return. Its legions of evil demons descended again, as they had every thousand years, to end an age of progress and plunge the world once more into nightmare. This book is the story of two men and a woman, all about the same age, whose lives shaped the cruel history of their coming.

The woman was a miner's daughter born in far North Riding, near the wyvern border. A bold and hardy spirit who renamed herself Lyrane lo Lyrane because she liked the sound, she loved the hunters who rode to kill the raiding werewolves, loved their unicorns, and almost loved the wolves. She made the best of the unlikely accident that brought her as a most unwelcome guest into the sacred city of Quar, where no woman had ever been allowed, and made herself the speaker to demons, the actual voice of Xath.

One man was the primarch's son, born in secret to a lady of the court whose name was never known. Out of his favor by then and fearing the wrath of more recent consorts, she concealed her pregnancy, slipped out of Targon on the pretext of a pilgrimage to Demon's Island, and waited her time in a squalid village hut.

When the midwife had washed the baby and brought him back to her bed, she took a single glance in the flicker of a guttering candle, called him a hideous little monster, and declared she never wanted to see him again. The boy was orphaned to the Church. Brought up by hard-minded mages in their hard schools and taught the dark mysteries of Xath, he named himself for a demon and almost became a demon in his eagerness to welcome the kindred he recognized in the invaders from the scarlet moon.

If the demons found an ally in this man, or at least a useful tool, the other man became their ultimate foe. A more welcome child, he was the son and rightful heir to Rendahl ir Var, born in Dragonrock castle and christened Zorn ir Var as soon as his mother could leave her bed to carry him down to her garden shrine.

That moment of rejoicing was soon eclipsed by bleak misfortune. Zorn was not yet a month old when his uncle Thorg returned from Targon with the primarch's degree that deposed his father and exiled the family from Dragonrock to a rocky farm on remote Little River, far beyond the Wind River desert and the trackless Wolf Gap wilderness.

He grew to manhood there. His mother had been a student of ceramic art before his father carried her to Dragonrock. To keep the little family alive, she toiled at her wheel through the years of exile, peddling her plates and pots and pitchers in the nearby village.

Zorn had hoped for no more than to learn her craft of pottery, at least well enough to sell enough of his work to pay for care. The coming of the demons caught him untrained for conflict and unprepared for the terrors they brought, but he endured the disaster and played his own small part against them. His own account of that dreadful time is the most complete that has survived.

Wolf Bite

When we were exiled, I was still a baby. I recall nothing of Dragon-rock or Wolver Riding. My childhood world was the tiny prison farm on the rocky bank of Little River, which flows down from the high wilderness where dragons and wyvern ruled and werewolves roamed. My parents seldom spoke of any other past.

Their memories must have been painful, and I suppose they didn't want me feeling sorry for myself. My father never explained all the rules of his exile, but except for the tantalizing flights during which he was allowed to touch down nowhere else, he was forbidden to leave the farm.

He worked his little field of suncorn to feed our flying unicorn, Sharabok, dug clay and coal for my mother, and never spoke of the scar on his arm. A ragged blue ridge, it ran from his elbow halfway to his wrist. I used to wonder about it, but I never dared ask.

I spent most of my time with my mother, helping in the house and watching her work in the pottery. She, not so silent as he was, sometimes talked of the childhood she seemed to recall with sadly wistful pleasure. Motherless herself, she had lived with her father, a professor at the Institute in Targon, a city so far from the farm that it seemed as unreal to me as the worlds I invented in my dreams.

One day in the pottery I found courage to ask her how my father had got the scar.

"A wolf bite." She stopped the wheel with a look on her face that made me sorry for the question. "A werewolf bite."

All I could do was stand there wondering and afraid, shuffling my feet on the bare clay floor. She bent again to the lump of clay on the wheel, but straightened again in a moment with a troubled look in her eyes.

"You know about the werewolves?"

I shook my head; the little I knew terrified me.

"They live in the high wilderness west," she said. "Ugly brutes as large as men. Sometimes in the winter they come down to raid the riding. Once it was your father's duty to keep them driven back. A dangerous duty. One of them bit him."

Absently she was kneading the clay.

"It was a terrible thing, because the bite of a bitch wolf can change a man. If she is in heat—if she wants a mate—the bite can transform the man into the mate she needs. At first I was terribly afraid your father would be changed."

"He wasn't." With a grim little smile, she shrugged and leaned back to the wheel. "If he had been, we wouldn't be here."

Though I longed to know more, that was all she said. Perhaps she shouldn't have told me anything. My father was a wild-bearded giant, nothing wolfish about him. Commonly quiet and sometimes moody, he was always kind and often jolly. Yet at night on my pallet in the corner of the kitchen I used to wake to dark imaginings that he might yet become a black and dreadful beast, hungry to kill us.

The first I knew about my birthplace came from a pencil drawing my father found in my mother's sketchbook. Only half-finished, it showed towered walls standing on a high rock. He asked her to let him hang it over his desk in the corner of their bedroom. I asked her if the tower was real.

"Dragonrock," she said. "The great castle in the riding."

I was learning to help her in the house. She had been showing me how to make the bed, but she stopped to look at the sketch. I thought her eyes were sad. I asked her where the castle was.

"Over the mountains." She gestured north and added, perhaps on impulse, "You were born there."

"So why do we live here?"

Something pinched her face.

"The wolf bite," she said. "And bad men."

That was all she wanted to say, but I begged her to tell me more about the castle until she described it and finally made a better picture for me on my birthday, painted in blue on a white porcelain plate. I loved the picture: the dark rock itself jutting above the canyon of Dragon River; the massive walls that rimmed the summit; the great square donjon on the highest peak; the high stage where the unicorns rose and landed.

She helped me find it on the map: a black dot on Dragon River, which ran out of the Dragon Mountains down across the yellow emptiness of Wolver Riding to twist around three sides of the castle before it flowed off the scarp and on down by Dorth and Targon in the lowlands, at last through Delta Lake and out through the five mouths into the eastern sea.

I used to dream about Dragonrock, and I remember telling her once that I was going back there when I grew up. She let her wheel stop and sat for a moment staring at a half-shaped bowl before she drew a long breath and turned to frown at me.

"Better forget it." Her voice was sharp at first, almost scolding, but she paused to warm it. "Too far away. Too many wolves in the mountains. Too many banshees howling in the desert and watching everything we do."

"I'd have a unicorn," I said. "I'd fly."

"Nothing there for you." She shook her head and spun the wheel again. "Not even if you reached it. The people at the castle wouldn't let you stay."

Yet I kept the dream alive. Playing alone on the riverbank, I built little mud copies of the castle she had pictured. I caught butterflies and let them fly like unicorns from the tiny stage. I invented my own adventure tales, always about fighting my way to Dragonrock and somehow claiming it to be my own.

I'd decided that if I had no money to buy a unicorn, I would capture a wild one and tame it. Or perhaps I would go on foot to climb the mountains and fight the werewolves and hide from the wyvern till I reached the castle. If the people there didn't want me back, I would find out why, and change their minds.

I knew that dreams were only dreams. I never hoped even to see the castle, not until that wonderful day when my father carried me over it on Sharabok. Even then, he said nothing about that ugly blue scar. When I tried again to query my mother, she had always put me off. She had no time. The story was too long. I wouldn't understand. Some things were best forgotten.

Growing up in puzzlement, I gathered hints and clues and bits of information until I knew that my father had been the Wolver Rider till his brother Thorg seized the castle and the riding and sent us into exile, but the bite and its ragged scar were still haunting mysteries until after I was grown.

When at last I heard the story, it came from Scorth, who had been my father's unicorn trainer. We had camped one night in the dry bed of Wind River, where water no longer ran. We were sitting squatted together on the sand beside our dying fire, surrounded by grotesque masses of eroded sandstone.

The demon star had risen, already swollen to a disk and so bright that it turned midnight to a baleful crimson dusk, transforming those dead rocks into crouching monsters as ominous as the wyvern and the dragons themselves. An eerie howling echoed through them, as if they were awakening.

"Banshees!"

Scorth was hard to see in that dim red gloom, a tiny, wiry man, his oddly hairless face and scalp withered under the desert sun and browned to the color of old hopper leather. The rhythms of the unicorns echoed in his voice.

"Ugly, stinking things the banshees are, with poison spines and poison bites. They're sly and quick and black, hard to see when they come out of their dens at night to look for the carrion they eat. Their wailing is said to warn you of death to come.''

The howling paused and came again, paused and came again, an unearthly sound that lifted the hair on the back of my neck. A single beast or a scattered pack? Sometimes so far-off among the red-lit rocks around us that I thought it had ceased. Suddenly so loud, the creature or creatures might have been beside us.

''True enough, I heard the Lord Rider say, if you don't ask the date.'' Scorth shrugged and stirred the dead coals. ''Their howling terrified your mother. He fretted more about the evidence that they're sneaking spies for the wyvern and the wolves. Your noble mother dreaded something worse.

''I loved her.'' Surprised that she had told me so little about the rescue, he seemed apologetic for her. ''Rode with her and tried to save her from the consequences of her rashness. If they never spoke of the bite, that's no wonder. A dreadful thing for her—your great father was too far out of his head most of the time even to know he'd been bitten. Nothing they'd ever care to talk about.''

When I begged for it, he told me the story.

''Not that I can brag of anything I did.'' He poked the coals again and still found no fire. ''As you may have heard, your father and I had killed a wyvern wyck and chased the mother queen and her surviving wyck far toward their lair in the Dragon Mountains. Your father was on Zeldar, a great bay stallion we both of us loved. I was on Sharabok, Zeldar's son, still too young to have his sire's full strength.

''The wyvern had led us too far and too high for Sharabok. We were over a great glacier with a mountain wall beyond it. Zeldar had carried your father a good way ahead of us, and higher. He never told me what hit them there; the wolf had got him before I saw him again, and I'm not sure he remembered.

''Something did happen. Zeldar was knocked down. I never knew how, though Sharabok felt him die; unicorns have a sense for each other. He never sang me anything about it, but it left a terror that's still in him. Zeldar fell on the ice. He never moved again, and I had to leave your father.

''You may call me a coward for that, but the fact is, I had no choice. I saw your father walk away alive. He saw the situation, knew Sharabok was too far gone to carry double. Stricken with grief for Zeldar, too, and barely able to stay in the air. Your father waved us to go on. We did, and I beg you not to blame me.''

He stopped to squint at me in sardonic inquiry. I told him I didn't blame him for anything. He grinned and shrugged and stared off into the crimson dusk, remembering.

"We had to leave your father where they fell, but Sharabok brought me back to Dragonrock alive." He hunched himself against the wind, with a wry squint at me. "That's the tale I had to tell your mother. If you'd known her then—''

He caught himself, remembering that she had been already pregnant with me, and cocked his leathery head to listen again to that uncanny howling.

"Still the Lady Rider!" He spoke with rueful admiration. "With a will of her own. She took my breath when she said she wanted me to take her back to rescue her husband. Not a chance, I told her. The wyvern would surely dive on us long before we got near the glacier. The Lord Rider was probably already dead. Her first duty, I tried to tell her, was to care for his heir. Old Nanda put it more plainly; I heard her call your mother a hopper-brained idiot.

"The rider had left his brother Thorg in command of the castle garrison. A slimy schemer, if you'd let me say it. Claiming to be as anxious about your father as your mother was. He urged us to go. Hoping, of course, that we'd never get back.''

Bleakly he grinned.

"She wanted to set out at once, but I was near dead. Sharabok too. We had to eat and rest. I slept half that day and all the night. She wanted me to exchange Sharabok for a fresher mount, but he made me take him, exhausted as he was. Out of his own love for your father and I think a sense of duty to the memory of his own. We left next morning at dawn. She rode Falcon Child.

"A flight I can't forget." The banshee seemed far off among the sandstone demons, but he paused and stared again into the red shadows among them as if searching for it. "We flew west and north and west again into a blizzard, and never outran the banshees that kept howling under us. Gleeful I guess they were, from their feasts on human carrion.

"Your mother endured everything bravely, but I made her stop at Iron Hill. A lonely fort in border country. We found it almost abandoned. Captain Yarcho had gone to fight the raiders, leaving only a handful of men. All on edge with fear, but they put us up and fed the unicorns. I'd hoped the blizzard would end, but next morning it was still whistling, the snow drifting deep.

"I begged her to wait at the fort, and let me go on alone. Begged till she grew angry. We went on together. At first we had to fly low against the storm. The banshees cried behind us all the way. We came out of the clouds, but the snow lay deep and the cold was merciless as your Uncle Thorg."

By daylight, Scorth had odd yellow eyes nearly the color of a unicorn's. They were invisible now, in the red dawn of the demon star, but I heard the irony when he paused, frowning at me as if to sense what I thought of Thorg.

"My father never spoke of him," I said. "My mother hated him."

"Who could love him?" A grunt of contempt. "She didn't like leaving him in command of the castle, not that she ever stopped to worry as we flew on beyond the border. Sharabok took us back the way the rider and I had followed the wyvern, climbing over dead white summits into a dead white world. I got numb to the bone. The banshees had gone silent, the cold too savage for them.

"I expected the wyvern to meet us before we reached the glacier, but we never got there. The ice blinded me, but Falcon Child had keener eyes. Far down the canyon under the glacier, she picked up the trail of a lone man on skis. The Lord Rider, she thought.

"Impossible, I told her, because your father had no skis, but your mother's a Mystic. Believes what she believes, no matter what you say. She made me follow—and I later learned that he'd found them with the bones of a man who died trying to climb into the Dragons two hundred years ago.

"We lost the trail where new snow had fallen and found it again farther down the canyon on a frozen river—it must have been the upper Dragon. On down below the timber line, we found the tracks of a wolf on the trail ahead of us. A bitch, your good mother feared, in heat and hungry for the rider's soul. I heard her praying the Three to preserve him.

"Your noble father!"

Scorth squinted at me through that red dusk as if trying to guess whether I would ever measure up.

"The creatures had hunted him hard, but he fought them like the Var he was. We found the wolf and the ashes of a fire in a little hollow with the snow scraped away. Circling low, we saw that one ham was gone, all except the bone. Skinned out, roasted, eaten. I had to laugh.

"The ski tracks led us on across another empty valley, where nothing had followed. Your mother felt better and my own hopes rose higher, till we heard the banshees yelling again and found the prints of another wolf on the trail.

"It, too, had died. Hovering, we read the story in the red and trampled snow. Tracks and bones and scraps of skin, where its own evil folk had fed on it. Not much farther, we found the rider, trapped against a cliff above a river bend. Already bitten. His leathers ripped to shreds. The sleeve torn off and one bare arm already red with blood. I'd hoped your mother wouldn't see, but I heard her gasp and heard her praying.

"Injured as he was, your father was still the valiant Var, swinging a broken ski against three gaunt gray wolves. One was standing, clubbing at him with a charred driftwood pole. Another, with a long steel blade, crouching to spring from the bluff behind him. A third, down where wind had swept the snow away, gathering rocks to throw.

"If we'd come later—"

Scorth stopped, crouching from a sudden gust of wind that stirred the dead ashes. Higher now, the crimson star had found new monsters around us and begun to reveal Scorth himself, a bald brown gnome with a perpetual infant grin that made him seem almost as strange as they.

"The wolves yelped and ran when they saw us, and our unicorns came down safe on the ice. Nearly done for, the Lord Rider floundered toward us and collapsed in snow too deep for him. Your mother helped me lift him onto Sharabok. We got him back to what was left of Battle Bluff and finally on to Iron Hill.

"Wolf weather delayed us there. Wolf weather and your father's wound. The fever from his torn arm nearly killed him. Though he swore to your mother that the creature that bit him was a male, the men at the fort kept him locked up in their guardhouse as if he'd already been transformed. For many days he was out of his head, fighting those wolves again.

"Your brave mother stayed with him in the room. Prayed to the blessed Three. Gave him water when he could drink. A bad time for both." He shook his naked head. "When his fever finally broke, she knocked and begged at the door, but it had left him so gaunt and wild and strange that another day was gone before I could get the men to let them out.

"We had to keep him there another week, till he got strong enough for the flight back to Dragonrock." He shrugged in the scarlet dusk, blinking at me shrewdly. "I guess you know what had happened there?"

I told him how little I knew.

"I hate to think about it." The banshee's howl seemed suddenly near, and I saw him shiver. "Your grandfather, the old rider, had been a true and noble Var, but in his final years the Three had somehow forsaken him. His first wife had been your great father's mother. As fine a woman as your own mother is. She died when he was still a boy, and he took another wife. The Lady Vlakia sar Sardek."

He mouthed the name like something foul.

"A great beauty once, and once the primarch's favorite mistress, but nasty when anybody crossed her. I remember all the ugly names she called me, once when she wanted to ride a unicorn that didn't like her in the saddle. She bore Thorg and Slarn in the old rider's bed. Let him believe he'd sired them, though I was never sure. Took them back to Targon and left him groaning through his last years alone while she tried to win the old primarch back.

"She'd always lived in scandal. . . ."

He paused to listen at the banshees and sat staring moodily away into the crimson shadows till I begged for the rest of the story.

"A sad business," he muttered. "When Thorg heard about the wolf bite, he went down to Targon with his tale that your father was now a wolf, locked up at Iron Hill. The Lady Vlakia had faded into a wrinkled witch by then, but Slarn, her younger son, had learned to amuse the old primarch as well as she ever had. Or so the rumors went.

"Slarn persuaded him to sign a decree the made Thorg the new Lord Wolver. Your uncle Thorg!" His voice wryly sardonic, Scorth tossed his shoulders. "His bite was worse than the wolf's."

That night I lay a long time awake, listening to Scorth's rattling snore and the banshees' eerie music, while the dull red disk of the demon moon climbed hour by hour above the sandstone dragons crouching around us. Shivering under a blanket too thin for the cold, I wondered how my mother could survive alone on the prison farm and wondered again what Thorg had done to my father. I dreamed of revenge—and tried to make my clenched hands relax, because I knew I was no killer. At least, unhappy as Scorth's revelations had made me, I felt grateful for a better understanding of my life.

—— 3 ——

Xath

Xath, so the mages preached, was the demon who loved mankind. He had stayed behind when the long orbit of his burning world carried his celestial fellows away, stayed to guide and comfort men and ready them for all the blessings of the foretold millennium when his crimson moon would rise again to end the cycle of time.

Invisible except to the archimage, he dwelt in his great wooden fanes on the Isle of Paradise, appearing only rarely in the eternal flame kept burning black in the crimson-domed temple in holy Quar. His visitations there were to instruct the faithful and ask for gold and receive the worship due him in return for his benedictions. Fire was the garment of the celestials, and gold their favored food. Dutiful obedience would earn everlasting bliss.

Men were damned, his mages preached, born with fatal evil festering in every infant heart. Seeking redemption, the faithful were commanded to restrain appetite and impulse, to fear women, to revel in hunger and cold and pain, and to scourge themselves until their flowing blood washed away all the inborn longings of the beast.

Loyal to his sovereign will, the archimage marshaled the lesser mages for their sacred crusade against the Realists and the Mystics. The principal issue was the doctrine of transincarnation, was the miraculous redemption of the doomed through the sacred rites of privation, pain, and ultimate ecumenism with the celestials in the black flame of Xath.

The Realists, in their blasphemous defiance, called that doctrine pernicious nonsense. Realist philosophers traced most human ills not to that tainted heritage, but merely to ignorance and stupidity. Their remedy was not purification through agony, but the arrogant folly that man might redeem himself through worldly acts.

In this age of rampant heresy, the Realists had led souls astray with all the ease and convenience created by the so-called science they had stolen from the mages. Honest walking was no longer good enough; steamboats ran up and down the Dragon River, and steam carts and trains were puffing all across the lowlands.

The Mystics were less certain of themselves and their world, claiming that they sought a path of peaceful sanity through a universe of unknowable mystery. The Mystic way appealed through a deceptive simplicity: release from fear through love.

As the mages taught, the Mystics were fools, stumbling into hell through their mistaken faith, and the Realists were equally doomed by their foolhardy trust in their own blundering minds. They were, taught the mages, malevolent fiends besides, claiming that the stolen powers of Xath that drove their dynamos and steam carts had been inventions of their own.

Powerful once, the faith of Xath had waned as men forgot his scarlet moon. Unexpected when at last it shone, his herald star ignored by his temple watchers, the actual descent of the celestials caught the archimage unready for the battle to restore his diminished dominion.

4

The Serpent Staff

The police watched us.

Gray men with long guns, they came up the river riding unicorns, sometimes one alone, more often two, rarely three. They dived to circle low over the farm, leaning in the saddle to search through glasses until they found my father. He never looked at them. And they never landed, not so long as he was there.

The unicorns excited Sharabok. He always sensed them far away and ran to where my father was, neighing to tell him. I think he was lonely for his own kind, but my father kept him on the ground. He would stand looking after the unicorns, nostrils distended and white horn high, till they had gone on upriver to patrol the wilderness border.

When I asked why they came, my father shrugged as if it didn't matter and said they were only doing their job. He never explained the job, or told me why we had to stay there. All through my lonely childhood, I wondered who I was and wrestled to unravel the clues I could uncover.

Wistfully he and my mother sometimes spoke to each other of their happier years as classmates at the Institute in Targon. He had gone there already a Realist. Their friendship had begun when he teased her about her Mystic faith. Hurt by his teasing, she cried. He apologized and took her flying on his unicorn. They fell in love.

Listening on my pallet when they thought I was asleep, I learned that he was still a Realist, but what that meant, I didn't know. I knew her father had been a professor of Mystic philosophy, and sometimes I heard her praying for the loving Three to save us from the demons and their evil moon. I felt afraid to ask what the demons were or how they might hurt us, but often I lay awake and wondered.

I thought we must have once been rich. My mother treasured the shining diamond ring my father had given her, too precious to wear while she was working clay. My father's books were printed with what my mother called the sigil of the Vars: a unicorn's head outlined in blue, with golden eyes and horn. Sharabok's saddle was polished hopper-hide, mounted with silver and precious green malachite.

Yet somehow we were now very poor. Our house was built of rough fieldstone my father had laid up himself, with mud for mortar and a grass thatch instead of tile. It was only two small rooms and the narrow hall between. My father's desk and shelf of books took one side of the bedroom. My own bed was a pallet rolled down every night in the kitchen.

Our farm was a lonely strip of steep and stony land on the bank of Little River, which rushed white and swift over the rapids below the house. Above the rapids, it came down out of the high mountain wilderness where no human people lived, but only such evil creatures as the wolves and banshees and wyvern and dragons.

My mother used to tremble and kneel at her tiny shrine in the corner of the bedroom when she heard the banshees howling, though my father always told me they were slinking, cowardly things that would never trouble us.

We had no money. The suncorn my father grew in the narrow field was barely enough to keep Sharabok alive. He cultivated the kitchen garden and dug coal out of the cliff above the house to fire my mother's kiln. She earned most of our living, making the pottery we carried to the village.

That was a dozen miles down the river. I met a few of its people when she let me go there with her, walking ahead of the donkey. Mr. Yggs herded spotted cows and preached in the chapel. Mrs. Yggs sold milk and butter. The Ulors grew cherries in the spring and sweet melons in the summer and apples in the fall. Mr. Keroth made boots and shoes. Mr. Gornal built houses. Mrs. Emok ran the general store. Mr. Alu was the blacksmith.

Miss Penra taught the school, but it was too far for me to walk. My father helped me teach myself to read, though most of his books were too hard for me. He showed me how to use his counting frame, which had wooden beads that slid on little rods. I had no friends. Sometimes I felt unhappy. My parents tried to be kind, even when they didn't want to talk about themselves, and I loved them.

My mother was a neat little woman with bright brown eyes and deft brown hands. She could be quick as a bird, but she liked to sit all day, busy at her wheel. Sometimes when I begged, she would sing. Her voice was music, and I loved the ballads about the times long ago when the noble Vars were fighting the demons and wyvern, and the cunning wolves that had been men.

My father was a tall, copper-haired man who teased my mother and betimes played his flute for Sharabok. Sharabok grazed on the hills above the house and came to beg my father for suncorn, singing for it in his own strange language. His songs always puzzled me, even when my father tried to translate, but I loved their music and knew when he felt sad or lonely, or more often happy, because my father loved him.

I longed sometimes to ride in the sky with my father, yet Sharabok frightened me. He was taller than a man. His odor was strong and strange. I never understood the look of his great golden eyes, and I felt afraid of the shining ivory horn, which was sharp as a knife and longer than I was tall.

We were exiles.

The word was strange when I first heard it, listening as I lay on my pallet at night. I kept wondering, till I finally dared myself to ask my mother what exiles were. She was grinding blue pigment in her mortar, and I stood waiting till she stopped to raise her head, her face set hard.

"Look at me." Her voice was quick and sharp. "Look at your father. Look in the mirror. Exiles are what we are."

"I don't understand."

"You will when you are older. No need to fret about it." I saw her lip quiver. "We must learn to take what we have and try to be happy with it."

I liked the times I spent exploring the sandbars and searching for bright pebbles when the river was low, or riding the donkey when I went with my father up the hill for coal, or watching my mother shaping and burning and painting and glazing her plates and bowls and lovely vases.

I was always glad when she let me come with her to the village. We led the donkey packed with pottery, and camped overnight on the trail. We saw birds in the trees and sometimes fish leaping up the rapids. Sometimes we heard a banshee howl and my mother would kneel to pray, but there were never any wolves.

Mrs. Emok smiled to see us because she wanted the pots, but most people seemed afraid to speak to us. The only village boy I knew was Bastard, who worked the bellows for Mr. Alu in the blacksmith shop. Mr. Alu went home when he could to tend the still where he made the untaxed brandy Mrs. Emok sold through her back door, and he used to leave Bastard to watch the shop.

Bastard was always hungry. When I offered to share my lunch, he brought water in a gourd to drink with the bread and cheese. We sat on a flattened log in front of the shop, and Bastard talked. He had no father. When he was still a baby, his mother ran away with the captain of the trading boat that came up the river from Dorth. Mrs. Yggs kept him till he got old enough to do odd jobs around the blacksmith shop. He always stopped whatever he was saying to watch Miss Penra when she went by on her way to school. I thought he longed for her to like him, but she never even seemed to see him.

I asked him about dragons and wyvern and wolves. He looked warily up and down the muddy street and leaned closer before he would say anything about them. They were dreadful. Mr. Yggs said the Three had let the serpent-god Xath send them to punish people for cheating on their taxes and tithes or for talking treason against the primarch.

"The wyvern . . ." He looked up the street again, and his voice sank lower. "Mr. Yggs says they're half as big as dragons. They fly like unicorns and fight with long black fangs and great black claws. He says they can kill unicorns. And they eat everybody they can catch."

I asked about the werewolves.

"They're bigger than men," Bastard said. "They run on all fours, but walk on two feet when they like. Their forepaws are nearly like hands. They can throw rocks and carry weapons and fight like men, but they are covered with hair and look more like giant dogs. Mr. Yggs says they suck human blood, while the victims are still alive. The male wolves kill you. But people say . . ."

He hushed his voice.

"People say they're half demon, born of human women the demons bred with. And they say a bitch wolf's bite doesn't kill you. Not if she's in heat. It just makes you the mate she wants."

Horrified, because I hadn't really understood what my mother said about them, I stared into his grimy face.

"I know." He leaned closer. "Because that's what became of Mr. Emok. Last year he went hunting up in the foothills and never came back. Mr. Alu went with the men searching for him. They followed his trail to the last place he camped, and Mr. Alu found blood on the rocks and the weeds torn up where the bitch wolf caught him. Two sets of wolf tracks going away.

"Queer tracks!" His pale eyes went wider. "Because the wolves have queer feet. Mr. Alu says the wolf tracks were like tracks of fat human hands."

I shivered at that, but he hadn't finished.

"They'll eat you if they catch you," he whispered. "But you better never see a banshee."

I gulped and leaned to ask if he knew about the demons. He caught my arm to hush me. Two boys were walking up the street on their way to school. They yelled something I didn't understand. Bastard went red in the face and said he had chores to do before Mr. Alu came back.

I learned more about the world from a book called *The Legend of the Land.* I'd found it on a rack in Mrs. Emok's shop, back before I learned to read. The colored pictures looked so wonderful and strange that I begged my mother until she traded a blue plate for it.

My father helped me spell out the opening chapters, about how the first settlers had come across the great ocean and found the land. They were happy in the beginning because it had rich soil and great forests and no people except the singing unicorns. The werewolves hadn't learned to hunt people then.

They sailed up the great river to Granite Ridge and knocked the timbers off their ship to build a fort at Targon. They learned to hunt the wolves and the wyvern that had hunted the unicorns. The unicorns got to be their friends. Spreading over the smiling land, building new towns and exploring as far as the foothills of the Dragons, they'd lived in peace for centuries, till the demon moon came into the sky.

The book had pictures of that moon. It was huge and red, with dark marks that made a snarling face. The demons had come down from it, blazing like comets at night. They brought the dragons and taught the wolves and the wyvern to burn cities and hunt people. The book gave me nightmares, and I was afraid to read on.

"It's only a legend," my mother tried to cheer me. "You mustn't be afraid."

She made me finish the book. It told how the demons had taken over nearly all the world before the great Nuradoon the First fought them from behind the magical Dragonshield. He drove them off the planet, but they had left the dragons to command the wolves and the wyvern in their endless war against us. The book ended with a prophecy that the demon moon could rise again.

"Is it true?" I asked my mother. "Will the demons come again?"

"Please, dear." She stopped her wheel to shake her head at me. "The book is only a legend, handed down from people who had almost forgotten how to write. It says they'd come here from some-where beyond the ocean, but the maps will show you there's no land anywhere beyond our few islands. Men looking for it have sailed all around the world and found no other continent. Forget about the demons, and learn your spelling lesson.''

But of course, I couldn't forget. If there had been no demons, why did people fear them? Who had brought the dragons? Who had taught the wyvern and the wolves how to kill us? When she leaned back to her wheel, I decided to ask my father.

I found him at work under the cliff above the house, bagging broken coal. Careful with the question, I offered to hold the bags to be filled and asked about the print of a leaf I found in the coal. He explained how coal was made from plants that lived in swamps back when the world was new, and showed me odd little rocks he said were the fossil teeth of a creature that had eaten them.

''I was reading about the demons and the Dragonshield. Were they—'' I tried not to seem too anxious. ''I wondered if the demons were real.''

He had bent for another scoop of coal, but he straightened to frown away for what seemed a long time at the blue foothills of the far-off Dragons before he looked back at me. His face looked grim beneath the streaks of black coal dust in his beard.

''Something did happen to the world.'' He nodded, his voice low and slow. ''Something so bad, nobody was left to write good rec-ords of it. My professors at the Institute never made much sense of the old documents they had.''

''The Dragonshield?''

''It's real.'' He nodded, looking no happier. ''It belongs to the Vars.''

''You've seen it?''

''I've held it in my hand.''

''Where is it?''

"Still at Dragonrock, I suppose." He shrugged. "Not that it can matter now. Not to us."

"If it's real . . ." I shivered. "Does that mean the demons will raid the world again?"

"Don't fret about it." I saw he wasn't sure. "You'll hear people talk. The mages of Xath expect it back, but they've been expecting it the last thousand years. My Realist professors at the Institute said most likely it was a one-shot comet that would never be back. You'll have enough to do growing up, without fretting over dangers that maybe don't exist."

"But maybe they do?"

"Nobody knows." He stooped to catch my shoulder with his dusty hand. "Your business is to grow up and be ready if they do come back."

I spent a minute wondering how to be ready for demons. With no idea, I asked if the werewolves were real.

"Real enough!" He made a bitter face. "There's a story that they used to be men, turned into werewolves because they tried to fight the demon, but the unicorns say they were always here, preying on their foals. Nobody knows. Whatever happened a thousand years ago, it's nearly all forgotten."

Gently his big hand squeezed my shoulder.

"So don't brood about it." He tried to warm his voice. "Whatever the red moon was, it may not come again. Surely not while you're alive."

"The prof—prophecy?" The new word was hard to say. "It says the red moon will rise again and bring the demons back."

"But not without a warning." He looked away again, toward the far blue Dragon Mountains. "The prediction is that a warning star will appear in the constellation Capricorn. It will be red and very faint at first, but it will grow and move among the other stars. We can know it because it won't twinkle—"

He broke off abruptly and bent for another scoop of coal. I wanted to ask how he knew so much, or if perhaps he did believe the prophecy, but I held my tongue until one dark night not long after, when I found him in the yard outside the house, looking up at the stars through his pocket telescope.

"Of course I watch." He laughed when he saw me. "You probably will, when you're grown-up. Not because we really believe in demons or the black magic of the mages, but if that star ever does shine to warn us, we'll want to know.''

He showed me how to focus the telescope and sweep the faint stars of Capricorn, and we stood watching in the dark. One bright meteor left a green-glowing trail across the sky, but not in Capricorn.

After that he sometimes let me go out late to watch with him. We never saw any strange red star in Capricorn, and I tried not to worry. Perhaps the demons and their red moon had never been. Even if they were real and planning to return, that might not be for another thousand years. Or if they did come, somebody could surely use the magic Dragonshield to stop them.

Late that winter a terrible thing happened to Bastard.

My mother and I were in the village again. When Mrs. Emok told her that a mage was coming to preach, she said my father would want to know about him. The weather was bitter, with snow thin on the ground, but Mrs. Emok let us stay overnight in the barn where Mr. Emok had kept his hoppers. We waited for the mage with a little crowd on a vacant lot.

He was lame, a lean, gaunt man in a long black robe. He came limping quickly on a long black staff. His terrible face looked lean and stern and angry, even before I heard him yelling about the demons. Frightened, I caught my mother's hand, and we all stood far back.

I stared at his strange head, and stared at the staff. It was black wood, carved with the scales and head of a snake, and thicker and heavier than it needed to be. The eyes were red stones that shone in the dusk, brighter than the torch he had planted beside him.

The staff was merely ugly; the mage frightened me. When he threw his black cowl back, his bony head had no beard or hair. His naked skull was bright red. His long teeth were black and sharply pointed, shining through wide blue scars that gave him a ferocious grin.

"Mr. Yggs says their faces are tattooed." Bastard was standing near, and he jogged my arm to whisper. "He says they have to file and dye their teeth. And they use drugs and salves to kill the hair and leave their scalps the color of the demon moon."

Mr. Alu muttered to hush him. The mage jabbed the tail of the snake into the snowy ground to let it stand beside the torch. He made a harsh bark to clear his throat.

"My name is Gark ru Garo." His voice was loud and raspy. "I came from the sacred city, Quar. I am an anointed mage of the Eternal Xath, and I bring you a message from his archimage, a message meant to turn you from your paths of reckless evil into humble contemplation of his awful truth.

"Heed me well, for I speak for Xath. He is the Creator. He is the Destroyer. He is all you need to know. Reigning through all the cycles of infinity, with neither beginning nor end, he forms all the world from ice and finally consumes it again with fire. Yet no termination is ever the end, because the fire burns out and the flames freeze to ice and darkness, which he thaws to form the world again, to let men sin and suffer and finally burn though another cycle and yet another, time upon time forever, an everlasting trap of pain and darkness for your moaning souls, except for the fortunate few he may elect to rescue.

"The fools among you who defy Xath and dare deny that he exists, who call his eternal celestial messengers evil demons, who laugh at the blessed mages who come to save you from the manifold follies of your blindness, I beg you to hear his truth and follow me, because we who come humbly walking with our simple staves, we are the chosen, who have found eternal fulfillment in his holy flame.

"His cycles are a thousand years. When he returned at the turning of the last, he found himself offended by men who had forgotten his commandments and denied that he was real. He sent his celestials down to subdue their arrogance with fire, which left the skies black with smoke; and justice that flooded the street with blood. . . ."

Appalled by his strange look and cruel voice, and the words he screamed, we were all drawing farther back. He stopped to glare at us, his eyes mad and terrible.

"Do you dread his holy truth? You who have to face the holy mages who have interceded for you, who have sacrificed themselves and all their goods to atone for your blindness and your folly? I beg you not to fear me. It is from humble love that I come to warn you that your cycle of time has run to its close. Learning nothing, mending nothing, regretting nothing, you are condemning yourselves and all your world to perish when the world burns again."

He snarled at us, black teeth gleaming in the red torchlight.

"If you shrink from me, you should be crawling on your bellies to pray for mercy from Xath, because your days of lust and greed are done. The cycle closing, the black flames will burn again, and the celestials will be descending from their moon to find you cowering in your huts. They will be thirsting for your souls."

Clearing his throat, he growled like some strange animal.

"Yet even now, in this last hour, the doors of your fate are not finally sealed. Even now, in this dreadful twilight of your dying world, you may still save yourselves. I beg you to follow me. Give your worthless gold to Xath, and throw yourselves into his blazing arms, and you may live again among his blessed celestials in the scarlet splendor of his new creation."

I saw Bastard crouching farther back, shaking his head. The mage, glaring at him out of that blue-scarred mask, snatched the black staff from the snow where he had planted it.

"You!" He pointed the staff at Bastard, as if the serpent's red-eyed head had been the blade of a spear. "You banshee-bitten fool! Do you hear the holy truth? Are you wise enough to yield? Will you now surrender your gold on the altar of Xath and swear your blood-sealed vows to heed his will forever?"

"No, sir." Uneasily Bastard shrank farther back. "I don't believe—"

"You don't believe?" A mocking yell. "Who are you to say that the Eternal Xath has lied?"

"I—I didn't," Bastard stammered. "I don't know what he said."

"I'm here, you craven idiot, to tell you what he said. He promised that those who accept his truth and follow his blessed path will live to serve him forever. But those fools like you who dare deny his everlasting power will die and die again in the hells he builds for you, feeding the wyvern with their bodies and their souls, and becoming wolves themselves. His grace allows you the choice between celestial incarnation and everlasting horror.

"So which do you choose?" He stabbed the staff at Bastard. "Which do you choose?"

"Please!" Bastard begged him. "I don't choose. . . ."

"You choose not to choose?" The mage thrust the snake's red-eyed head into his face. "Tell me why."

"Because I went to chapel, sir." Bastard stood his ground. "I heard Mr. Yggs say that we need not fear the demons or the mages who worship them, because the Three will defend—"

"Sacrilege!" the mage thundered. "Who is this blasphemous idolater?"

Bastard pointed at Mr. Yggs, who retreated uneasily.

"Let him beware the wrath of Xath!"

"Sir, I believe in the Three." Bastard shrugged and faced the mage again. "I trust their love and the healing powers of the seed and the bloom and the fruit—"

"Try them!"

The mage turned to glare at the rest of us. I crouched closer to my mother. Bastard and the red-skulled mage stood alone at the center of the circle, the torch blazing strangely red behind them. The mage flourished the staff like a lifted lance.

"Let them save you!" A gasp of fury. "If they can!"

He hurled the staff. It changed in the air. Suddenly a real, thick-bodied snake, it struck Bastard on the shoulder and wrapped around him. The staring head whipped into his face, black fangs yawning. It made a hissing scream, so keen it hurt my ears. The coils contracted.

I heard Bastard's bubbling moan as the serpent squeezed out his breath. I heard his bones snapping. His eyes bulged. Blood spurted out of his gaping mouth. Nearly hidden in the thick black coils, his body crumpled down into the snow.

People around us gasped and stood frozen. I heard no other sound until Mrs. Ulor screamed and fell over. The snake was unwinding from the little pile of red rags. Its head rose to look at us,

the red eyes bright and dreadful. The mage barked a word I did not
know and it slithered back toward him, leaving a twisted trail of
blood across the snow. Lifting its great flat head to his outstretched
hand, it stiffened and turned back into the wooden staff.

"The wrath of Xath," the mage snarled at us, his deep-sunk eyes
as angry as the snake's. "If you fear it, follow me."

He stood a moment glaring at us and limped off into the dark.
Nobody followed. Mr. Ulor knelt beside his wife. Their little girl
began to cry. My mother's cold hand caught mine. The torch was
left still flaring, its red light flickering over the dark stain slowly
spreading around what had been Bastard.

5

The Primarch's Child

Never wanted, never named, the boy spent his first few years in the indifferent care of a hopper herder's widow in the hill country far south of Targon. She was an arthritic cripple, haunted by a terror of Xath she tried to instill in him. She made him listen to the endless horror tales she read in a droning monotone from a tattered *Book of Xath* some wandering mage had sold her, and the whippings she gave him for anything or nothing were always done to save his evil soul for Xath.

"Demon bait," she used to call him, after he learned to sneer at the wrath of Xath. "He'll send his demons after you."

Bruised and scarred from her constant beating, shivering through the winters in his filthy rags and hungry all the year, he hated her and mocked her faith in Xath. His mind was keen enough. When he found that the marks on the tattered pages stood for words, he begged her to teach him what they meant and longed for learning she had never glimpsed. Never afraid of her or Xath, he promised her that he would grow up to become the archimage and send his serpent staff to drag her off to hell.

When she said he had no name, he named himself Argoth, after a powerful demon who had descended with Xath to command the wyvern and the werewolves against his enemies while the red moon was in the sky.

She whipped him for taking the name, called him a demon brat and a blasphemer condemned to feed the wyvern in hell, and whipped him again every time he claimed it. She said the demon's name would shrivel his soul to ashes. He promised her that he would shrivel her own when he became the archimage. And he kept the name.

He never ran away, because there was nowhere to run, but sometimes she let him play with the grubby youngsters who brought their marbles and tops to the vacant field across the road. They laughed at his demon's name and laughed at his rags and laughed because he had no father.

"You won't be laughing when I'm the archimage," he told them. "Not when you feel the coils of my black serpent staff. I'll send it after you, to let you see the primarch crawling in the dirt to kiss my feet."

"Better wait till somebody patches the seat of your pants."

"You'll see. . . ."

He stared at the other boys, and they all stumbled back from the light in his eyes. One by one, they turned and slipped away.

6

Questions of Evil

Nobody spoke as we watched the black mage hobbling off into the dark. The people around us muttered uneasily among themselves when he was gone, and scattered to their homes. Mr. Alu and Mr. Gornal rolled Bastard's body into a blanket and carried it to the blacksmith shop, Mr. Keroth walking ahead with the torch the mage had left.

I went back with my mother to our bedrolls on the floor of Mrs. Emok's barn. The barn was cold, and the dirt floor still had a rank stink of old hopper dung. Something squeaked and rustled all night in the bales of moldy hay. Banshees began howling, and I wondered if they were trying to get at Bastard's body.

I lay chilled and shivering a long time, and woke too early from a dreadful dream. I thought Bastard's body was changing into a wolf. It was all red and dripped blood; too broken to be whole again. Still more crippled than the mage, it rose to chase me, limping faster than I could run, howling a banshee's howl.

The red-skulled mage scuttled close behind it, the red-eyed snake coiled on his black-cloaked shoulders. Trying to get away, I was trapped in a rain of blood that fell from the demon moon and clotted into bottomless mud. I lay there afraid to sleep again till at last I saw white daylight in the window and Mrs. Emok brought us a pot of hot rockwheat porridge.

We stayed for Bastard's funeral. It was late that morning in the graveyard at the edge of the village. With no coffin, his body was still rolled in the blanket, which now had dark stains soaking through it. Mr. Ulor spoke at the grave, never calling him Bastard but only our unlucky friend.

A modest, hardworking young man, Mr. Ulor said, he had died well. Deeply as we mourned his tragic passing, which only a Mystic could understand because its justice was invisible except through meditation, we could only pray that he might rest in peace and wake whole again within the healing vision of the Three.

Mrs. Ulor knelt to toss a paper rose and a withered apple and a few grains of suncorn after him into the grave. What good were they, I wondered, against the terrible power of the serpent staff? We all stood shivering in a cold west wind while the men filled the grave and made a neat mound over it.

Miss Penra had come to stand among us. Her eyes looked tired, as if she hadn't slept. I heard her ask Mr. Alu why nobody had tried to stop the killing.

"To stop a mage of Xath?" He blinked as if the question startled him. "Even the primarch wouldn't dare."

We had a long walk home, leading the donkey up the slippery trail beside the ice-rimmed river. My mother didn't want to talk about Bastard and the snake, and I couldn't think about anything else. We got there late, stumbling the last few miles in the long winter dusk.

My father had waited up with a candle at the window. He had a pot of redbean soup hot for us. Helping my mother unpack the donkey, he stopped to stand very still while she told him what happened to Bastard. His face set hard behind his beard, but he said nothing at all.

I was tired and aching from a fall on the ice, but even safe on my own pallet, I lay awake most of the night listening to a banshee's dismal howl. My mother was up early to make an omelet and rockwheat cakes for breakfast, but nobody ate much, and nobody talked. She went to work in her pottery, and my father rode away on Sharabok, into low clouds and a bitter mist.

I washed the dishes and walked down to the river. Shivering in the wind, I felt too sick and miserable to do anything else. Thaws must have begun somewhere above us, and I stood a long time on the high bank, watching the wild white water that foamed and roared over the rapids below me.

The wind got colder. Fine sleet began to sting my face, but still I stood there, held by the power of the thundering water. Boulders rumbled, grinding down the riverbed. The river seemed stronger than Xath. One quick jump, I thought, would let me forget the red-scalped mage and his terrible snake.

I didn't hear my mother till she caught my arm.

"Zorn, dear! You mustn't!"

"Why—why not?" I tried not to sob. "You saw the snake."

"An evil thing." She kept her hold on my arm. "The mage was evil. Xath is evil." She must have run to reach me, because she was breathing hard. "But there is good in the world. You must learn to love and seek the good."

"What is good? Where is any good?"

"The Three are good."

She bent her head to breathe a prayer for them to help me.

"What did they ever do for Bastard?"

"We are not the Three." Her voice was soft and patient. "The truth we know is never whole. There are questions we can't answer, but we must trust the Three to keep the world in balance. There is darkness, but also light. Winter but also spring. Death but also life. Opposites cannot exist without each other. Bastard did die in a very horrible way, but you are still alive." She held me closer, and I felt her fast-beating heart. "You must stay alive!" Her whisper quivered. "Because we love you. It would kill me—"

Her voice was gone, but she held me there a long time. The mad water roared just below us, and I shivered in the spray. At last she stood up and pulled me farther from the bank.

"We must speak to your father." Her voice was suddenly firmer. "You'll want to stay alive when you know who you are."

She made a pot of stoneflower tea and had me put new logs on the fire. We waited in the kitchen till he came in from his ride, clapping his cold hands together. He sat with us before the crackling blaze while she poured big cups of the tea and passed a little bowl of hard blackmint candy to sweeten it.

"Zorn." My father's voice was sternly scolding. "You frightened your mother. She thought you were about to destroy yourself."

"The snake—" Something choked me. "It was too—too dreadful!"

"I'm sorry about your friend." His voice suddenly kinder, he set his teacup on the hearth and shook his head in sympathy. "I didn't know you were taking it so hard."

An ache closed my throat when I tried to say I couldn't help it.

"I know you are terribly hurt." He put his strong hand on my shoulder, and I caught the sharp unicorn scent of his sleeve. "But there are things you must understand."

I didn't want to understand that hideous snake.

"There is dreadful wrong in the world." He put his hand on my mother's, with a quick little smile for her. "We have suffered from it, your mother and I, but she has taught me to search for the right."

My eyes were blind with tears. The yellow flames swam and blurred, and I could imagine no spark of goodness in the red-crowned mage or his horrible staff.

"If the Three have power—" not used to questioning him, I turned to my mother instead "—why didn't they stop the snake?"

Looking unhappy, she waited for him to answer.

"An old question." Frowning as he thought about it, he picked up his teacup but forgot to drink. "Good people have been wondering for a thousand years."

"That mage." I needed terribly to know. "How could anybody make a stick of black wood change into that terrible snake?"

"How can a she-wolf's bite change a man into her mate?" His

tone low and sober, he looked hard at me. "The world is full of such questions. Terrible questions, sometimes with answers that are hard to find."

I shivered, remembering all Bastard had told me while he was still alive, remembering the mage and the snake and the howling banshees.

"We've had our own hard lessons, your mother and I." His blue eyes warmed with fondness when he nodded at her. "Beginning, I guess, when we were students back at the Academy."

The tea was sour in my belly in spite of the blackmint, and his words meant nothing.

"She was a Mystic." He smiled at her, but I knew his lesson was for me. "I was a Realist. We never agreed on anything—except that we had fallen in love."

"What's a Realist?"

I asked the question just to please him. I knew the snake would haunt me for the rest of my life in spite of whatever he said.

"A question of belief." He spoke very slowly, thinking how to say it. "We Realists believe in ourselves and the power of our minds. We keep asking why, trying to learn enough about our universe to become the masters of our lives. The Mystics are afraid to ask." He shook his head at my mother, his tone gently teasing. "The Mystics see themselves as blindfolded victims of a world they're afraid to understand."

"There is darkness, and evil magic in it." My mother spoke more seriously, perhaps a little hurt. "I fear Xath and the black magic of the mages. I don't want to understand their ugly secrets. But I do find comfort in the holy Three. They are life and love and hope."

"A noble hope!" He grinned at her and turned very seriously to me. "You must choose for yourself. The Realist thinks and inquires. The Mystic feels and imagines. The Realist looks for laws. The Mystic kneels to Powers. The Realist seeks knowledge and trusts himself. He believes every question has an answer, if he can only find it. The Mystic prays for peace instead of answers."

"Because there are no final answers," my mother said. "None that we can know or I can believe."

"If you know the answers—" feeling desperate, I looked back at him "—what changed that stick of wood into the snake?"

"I don't know, or even need to know." He shrugged as if it didn't really matter. "But I think the mages could tell you if they wanted to risk exposing the cunning tricks that make their magic."

"Forget the mage," my mother urged me. "He's pure evil. Evil is hate and destruction and death. I hope you'll learn to trust the Three. Their goodness is love and life itself. Your father and I have had sad times. We may have more, but my faith in the Three lets me laugh at most of them."

Feeling sick and miserable, I could only shake my head. Nobody could laugh at the mage and the snake.

"The Realists wants more than comfort." My father's voice had quickened. "His faith is in the courage that comes from understanding—"

"What good is understanding?" Her voice turned sharp. "Look at the mages! They boast of all their secret knowledge—the dark secrets they say they learned from Xath—and it has turned them into evil monsters."

"Evil enough." Wryly he nodded. "But is the evil in the understanding? Or in those who misuse it?"

"Knowledge is power." Lost for the moment in their old debate, she had half forgotten me. "Power corrupts. The mages know too much. They have enjoyed power too long. Xath is total evil!"

"Is Xath a god?" I asked her. "Stronger than the Three?"

"A demon!" Her voice grew savage. "Perhaps a man who used his evil secrets to turn himself into a demon!"

"Perhaps. If the historians are right." My father turned to me. "The mages are certainly evil, but they themselves are merely men. Realist science can explain most of their magic. Their powers are sometimes frightening, but they don't rule the world—"

"They want to!" she cried. "They plan to help the real demons conquer it when the red moon rises."

"If it rises," my father said. "Perhaps it never will."

"Will it?" I looked back at her. "Do the Mystics know?"

She waited again for him to speak.

"Nobody does." He shrugged. "Something bad did happen to the world a thousand years ago. Archaeologists have found relics and ruins that seem to date from some great disaster. The mages do expect the red moon to rise again. They believe its real demons will descend to wake the sleeping dragons and arm the wyvern and the wolves against the infidels.''

"We—'' I had to gulp at the sour tea burning in my throat. "We are infidels?''

"I am.'' He nodded, with an odd quick glance at my mother. "We Realists don't believe in tales that can't be proven. The Mystics never know.''

"Please, Rennie!'' She shook her head in patient protest and spoke to me. "I don't believe all the claptrap of the mages. I suppose they'd call me another infidel.''

"Will I be one?'' I could only whisper. "Will the demons come hunting me?''

"I hope not.''

My father was laughing at me.

"Rennie!'' She scolded him more sharply. "Please!''

"Forgive me, son.'' Suddenly he was very serious. "Terrible things do happen, but your mother and her Three live for better things. You may never forget your murdered friend, but you're a Var. No true Var would destroy himself. Will you remember that?''

He waited, but I found no will to speak.

"I think your mother will agree. . . .'' He waited for her quick nod. "I think we've tried too hard to shelter you from all the badness in the world. I think we should tell you why we're here and who you are.''

She nodded again, tears shining in her eyes.

"So let's make a bargain.'' He grinned and offered me his hard-callused hand. "You were born at Dragonrock castle. I don't think you've been told that it should have belonged to you.''

I'd imagined that, but never dared believe it.

"Promise me you'll never destroy yourself,'' he said. "And I'll take you to see Dragonrock.''

7

The Grugarn Lectory

The black curtains kept the boy blind, and the police only shook their heads when he asked where they were taking him. Smelling of fire and hot steam, perhaps of the demons themselves, the cart wheezed and rocked and jolted all night and most of a day. Once they let him out to vomit, and twice when he needed a toilet, but woods and stars were all he saw till they stopped in a yard with high stone walls.

This, they told him, would be his new home. It was a lectory in Quar. He would have to mind the lectors, grim, lean men with scar-carved faces, who wore long black robes and filed their black teeth sharp and dyed their hairless skulls the color of blood.

Growing up there, he learned the hard discipline of Xath, who was the Eternal One, the Celestial Guest, the Flame of Darkness, the World Maker and World Destroyer. The lectors were not cruel to him, except in the many ways they were cruel to themselves. Their food was poor and scant, and the lectory had no heat in the winter. The head lector woke them early to kneel naked on the cold stone floors and repeat the rituals of Xath. Most of them never spoke, except to chant their endless chants or to teach him his duties to Xath. He learned the chants and the special forms of humble respect due the demimages and the mages and the master mages and the archimage above them all.

''The archimage is the voice and the sword and the torch,'' they told him. "He kneels to the black flame in the temple to hear the words of Xath and speak his sovereign will. When the celestials come, he will command them."

He found a fierce joy in the cold and the hunger and the pain, because they were steps on his way to become the next archimage and the voice of Xath.

8

Dragonrock

"How about it, son?" We were still in the kitchen, before the dying fire, and my father was waiting for me to take his strong, sun-browned hand. "Want to fly over the castle?"

I had to look away to hide a sudden flow of tears. I don't know why I cried. Perhaps because I knew my parents loved me and I felt sorry I had hurt them. Perhaps because of grief for Bastard. Perhaps only from helpless, hopeless hatred of the black mage and his snake.

Too many feelings I didn't understand. Yet, in spite of all they had said about Realists and Mystics, I had a dull cold conviction that nothing really mattered. I had seen the evil of Xath, and something inside me was dead.

"Dragonrock?" I sat wondering if I really cared, until the breathtaking reality rocked me. I caught my breath and blinked. "Will we ride Sharabok?"

"How else?"

Sharabok had always frightened me, so splendid in his sleek black power, with his white-shining horn and his immense black wings, but also terrible and strange. I had always longed to ride him, and wondered if I would ever be strong enough and brave enough.

But the mage had changed me. Falling off Sharabok could be no worse than dying in the high white water and the boulders grinding down the river. An aching lump had closed my throat, but I gulped and gripped my father's hand.

"Rennie!" My mother's voice quickened. "I wanted just to tell him. Not to fly there!"

"I know the rules." He laughed at her dismay. "They let me ride Sharabok. Just so long as we never come down anywhere off the farm."

"But flying over the castle!" She reached for my arm as if to hold me on the ground. "Isn't that a dreadful risk?"

"I suppose I'll always be at risk." He nodded soberly. "So long as my little brother's the rider and his good mother has her connections. But we'll respect the rules. All I want is one quick look, from high up and far away."

"Enemies may see you."

"They're always watching." He shrugged. "But the primarch does remember when he owed debts to me. That's why his decree let me keep Sharabok, with the right to ride."

"But Zorn—"

"We've shielded the boy too long. He needs to know the world we live in. If he's to be a Var, he must learn to live with risk."

He looked at me. "Are you game?"

"I—" I tried to find a better voice. "I'm game."

"Rennie! He's too young!"

"My father gave me Zeldar when I was five years old." His keen blue eyes came back to me. "How about it, son? Want to learn what it means—what it ought to mean to be a Var?"

Trembling, I had no breath to speak.

"Wait till you're older!" she begged me. "The castle will keep."

Uncertainly I looked back at him.

"It's time he saw his birthright," he said. "Dragonrock could be the medicine he needs."

"Perhaps." She was still afraid. "Perhaps."

"I'll try to keep us out of sight," he promised her. "And hope we aren't observed."

"The banshees," she whispered. "Always watching."

"Maybe spying for the wyvern." He laughed. "I don't think they talk to Thorg."

We had to wait till the snows were gone. At last, on a fine spring morning, my father looked at the small white cloud puffs building over the mountains west and north, and said they would give us the cover he wanted. He put on his worn flight leathers and blew a long note on his flute to call Sharabok.

The great black stallion came down to us off the hillside where he had been grazing, running on four legs like a horse, bright black hooves ringing on the rocks. He dropped his huge head to lick up the yellow suncorn when my father poured it into the trough. His hot scent washed me, a sharp fragrance like sweetwood smoke, and I dared myself to touch the tip of his long ivory horn.

My mother pulled me away from it, and made us wait while she ran back to the house to get a cap and jacket for me. I stood there trembling, staring up at Sharabok. He was larger by far than any horse, and very different. His front hooves were on his elbows. His wings were long, stretching far out when his strange forelegs unfolded in the air. They were sleek black velvet, grown to his flanks and muscled from his rump.

My mother came back to hug me and help me into the jacket. The suncorn was soon gone, and Sharabok raised his great head to pipe something like another chorus to the song of the flute. Careful with the needle-pointed horn, he dipped his delicate muzzle to touch my father's forehead before he knelt for the saddle.

It was a precious thing, carved hopper leather inlaid with silver, and my father kept it bright with oil and polish. With the flute in a sheath at his belt, he buckled the collar and crupper that anchored it and stepped over Sharabok's bent wing into the stirrup.

"Ready, boy?"

He reached down for me, but I stood paralyzed.

"Rennie, please!" My mother's voice was sharp. "Let him wait!"

I was quivering with eagerness to ride into the sky, to see the real Dragonrock, to know more about the Vars, yet I felt afraid. The needle tip of Sharabok's long, bright horn came too close when his muzzle swung around toward my head, his great eyes fixed on me. They were long and golden, flecked with blue. Perhaps they were merely curious, but I shuddered when he whistled softly to me in the unicorn language.

"He begs you to be brave," my father said. "He knows you are still a very young colt, not yet at home in the air. He will take good care not to let you fall."

I raised my trembling arms, and my father hauled me off the ground. Sharabok made a cooing neigh and lurched upright. Suddenly I was looking far down into my mother's anxious face. I wanted to tell her I would be okay, but she was already stumbling away from Sharabok's hooves.

The saddle swayed under me. Sharabok was suddenly running, and the wind blew cold on my face. The saddle tipped as his forefeet lifted. The rear feet hammered the rocks, faster, faster. The black wings spread, as wide as threshing floors. The ground blurred. A hard knot of sickness tightened in my stomach. I had to shut my eyes.

When I opened them, the world had spun beneath us, and it was strangely changed. My father pointed, yelling past my head. I had to follow the narrowed silver river to find our grass-roofed house, already nearly too small to see. My mother was a tiny doll, waving something white.

And sheer joy swept my fear away. The world under us had shrunk to a harmless toyland. Soaring on mighty wings, we were already too high for anything to touch us. I twisted in the saddle to grin at my father, who grinned back for a moment through his red-gold beard and then looked very grave.

"There is a risk." Wind was rushing past us, but he held me high against him, his voice close to my ear. "But we'll hope nobody sees us."

His strong arm tightened around me.

"You were born a Var." His voice had turned more solemn. "You must discover what that means."

Sharabok had flown eastward down the valley as we climbed. Leaning to look, I found the village and the small green squares that were farms around it. The houses looked smaller than the mud models of Dragonrock I used to build on the riverbank: the white spire of the toy chapel, the fleck of red tile that roofed Mrs. Emok's store, the bright metal glint of the blacksmith shop. All I'd ever known, dwindled to nothing.

"A world you've never seen." Again my father spoke through the whistling wind. "We came from Wolver Riding. It lies yonder, beyond the Wolf's Head range."

He pointed at the mountains north and west, and I felt jolted out of my joy. The thin bright thread of Little River was lost in low green hills with higher hills and bluer hills beyond them, and finally in the far west the Dragon Mountains, a wall of jagged peaks tipped with white I knew was snow. I shivered when I thought of the dragons that lived under those unreachable summits and the wolves and wyvern hunting through the nearer wilderness.

"Back when you were born—" his voice was close to my ear "—the whole riding was ours. It has always belonged to the Vars, ours to rule and guard, ever since we took it back from the wyvern and the wolves. We had always been loyal to the primarchs, but they are far off and they had never meddled. They knew we needed imports from their lowlands, and they needed us to hold the border safe. I was lord of the riding when you were born. Your mother was the Lady Wolver. We were expecting a happy reign, till things went wrong.

"Terribly wrong."

He stopped with that. Sharabok was lifting us into the west over a world I had never seen. The valley had become a narrow canyon under us, Little River a thin white thread between great dark cliffs, and the bright-peaked Dragons looked higher, still very far ahead. The wind sighed a long time in my ears before he went on.

"I don't think you know much about my half brothers, Slarn and Thorg. They were off at Targon when you were born. They lied about me to the primarch, and Thorg came back with the decree that gave him the riding. A bad accident had left me too weak to fight, and he sent us into exile here. He's the rider now."

"Thorg?" Listening on my pallet, I'd heard the name. "Do you hate him?"

"My father's son? Yes." His voice seemed sad. "Born a Var, he disgraced the family. He has done a great wrong to you—and many another. You should have been there in Dragonrock and heir to the riding."

"But I'll never be?"

"Not likely." His voice went harder. "My brothers are clever. They have powerful friends, and a powerful mother who always hated me. Our exile is forever."

The wind was growing colder as we climbed. I buttoned my jacket and leaned back against his body for warmth. The world had flattened under us until it looked like a wrinkled quilt, green beneath us, edged with white on the farther mountains.

"Forever." I barely heard the word above the wind. A long time passed before he went on. "You've heard about the Dragonshield. We Vars have always been its keepers. But for Thorg, you should have been its next custodian."

"Is it magic?" Remembering Bastard and the dark magic of Xath, I turned my head to ask him. "A magic weapon?"

"Don't ask a Realist." I saw him shrug. "It looks like a small glass lens, except that it's black. You can't see through it. What it is and what it does, I was never told. I don't think anybody knows, but my father hoped it could somehow help us save ourselves from the demons if they ever come again. He was more Mystic than Realist, trusting the Three more than the Shield."

"Thorg kept it when he sent us away?"

"He kept it. Not that he'd ever fight the demons with it." My father's laugh boomed against the wind. "Not if he can run away."

The great wings beat, slow and strong. The wind felt colder. The wrinkled world slid slowly back beneath us, the Dragon Mountains still dim and blue with distance. I clung to the saddle's double horn, shivering to more than the chill of the wind. All this was too much to take at once: my fear of the flight and the thrill of it, the truth of who I was born to be, the mystery of the Dragonshield, the pain of all my future lost.

Yet all that eagerness could not erase the dread that had driven me to the riverbank. I wanted to believe Xath was only the cunning invention of the mages, as my father thought, but I couldn't forget that terrible staff or my mother's fear of evil powers too strong for the Three.

The Realists saw a world we could know and manage, but I saw no way to understand a stick that became a dreadful snake. The Mystics saw a world of mystery, where only the Three could aid us. They had not saved Bastard. I had trusted my mother's love and my father's strength, but my bad uncle Thorg had beaten their goodness.

I saw nothing worth hoping for, yet the ride was still exciting. Watching strange new landscapes slide under us, I tried not to think of Thorg or the mage or the demon moon. We flew west a long time before my father pointed north over bald brown mountains that fell away ahead of us toward a hazy red and yellow horizon.

"Dragonrock," he said. "Beyond a field of old volcanoes and the Wind River desert. That's where Nuradoon the Ninth was lost. Still too far for us to see. We'll circle farther west, flying over wyvern country. That'll be safer for us than my brother's riding."

He said no more of Nuradoon, and I was too full of other things to ask how he had been lost. We flew on above the flattened wilderness, west and north and finally east again. I leaned out of the saddle to search for signs of wolves or wyvern. Of course, there were none. The werewolves opened no roads, cleared no fields, built no houses. Yet I knew they were there, hiding in their caves and dens, cunning and cruel and hungry, perhaps watching us.

I looked for Dragonrock.

The sky at home had been blue and clear, with only a few small clouds far off in the North. Those little white puffs had grown gigantic before Sharabok carried us back among them. Staring up at them, I shivered with wonder.

Clouds had always seemed magical to me, growing out of nothing into cities and jungles and armies of monsters, strange as dreams and impossible to touch. Here they were huge and close, so bright they hurt my eyes. They were all flat at the bottom as if they stood on an invisible floor, but swelling upward as high as I could see.

My breath caught when Sharabok dived with us into a shining

cloud-wall. It turned to icy fog around us. Lost in it, I felt cold and afraid. The whole world was gone, and only Sharabok seemed real, his sleek black shoulder burning hot when I leaned to touch it.

"He does get hot." My father had seen me reaching. "Flight takes power. Unicorns have their own metabolism. It's more efficient than ours, but still they have to eat a lot of suncorn."

My jacket seemed too thin, and I dropped flat to warm myself on that sleek velvet coat. It was steamy with sweat, strong with the peppery unicorn scent. I clung there a long time, happy for Sharabok's wonderful power and hoping I could grow up to ride like my father.

"We're over the riding now." His voice was hushed. "There's Dragonrock. Take one quick look."

We dropped out of the freezing mist, back into hot sunlight. A vast shallow valley spread below. Long, dark hedges and thin white roads wound through a bright patchwork of farms, green and gray and yellow, flecked with red dots that must be roofs. A wide green-edged river swept in shining curves down the valley from a long blue lake.

I found the castle before my father pointed with the flute. It stood on a great dark rock, the river sharply bent around it. More oblong than square, the castle was shaped to fit the rock. I saw shining water in a deep ditch cut across the bend, and a bridge across the ditch to the castle gate. That made the hill an island, really. It looked safe from every danger—except, of course, from my father's crafty brothers.

"The keep." The flute pointed at the great square tower on the highest point, inside the walls. "You were born there."

I saw the level platform that topped it, and something moving on it. A scuttling insect was spreading its wings. A tiny brown unicorn sailed out beyond the walls.

Climbing after us?

My heart came up in my throat, but I saw no fear when I twisted to look at my father. He was shaking his head, his blue eyes sad. A long moment passed before he sang the command for Sharabok to lift us back into the chilling mist. We flew there forever.

My face grew wet and stiff, and I leaned again to warm my hands on Sharabok's shoulder. The black wings whispered faintly on each slow beat. Their tips were lost in the fog, and suddenly I felt afraid that Sharabok himself was lost, turning in circles, going nowhere. For one sick instant, I thought we were flying upside down.

"Does Sharabok—"

My tight throat caught, but I heard my father laugh.

"We're okay," my father said. "His compass is his horn."

Suddenly we were back in sunlight, the icy towers all behind. My father sang again, and Sharabok turned back southward over the wrinkled wilderness. The air grew warmer and the sun felt good on my skin.

"You saw the keep." My father twisted in the saddle to look back, but the castle was lost in the haze behind. "It's a monument, built seven hundred years ago by Nuradoon the Ninth. Generations of Vars before him had been elected primarchs of the lowlands as they were then, but it was the ninth Nuradoon who took these highlands back from the wyvern and the werewolves. He built the keep to hold the riding against them, and died somewhere in the desert, chasing them back toward the Dragons. A great man. Remember his name. Nuradoon ir Var."

"Nuradoon." I felt a thrill of pride that my name was also Var. "I'll remember."

Remembering the castle and that lost heroic Nuradoon, I felt a new wave of sorrow for my father and mother. If Thorg had taken Dragonrock from them, what was the use of being a Var? My father's voice surprised me when I heard it again, because it seemed so cheerfully matter-of-fact, with no sadness in it.

"The unicorns sing a story of the first Nuradoon. In the story it was he who began to kill the wolves that killed their foals and learned to sing their language and began to grow suncorn for them. I'm not sure it's true. Perhaps they tell it just to make us happy, because they cherish happiness. But they've been our friends ever since."

Sharabok's neat little ears had been cupped back, listening. He whistled softly. My father sang an answer, and I knew from the songs that the friendship would never end.

We were dropping lower now, veering east. The leveled landscape took shape again, and I saw the thin bright ribbon of Little

River. Looking for the gray grass roof of our tiny house, I was sorry for the flight to be over.

"Now you know who you might have been." Something in my father's voice made me turn to look up at him. He shook his head at me, a small wry smile behind his wind-twisted beard. "Now you must learn to live with who you are."

The saddle rocked. Sharabok bugled.

"Hang on!"

I heard my father's shout and then the flute, playing a fast tune that made my pulse pound. A gust of wind swept the sound away. The world tilted under us. Eyes half-shut against the rushing air, I saw tree-tangled mountain walls rushing back around us and white water close below.

Suddenly weightless, I clutched the saddle's two horns with both desperate hands till I grew suddenly heavy again, as heavy as lead. Foaming water flashed back beneath us, and I saw something moving on the riverbank just ahead.

It was stooped and gray and ugly, with an odd hump on its back. Running on two legs like a man, it was darting back and forth like a frightened rat. I blinked to clear my blurry eyes and saw that the hump was a bundle of something like black sticks. It stopped and turned. I saw that it was not a man.

9

Eighty–Nine

He was always hungry, often in pain. He was stripped and whipped when he was clumsy or forgot the lectory rules, but he tried to endure it all without complaint because the lectors ate no more than he did, because he saw the other acolytes stripped and whipped as often as he was, and because of all he planned for.

Yet he never loved Xath. He hated the hard rules and most of the lectors. Once he tried to run away. He left a dummy on his cot, made of the pillow and his laundry, and hid in a hallway until he could slip past the night-duty lector. The road outside the quad led to an iron-barred gate in a wall he couldn't climb. They caught him when day came, and took him back to the head lector.

"So you are Eighty-Nine?" His name was still Argoth, but he had learned not to say it. The head made a sour face and looked up his number in a black-backed book. "Why did you offend?"

He had grown used to the black robes and black teeth and red scalps by then, and he thought the stern old man seemed more sad than angry. Feeling no hatred, he tried to stand straight.

"I wanted to know who I am and why I'm here." That wasn't all the truth, but it was what he said.

The head frowned as if surprised. "Weren't you told?"

"Somebody said it was something about my father."

"With better luck, you might have known the truth and led another life." Thin lips tightened judicially against the sharp-pointed teeth. "But luck ran against you. You are here without a name because you don't exist."

"Why?" No sound came, and he had to catch his breath. "Why don't I exist?"

The head studied him and took a long time to answer.

"Because the world requires order. Existing, you would have posed a threat to order. Entered on the census lists under any name you might have had, you would have been erased. It is only here, under no name at all, that you may remain alive."

He waited, trembling on his feet.

"A bit of secret history." At last the head spoke again, the dry old voice precise and slow but not unkind. "If you have not been told, your father was the primarch—"

He caught his breath, blood pounding in his ears. For a moment, remembering the hopper herder's widow and the jeering neighbor boys, he was deaf to what the old man said.

"—jealous," he heard the patient words again. "Your mother concealed your birth and ordered the midwife not to save you. She was disobeyed by others who hoped to use you in their own plays for power. They were found out and had already suffered for it, but Xath protected you. You may live safe here, so long as your story is not told."

The shrewd eyes studied him. "Do you understand?"

He felt a savage anger, but made only a very tiny nod.

"One question, sir," he whispered. "My mother's name?"

"You would be wiser not to ask," the head told him. "Most of those who ever knew have died."

The head sent him back to his cell with no penalty at all, and wiser for the escapade. He had not yet seen the archimage, but the whipping post was on the lectory roof, and from there he had glimpsed the vast scarlet dome of the temple on the fortress hill, and the tall black tower behind it where the mages waited for their message that Xath was descending to close another cycle of time. He felt glad to know the bit of truth he had been told. That great temple was the archimage's home. It was where the primarch's son should live, free to whip whomever he liked.

10

The Banshee

I caught a glimpse of something else as we dived past the diving wolf. Some small scaly creature, the gray color of the rocks where it had crouched to stare up at us. Needle spines stood up along its narrow back, and a thin scorpion tail curled above them. Its eyes caught the sun as we neared it, flashing red as the eyes of the serpent staff.

It was gone before we passed, slithering into a crevice in the rocks. We climbed fast, the canyon shrinking to a dark little groove in the green wilderness under us. Looking back at my father, I saw his troubled frown.

"Did you see that?"

"The wolf?" I asked.

"The banshee." He shook his head. "I hate to tell your mother."

We were soon high again, following the river's shining ribbon toward the far white chapel steeple and the red village roofs around it. I found the narrow yellow rectangle of the suncorn field and at last our own small gray roof.

My mother came running with tears in her eyes to watch while

Sharabok knelt, and caught me in her arms when I slid down out of
the saddle. She felt me shivering and said I must come inside for a
mug of hot stoneflower tea.

"I'm okay," I told her. "We saw the castle! We killed a werewolf!"

Though I said nothing about the banshee, I saw shock on her
face.

"Rennie!" She turned to frown at my father. "You didn't!"

"Not really." He laughed at her alarm. "Just jumped him into
the river. Wolves can swim."

"A wolf?" Her voice went sharp. "Why?"

"Sharabok's a wolver. I couldn't have stopped him."

"Were you seen?"

"I hope not." He hesitated, his easy grin fading. "Except by a
banshee. It was perched on a rock, watching when the wolf
jumped."

Her face gone white, she turned and walked back into the house.
I stayed with my father. We unsaddled Sharabok and rubbed the
white lather off his flanks and gave him a basket of suncorn. Back in
the house, we found her in the bedroom, kneeling at her tiny shrine.
I was hungry, and my father found bread and cheese for us. She
came out at last, her face streaked with tears, and filled our mugs
with tea.

"We never touched the wolf." He shook his head, solemnly
apologetic. "As for the banshee, they're ugly enough but only
slimy little animals—"

"They're evil!" Her voice was quivery and sharp. "Their howling is the voice of Xath, and they watch with the eyes of his ser-
pents."

"Joy, please!" he begged her. "We broke no rules. We did no
harm except to give that wolf a bath. And I gave Zorn a glimpse of
Dragonrock and his lost birthright."

"Better forget it." She frowned at me, her low voice almost
scolding. "Your uncle Thorg's the rider now. If you want to call
yourself a Var, you'll have to earn the name."

"True enough." My father nodded. "But I wanted you to know
why you must."

"No easy task." With a tired little shrug for me, she turned to my father. "Not from here." Her voice hard and flat, she gestured at the rough rock-and-mud walls of the little kitchen. "Existing at the primarch's mercy, which could end tomorrow."

"Please, Joy!" he begged again. "Can't you forget the banshee?"

"Rennie, I'm sorry." She turned away for a moment to wipe at her eyes. "I must try to trust the Three." She gave me a thin little smile. "The mages may seem frightful now, but in the end the Three will surely prevail."

"Trust them if you can." Smiling through his sun-bleached beard, he nodded approvingly at me. "But you *are* a Var. You must learn to trust yourself."

"And learn your numbers now." She was on her feet. "I've got pots to paint."

The lesson done, I went out with my father to help him seed the kitchen garden. He was whistling a unicorn tune, and I felt happier. At least, even if the castle was gone forever, I had something new to think about, something better than the mage and his dreadful staff.

One morning a week later I found the wolf washed up on the sandbar below the house. Its shaggy gray body was bloated and stinking. Open wide, its green eyes stared so strangely that they looked almost alive. Yet it was very dead, the swollen legs stuck straight out.

I stood there shuddering, staring at its feet. They were queer feet, almost like wide three-fingered hands. The thick fingers ended in cruel black claws, but they could be retracted. The tracks, I saw, would look like the tracks of fat human hands.

Had the wolf been Mr. Emok? Slipping back to rob the village he remembered? Afraid even to wonder, I ran to tell my father. He brought a pick and shovel, and the wolf lay gazing at me with those terrible eyes while he dug a grave for it. Its evil odor put a knot in my stomach, and even in the pit its ugly feet stuck up so high that they were hard to cover.

My mother looked sick when she heard about it.

"If you killed it . . ." She shook her head. "What will happen?"
"Nothing, I hope." My father grinned at her dread. "It
shouldn't have been there." I saw his lips twist. "Unless my dear
brother is neglecting the wyvern border."

"What was a wolf doing here so near the village?"

He didn't answer, but I got a clue a little later, on one of our trips
to the village. While she was bartering her mugs and plates and
bowls to Mrs. Emok, I led the donkey to the water trough behind the
blacksmith shop. Mr. Alu was gone to lunch, but I found a boy
younger than Bastard sitting on a cot at the back of the shop. His
name was Klarn.

I told him Bastard had been my friend. He was Bastard's cousin.
His father had sent him from a town somewhere down the river to
live with Mr. Alu and learn to be a smith. Or actually, I gathered, to
escape some trouble he didn't want to talk about.

"I have to sleep here in the shop." He was already as ragged as
Bastard, and just as black with smoke. "Because somebody robbed
it. Broke in and took a lot of tools. Even the bellows off the forge."
He blinked through the grime. "Who would steal tools?"

I didn't know, not then. Later, when I thought of the wolf's
hand-shaped feet and the black sticks it had been carrying, I felt
sure the wolf had really been Mr. Emok, who must have wanted to
make weapons for the wolves.

That winter the police came for my father.

A light snow had fallen in the night, but the sky was clear and the
air very still. I had gone with him up the cliff to the coal seam. We
were loading bags of coal on the donkey when we saw Sharabok
running across the pasture, head high and white horn shining.

He had seen four unicorns floating out of the dazzle of the low
morning sun. My father gripped my arm hard and stood watching
till they touched down near our little house. I saw that one of them
had no rider.

That frightened me, and I looked at him.

"No surprise." He shrugged and nodded for me to hold another bag for him to fill. When he spoke again, his voice was tight and quick but very low. "Just remember who you are, and try to take care of your mother."

"I will," I promised, not sure what he meant. "But what . . ." I didn't know how to finish the question.

"We'll see."

He released my arm and caught the donkey's halter to lead it down the hill. Two of the riders hadn't waited for their unicorns to kneel. They jumped off the folding wing and ran toward the house. The other sat watching from the saddle. They all carried long guns.

"Who are they?" I whispered. "What do they want?"

He stopped and raised his hand to shade his eyes. I saw my mother running from behind the house with a bundle in her arms. She came behind the pottery and the suncorn crib, where the men didn't see her. After a moment he muttered something to himself and nodded for me to follow down the trail to meet her.

"I knew it!" She was breathing hard, her face strange and cold. "Your brother—"

"Half brother." He was very quiet. "Only half."

"More than half a devil!" She offered him the bundle. "A blanket," she whispered. "A knife and a loaf of bread."

"My Joy!" He shook his head at the bundle and took her in his arms. "Take care of Zorn."

"You must run!" She kissed him and pushed the bundle at him again. The loaf of bread fell in the snow. "Climb the cliff and hide in the woods. I'll have more food and your leather jacket ready when you can slip back—"

"No." He spoke sharply, looking down toward the house. The men were hammering with their guns, breaking the front door. "They'd misuse you."

"What will they do to you?"

He put his arm around her. She stood stiff for a moment and then gulped hard. The blanket fell out of her hands, and they walked on together, arms around each other. Suddenly cold, I picked up the blanket, wrapped it around me, and led the donkey after them.

The mounted man had seen us now. He shouted to the others and came on the walking unicorn to meet us. It was golden, as tall as

Sharabok, and it moved proudly, even on the ground. The man was lean and tall, with long black hair that fell around his neck. He wore black leathers, with a shining badge on his chest and a smaller gun belted at his waist. He stopped ahead of us on the trail, long gun lifted.

"Captain Mogard ir Barlik." He yelled his name. "Here in the primarch's service." His eyes were small, bright gray and hard as marbles. "Are you Rendahl Var?"

"Rendahl ir Var," my father said. "Exiled to this farm by the primarch's command."

"Rendahl Var, your exile is abrogated." Captain Barlik's voice was still too loud, as if he thought my father were deaf. "You are under arrest and ordered to accept the primarch's justice."

"I have accepted his justice." My father's voice was quietly patient. "I have observed the conditions of exile."

"Hear this, Rendahl Var." Barlik pulled a flimsy yellow paper out of his black leather pocket. "You are hereby informed of new accusations laid against you by Wolver Rider Thorg ir Var. He charges that you have violated the terms of your exile, that you have joined the monsters of the outlands in their invidious conspiracies against the lawful rider, that you have aided their raids into the riding and their efforts to secure illicit arms."

He flourished the yellow paper. "Rendahl Var, you are charged with treason."

"I am innocent—"

"Innocent?" Barlik shouted. "The evidence condemns you. You were seen crossing the wyvern border to meet with your confederates and later burying one of them who died near your dwelling. We'll be asking how it died."

My mother gasped and shook her clay white fist.

"Evidence?" My father stepped to put his arm around her. "Evidence of Thorg's ugly lies!"

The other men had come out of the broken door. They stood waiting, and Barlik gestured toward them.

"Come," he told my father. "Walk ahead."

My father and mother went ahead, close together, keeping step. Barlik slid the long gun back into its scabbard on the saddle and followed them on the golden unicorn, the small gun in his hand. I led the stubborn donkey after them, feeling sick.

The house made me sicker when we got inside. The men had wrecked it, tearing the bed apart, spilling books off their shelves and everything out of the cupboards. Two of my mother's lovely unicorn vases from the mantel lay shattered on the floor.

Barlik said they were hungry. He made my mother spread the table with the food she could find, a bowl of corn and redbean chowder, a slab of Mr. Ulor's goat cheese, another loaf of bread. They were angry when she offered to make stoneflower tea, and she found them a jug of iceberry cider.

When they had eaten, they shut me and my mother in the bedroom while they questioned my father in the kitchen. My mother made up the bed and we sat huddled together on the edge of it, trying to listen. We could her Barlik's angry voice, but nothing my father said.

Winter air had come in through the broken door and I was shivering, even with the blanket still around me. I wanted to ask my mother what was going to happen to her and my father, and finally to me, but a hard knot kept aching in my throat.

Her turn came next. They took her into the kitchen and one of the men came with my father into the bedroom to make him pick up the books and papers they had scattered on the floor. Once my father looked at me and winked. A sad wink, I thought. When he tried to speak, the man shouted to stop him.

I was the last. Barlik and another man sat at the table with their long guns leaning on it, drinking mugs of my mother's good cider. They made me stand near the outside door, shivering in the gusts of wind. Barlik emptied his mug and lifted it to look at the bottom.

"Your mother's mark?"

"She made it, sir."

"A bowl with this same mark was found farther up Little River in a tunnel the werewolves had dug." He looked hard at me. "How did it get there?"

"I don't know, sir." I might have guessed, but I didn't want to make trouble for Mr. Alu or Klarn. "Perhaps a wolf stole it."

"Where does your father go when he rides his unicorn?"

"Nowhere," I said. "He just flies and comes back here."

"Don't you ride with him?"

"Once, sir." My voice quivered. "Only once."

"On that occasion, where did you go?"

"Nowhere, sir. We flew over the mountain, up into the clouds, and came back here."

"I believe you met a werewolf?"

"Sharabok dived at a wolf, sir."

"And killed it?"

"No, sir. It jumped into the river."

"Why did you attack it?"

"Sharabok's a wolver, sir. He's trained to fight wolves. He did dive, but his horn didn't touch it."

"Sure?" His cold voice mocked me. "Why it is buried here?"

"I found the body of a wolf washed up on the sandbar. It stank. My father buried it because of the smell."

Barlik wrote something in a little notebook and laid it back on the table. He nodded at the other man and scowled again at me.

"If you want to help your father, tell me the truth." His voice was hard and flat. "Was he trying to bribe the wolves and the wyvern to make trouble for the primarch and the rider? Was he taking weapons to the wolves, or tools to make weapons? Did he kill the wolf when their plot went wrong?"

"No, sir!" My voice was a hoarse little whisper. "If anybody says that, it's a terrible lie."

"Of course." He nodded, with a twisted smile. "You can't accuse your father."

They made my father dig up the stinking bones of the wolf and spread them out on the sand to show that they were only bones, nothing else buried with them. They made him cover them up again. And then they took him away.

Not on Sharabok. Barlik tried to give him to one of the other men, but he snorted and waved his bright horn and made them all afraid. They loaded him then with the saddlebags that held my father's books and papers, and put my father on the scrawny little yellow mare they had brought.

Hunched against the wind, I stood with my mother in the snow-covered yard to watch them go. My mother was silent, tears running down her cheeks. My father waved and tried to say good-bye, but still they wouldn't let him speak.

The two lieutenants went first, their unicorns pounding down the snowy pasture side by side. Captain Barlik sent my father next on the little mare. She limped on one hind leg and took a long time to rise, but her yellow wings seemed strong enough when she was in the air. Hooting at my father, Sharabok followed close behind. Barlik bowed and smiled at my mother, and said he hoped she would forgive the inconvenience.

She spat on the ground.

Barlik smiled again, and raced the golden unicorn to overtake the others. They circled over the valley and came back low over the house. My father raised one hand when my mother waved. Sharabok made a bugle sound I didn't understand. I stood trembling with an ache in my heart while they grew small in the air above the eastern hills and finally vanished in the sky.

I felt terribly alone.

11

Acolyte

Argoth had two rivals. Gamel was the son of some minor court functionary who had sent him to Quar to save him from prison for some offense he never spoke about. A thin, weak-chinned boy, he wet his pallet at night and whimpered when he had to kneel and speak at open confession and howled miserably when he had to be whipped.

Kethek Ayc had come with gold bars as a gift to Xath. The gift was from a devout merchant who had found him lying in a Targon alley, so near death from sickness and hunger that the grace of Xath shone in his eyes. He never had to be beaten, not even after his strength came back.

Argoth pitied them both. He never reported Gamel for stealing bread from the pantry, and he helped Kethek learn to read. Yet he always drove himself, mastering his astral science and enduring his ordeals and answering quickly and correctly when they knelt together to be tested for advancement in the pitiless grace of Xath.

He became an acolyte. His hand steady in the black eternal flame, he repeated the ritual that bound him forever to the will of Xath and gulped the boiling crimson stuff they called the blood of Xath. It burned his mouth and made him sick and gave him dreadful dreams he never forgot.

The days of an acolyte were long and cruel, but he bore them because an acolyte could become a lector, and a master lector might become a demimage and then a mage, and a fortunate master mage might be anointed as the archimage, the terrible vessel of Xath.

On bare knees again, before the scarlet-skulled head lector, he learned the secret mysteries.

"Forget your human father and your human mother." The toneless drone was cold as the hard stone floor. "Forget the human friends you loved and the enemies you hated. Forget the folly of the human Mystics, who hope to save themselves with a rotten apple and a withered rose and a grain of corn. Forget the blind arrogance of the human Realists who hope to learn the language of the birds and the motions of the stars, and yearn to seize the power of the storms—before they know magic enough to stop a stinging gnat!

"Entering the house of Xath, you have left your human heritage behind. Cleansed in the black fire of Xath, you are reborn into his undying body. His will is now your soul. As his chosen arm, you will learn to seek out and punish deviation from his eternal plan and guide his servants through their cycles. Yet you must defend yourself, more than any other."

The head's black teeth flashed through a grin that frightened him.

"Your own conceit can damn you, for he cuts down the tallest and destroys the strongest. He is the Awakener. Returning when his red moon rises, he will punish human pride, humble human insolence, turn arrogance to agony. Even your own."

12

The Warning Star

My mother's cold hand caught mine, and we walked through the snow back to the empty house. I did what I could to help her fix the broken door and straighten up the mess in the kitchen. She washed the dirty dishes. I went out to get wood for the fireplace.

She was in the bedroom when I came back, kneeling to sob at her tiny shrine. Now in winter the bare clay altar held only a paper rose and a hard little apple and a few yellow grains of suncorn, but she stood up when she heard me drop the wood and said the Three would surely give us strength to stay alive and wit to find help for my father.

"I'm going to ask your uncles," she told me. "If they call themselves Vars, they are bound by family duty to rescue a brother in trouble."

No help would come from Thorg, I thought, not if he had stolen the riding and caused my father's arrest. I asked about Slarn.

"He's younger." Her mouth tightened as if from some bad taste. "Smaller than your father. He struts when he walks and wears bright colors and curls his yellow hair, hoping to impress the ladies. He tried to flirt with me, even at the wedding. He's now in Targon, where his mother lives."

His mother was the Lady Vlakia, my father's stepmother.

"I used to hear about Vlakia. She'd been the primarch's favorite when she was young. She never liked Dragonrock or wanted to live there, not even after the old rider married her. She and her sons moved back to Targon when they could. It was their lies and schemes that sent us into exile.''

In spite of that, she wrote the letters and we walked through the snow to the village to send them from the post office Mrs. Emok kept in the corner of her store. Mail had to go down the river on the boat that came every other week from Dorth, and on from there by steam train. We knew there would be no quick replies, but all that spring we were waiting in the store every other week when Mrs. Emok was sorting the mail.

No answers ever came.

People in the village must have heard how my father was taken away, because now they seemed colder toward us than ever. When I stopped once at the blacksmith shop to see Klarn, Mr. Alu told me sharply that he didn't want me there. I was walking away, choked with pain and anger, when he called back.

''Sorry, son.'' His voice was softer, and he really did seem sorry. ''No fault of yours, but I can't afford to have you here.''

Mrs. Emok had been our lone friend in the village, but now she told my mother to stop bringing pottery. She had no market for it. With none of the meat and flour and sugar and cooking oil she had always traded for my mother's pottery, we lived that summer on suncorn meal and what we could grow in the kitchen garden.

I was worried about how we were going to last through the winter, until Mrs. Emok found another market for the pottery in a town down the river. It paid so little that we had to live like hermits, ragged and sometimes hungry, but we stayed alive.

Later that fall, when we had waited on the landing for the riverboat to pick up our crates of pottery, my mother begged the river boat captain for anything he might know about my father. Captain Thrack was a big, red-faced man with dragons tattooed on his arms. He scowled at first and tried to wave us away, but when he saw my mother's tears he looked at me and looked back at her and dropped his voice to ask us into his cabin.

"I shouldn't be speaking to you." He shut the door and pulled a curtain over the porthole, then poured wine for my mother and himself. He gave me a delta orange, the first whole one I'd ever had. His voice was quick and quiet. "You know the danger."

"We're desperate." My mother raised her glass to thank the captain, and forgot to taste it. "I shouldn't trouble you, but I keep hoping for news of my husband. Rendahl ir Var." Staring at him, she wet her lips. "Do you know—"

"Nothing." His big hand lifted impatiently. "Not since the arrest. I don't expect to. The authorities don't talk."

"I must ask—"

"For the boy's sake, you shouldn't." I was about to peel the orange. It had a rich, exciting smell, but I stopped when he looked sharply back at me. "Better thank the Three for your good luck and leave things as they are."

"Captain, please!" My mother was whispering, and I saw her gulp. "If you hear anything—"

"I'll let you know," he promised her.

She tasted the wine and thanked him again and stood up to go. He winked at me when I thanked him for the orange, but I thought he looked unhappy for us. Afterward, we tried to be waiting on the landing when he docked. He never spoke to us again, not even when we had pottery to load, but he would still look for me and shake his head.

Perhaps we should have been grateful for good luck. Men on unicorns still came to circle low over the farm on their way up the river toward the wyvern border. Now and then Captain Barlik or another officer came down to our empty pasture and dismounted to question us. My mother, with hope that never faded, always asked for any news about my father. The answer was always the same hard frown, without a spoken word.

Yet they never took us away.

The lonely months stretched into lonely years, and we survived. I did all I could for my mother, helping clean the house, helping in the kitchen garden. When Mrs. Emok wanted more pottery, I helped my mother dig clay to form it and coal to fire it.

She became my teacher, using books of my father's the primarch's men had left on the shelf. Texts on mathematics and world geography. A history of Wolver Riding, which thrilled me with pride in the old warrior Vars who had taken it back and held it so well from the wyvern and the wolves.

I used to puzzle through three worn and water-stained volumes called *Records of the Demonic Invasion.* The records were never whole, but only scraps of letters and diaries, fragments said to be the recollections of survivors, inscriptions archaeologists had read or reconstructed from tombstones and ancient monuments, descriptions of broken and corroded tools and weapons, summaries of desperate campaigns against the wyvern and the wolves, fought long centuries after the invaders were gone. The words often seemed quaint or strange, always hard to understand.

My father had written comments in the margins. "Guesswork." "Pure fiction!" "Idiotic!" Now and then a kinder comment. "Likely." "Maybe." "Perhaps." And on the last page, "They appeared here when their red moon rose. They departed when it set. That's all we're sure of. What they were and why they came—I hope we never know."

After the first year, my mother seldom spoke of my father. Because it hurt, I suppose, or perhaps because she thought it would hurt me. I felt afraid to ask if she thought he was still alive, but I tried to imagine him free somewhere, safe and well, longing for us but afraid to come home because he knew the police would be watching for him here.

Though the village folk were never glad to see us there, one year we found a friend. He was Arad Narchalgo, a tall, quiet man who was something of a mystery when he arrived on the riverboat with no apparent business in the village. We met him in Mrs. Emok's store when he was buying dishes my mother had made.

"Var?" He looked up from a cup to stare at my mother. "Is that your name?"

She nodded, and he lowered his voice to say that he had known my father. She asked, anxiously as always, for news of him.

"Not a word." He glanced around us to be sure nobody was listening. "I was in the riding, living in the town below the castle, when he was exiled. Afterwards, people were afraid to say his name. It was only by accident, from a unicorn trainer's chance comment, that I learned that he was exiled. I'd hoped to find him here."

She asked where he had known him.

"We were students together in Targon." A wistful smile crossed his face. "We kept in touch, and he brought me to Dragonrock when he was planning to set up a Realist academy. Hired me to teach math and science."

"I remember." My mother's face had the shadow that came with recollections of my father. "He had grand plans for the riding."

"If he'd been able—" He caught himself when he saw her hurt look. "Lady Rider, I am sorry."

"Forget the title," she told him. "What happened to the school?"

"Under Lord Thorg?" Cautiously he looked around again. "Your husband had finished the building, and the young people were eager enough to learn. We were going to offer courses in mechanics and mining and agriculture—skills the settlers really needed. We'd made a good start. . . ."

With a bitter little shrug, he shook his head.

"Till Thorg came back from Targon to throw out Rendahl, and brought a mage of his own."

I shivered, remembering the serpent staff.

"A black mage of Xath. He called us heretics. Called our science blasphemy. Threatened our students that their souls would feed the wyvern in hell forever, he said, unless they threw their books into his sacrificial fire. I don't think many believed him, but Thorg closed the school."

On his next visit to the farm, Barlik questioned us about Narchalgo. How had we come to meet him? What had we discussed? What had he told us about himself? When were we planning to see him again?

We had made no plans for that, but Mrs. Emok gave us a note from him when we were at the store again. He asked us to visit him in the little house he had rented at the edge of the village. At his door, my mother warned him that we were dangerous to know.

"No more than I." He nodded, with a stiff little smile. "I've taught Realist science, which has been outlawed in the riding. Old friends are afraid of me. That's why I'm here, looking for a quieter life. With no teaching job, I'm writing a monograph on the cult of Xath."

"At your own risk," she said. "Don't talk about it."

He shrugged and promised to be discreet. He asked us to come back, and we saw him several times. He loaned me books of science and math. My mother gave him a porcelain teapot and a jar of dried stoneflowers. We talked about Xath and the demons.

"I had Realist friends at the Academy," he said. "We looked at what there is to know about their red moon and their invasion, which isn't much. Some suspected, in fact, that they were sheer mythology. Others wondered if their moon might have been some unknown astronomic object passing near us. Nobody had any concrete evidence, pro or con."

"Xath?" my mother asked.

"A raider from that object?" He shrugged. "Who returned to it before it disappeared?" He paused a moment, frowning at me. "Whatever the truth, I'd like to know."

When we passed by his house again on our next visit to the village, we found it locked and empty. Mrs. Emok whispered that the unicorn police had taken him away. Captain Barlik was waiting at the farm when we got back. His men had searched the house again, and he seized the books Narchalgo had loaned me.

He spent the rest of the day demanding facts we didn't know

about Narchalgo and the Realist scientists he had known, but finally
he seemed to believe my mother when she swore on her faith in the
Three that she had never shared my father's forbidden beliefs or
read any of Narchalgo's writings.

Until I grew old enough for heavy labor, my mother hired Klarn to
dig coal for the kiln or help me plant and harvest the narrow field.
Working in the suncorn field always gave me sad recollections of
my father and Sharabok, but the crop was something we could bar-
ter or sell to keep ourselves alive.

As soon as she would let me, I learned to help her in her work,
mixing and shaping and firing and painting the clay. Though my
first efforts came out misshapen and ugly, I began in time to share
her joy in the beauty we could find in form and pattern and color. I
felt elated when at last she smiled at a piece of mine and found it fit
to offer Mrs. Emok.

"You'll make a good potter," she told me. "Perhaps you should
content yourself with that. Better than staying alive to hate your
uncle and pine for a legacy you'll never recover."

Time went by. I did become a potter, though never as gifted as
she was. I longed to help relieve her endless toil, but we were still
prisoners. Captain Barlik still came on the golden unicorn to watch
us from the air. Landing when he chose, he questioned all we did,
but never spoke of my father, or even of Narchalgo.

Yet life offered pleasure. I had my mother and our craft. I had
those precious books that had been my father's, and his little telescope which I kept hidden where he had left it, under the thatch
above the kitchen door. On every cloudless night when the constellation Capricorn was in the sky, I stood outside to sweep its stars.

Nothing changed there—not until one crisp spring evening the
year I was twenty-two. We had come back late from a trip to the
village. The donkey unpacked and fed, we had made our own quick
dinner on what was left of the lunch we had carried for the trail. My

mother went on to bed. Tired as I was, I walked outside with the telescope to search Capricorn.

There it was!

A faint red star, where no star had been.

13

Novitiate

Leaving all his rivals behind, Argoth mastered *The Esoterica of Xath* and subdued his own emotions. Suffering through the required ordeals and conquering the tests, he was raised from acolyte to the rank of novitiate lector. No longer whipped or beaten, he himself sometimes had to beat the groaning Gamel and once even Kethek Aye, who had uttered a forbidden impiety.

He was still waiting for confirmation, however, his face still bare of the lector's ritual tattoos, when he was called from his dawn devotions to the head lector's office. The head congratulated him on his piety, wished him unbounded joy in all the cycles of Xath, and informed him that his first sacred service to the celestials was already required.

"The master mage has orders for you."

Standing bowed in silence, he shivered with forbidden elation. Sacred service? To the celestials? Under the master mage, who was the first legate of the archimage himself? He dared not ask and the head did not say, but dangerous emotions quivered in him when he heard the iron wheels of the guard cart that came clattering over the cobbles to carry him to meet the temple of the black flame.

Too often he had seen its blood-colored dome from the whipping post on the lectory roof, but still far across the ancient black-tiled roofs of the holy city. It stood on the crown of the walled citadel in the heart of old Quar, a sanctuary the primarch himself had never been allowed to enter on his pilgrimages of atonement.

As the cart jolted fast through narrow streets laid out for men and mules, he sat, wondering, yet trying to stifle his unholy eagerness. With Realist steam hardly more welcome here than women, he had to leave the cart at the temple gate, strip for the guards, and crawl naked on all fours through the great doorway. On his feet again at last, reclad in a black temple robe woven of something rough and coarse, he was guided down dark and soundless corridors to a cell as bare and narrow as his own.

"The master." His escort bowed. "Master Chero li Chark."

Himself naked to the waist, his old skin stretched tight over thin old bones and dark with its web of holy symbols, Chark sat bolt upright on a hard stone bench behind a black granite slab, a long black serpent staff leaning on the wall at his hand. His red skull shone dimly in the gloom, dimly glowing with its secret dyes and pigments.

Overwhelmed with awe that was itself a sin, Argoth knelt.

"Stand," the master commanded. "Now you need kneel only to Xath."

Silently he stood, breathing the strange temple scents of stale incense and moldering parchments and slow decay. A single candle flickered crimson on the corner of the granite slab, feebler than the gleam of the master's scalp, and a distant gong sounded the second hour.

Beneath the dimly shining brows, emotionless eyes surveyed him.

"You came here with a demon's name."

"I chose it, sir."

"A demon's errand for you." Black teeth glinted through the blue-scarred grin. "We hear rumors of malignant heresy at the Academy in Targon. Realists there are said to be challenging our theology and denying the divinity of Xath."

"Yes, sir?" The mage paused until he added, "Such vile heresies must be extirpated."

"A sacred duty now, as we prepare to welcome Xath's foretold return." The bare skull nodded. "Acting under cover, as I no longer can, you will go to Targon and matriculate at the Academy as a student of astronomy. You will determine the truth of those rumors.''

''If I find them true?''

''You will do as Xath compels you.''

''I seek to know and serve his will.''

''You know it well.'' The master regarded him again. ''I believe you will be a stranger in Targon?''

''I have never been there.''

''You will find it a festering hive of iniquity.'' The burning eyes probed to his soul. ''Mystic infidels and Realists worse than they. All contemptuous of Xath, they will test your faith with deceits and temptations you have never known. Defend yourself!''

14

The Nuradoon Helmet

I waited for months to tell my mother. That faint red star was something I simply didn't want to talk or even think about. Gazing back into Capricorn night after night, I kept hoping it would turn out to be only a passing comet, vanishing with no harm to anybody.

But it stayed. Night by night, it grew brighter. Never twinkling like the good stars did, it glowed steadily and sullenly red. It crept along its own ominous path among the unsteady stars. A night came at last when I saw that it was no longer a point, but a tiny disk. I stood shivering to something colder than the wind until I heard my mother's anxious call:

"Zorn? What is it?"

I put the little telescope back under the thatch and came inside. She met me at the kitchen door, a flickering candle in her hand. Time had left gray streaks in her hair and cut sharp lines around her eyes. Her shoulders had bent from years over the wheel. She had already endured too much, yet she listened with a calm that surprised me.

"I thought so." She set the candle on the table and went to the cabinet for two small glasses. Filling them from a bottle of Mrs. Emok's brandy, she set them on the table and bowed to pray, "Let the Three be with you!"

Her tiny fire was dying on the hearth, and the chill of the star had come inside with me. I stirred the embers and added another log before I sat with her to sip the burning brandy.

"We don't know what I saw." I tried to offer more hope than I felt. "Even if it is the bad moon, it should be a long time getting here. About the demons, we don't really know—"

"Son!" Reprovingly she shook her head. "You can't hide."

"Can anybody?"

"A Var can't."

"I'm not *the* Var." I shook my head. "It's my uncle who owns Dragonrock and the Dragonshield."

"Thorg?" Her voice was cold with contempt. "Imagine him against the demons!"

Sitting with me there at the rough-timbered table my father had hewn from logs he felled himself, on the heavy bench he had carved from another log, she waited expectantly for me to speak. Finding no words, I shrugged at the mud-plastered rock walls around us, walls my father had laid up himself, shrugged again at the frayed straw mats on the hard clay floor where I used to sleep.

"You're asking me?" I had to laugh. "To imagine myself fighting demons?"

She nodded silently, her face drawn grim.

"I used to dream," I told her. "When I was a kid, and excited at first to know who I was. I used to imagine I could catch and tame a wild unicorn. I would ride it back across the mountains and the desert. Thorg would come up to meet me, and I would fight him in the sky. I couldn't kill him, because Vars don't kill Vars, but I would run him out of the riding. I would land on the high stage, to claim Dragonrock castle and hold it till my father came—"

"If he ever came."

I'd never really believed he would, or felt sure of anything else, but I used to think my mother would be happy when I could send for her. I'd try to rule the riding as wisely as my father had. I hoped for skill and courage to fly against the werewolves and the wyvern if they ever dared to come back. But I'd never wanted to think about the red moon returning. After I watched the black-robed mage kill Bastard with his serpent staff, I tried not to dream of demons.

A wistful smile had lit my mother's face for an instant, as if my words had awakened some fond recollection of her own.

"That dream was long ago," I told her. "I'm no hero now."

"You were born a Var." She shook her head as if to reprove me. "You can't escape the duty that would have fallen on your father."

"What can I do?" I spread my empty hands. "What do I know how to do? How to work the farm and dig clay to make a pot and lead the donkey to the village. I've no unicorn. I've no weapons. I was never trained to be any kind of hero. All I really want is to learn to be a better potter and work here with you."

"I used to hope." She sat a moment, staring sadly into the candle's flame, and shook her aging head. "Too late for that. Thorg has the Dragonshield, but the times call for a better man than he is."

"Not for me."

"Your fate is yours to find." Looking hard at me, she finally shrugged. "You must at least warn him of the prophecy and teach him how to use the Shield."

"When I don't know?"

"I can tell you more than your father ever did." I saw a quick little quirk of her lips. "Because he was the Realist. The unbeliever. The Shield to him was only an emblem of the Vars. He used to laugh at my Mystic beliefs, but he let me hold it in my hand. I felt more than he could see."

She was silent a moment, remembering.

"Not much to look at. Just a lens shape of something like black glass. He let me hold it against the sun to see that it was not a lens, but I thought I saw a spark of light dying in it afterward. And I felt something. . . ." The memory hushed her voice. "It tingled very strangely in my fingers."

Remembering my father and all he had taught me, I thought I wanted to be a Realist. I longed for a sane world, one where events made sense and effects followed causes that could be understood. A chill ran down my spine when I thought of that red-skulled mage. The monstrous magic of his staff had no cause that I could even guess.

"What does the Shield do?"

"I asked your father." She looked away from me into the candle's uneasy flame. "He laughed at me, but I asked again. He told me then what the old rider had tried to tell him. That it was a magic talisman that had guided and aided the Vars to all their victories against the demons and the wyvern and the werewolves.''

"Could it really be?''

"Not to Thorg!'' Her face set hard. The little glass was quivering in her hand, and she set it down. ''A coward and a thief!'' Old anger quivered in her voice. ''He took it and kept it as a token of his stolen power, but he has no notion what it really is. He has to be told.''

"Will he listen?''

"He must be persuaded.''

She paused to draw a long, unsteady breath before she spoke again.

"Your father had sad times, Zorn. Sad times. Giving up the riding wasn't easy. He never wanted to talk about Thorg, or all he had lost. He'd let me see the Shield, but I had to beg for the rest of the legend.''

Flame had wrapped the crackling log. I drained the last sip of brandy in my glass and waited while she sat remembering.

"The primarch's men had just brought us here. The house wasn't even begun. We were still camping down on the riverbank while he felled trees and squared the timbers. They had let him keep the telescope. When I asked why he wanted it, he had me wait till dark and told me the story of the Shield while I held you in my arms.

"Told me—and laughed at me for wanting to believe. It begins with the story of an ancient warrior named Nuradoon, who led a revolt against the demons. The Dragonshield was his weapon—or maybe not really a weapon, because it was not made to kill. The old rider believed the story. Your father didn't. There was nothing in the story about how to use the Shield, but the old rider thought it would explain itself if the need ever came.''

She pushed her empty glass aside and leaned across the table.

"Trust the Three,'' she urged me. ''Trust the Shield. Persuade Thorg to trust it—if you can.''

"If I can.''

I hated to leave her. Even as exiles, we had enjoyed a sort of security. The villagers had always kept their distance, but they left us alone. And the unicorn police would surely make trouble for her when they found me gone.

"So?" She shrugged. "I'm used to trouble."

I knew no way to Dragonrock across that vast wilderness of forest and bare mountains and yellow desert I had glimpsed from the air when I rode with my father. If I tried to go by boat and steam train or wagon, the police would doubtless be alerted to stop me.

She sniffed when I spoke of that. If Thorg or the primarch got news of the red star from anybody, it would be from the worshipers of Xath, who would welcome it as the happy omen of their demon-god's foretold return. They would know nothing of the Shield, and they had no reason to fear me.

"There's a way to Dragonrock," she told me. "A path your father mapped."

The room had grown cold by then, and the candle was guttering in the saucer. She paused to stare a moment at the last embers dying on the hearth, or perhaps at her own recollections.

"That was years ago, when you were still a baby and he still had friends in the riding who hoped to bring him back. He never really believed in their schemes, or took any active part, but he did ride Sharabok over the mountains as far as he dared, surveying a path that he thought a little group of men might follow on foot if the time for action should ever come."

I sat straighter to listen.

"Of course, they failed." She shook her head, with a bitter little twist of her lips. "Thorg got wind of the plot and hanged the plotters he caught. The police came here to question us and search the house again. We were lucky. Your father had been cautious. They had no witnesses against him, none still alive, and they didn't find the map."

She lit another candle and took a kitchen knife to chip at the mud plaster over the mantel till she could pull a thin roll of brittle yellow paper out of a hole between the rocks.

"Here's Little River." She smoothed it on the table, and I saw my father's blue and gold unicorn sigil printed at the top. "The route begins here, in the gap in the cliffs above the coal seams.

You'll climb northwest through the foothills toward a V-shaped pass. A long trail, and difficult, but he said it should be possible. At least to the crest of the high divide, where the land slopes down beyond, toward Wind River. I persuaded him not to fly any farther. He said he saw old lava flows and volcanic cones below, and finally the edge of that dreadful desert where the last Nuradoon died. Beyond the map—''

She gulped, and her voice had turned husky when she went on.

"I asked about that desert. Bad country, he said. Fit only for ghosts and banshees. Nobody has ever lived to get all the way across it. Not even Nuradoon. Nothing flows in Wind River. Nothing but windblown sand. Except perhaps in spring, your father said, when there might be a little water from thawing mountain snows. He hoped the crossing would be possible in spring.''

We sat there the rest of the night with the dead fire and the empty brandy glasses, talking of all our hopes and fears. She had to remind me twice that I had been born a Var. Half the spring, she warned me, was already gone.

Dawn had come before I knelt with her at the little altar in her bedroom and repeated the pledge my father had taught her when they married, the pledge that made her a Var. It was a solemn vow, witnessed by the holy Three, to defend the Dragonrock and hold the wyvern border and guard the honor of the Vars.

My hand, she said, should have been placed upon the Dragon-shield. With no Dragonshield, she had me touch the earthen altar. The house was cold by then, but it was awe at that task that sent a shiver through me as I bent with her to kiss the paper rose, the withering apple, and the tiny pile of golden suncorn grains.

Next day she helped me make a pack, as heavy as I wanted to carry. Dried meat and hopper cheese from Mrs. Emok's. Dried fruit from the Ulors' orchard. Hopper ham and bacon they had cured. Yellow meal ground from our own suncorn. Blanket and tarp and waterskin. And the brass telescope, though now the star was plain to see without it.

That last night I slept very little, haunted by dread at what might happen to my mother, dread for the world, dread for myself. Nothing in my life had prepared me to trace that untraveled trail, or to cope with Thorg, or to face whatever the red star foretold.

I was out in the yard at sunrise, searching the sky for storm clouds over the mountains or the police patrol flying up the river. I heard the tension in my mother's voice when she called me back inside, to the warm scents of ham and hot bread and her stoneflower tea. Breakfast over too soon, we knelt a last time together. I kissed her, holding her thin body close, wondering if I would see her again. She helped me shoulder the pack.

"I'll pray," she whispered. "And I trust you."

Looking back from the top of our old trail to the coal seam, I saw her standing beside the tiny square of yellow thatch, waving her white apron. Gulping at the ache in my throat, I waved my hand till her image dissolved in tears. Turning then, I stumbled on to find and follow the path my father had tried to chart. The pack seemed awkward at first, but soon I forgot its weight.

The world ahead was all unknown. Mountain passes and desert canyons where no men had ever walked. Banshees, perhaps, if the land was really fit for banshees. Werewolves, if they had ventured this far from their western wilderness. Thorg, if I ever got to Dragonrock.

Somehow those uncertainties lifted my spirits, suddenly as intoxicating as Mrs. Emok's brandy. All my life had been chores to do, lessons to learn, the potter's skills to master. Burdens I felt relieved to shed. I studied the map again and hitched the pack a little higher and did not look back.

For the first dozen days, the map served me well. The winding line of tiny crosses guided me up the stony slopes and through the gaps and gorges beyond. Always I found wood for a campfire, sweet water to refill the skin, a level spot for my bed, with never a sign that Nuradoon or anybody else had been there ahead of me. Searching the sky for police unicorns, watching the ground for the fat handprints that were werewolf tracks, listening for banshees, I encountered no cause for fresh alarm.

The nights grew colder as I climbed, the air so thin, I sometimes had to stop for breath. The line of little crosses on the map led me into the last high pass, and ended there. Able only to guess the features of the falling slopes beyond, my father had left a wide blank space, empty except for a black question mark and a few such legends as "salt desert," "Wind River," and "Black Rock range."

Dusk had already darkened the pass, and I was aching with fatigue, but I climbed a last treeless crest to look ahead. The shadowed canyons behind me still held winter snows, but those below looked dry. A few wind-twisted trees clung to the cliffs, but most of the slopes below were black and barren lava flows from old volcanic cones. The desert beyond them was a baffling haze of fading daylight.

With no firewood I could find, I spent the night there, wrapped in my tarp and a blanket too thin for the gusty wind. Capricorn crawled above me, and under the brilliant mountain sky I needed no telescope to see the demon moon, a dull red globe that had swollen surprisingly. Too cold to sleep, I packed my gear at dawn and began the long descent.

The next dozen days were not so easy. Here beyond the map, I could only test the dry ravines and canyons for paths that looked fit to follow, searching always for chance pools the thaws had fed. Those grew rare and finally ceased. There was no more firewood, never a hint that anything alive had been here before me.

Knife-edged lava cut the sole off my right boot, and I wasted half a day sewing a clumsy repair. Below the lavas, the desert was no kinder. In some wetter epoch, flowing water had carved an enormous valley here between the ranges. Its floor was yellow sand and red sandstone cut by wind storms into pillars and castles and monsters as strange as the wyvern.

Here beyond even my father's hints and guesses, I had no clues to anything. In blinding dust, I blundered into canyons too deep to cross and mazes that lost me. My pack grew light, the moldy cheese all gone. I baked the last of the suncorn meal and the last of the rancid bacon into three small cakes and rationed them to one a day. Still I stumbled on, clambering through gullies cut by ancient floods, until at last the land sloped up again toward a far rust red cliff, a barrier that looked impossible to climb.

I sucked the last sour water from the skin and staggered all day toward that endless wall, afraid that if I stopped, I would never move again. The blazing sun went down, so luridly red with wind-borne dust that the bloody glow of the swelling moon hardly changed the sky. I heard a banshee howling, a long wail of utter desolation, which quavered and changed until it was piercing pain and finally filled with the bleak despair I was fighting not to feel. Far and near and far again, it came from ahead and behind. I remembered Bastard's dread of it, and the howling after he was dead.

With nowhere to stop, I toiled up a rubble slope almost too steep for me, and reached the cliff too sheer for me. Groggily relieved to see no way to go farther, I staggered along its foot, searching for any flat spot where I could sleep.

I can't remember how I found the cave. All I recall is waking on its dry gravel floor from a dream in which I had been back with my mother on Little River, about to fire a vase I had painted with the figure of the ninth Nuradoon following banshee tracks through that maze of sandstone monuments—tracks that had the shape of fat, long-clawed human hands.

"You're a good potter," I heard my mother saying. "Too good to waste your time chasing demons."

An icy dawn had come when I woke again, shivering and hungry. Gray daylight from the entrance showed rough black rock around and above me. Stiffly fumbling, I found the gravel under my blanket, and something smooth and round and cold that rattled when I touched it.

I sat up and found the object: A bucket shape of red-rusted iron. When it rolled away from my reaching hand, I caught the glint of precious metal. On each side of it, a unicorn head was inlaid in hardly tarnished silver, with bright golden eyes and shining golden horns.

The sigil of the Vars!

I caught my breath and reached again to pick it up. Something rattled again, and I found a white human skull inside it.

"Nuradoon!" A childish voice echoed from the rocks around me. "Nuradoon, hello!"

15

Infidels

He took the steamer upriver from Quar to Targon.

Used to the lectory's disciplined order, he felt lost in this unholy outside world. The casual blasphemies of his fellow passengers angered and sometimes frightened him. They jeered him rudely in the dining room when he expressed offense at their intolerable impieties. Overcome by such inordinate evil, he stalked out and spent the rest of the voyage in his cabin.

Targon was worse than the boat. Shrinking from all its monstrous godlessness, its marching mobs, its reeks and filth and roaring disorder, he hired a steam cart to take him from the docks directly to the Institute. A room was waiting for him; the mages had arranged his welcome as a transfer student from a school of mines in the far North Riding, but he found the campus a kind of hell.

Infidel were everywhere. Even the janitor sweeping the hall mouthed the holy names without reproof. The students spoke a jargon he hardly understood. They lived in a perpetual mad disorder. He was used to the tranquil peace of the holy city, where every person had his place and observed his duties, to the mages and the archimage and Xath. The people of Xath knew who they were and did what they must. Life flowed smoothly.

Not here. Nobody had any duty at all. He felt lost, drowning in a sea of perplexing uncertainties. Life was a hazardous game, played with conflict and compromise. Blasphemous debates raged around him, between Realists and Mystics and skeptics of everything. Students scorned the mages, laughed at magic, defied the commandments of Xath.

The women were the worst. He was appalled to find them quartered on the lower floor of his own residence hall. He had never known a woman, not since the hopper herder's widow, and all his old hate and scorn still rankled when he thought of her. Women, as the sacred books declared, were she-demons created to test the sanctity of men. Things without souls, they were justly forbidden in holy Quar and denied the hope of paradise.

Baffled when he couldn't avoid them, because the campus had no building they had not infested, he could only try to ignore them. That proved impossible. They crowded the halls, served his meals, taught classes he had to take, sat near him in the classrooms.

He yearned for the signal star to flash in sacred Capricorn, for the red moon to rise, for the celestials to descend again and set the world to right. His mission here was to clear their way. A difficult mission, perhaps, but they would crush these vermin when they came, like noxious insects.

And surely they would reward their friends.

Demon's Island

Stumbling out of the cave, I must have looked a scarecrow. Unshaven for weeks, I was unwashed and ragged, blistered from salt and sun, weak and giddy with hunger. I had left the skull among the scattered bones, but the helmet was still in my hand.

The creature that faced me outside was no child, but an odd little man, as ragged and grimy as I was. His bald head was burnt browner than the rusty helmet, his face round as an infant's but wrinkled into an impish leer. His eyes were what held me. They were wide-spaced and bright, oddly yellow.

"Greetings, Nuradoon." He bowed to me, but in a way that seemed more ironic than sincere. His voice had taken on a fluent power, surprising for such a tiny man. "If you really are Nuradoon the Ninth?"

"I'm not."

"Yet you wear his sigil." He shrugged, unsurprised, and nodded at the helmet. "A curious circumstance, here where I was expecting nobody. Certainly nobody alive."

"I was not expecting you." Still barely awake and totally astonished, I gestured at the cave. "There is a skeleton in there. I suppose it could be Nuradoon's."

"Perhaps." Enigmatic eyes narrowed shrewdly. "Though that still leaves a question. Who are you, sir?"

"A simple pilgrim." I hesitated to give my name. "Searching for the sacred springs that feed the power of the Three."

"Nameless?" His skinny head was brown as his face, as hairless and slick as if he kept it oiled. He cocked it critically aside, inspecting me. "If I may say so, sir, you have the aspect of a Var. The features, in fact, of one I served and loved. Could you perhaps be a kinsman of Lord Rider Rendahl ir Var?"

"I'm his son."

"So I'd suspected." He gestured at my pack, where I had dropped it at the entrance to the cave. "I found his sigil on your map, and notes written in his hand, if you'll forgive the liberty. Sir, what may I call you?"

"Zorn."

"Zorn ir Var?"

"Not yet," I said. "My parents did give me the title, but I should earn it before I use it."

"Call me a friend." He was bowing again, no longer with irony. "My name is Scorth."

"Scorth?" Recollections woke. "You trained my father's unicorns?"

"I rode with him." His leather face lit for an instant, and furrowed again with concern. "And loved your lovely mother. How is she?"

"I left her well, though I'm afraid of what will happen when the police miss me from the farm."

"I was on my way to look about her." He turned to scowl across the red stone desert the way I had come. "A confusing trail to follow."

"You may take the map," I said. "It's no good here in the desert, but it can guide you across the divide. The going will be easier beyond it. She does need you."

"You left her alone?" He was almost accusing. "Perhaps in danger?"

"Her decision more than mine. When we saw the demon's moon."

He froze for a moment, squinting sharply at me.

"The demons?" His voice had lifted sharply. "Only the mages

speak of them. Or call them celestials. To the Realist, it's only an unpredicted comet.''

"My father was expecting demons," I told him. "The object appeared in Capricorn, where he used to look for it. It's the color of blood. It never twinkled. It has moved among the stars. Now it shows a disk.''

His lean-boned frame seemed to sag, and he stood for a time staring blankly past me.

"The Lord Rider spoke of it," he muttered at last. "Though seldom, and always as the skeptical Realist. He expected—he hoped never to see it.''

"I've watched it every night," I said. "I think we've passed the time for hope.''

"The mages are already rejoicing the miraculous return of Xath, Lord of Fire." His bald head bent in sardonic bow toward those red stone monsters crouching around. He gave me a crooked grin. "Will you join me for breakfast?''

Gratefully I followed him down the rubble slope beneath the cave. A wonderful aroma rose out of a smoke-black pot propped on rocks around the embers of a tiny fire. His scant camp gear was tidily stacked, and a small brown donkey grazed farther down the ravine.

Generous with his waterskin, he let me drink and poured enough to let me wash my grime-gummed eyes. There was hard bread with the stew, and ripe figs he said he had picked at a spring a few miles back down the ravine.

"I loved the Lord Rider." Listening as we ate, I tried not to wolf down the stew too rudely. "He trusted me enough to speak of all his troubles with his brothers." He looked up at me, his voice grown sharper. "Why are you here?''

"On my way to Dragonrock. My mother sent me, really. I'm not very hopeful, but I promised to try to alert my uncle Thorg. To inform him of the danger, if he doesn't know it. To tell him what I can about the Dragonshield. A possible defense against them.''

"Thorg ir Var?" He seemed amused. "You'll make him a demon killer?''

"He owns the Shield. He should use it.''

"He'll hang you.''

"My own uncle?"

"He'll laugh." His grin grew bitter. "As he watches you jerking in the noose."

I was scraping up the last of my stew. He poured what was left into my bowl and watched in thoughtful silence while I ate. Though we were utterly alone, he glanced warily behind him and lowered his voice before he went on.

"I know your father's brothers, far too well. And the Lady Vlakia, his stepmother, who is somewhat less than any lady. The old primarch was once her lover and said to be Slarn's actual father. I was still training unicorns at Dragonrock when they sent your father into exile.

"And I knew his unlucky friends." His hard brown face twisted with remembered pain. "One unlucky man was heard to regret his exile. Thorg hanged him, and then a dozen others."

Silently scowling, he was scrubbing the empty pot with dry sand.

"Back when I was a kid—" my own dark memory fell like a cold shadow over me "—I used to nurse a silly dream I'd grow up to help Father get Dragonrock back. Until I watched a black mage murder a friend of mine."

"Silly?"

He laid the pot aside and looked up to inspect me again, his odd eyes critically narrowed.

"I take you for the Lord Rider's actual son." He nodded at last, with a shrewd half smile. "You carry his sigil. You have his eyes and his copper-colored beard. I never thought to meet you here, but there's something I must tell you—if you care to face a risk you'll hang for."

"Something about my father?"

"The true Lord Rider." He gestured at the rusty helmet, and his voice fell to a solemn undertone. "If you'll place your right hand on Nuradoon's helmet and swear upon your sacred honor as a Var that you are in fact the Wolver Rendahl's son."

"I do." My hand was on the ancient helmet. "Is my father alive?"

"Who knows?" He inspected the pot and pursed his lips to blow away the last grains of sand. "Unicorns listen, and sing their secrets to trainers they trust. I heard of that reckless plan to restore your father to the riding, and knew the careless speaker who betrayed it. I warned the men I could and escaped with a few of them into the lowlands. We lived in hiding there. No easy life, because we had a deadly game to play.''

Absently he peered into the pot again and brushed at imaginary sand.

''Our goal was more than just to find and free your father. We wanted freedom for all the nation, hoping finally to bring him down to Targon as the next primarch.'' That took my breath. ''Thorg and the primarch hoped, of course, to catch and hang us all. They've come near enough. And if you wonder . . .''

Frowning as if uncertain how much to tell me, he stopped to stare moodily away into the forest of grotesque stone monsters around us.

''If you wonder why they left your father so long on Little River, and left you and your mother there so long without him, it's because they were using you for bait, hoping to trap us when we came there.

''The primarch!'' A grimace of hatred twisted Scorth's deep-seamed face. ''He's old and fat and rotten with his vices, but still cunning as a wolf.''

''What has he done with my father?''

''I've spent the last half of my life at the search.'' He let his lean frame sag as if the effort had worn him. ''The police gave him to the mages, who never talk to anybody. I knew years ago that he had not been hanged, not in any recorded execution. He was not in any prison where I could reach the records. To discover anything, I had to convert to Xath, or pretend to. Dye my scalp and endure the whip and mouth the hymns of praise to eternal Xath.''

With a wry grimace at the memory, he paused to rub a sunburnt hand across his hairless skull.

''And then?'' I couldn't wait. ''Do you know where my father is?''

''Demon's Island.'' Ruefully he shook his head. ''The mages have another name for it, but that's the one that fits.''

It had chilled me again with an old terror of my childhood, when my book of early legends used to give me nightmares. Pictures of the island showed horrible black-fanged things flying over great black cliffs where high waves were breaking. Those monsters had always haunted me, even after my mother said they couldn't be real.

In the sudden flood of childhood memory, I was back on the farm with my father, holding coal sacks for him to fill; riding with him on Sharabok to see Dragonrock and diving at the wolf; watching with my mother when he turned to wave good-bye from the back of that scrawny yellow mare when the primarch's men were taking him away.

"My mother—" I gulped to find my voice. "My mother said the secret island was probably just an ugly myth."

"Ugly enough." He had begun to pack his cooking gear, but he stopped to nod his bare skull at me, his face gone grim. "But more than myth. I earned my own way there, with three strange years as an acolyte of Xath: Well enough regarded by my masters, if I may say so, even though they never told me anything about your father.

"My first word of him came on a pilgrimage to the island. My reward, if you wish to believe it, for outstanding zeal and aptitude! My master lector said he could sense the holy spark of Xath burning in my soul. He herded a chosen few of us aboard a sacred ship. We sailed down the river from Quar and on into the sea.

"Where Xath forgot us." He leered at the name. "The island is a wooded mountain in the track of the storms that come howling off the northeast coast. Our craft was old and leaky, unfit in truth to leave the dock. High winds drove us past the island and kept us five days at sea, sick and sweating at the pumps, before we finally docked.

"The island's sacred to the faithful, because they believe it's where the demons descended to begin their visitation. The mages have spent the last thousand years preparing to welcome their return. We were brought to aid the effort. Treated more like slaves than holy men, we were marched inland, up a stone-paved road to the temples on the highest point of the island. The temples are all wooden, built of heavy axe-hewn timbers. Another sacred city! Chapels and fanes and shrines stand spaced along winding avenues of great wooden pillars, all painted red."

"You found my father there?"

"I never saw him." With a wizened scowl, Scorth shook his head. "All I heard were tales from men who may have been honest rebels, or more likely informers for the mages. Your good father was said to be in one of the labor gangs, slaves toiling to complete the temple complex before the celestial lord returns. Felling trees, hauling logs, hewing timbers and raising them, splashing everything with blood-colored paint.

"Built to burn! Xath dwells in fire. The true believers must cleanse themselves in fire before they can rise to meet him. When the red moon rises, they're to be ferried down the river and out to the temple. The entire complex is designed to burn. The final duty of the mages will be to set it off, and the acolytes will be provided with vats of red-stained oil to douse the faithful and hasten their ascension.

"Can you believe it?"

He was grinning, his voice sardonic, and for an instant I saw him as an actual mage of Xath, his hairless skull dyed scarlet, his teeth all black, the lean-fleshed grin so malevolent that I shuddered.

"I never thought the master mages could be so cruel, or their converts so stupid, yet they all toil together with their slaves to build the pyres where they plan to burn themselves alive." Suddenly himself again, the grin painfully human, he drew a long breath. "I've never understood it, unless perhaps the temple drugs have turned the mages into human demons."

"Xath?" I asked him. "Who—or what—was the actual Xath?"

He shrugged, with a puzzled scowl.

"An actual demon?" He shook his head. "They're inventions of the mages. What else could they have been? How could they have got here? What's their bargain with the mages? If they ever made a bargain.

"I've thought enough about it. The mages hound the world for money. Gold and silver coins; they don't like paper. They claim it's all for the demons. Don't ask me where demons spend it, but the mages have their slaves filling the temple vaults in Quar with gold and silver, piled up by the ton.

"To pay for their own cremation?"

He grinned at me ghoulishly, contemplating that.

"Some few, of course, don't care to burn, though saying that can get you whipped or even burned alive ahead of schedule. One such skeptic was the captain of our ferry. He'd known your noble father, or so he told me when we came to trust each other.

"Your father had planned a slave revolt, he said, but had not yet attempted it. The ferry captain was hatching a larger scheme. People everywhere hated the mages and their evil magic. Hated the corruption of the primarch's rule and all the extortions of his tax men. The world was ripe for rebellion.

"If your father and his confederates could break free, the captain planned to take him and his best men with us aboard the ferry. We were to sail back to the mainland and on up the river to spread revolt against the archimage and the primarch. We would take Quar and go on to Targon. Proclaim your father the new primarch.

"A grand plan." With a dismal shrug, he paused to pack our scoured bowls into the empty pot. "Or perhaps a cunning ploy of the mages, invented to trap the silent enemies of Xath. I was never sure."

"So?" I tried to hurry him. "What happened? Happened to my father?"

"I never got more than hearsay." A helpless shrug. "He'd been the most famous prisoner. His name was the life of the plot—or bait for the trap, if it was a trap. Perhaps the captain really hoped to make a primarch of your father. Perhaps he was an informer for the archimage." He shrugged again. "Either way, we were betrayed."

He spat into the ashes and made me wait while he made a neat little stack of his gear, ready to pack on the donkey.

"With no hint of trouble, we left our cargo on the island docks and put back to sea. Midway to the mainland, we doubled around to a cove on the north coast and waited there for your father and his men. The mages came instead, like a pack of werewolves to track us through the forest. Most of the crew were caught. Probably burned or hanged.

"I swam ashore and lived however I could till I saw a unicorn landing, bringing the archimage on a tour of inspection. Thanks to the Three, the unicorn was your father's great black Sharabok, unhappy with the mages and glad enough to carry me back to the riding.

"Not that I found any real refuge there—too many enemies had known my face. Too few of my old friends were still alive, though one brave man risked his life to fit me out for this trek. If you wonder how I came to meet you here where Nuradoon died, it happened because this is the trail we mapped for your father when we hoped to bring him back from exile. I wanted to reach your lovely mother with that news of the rider, sad as it is.''

"My father?'' I had to prompt him. "What became of him?''

"I wish I knew.''

"Can we—is there any way we might help him?''

"How?'' He spread his empty hands. "I once thought there was a chance, but the primarch and the mages have hanged or burned the best of my friends.''

A north wind had sprung up, stirring snakes of yellow sand. He squatted back to watch them crawl away among the great red rocks that had tumbled down from the tall red cliff behind us. He drew a long breath at last, and turned back to me.

"Perhaps . . .''

He made me wait again while he watched the crawling yellow snakes. Shivering from a fresh gust of wind, I looked around us at the ancient helmet where I had dropped it on the sand and the dark cave mouth were I had found it, at Scorth's brown donkey nibbling at the sere yellow brush in the ravine below and the wind-shaped dragons of red sandstone in the desert beyond.

Somewhere a banshee howled.

"I wonder . . .''

Squatting there at the edge of the ashes, Scorth squinted at me owlishly, while I wondered what he wondered, wondered at his tale, wondered how far to trust him.

"A hard task you've set yourself.'' He shrugged and spread his gnarly hands. "But I'm with you if you want me. You see me as I am, weaponless and penniless. Friendless since so many hangings. Yet, if you want me, I'm still a servant of the Vars.''

"I—I thank you.'' He looked so childish for a moment, so helpless and pathetic, that a lump closed my throat. Yet his story had made him so able and so clever that I couldn't quite believe it. "What's left that we could hope to do?'' I asked him. "When all your plots have failed?''

His amber eyes had narrowed, falling to the old helmet where it lay beside us in the dust.

"We must trust the Three.'' Abruptly on his feet, he bent to pick up the helmet and set it on my head. "I think we can. They've made a miracle to save us!"

I blinked at him, bewildered.

"Don't you see it? You're no longer the exile's fugitive son. You're now in fact the reborn Nuradoon the Ninth, our ancient hero awakened from the grave to defy your evil uncle and defend the world against the archimage and all the demons of Xath."

17

She-Demon

The ravening women. The ceaseless blasphemy. The insane disorder. The accents he didn't understand. The obscenities that shocked him. All intolerable. Yet, for the sake of his mission, he had to endure. Unable to avoid the verbal duels that made the Institute an academy of fools, he declared himself a Mystic, skeptical of everything except the saving grace of the human spirit.

For a secret agent of Xath, that seemed a safe disguise. Most of the time he was able to keep silent, but one day in the classroom he came close to a dangerous explosion. The mages had enrolled him in basic astronomy, where the professor was a wizened little hunchback named Kallenayo, whose arrogant stupidities drove him to the brink of defiance.

Enjoying "battles of ideas," Kallenayo took a particular pleasure in ridiculing what he called the superstitions of Xath. Lecturing one day on the origins of the solar system, he outlined half a dozen theories and finally paused, blinking at the class through heavy black-rimmed glasses as if inviting a challenge from some foolhardy student.

"Theories!" In combat, or even the hope of combat, his rusty voice became a wheezy screech. "None of them with any better proof than the claim of the mages that the universe was created by their devil-god."

The lectors had trained Argoth in logic aimed at Realists and

Mystics and all such monstrous infidels, but he tried to swallow the hot reply on his lips.

"I've bad news for the mages." Kallenayo stood, teetering on tiny feet, scowling at him through the thick glasses as if he had made his protest aloud. "Xath is dying." Basic astronomy dealt chiefly with the motion of objects in space, but Kallenayo liked to brighten mathematics with melodrama. "Realist science is killing him. I'm about to deal Xath his deathblow."

Trembling, jaws clenched, Argoth glared back. Listening in silence, he could almost hear the screams of the blasphemous fool tied as he would be to a whipping post when Xath descended, stripped and bleeding.

"I know the archimage is preparing his reception." Kallenayo's wheezy voice dripped sarcasm. "If you didn't know, the mages are watching the constellation Capricorn for signs that the gates of paradise are readying to open. Xath himself is going to emerge in a ship of red fire, coming with his host of demons to end our own dismal cycle of time and carry the few fortunate back into heaven for the new creation."

Huge behind the lenses, his cold pale eyes scanned the room again in search of opposition and came back to Argoth.

"Perhaps the mages have a telescope?" He paused for an instant as if expecting Argoth to answer. "If so, our own new instrument is certainly better. Using it to search Capricorn, I failed to find the gates of paradise." His shaggy head shook in ironic regret. "What I did find is a very ordinary star."

Though the mages kept watchers in the tower behind the temple, they had always urged the infidels not to wait for any signal of Xath's return. He would appear with no warning, when he was least expected, to catch them in the full flower of their infidelities. He grinned to himself, contemplating Kallenayo's consternation when that took place.

"Only a small red dwarf," the scornful screech continued. "Though our observations have just begun, I believe it is a faint companion of our own sun, moving on a long-period orbit that brings it back to perihelion about every thousand years. The fantastic mythology of Xath and his demons is probably no more than a distorted folk memory of its last perihelion passage." Triumph flushed his long hopper face. "Nothing, I'm sure, that Realist science cannot explain and deal with."

"Sir, how do you know it's a star?" Tired of concealing himself, he was finally goaded to his feet. Skepticism made the best sword against the skeptic, so the lectors taught. "Aren't you making too much of a speck of light we can't see without your telescope? Couldn't it be a harmless comet? Or perhaps an insect in your instrument?"

Taken by surprise, Kallenayo gaped at him like a fish out of water.

"The demons were real."

A woman's voice. Argoth shrank from it, so shaken that he forgot the startled astronomer. Though he kept his eyes away, he felt her near him, standing to speak as boldly as a man.

"You're sure?" Kallenayo caught his breath to sneer at her. "Really sure?"

"I'm from border country." She sounded young, and as confident as he was. "An ancestor of mine was a warrior who fought with Nuradoon the Ninth in the highland wars. My family has lived there forever. My father used to sing the old ballads of Nuradoon the First, who fought the demons centuries before. He carried a magic shield against the dark magic of the demons and finally forced them off the world.

"He always believed—"

"Please . . ." Kallenayo raised his raucous voice to interrupt her. "Please sit down. I've heard the ballads of Nuradoon. They do tell stirring tales, but they are not historic evidence. I doubt that he or his magic shield ever existed."

He waited till she sat and turned to blink at Argoth.

"As for that fleck of light, faint flecks of light are the whole subject of astronomy. I have no doubt that this will prove to be a dwarf star in orbit around the sun. What I don't expect is to see any devil-gods there, or be receiving any celestial guests."

Argoth hurried out of the room after the class, eyes devoutly on the floor, eager to escape all the mockery of Xath, the brazen blasphemy, the female demons. He shuddered when he heard the woman's footsteps following him and felt her eyes upon him, but he did not look back.

"Mr. Ayth?"

He heard her voice close behind him in the corridor outside. Resolutely blind, he walked on till the quick tap of her feet overtook him.

"Mr. Ayth?" Her voice seemed amused. He caught her flower-like scent and felt her hand on his sleeve. "You aren't deaf?"

He flinched from her touch, but he had seen her. Only one careless glance, yet enough to let him feel her witchery. Feeling already damned, he shivered and looked again. She was smaller than he, slim as a boy, with pale gold hair that fell in soft curls around a fair oval face that concealed her incarnate evil behind a smile of childish innocence.

"No." He dragged his eyes away. "I'm not deaf."

"You make me curious." Her tone seemed lightly playful. "May I walk with you?"

He shrugged and looked ahead.

"I've been wondering." Her gentle voice was as insidious as her smile. "Where's your home?"

"Gold Fort." The mage had invented the name and data on his admission card. "A small mining town in North Riding, near the wyvern border."

"Really?" She seemed to doubt him. "Does your family live there?"

"I have no mother." That was his story. "My father is Anthel Ayth. He owns a gold mine."

"Does he?"

He tried to turn away, but her arm had slid through his. He shrank from its quick pressure and the hateful abomination of her scent.

"Forgive me, please!" She was suddenly contrite. "Your home is really no business of mine, but I happen to work part-time in the admissions office. When I saw your records, I wondered if there had been an error you might want to correct."

"Why?" Stronger than it looked, her small arm held him when he tried to pull away. He had to look again. Her eyes were violet and wide, fixed on him so intently that he could not escape. "Why do you care?"

"No reason." She laughed softly, tossing back her shining hair. "Just that I wondered. It happens, you see, that my own home is Gold Fort. My father is a mining engineer. He manages the mine, the only mine there. I know the owners, and I never heard of any Anthel Ayth."

18

Scarlet Nights

Scorth knew the unicorns' music, which was also their language. He was cheerily whistling unicorn songs as he packed his camp gear on the little brown donkey and guided me away from the cave and back the way he had come, toward Dragonrock.

Plodding after him over dunes of loose red sand and reefs of bare red stone, I began to envy him, though he still made me uneasy. He was a grotesque little gnome, still a stranger to me, and a puzzle: sometimes childlike, sometimes sage, warily intrepid. I found it hard to trust his opaque yellow stare, yet I almost believed his tale of long loyalty to my father.

"Demons beware!" He slapped the donkey's rump. "The mages may be after me, and your uncle would surely love to hang you, but they won't be expecting Nuradoon."

I trudged after him, still nagged by concern for my mother and dazed by his audacity. In all my life, except for that single flight over Dragonrock with my father, I had never been beyond our little village. I had none of his casual readiness for anything, and I certainly was no Nuradoon.

He said no more of any actual plans. Yet following him across the drifted dunes and waterless ravines, envying his dogged endurance, I began to catch something of his spirit. Trusting him more than myself, I felt a growing eagerness to see him test the temper of my uncle and the wrath of the mages and whatever might descend from the demon moon.

On that first day, I must have been a poor companion. Even filled as I was with his hard bread and stew, I was still weak and reeling from near starvation. He slowed the pace when I lagged and let us rest through the blazing noon and put me on the donkey for the last mile or so to the spot where we camped.

Our camp was on an ancient sandbar in the bed of Wind River, near the seeping spring where he had picked the figs. The little basin he had scooped in the sand had filled again with water for us and the donkey, even enough to let us wash our grimy faces. We filled ourselves with ripe figs, and he found dry brush to heat his cook pot for another stew.

I slept poorly that night, watching the red moon. It rose at sunset, already half the size of our own pale white satellite and many times brighter. It shone bloodred on the rocks around us and clotted the shadows with a darker scarlet. The wailing of the banshees echoed through the canyons as if they reveled in its ominous light.

"Hear them howling!" Scorth muttered. "A chorus to greet the demons."

They fell silent when the moon went down. I slept at last, my dismal forebodings turned to uneasy dreams. Scorth woke me, happily humming his unicorn tunes, gave me hard bread and bitter tea for breakfast, and led us on again. We were three days climbing out of the waterless river and four more skirting the fringes of the great salt desert to reach the Black Rock range. Beyond it, we came down at last into kinder country, a world where rain fell, water flowed, and green trees grew.

The mountains flattened into foothills. We began to see the footprints of wild hoppers. Fleet bipeds, they were mottled with gray and green that made them hard to see, but Scorth stopped me once to point out a herd, rising and falling in living waves on a distant trail that took them quickly out of sight. That night he set a snare and caught a young calf, which gave us a fat haunch to roast and smoked meat to carry with us.

My boots worn beyond repair, I was barefoot and limping before we reached what Scorth said must be a hopper ranch. Several hopper species had been domesticated, the lesser grown for slaughter, the males of the largest trained for the saddle. We came upon two ranchers following a grazing herd.

One of them came with soaring leaps to intercept us. Scorth's donkey, not used to such monsters, panicked and dragged at the halter. The rancher was a heavy, black-bearded man in worn and thorntorn hopper leather. He stopped to watch in bleak amusement while Scorth calmed the donkey.

"Private property," he snarled at us. "Trespassers beware!"

He was sliding a long rifle out of its scabbard as he spoke, scowling as if he meant to use it. I looked at Scorth, waiting while he led the trembling donkey back to my side.

"I want no hopper thieves," the man snarled at us. "Nor rascals of Xath with their demon snakes!"

"Sir, we beg your kind indulgence." Scorth bowed to him, grinning blandly. "We're neither thieves nor magicians, but only unlucky prospectors, returning from a long search for gold in the sands of Wind River."

"Then you're hopper-brained fools!"

"Sir!" Scorth looked hurt. "We did find gold."

"Hah! Let me see it."

"Believe me, sir!" Scorth spread his empty hands. "I swear it's there. I could show you how to reach it, but the good Three sent no rain to let us wash it out, nor even a good breeze to winnow it. We stayed too long, until that demon star was rising and the summer heat killing us. We were lucky to escape. . . ."

"Lucky?" he sneered. "No longer."

"Sir, please, we only beg to pass—"

"Across land you never owned?" He was cocking the rifle. "We've held this ranch for five generations, against the wyvern and the wolves and the primarch's thievish taxers. We intend to hold it, and we've no room for beggars." He swung the gun back to Scorth. "If you have prayers to make, to Xath or any other demon, say them now."

"Time for the helmet," Scorth murmured to me. "Put it on."

It was slung on my back. The rancher held the gun on me as I fumbled for it.

"Sir!" Urgently Scorth stepped between us. "I beg you, sir, in the sacred names of the Three, don't act rashly! Our story will amaze you. When I saw that star of evil burning in the east, I prayed to the powers. They answered with a miracle—"

"You need a miracle."

"Here you see a wonder!" His voice hushed, he bent his bald crown at me. "The all-seeing Three perceived the demons descending to waste our world, and they awakened an ancient hero to defend us."

"Hero?" the rancher snorted. "Heroes in rags! Leading an ass and peddling lies!"

"Hear me, please!" With a wounded look, Scorth bowed again. "It's true I'm nobody. True we're penniless and sadly ragged. Yet I beg you to consider my companion. Take a moment to inspect the sigil on his helmet, and you'll agree that he's a living miracle."

He lifted the helmet off my head and held it up to show the inlaid figure of the unicorn's head. The rancher scowled at it, and scowled unbelievingly at me.

"The sigil says it, sir. It proves an actual miracle, which the world must believe. And will believe, sir, when events begin to prove it. This man is in fact Nuradoon ir Var. Nuradoon the Ninth. Surely you know of him. The man who conquered this land where we stand from the demon's fearful spawn and began the building of Dragonrock."

"Var?" An incredulous bark. "What right have you to speak that ancient name?"

"The right of the actual Nuradoon, our historic champion! The invisible powers have awakened him to battle the demons again as he did so many centuries ago."

"You?" He leaned to peer at me. "Where were you born?"

"Drag—" I caught myself, uncertain of any facts about the actual Nuradoon.

"A dragon's den," Scorth said. "So he meant to say, creating a metaphor to name his birthplace down in the lowlands in that evil age when the demon's hideous breed still ruled half the world. But I beg you, sir." He shook his head at me, a hint of malice in his grin. "His voice has not yet returned. He can only whisper."

Staring at Scorth, staring at the helmet, the rancher reined his hopper away from us and beckoned the other rider to join him. A younger man with the same broad hopper leather hat and hopper leather leggings, he had the same wide, dark-weathered face. Perhaps a son. He leaned in his saddle to take the helmet from Scorth. They squinted at it, muttered together, and peered doubtfully at me.

"It is the Var sigil." The older man nodded reluctantly, but kept his gun ready. "I know it from the land grant, the deed given our family to reward our frontier service." He turned to Scorth. "Mister, where did you get this?"

"A miraculous gift from the Three." Speaking with a glib assurance, Scorth gestured at the distant peaks behind us. "Bestowed upon us in the dreadful desert beyond those mountains. I was there as I told you, sifting for gold in the sand of dry Wind River."

His fluid voice had begun to ring with the rhythm of his unicorn songs.

"Believe me, gentlemen!" Yellow eyes shining, he appealed to the younger rider. "The gold is there. Every blazing morning, I knelt to pray to the unseen Three for a drop of rain to wash it out, or a breath of wind to take the dust away. Rain never fell. No wind came. The summer sun burned hotter every day, till I thought the Three had forgotten me.

"I stayed too long, till my water and food were gone, and my faith with them. I'll never forget the evil dusk when I first saw the demon star. I felt the terror of it then, and implored the Three to save us.

"That night was cold." He swung to the rancher. "Perhaps you know the desert, sir? Hot by day but cold by night. The red star burned and the banshees howled their hymns to greet the demons. Shivering from the bitter wind, I crawled into a cave for shelter and prayed again before I slept.

"The powers heard."

He bowed toward me.

"Here their sacred answer stands. He lay beside me when I woke next morning in the cave, his body crusted with the dust of many centuries but miraculously preserved. His helmet lay near him. I wiped the dust away and found the unicorn's gold-horned head.

"The sigil you see!

"I knew at once that he was the restored Nuradoon, who had never returned from his final expedition. Alive again! Don't ask me how; the Powers keep their secrets. But he moved when I touched his shoulder. He sat up in the dust to whisper at me, asking if I had seen the demon star."

"Nuradoon?" The younger man frowned from his hopper. "If you are Nuradoon, what's your business now?"

Scorth stayed silent, and I had to answer.

"I woke—" My first whisper came too faintly, and I tried again. "I woke to fight the demons."

"How? What's your weapon?"

"My weapon will be the Dragonshield."

"Dragonshield?" He shook his head in puzzled disbelief. "A tool of magic?"

"White magic," Scorth said. "The magic of life, which flows from the eternal Three."

"Let's see it."

"We seek it," Scorth said. "Expecting to find it at Dragonrock."

"The rider's castle?" He laughed. "Rider Thorg holds a magic weapon for you?"

"He'll yield it to Nuradoon."

"Thorg? Not if he can keep it."

They pulled their hoppers aside, muttered together, and came back to sit staring skeptically at us. I was sweating, but Scorth moved to face them with a wary grin.

"Dead men don't live again." The older man paused to scowl at him and then at me. "Yet your gold-eyed unicorn is in fact the sigil of the Vars. In this evil time, with so many already crazed with terror, few speak of fighting demons." He glanced at the other. "We can't agree—"

"We have agreed!" The younger raised his voice and spoke to Scorth. "My father doubts your miracle, but we do agree to welcome you as three-day guests, in the tradition of our hospitality."

The father rode back to their herd. The son escorted us to the ranch headquarters, a cluster of buildings with parapets around the roofs. He asked if the wolves had been after us. Scorth moved his fingers in the gesture of reverence and the Three for our escape.

"No end of trouble!" he muttered. "They've got bolder now since the red moon came. Crafty varmints, sneaking down out of the mountains to greet the demons. The banshees watch for them, and howl to warn them of anybody with a gun."

The ranch buildings were a kind of fortress, clustered inside a high rock wall. The rancher's wife was dead, but three of his sons lived there with their women. A daughter kept the house. A plain-faced woman with one wild eye who looked older than the sons, she seemed eager to make us welcome.

An eldest brother, she told us, had been mauled and taken by a bitch wolf in heat. The pair had denned in a cave in the foothills, preying on the hoppers till the younger brothers tracked them there, smoked them out, and got them both, the bitch already heavy with twin cubs.

She showed us the male's rough dark hide, a strange family relic, stretched on the wall over the fireplace. Her voice quivered when she spoke of him, and tears welled from her errant eye.

Though the father never wanted to believe our tale of Nuradoon, the daughter made him keep the full three days their tradition allowed us. We ate huge meals with the family and slept in the hopper barn. Scorth entertained them with his unicorn songs and long tales of his service in the old rider's campaigns in North Riding.

The daughter gave me a fine leather suit nobody in the family wanted to wear because it had belonged to that unfortunate brother, and even a sturdy pair of his hopper-hide boots. She had to stifle a sob on the morning when her hard-voiced father announced that our third day was gone.

"Nuradoon!" she begged me. "Promise you'll be back!"

I had to remind her that I hoped to be fighting the demons, with no idea where or when. She lifted her lips. I kissed her, feeling no kind of hero, and left her standing in the hall beneath the hide of her transformed brother. Scorth met me with a sardonic grin when I came outside, but I felt sorry for her, haunted as she seemed by demons of her own.

The youngest son, a slender redhead not yet married, was nearly as friendly. He traded Scorth an outgrown suit for the donkey, volunteered to take us on to the nearest market town, and even loaned us hoppers to ride.

My mount was a young green-spotted male with baleful black eyes and brains enough to sense that I was new to the saddle. He flexed his long head to bare yellow teeth at me as I climbed into the saddle, and his first long leap tossed me half out of it. The old helmet went rattling to the ground. Scorth recovered it. I got my seat again, the boy cracked his whip at the hopper's rump, and we left the ranch behind us.

Even now, so many centuries since the conquest, the riding was still a flinty border strip between the fertile lowlands and the forbidden wilderness. The wyvern and the werewolves had never stopped their raids. The land here was rough and poor, rainfall scant. The inhabitants were few, a hardy and self-sufficient sort.

Beyond a long stone fence, we came down off the prairie into a more fertile valley where the settlers had built their clusters of barns and silos and dwellings around huge wooden windmills. We stopped that night with a hospitable farmer who listened with no show of doubt to Scorth's tale of how he found me, and came out with us into the scarlet dusk to listen to the banshees and watch the swollen moon.

When we rode into the town late next day, the young rancher took us to an inn, paid for our room, and departed with the hoppers he had loaned us. The tale of the Nuradoon helmet had followed us, and a crowd was waiting in the bar when we came down to eat. I displayed the helmet, but left Scorth to talk. He drank and spoke with relish, improving his tale with every telling.

"The demons are here!" he finished. "Their scarlet fire has lit the sky, but the gracious powers have awakened Nuradoon to save us."

He raised his stein. Somebody ordered a second beer for me and wanted to see my magic shield.

"We seek it," Scorth said. "From the coffers of Dragonrock. It is reported to lie there, a neglected trinket of the ancient past. Nuradoon remembers its miraculous powers and recalls the skills to command them."

"True, Sir Nuradoon?"

"True," I whispered. "The helmet itself has magic to guide and protect its rightful carrier."

Hoping that might turn out to be the actual fact, I lifted it for people to see, but our little audience was suddenly dwindling, drawn to a rising noise in the street. I donned the helmet again, and we followed. A scarlet dusk had fallen. Two red-skulled men in black were planting a flaming torch in the open square across the street, and another stood shouting hoarsely into the scarlet dark.

He was a gaunt, black-toothed mage of Xath. That first glimpse of him chilled me to the bone. Turning from the black-robed men beneath the crimson-flaring torch, he marched to meet the gathering crowd, swinging his thick black staff like a weapon.

". . . cower before me!" His screaming rant was an echo from that dreadful night of my childhood when I stood with my mother, shivering in the snow-covered village square, and watched that great snake crush Bastard to crimson mush. "You should crouch and tremble in your huts, because you have reveled far too long in your ignorance and your sins."

For one sickening instant I thought he was the man who murdered Bastard, swinging the same dreadful staff as he howled the same message of doom, but he was larger, and when he strode among his apprehensive listeners, I saw that he had no limp.

"The demons have come!"

Two younger men came darting after him. Hardly more than boys, they were black-robed demons themselves, black teeth filed to points and naked scalps dyed crimson.

"Hear!" they chanted. "Hear the warning words of Xath!"

The mage swung his staff like a battle club, its ruby eyes reflecting the moon's lurid light.

"Hear and beware!" he shrieked. "You see their dwelling above you, washing you in their holy fire. They have come to judge you. They will judge you harshly because you have forgotten Xath. Burning forever in his most pitiless hell, you have none to blame but yourselves.

"Yet I come tonight, in this red twilight of your doomed and dying world, to allow you one last chance at eternal life, a blessing you have never earned. My acolytes will pass among you now, begging you in this final hour to yield yourselves and all you own to Xath. . . ."

I felt Scorth tug at my sleeve. He had shrunk behind me, and he stood trembling, wide eyes fixed on the mage.

"Come!" he whispered hoarsely. "Now!"

He ran. Shocked at his abject fear, I followed him back to the inn. He locked the door when we got into the room, and stood against it, breathing hard.

"Sorry!" he gasped. "I'm commonly no coward, but I've come too near the wrath of Xath."

I stood wondering, because I'd seen nothing to unnerve him so completely. With a rueful hunch of his shoulders, he came to sit on the side of the bed. His breath slowed, until at last he looked up at me with a wry little shrug of apology.

"I don't know if that moon is the eternal inferno the mages claim it is, but they've invented hell enough of their own for their acolytes. Those two men . . ." He shook his head, with a grin that became a grimace of pain. "We went through initiation together, lying on the temple floor in Quar, swearing that damned oath to yield our souls to Xath. If they'd recognized me . . ."

He shuddered and went to check the lock again.

Haunted as I was by the dreadful riddle of what the demons were, and worn and sore from the jolts and lurches of my ill-natured hopper, I lay awake half the night in the red gloom that seeped through the curtains, listening to the raucous yelling of the mage.

I slept at last, dreaming I was back with my mother on the snow-covered village square, watching the black mage toss his monstrous staff at Bastard again and yet again. Wheezing steam woke me, and the clatter of wheels on cobbles.

"Cop cart!" Scorth was out of bed. "The Powers save us!"

Heavy heels came thudding up the stair and down the corridor.

"Open!" Something hard hammered our door. "Open to the primarch's law!"

19

Lyrane

Her mother named her Narla and called her Baby Doll. On her first day in school, she said her name was Lyrane lo Lyrane, taking the name of a magic ring in one of the old ballads the wolf hunters sang. The teacher laughed and tried to call her Narla. She refused to answer to it.

She used to terrify her mother, climbing over the mine works to look down into the bottomless black shafts where the men were working, but she never hurt herself. Her best friends were the hunters who were her father's frequent guests, the hard, weather-beaten men who rode unicorns to kill the werewolves that came down across the border.

She thrilled to their tales of the wolves that had mauled them and the wyvern that had hunted them, and shuddered at the tragedies of unlucky men caught and transformed by ravenous she-wolves into their mates.

She was barely sixteen when one of the hunters brought her down in a mountain glade beyond the wyvern border and introduced her to sex. Her mother ran off with the same hunter a year or so later, and her father finally sent her to the Institute in Targon because he thought she had grown too wild for him to manage.

Argoth fascinated her, perhaps because he refused so stubbornly to look at her or any other girl. When she saw his admission card, with its claim that he was the son of a mine owner who did not exist, she took it to the director. He frowned and kept the card.

"The police know all about him," he told her next morning. "He is a protected witness. You can forget him."

She could not forget him. A compact, muscular man who moved with the grace and poise of a well-trained athlete, he was brighter and better-looking than most of the hunters, and he seemed even more exciting. She wanted to know what crime he had witnessed and why he needed protection.

He started as if in alarm when she spoke to him that morning outside the astronomy building. Glancing obliquely at her, he stopped in spite of himself to stare at her, dark eyes as wide as if he had never seen a woman.

Yet he took her questions calmly.

"I'm no criminal. The responsible authorities are aware of my identity. It is no concern of anybody else."

Scowling as if offended, he moved abruptly on.

Next day, when she came to her place at the desk next to his, he sat for a moment with his eyes fixed on her as if she terrified him, started when she smiled, and shrank stiffly back to his books. He sat there rigidly for a long time, breathing fast, before he turned a page.

Fascinated in her own way, she began a sort of game to break through his reserve, making excuses to look at his books or borrow pencils or erasers. Silently he gave her what she asked for. His eyes still avoided hers, yet she caught him glancing at her covertly, like a hunter watching a trapped and wounded wolf.

In many ways he puzzled her. When she had missed one of Kallenayo's lectures and asked to see his notes, he shoved them across her desk without a word. She found them as perplexing as everything else about him, filled with words and symbols that were nonsense to her.

In the classroom, he had an air of skeptical arrogance, doubting everything. Realist science, he muttered, was stupid claptrap, explaining nothing. Though he said he was a Mystic, he showed no reverence for the Three. When Kallenayo repeated his speculation that the mythic demon moon had been a companion star on a long-period orbit around the sun, he asked to check the computations as if he expected to understand them.

Spurred by curiosity, once after class she asked him to join her for a beer in the student hangout across the street from the campus. He scowled and walked away, but he surprised her the next day, offering to buy a beer for her. The first sip made him grimace as if the taste was something new, yet he sat a long time at the table with her, evading most of her questions but asking many of his own.

Had she seen a wyvern? Didn't it frighten her? Had she known men who were bitten and changed into werewolves? Did they remember what they had been? Had the herald mages come to Gold Fort to forecast Xath's return? How many believed them? He never told her why he asked, and the expression on his thin, dark face never changed as he listened to her answers.

In the class, Kallenayo announced that the detected motion of the red dwarf in Capricorn was already confirming that it was indeed the sun's companion star, now returning toward perihelion. When Argoth muttered his doubts, the professor invited them all to come to the observatory that evening and look for themselves.

At the appointed time, she waited for Argoth. He gave her no greeting, but climbed silently with her into the shadowy dome. Watching him at the eyepiece, she saw him start and heard the catch of his breath. Her own turn came, and she found a tiny point of light glowing dull red beside the faint cross hairs.

"So, Mr. Argoth!" When they all had looked, Kallenayo gathered them in a little circle under the instrument. "You were forced to admit that you could find no error in my orbital computations, and now you've seen our companion star returning to pass by again, as it passed a thousand years ago."

Argoth shrugged, his face a scowling mask.

"Proof enough!" After an instant of visible vexation, he swung to the others with undimmed glee. "You've all of you seen it. Proof that Realist science does rule the natural world. It ought to teach our Mystic critics that our cosmos can be understood. And I think it will confound the followers of Xath when their demons don't descend."

Silently Argoth shrugged again.

20

The Lady Rider Kye

Scorth scuttled to the windows, a red ghost in their crimson glow. I heard him scratching at the latches and heard another crash at the door. The lock clicked. A lantern dazzled me. Men in black swarmed in.

"Captain Kerrik," the leader yelled at us, waving his gun. "Primarch's police. Stand against the wall."

"Sir, please!" Scorth found his highest, most childish voice. "There's some error, surely. We are simple pilgrims on a circuit of the sacred sites—"

"Save it!" The harsh command cut him off. "You are under arrest, charged with high crimes against the primarch. You are hereby warned that your words and your possessions may be used as evidence against you. Do you submit?"

"I—we do." Scorth fell meekly to his knees. "I pray the great powers to preserve us, and I humbly implore you to explain how we can be suspected . . ."

Ignoring him, the officer ordered the men to search the room. The golden glint of the Var sigil led them to the helmet, where I had left it on the stool beside my bed.

"This object!" He thrust it in my face. "What is it?"

"My helmet, sir."

"Gentlemen!" Scorth assumed a look of astonished innocence.

"Allow me a moment to tell you the remarkable story of this man beside me—"

"Enough!" the officer grunted. "Save your lies for the Lord Rider."

Giving me no time to get into my hopper-hide jacket and leggings, they cuffed our hands behind our backs, dragged us out of the inn, and locked us in an iron cage on the steam cart waiting in front of the inn. All the rest of the night, it hissed and lurched and pitched and rattled through the scarlet night.

"What now?"

When I muttered the question, Scorth touched his lips and nodded toward our guards in the cab. Silent, sitting with him on a cold iron shelf, I peered when I could through a narrow slit in the door at the back of the cage. All I could see was the cobbled road retreating through clots of crimson shadow behind us. All I could do was fret about my mother and wish the demon moon had never risen.

It had sunk low before we jolted across the drawbridge and sighed to a halt inside a high-walled courtyard that Scorth whispered was Dragonrock. Recalling my mother's drawings and that brief glimpse I'd had when I rode from Sharabok, when they let us out of the cage I tried to see what I could. The great blocks of gray granite were so huge I wondered at the men who piled them up. The central tower loomed dark, crowned by the jutting lip of the flight stage against the narrow patch of open sky still flushed with the crimson moonset.

The guards gave us no time to stare, hustling us through a dark doorway and down a narrow stair into a maze of gloomy stone corridors. Dusty light bulbs hung from cables strung along the ceiling, glowing very dimly. Perhaps it was the same electric system my father had installed, which my uncle had never improved. We were shoved into a tiny cell. An iron door clanged behind us. Boots tramped away, and nobody answered when Scorth begged for breakfast.

When I caught my breath to speak, He touched his lips and shook his head again. Dressed only in my worn shirt and pants frayed to the knees, I was miserably cold, but I could only sit shivering there on the cold stone bench, with nothing to do but study the names and dates and unreadable legends scratched into the stone or written in black-dried blood. Faint taints of old sweat and old rot and old agony fouled the icy air.

Wryly I recalled my childhood dreams of Dragonrock. In imagination, I had been an actual Nuradoon. I'd caught and tamed a wild unicorn and ridden back across the riding to meet and defeat my uncle in the air. I'd recovered Dragonrock and given it back to my parents to make them proud of me. Never in my dreams had I come to any such dismal pass as this.

"I'm famished." Scorth spoke at last, raising his voice as if for the guards. "They've got to bring us bread and water. That's every prisoner's right."

No bread or water came. It seemed an eternity before I heard the thud of boots again. The door creaked open. Without a word, the guards cuffed our hands behind us and marched back through the musty corridors, back up the old stone steps, and out at last into an enormous room.

The great hall of Dragonrock!

It had been a place of splendor in my mind ever since my mother first described it. The lofty walls and massive granite pillars. The enormous ceiling beams. The Dragonrock itself—a huge dark mass of unshaped stone that jutted through the floor at the end of the enormous room. Always I had been enchanted by the legend of it.

"A sacred thing." I could almost hear her voice again, hushed with awe when she spoke of it. "Sacred to the Vars, as it had been to the wyvern and the werewolves when they owned it. They believe there was once a cave beneath it where the dragons used to lay their eggs. Nuradoon found a young dragon on guard, commanding the creatures fighting to defend the rock, and fought his greatest battle there."

The recollection gave me a moment of escape from the hard-faced guards and all my fearful uncertainties, escape to that happier moment of my childhood on the farm. Supper was over, and father sat with us in front of the fireplace in the rock-walled kitchen. I interrupted my mother to ask if dragons laid eggs like hens. He said he didn't know.

"I looked for the cave when I was a boy." He grinned at me through his wild sun-bronzed beard. "Never found it. Perhaps rock-falls have hidden it. Perhaps it never did exist."

"The legend tells how Nuradoon fought that dragon." Calmly my mother ignored the interruption. "Coiled on the very top of the rock, it called the·wyvern queen down out of the sky. She dived to attack but had to turn away when he raised the Dragonshield. Safe under the Shield, he knelt and prayed for the aid of the Three.

"The dragon came at him off the rock while he prayed, breathing death, but the Three had told him to lay a rose in its path. Its hot breath withered the rose. He placed an apple there, and a tongue of flame consumed it. When the dragon came on, he threw three grains of suncorn before it.

"The dragon's breath burned the first grain of corn and then the second, but it stopped and bellowed and flew away from the third. The wyvern queen followed it. The werewolves fled back into their wilderness. And Nuradoon built the first walls of the castle around the rock to hold it for men."

"Is the legend true?" My father's grin made me ask him. "Could one grain of corn frighten a dragon?"

"Ask your mother." He laughed. "She's the Mystic."

"I believe in the Three." She shook her head at him in a gently scolding way. "They are life: the seed and the bloom and the fruit. We must trust them, because in the end they will prevail."

"I'm the Realist." He winked at me. "I believe what I must."

Now, jostled between the guards, I yearned for my mother's faith in the Three. Nuradoon must have been an actual man, so I told my-self, bold enough to leave his helmet and his bones in that cruel desert where I found them. The legends were hard to believe. Certain I was no Nuradoon, I felt naked against the cold, dark mass of the Dragonstone itself.

It was huge, rising halfway to the lofty ceiling of the hall. A metal stair climbed one end of it. A massive chair stood at the very top, where the dragon had coiled. Carved of some lustrous red-brown wood, the high back of the chair was inlaid with polished gold and silver: The unicorn sigil of the Vars.

The great chair was empty now, as were the lower seats that flanked it and the rows of benches outside the railing where the guards made us wait. We had to stand, facing the rock. The guards scowled forbiddingly when I glanced aside to watch other guards dragging a gaunt-faced woman and a tiny man to our sides. Hands cuffed like ours, they swayed against the rail as if too weak to stand.

The guards kept us on our feet, facing the rock, till my legs ached and hunger began to gnaw. At last, from a hushed murmuring and the shuffle of feet behind us, I knew the benches had begun to fill. A red-sashed bailiff marched stiffly from behind the rock. At a signal from somewhere, he banged the floor with a tall official mace.

"Stand!" His bellow rolled down the high-walled hall. "All stand for the Lord Rider Thorg ir Var."

My uncle Thorg came around the rock. He was as tall as my father, and he may once have been handsome, with his jet black hair and thick black mustache, but he looked soft with fat, and I saw no family likeness. When he paused to look down the hall, I saw a dark bruise that ringed one eye and a neat white bandage above it. He waited a moment as if for applause. The patter of it seemed faint, but he bowed and climbed the steps to the top of the rock.

The noise in the hall was suddenly hushed, and I saw another man limping after him, a red-skulled mage of Xath, stabbing at the stair steps with a thick black staff. I knew him from the limp. Gark ru Garo, the human demon who had thrown that same snake-shaped staff to murder Bastard.

I shuddered from a shock of fear that he might recognize me, and shrank in spite of myself from his mad black eyes, though of course, I'd been only a timid child, clinging to my mother's hand. Searching him for anything human, I tried to imagine him as still a child himself, still with hair to comb and with a mother of his own, not yet a student of the dark arts. All I found, however, was the image of utter evil he had burned into my young mind: the black and sharp-filed teeth grinning through the hideous mask tattooed beneath his hairless, blood-drenched skull.

The bailiff hammered the floor again, shouting a command for the feeble man and woman beside us to stand forward to hear the Lord Rider's judgment. He began droning the charges against them in a legal jargon I didn't try to follow.

Scorth startled me again when I looked at him. Dread of the black mage had shaken him. He stood frozen, yellow eyes distended and fixed on the mage, seamed face gone stiff and pale with terror. I stood wondering blankly at him till Thorg startled me again, yelling at the bailiff.

"In the name of Xath!" Suddenly off his throne, he glowered from the edge of the rock. "I demand respect!"

I saw that the manacled man beside us had sprawled back across the bench.

"Forgive him, Sire!" The woman stood alone at the railing, her voice a pleading quaver. "He intends no disrespect. He is ill. He cannot stand."

"I will not be defied!" Thorg stiffened with anger. "Prisoners stand before me."

"Let them sit."

That quiet command seemed to freeze him. Flushed red, he sat back on his high seat, glaring down at a young woman tripping lightly from behind the rock. She paused to smile at the prisoners and turned to toss her dark head at Thorg. Clad very simply in plain brown slacks and a darker sweater, she waited at the foot of the stair for two older women who put her in a long white robe before she ran up the steps to the top of the rock.

"The Lady Rider," the bailiff bawled. "Lady Rider Kye."

She walked across in front of Thorg to reach the empty chair. Her eyes caught mine for an instant. They were green as good jade and luminous with a warm intelligence. I thought I saw a flash of interest in me, and a very fleeting smile. Had she heard of the Nura-doon helmet?

Even when her glance had gone on to the other prisoners, I couldn't help staring. Everything about her, the quick grace of her motion, the flash of sadness in her eyes when she saw the sick des-

peration of the two beside us, the glow of her quiet beauty, everything recalled my mother's definition of the Three.

She was life.

The bailiff let us sit, and Thorg turned from the huddled couple
to scowl at her with a cold malice that startled me. Even if her independence had vexed him, how could he—how could anybody feel
the stark hatred that twisted what I could see of his face? How, I
wondered, had such a man ever won her?

Jealousy stabbed me, so sharp and so far from any sane reason
that I felt astonished at the heat of my emotion. I wished again, with
no logic for it, that I somehow might have been the actual Nuradoon. Wearing the magic helmet, armed with the mythic Dragonshield, I could have leaped the railing, cowed or beaten Thorg, and
carried the Lady Rider away.

Or could have at least in the desire of that mad moment, before
reality hit me. But the helmet was gone, lost when the police
dragged us out of the inn. Thorg still owned the Shield, locked up
wherever he kept it. And I was still far from being any Nuradoon.
Scolding myself for yielding to such impossible dreams, I sat waiting, cheered a little just by looking at her.

Diamonds glinting on his pudgy hand, Thorg waved a signal.
The bailiff slammed the floor with his mace and glared down at the
silent woman who still clung to the railing with her shackled hands,
gazing up at Thorg in mute appeal.

"Bailiff," the Lady Rider called, "uncuff the prisoners."

The bailiff blinked and turned uncertainly to Thorg, who grunted
something I didn't hear. The guards unshackled all four of us. Rubbing my wrists, I turned to find Scorth still standing rigid, still staring in terror at the mage.

The bailiff thumped the floor again and droned his charges. The
prisoners were Ahran and Elra Morthan. Once a professor of history
in Targon, he had come to the riding after his removal from the Institute. The police had found seditious materials in their dwelling,
documents that implicated them both. Convicted of high treason,
they were under sentence to hang.

The bailiff let them speak.

"Lord Rider, I am my husband's voice." The woman dropped to
her knees. "I beg for his life."

"On what basis?" Thorg demanded.

"Humbly, Sire—"

"No basis exists." The bailiff thumped the floor to silence her. "Their own words damn them. They have conspired against the primarch's law and the peace of the riding. The verdict must stand."

"Lord Rider, look at my husband!" The woman caught the railing to pull herself upright. "Look at his poor hands!" The man was almost a skeleton, as if from long starvation. He sat trembling, shrinking from the cold eyes of the bailiff, until the woman cried again, "See what they've done!"

He raised his hands. They were twisted ruins, the fingers scarred and twisted stubs that had no nails.

"He was—was only a scholar." Her broken words were hard to hear. "His only crime was to search for the truth about the exotics—that was his word for those beings whose powers seem to defy the laws of Realistic science. The banshees and werewolves and wyvern and dragons."

"Why?" Thorg rapped. "No business of his."

"Why not?" Lady Kye answered, and asked the woman, "What did he find?"

"Little enough. He believed that their alien biology developed through natural evolution—"

"Heresy!" Gark ru Garo was on his feet, shrieking at her. "Heresy against the holy creed of Xath!"

"Speak." Thorg waved him on. "I allow no heresies here."

"A wicked lie!" The mage raised the serpent staff as if to hurl it at the woman. "The exotics were the native creatures of the world. Harmless once, before we men arrived. We were convicts, damned by Xath to exile here when he found us unfit for the paradise where our race was born.

"We came here with his blessing. Forgiving our monstrous sins, he had allowed us one more chance at eternal life, and once again we defeat his love. As always, we brought our evil with us. We ignored the warnings of the loving banshees when they begged us to mend our evil ways. We killed the gentle wolves for careless sport. We mocked the wisdom of the wyvern, and defied the dragons' laws.

"If we hate and fear those creatures now, their present nature is our just punishment. Xath transformed them with gifts sufficient to defend themselves. Powers no blasphemous Realist will ever explain, because such acts of Xath transcend human understanding.''

He swung the serpent staff toward the reeling woman and the huddled man.

''Denying that truth, these infidels have damned themselves. Let them hang!''

''Lord Rider, hear me!'' The woman fell back to her knees, frantic and hoarsely gasping. ''All my husband sought was the truth. He has already suffered unspeakable torture—''

''Enough!'' Thorg grated. ''Heresy is heresy. In the primarch's name, I confirm the action of the courts and order the execution—''

''No!'' The Lady Rider was on her feet, green eyes flashing. ''Honest doubt is no crime.'' She swung from Thorg to gesture at the bailiff. ''Set them free!''

I heard a stifled gasp behind us, and a choked whisper from the crippled prisoner. The mage blinked in black-toothed horror. Thorg came to his feet and stood a moment glowering at her before he rasped at the bailiff:

''Let them hang!''

White-faced, she sat slowly back into her chair. The bailiff made some silent signal to the guards. Hands cuffed behind them again, the two were taken away, the woman weakly reeling, the man clinging to her arm.

''Prisoner!'' I saw the bailiff pointing at me. ''State your name.''

My throat felt dry, and I hoped for an instant that Scorth would speak up with his tale of Nuradoon. Instead, he bent to a fit of coughing, his face buried in a handkerchief.

''Nur—'' I tried for a stronger voice. ''Nuradoon ir Var.''

''State the place of your birth.''

''The town—'' I knew no facts about Nuradoon. ''A small town in the lowlands, near Targon.''

''The date?''

''Long ago . . .''

My parents had never taught me how to lie. My voice faltered, and somebody behind me choked back a snicker. The bailiff snarled again, ''The date?''

"Time has dimmed my memory." My voice came back when I saw lively expectation dancing in the Lady Kye's eyes. "I beg your understanding, sir." I tried to borrow Scorth's style of speech. "I was born in a time when the wolves and the wyvern still roved the lowlands, and fighting dragons commanded them. I had no mother I remember. I was named for my father, who taught me the arts of war and made friends among the unicorns.

"His father had been another Nuradoon—"

My voice stumbled again, because all those early Nuradoons had lived before any accurate history was written, certainly any that I knew. Lady Kye's smile grew wider when I looked at her, and I drove ahead.

"A time came when my father had fought wolves enough. He gave me his helmet and the gift of the Vars. That gift was the magic Dragonshield, which had led him and Vars before him to victory in a hundred battles. He promised that it would serve again, against any peril."

Nobody had told me exactly that. It seemed the thing to say, however, though Thorg was hardly listening. Shaking his head and muttering at the bailiff, he had turned to glare at the Lady Kye.

"I left my father in the little town where I was born." She had cheered me with a tiny nod. "These highlands still belonged to the wolves and the wyvern. One hard winter a horde of them came down to raid the lowland towns, and my father gathered his old companions to drive them back.

"The wyvern raised armies of wolves against us, but we had the Shield to warn me of every move they made and guide our own attacks. Young men joined us, refugees from burned and looted villages, bitter men whose families had been killed. We beat the invaders in the lowlands and beat them on the scarps and beat them on the uplands till we reached Dragonrock and fought the dragon here."

I thought I saw a flicker of amusement on the lady's vivid face.

"If I seem bewildered, Sire, I beg your compassion." I bowed and spread my hands as Scorth might have done. "You see, I'm still a stranger here. All I knew has disappeared. My warrior friends are gone, the men who fought beside me to take these rocky uplands from the wolves and the wyvern. This whole world is new to me. This great castle was only a single tower when I left it."

Behind the bandage, Thorg wore a frown of baffled uncertainty, but the mage was seething, hollow eyes glaring out of the scarlet skull, black teeth gleaming through a snarl of fury. Lady Kye glanced at them and grinned, and I let the tale roll on.

"If you ask me how I came to be here, Sire, all I know is what I recall. When we had reclaimed this rock from the dragon, I built a lone tower to hold it. To make our victory sure, I set out with the Shield and a single daring man to follow the dragon to its den. We lost ourselves in a great desert of wind-carved stone where nothing lives because no rain falls. On the last night I remember, we had crawled into a cave to sleep. This man woke me."

I gestured at Scorth, and he coughed again.

"He tells me that seven centuries have passed since I fought the dragon here. I don't know why I slept so long, unless the holy Three preserved me to face our enemies when they rise again. My helmet was still with me, but the magic Shield was gone. Perhaps that companion carried it to get him safely past the perils of the desert."

The mage was on his feet, muttering at Thorg.

"Sire, that's who I am." I spread my empty hands. "And why I stand here bewildered, unsure of anything. I'm told that all my good friends are dead and long forgotten. I find strangers all around me, even their language hard to understand. I find farms and towns where we had fought the wolves through hostile wilderness.

"And I have seen a great red moon blazing in the sky. The demon moon, they tell me, that had risen and set again, so the old men used to tell us, in an age long before my time. I am told that the demons are returning with it to waste the world again, as they wasted it a thousand years ago. Can you tell me, Sire?"

Ignoring me now, Thorg had turned to stare at the snarling mage.

"Sire! Sire! Is that true?" Desperately I raised my voice. "If the demons have returned, perhaps the Three awakened me to battle them again. I am told, sir, that you own the magic Dragonshield, which can defend us and defeat the demons again."

"That man!" Flushed purple, Thorg was suddenly bellowing at the bailiff. "The rascal Scorth!"

21

The Esoterica

Drunk with triumph, Kallenayo kept the class in the observatory until they all had seen that faint red star. He had vindicated Realist science. He had made his own name. He had dealt the mages a deathblow. Even when the impatient janitors came to clean up the building, he could not stop talking. Reckless with eiation, he asked them all to join him at the campus pub.

Argoth scowled and muttered to Lyrane that he wanted no beer. "I hate the bitter stuff, and Kallenayo's a hell-blind fool."

"Kallenayo's making history," she urged him. "I want to hear it all."

"All he shows us is a tiny red spark lost among a billion more? That's history?"

"It's another sun." She had caught the little astronomer's excitement. "About to pass close again after all those centuries. Who knows what changes it can cause?"

"Not to my world."

Yet he came with her across the street. They sat together a little apart from the students around the professor.

"The Mystics are dead!" Kallenayo was already flushed and loud. "We've demolished their universe of magic and fates and mysteries too vast to explain. And we'll explode the cult of the mages. I've looked at their sacred book. Their little universe has room for just one planet. The sun and the moon are only curious lamps flying around it; the stars tiny holes in the sky with Xath's holy fire showing through.

"We've proved tonight that their little pinholes are actual suns, perhaps as bright as ours. We'll probably find that they have planets of their own, maybe larger than our world. Our companion star is new evidence that the actual universe is big enough to let it fly out of sight and back. The Realist Age has begun."

"And almost ended."

Argoth drained his stein and wanted to leave, but Kallenayo was ordering another round. Lyrane raised two fingers for more beers.

"Sir?" an uneasy student was asking. "Does this mean the demons—whatever they were—can come back to haunt the world again?"

"Hard to say what it means." Sobered a little, Kallenayo thought about it. "That last close passage was certainly catastrophic enough to set progress a few centuries back and obliterate most records of whatever happened. Perhaps the star does have planets. Perhaps they are inhabited. The so-called demons may have been raiders from space. If so, I suppose they might return."

"So we are in danger of invasion?"

"Danger?" He shrugged at danger and reached for his stein. "I don't think so. We're armed now with Realist science. I suppose we could have visitors; we may see military action, but I certainly see nothing to dread in the superstitions of Xath."

"Superstitions?" Argoth was on his feet, angrily shouting. "Hopper slop!"

She caught his arm. He flinched from her grip as he always did, but sank back into his chair. Some of the students stared, but all turned back to hear Kallenayo. Turning to face her, Argoth was trembling and strangely intent. He had learned to look at her now, but warily, as if she were some feral creature. She felt danger in him, the same alluring risk she had felt in the werewolf hunters.

"If you want the truth," he was whispering, "read *The Esoterica*."

"What's that?"

"I've drunk too much." He seemed abashed. "I should not have spoken." He glanced toward the others again, murmuring cautiously. "It tells the truth of the First Coming. Truth the Mystics and the Realists never knew."

"So?" Her impulse was to mock him. "What is truth?"

"I'm sorry." With a grimace, he shoved his stein away. "I'll do penance for revealing the mysteries. You could do worse for hearing them."

"You won't kill me." She smiled, leaning to look into his strangely shining eyes. "What is this remarkable truth?"

"More than a joke." He scowled at her, hoarsely growling. "Such secrets are too sacred for women." Yet her teasing smirk goaded him to ask, "You are sure you want to know?"

"Tell me," she breathed. "Tell me."

"You damn us both." Shuddering, he looked away to catch his breath before he met her eyes again. "The red point in the telescope is no star or moon. It is the great serpent's mouth, which glows with its own inner fire. The serpent winds around the world, and through the gates of paradise, and back to the beginning of time. It is striking toward us now, because our cycle of being has ended."

Her amusement roused him.

"Wait!" With a wary glance at Kallenayo's noisy circle, he lowered his angry tone again. "Wait till Xath descends to burn the damned and end the flow of time." Voice suddenly quivering, he leaned across the table. "If you can see your follies in time to make atonement—and I beg you to—he will carry you back with him through the belly of the serpent and all the splendors of paradise to be reborn as the eternal wheel turns again."

"Your own soul, too?" Her soft laugh mocked him again. "Can it survive the passage through the serpent's gut?"

"I'll make my own atonement." Kallenayo was yelling to hasten the barman, and he shrugged at them scornfully. "Blasphemous infidels! They'll never live again." Turning slowly back, he shuddered and bent so close, their faces almost touched. "Lyrane, I wish you were a man," he whispered. "I'd take you with me back to Quar to learn the secret truth."

"Thank you." Oddly, she felt touched. "But I am a woman."

His hard face had reddened. Suddenly he was breathing hard. Pushing his stein abruptly aside, he reached as if to take her hand

and pulled abruptly back. Trembling, he sat staring into her face. She saw his pupils widen.

"A woman," she whispered. "Have you ever seen a woman?"

He recoiled as if she had slapped him.

"Come," she breathed. "I'll show you one."

22

The Shattered Shield

For an instant the great hall was still. I glanced behind us. The benches had filled and people stood along the walls. Townsfolk and Thorg's retainers, I thought, terrified by the alien moon, cowed by the mages, perhaps amazed now at rumors of Nuradoon revived.

"Sorry!" Scorth had time to give me a rueful grin. "A great tale you were spinning—"

"In the name of Xath!" Thorg stood high on the rock above us, waving his arms and thundering at the bailiff. "Hang the rascals!"

"Hold them!" The bailiff hammered the floor with the butt of his mace. "Shackle them!"

Guards converged on us, guns drawn. The gaunt black mage came off his chair and hobbled to the rim of the rock, hoisting his serpent staff as if to call the demons down. Lady Kye sat alertly straight, intent green eyes watching them and watching us.

"Sire! Sire!" Scorth dropped to one knee before the guards could reach him, arms wide in the gesture of ritual appeal. "Hear me, Sire! Hear the truth—"

They hauled him to his feet. He tried to writhe away and his frantic voice quavered on, gone high as a child's.

"The powers save you, sir! Save you from a tragic blunder! You have mistaken me for my unlucky brother—"

"Shut him up!" Thorg bellowed. "Get them back to the dungeons."

"Not yet." Quick emotion flushed Lady Kye's vivid face. "Let them speak!"

Thorg muttered at her, muttered at the bailiff, and sat heavily back on his throne. The hall was hushed for a moment before she spoke again.

"This Dragonshield." She turned from Thorg to us. "It interests me."

The bailiff stood looking at Thorg, waiting for orders. When none came, he shrugged and waved the guards away from Scorth.

"The Three reward you, Lady Kye!" Scorth bent deeply toward her. "The magic of the Shield can save us from the demons if the Lord Rider will allow Nuradoon—"

Thorg stopped him with a bellow of disbelief.

"This Nuradoon?" With a withering glance at Thorg, she gestured for Scorth to go on. "The man with you?"

Her eyes were on me, a glint of amusement in them.

"Nuradoon the Ninth." Scorth nodded solemnly. "The legendary Var hero who reclaimed Wolver Riding, built the first tower of Dragonrock, and died in the desert seven hundred years ago. Believe me, Sire. . . ." He turned to Thorg with a stiffly formal bow. "The powers are merciful. They have awakened him to save us all."

Dark in the face, Thorg choked back a roar of outrage and sat scowling at the Lady Kye.

"You were speaking of a brother?" Her eyes were on Scorth, but her voice had a sardonic edge. Aimed at Thorg? Or at Scorth and me? "A rascal, really?"

"Sadly, my lady." The innocent child again, he raised his odd eyes to her. "My twin brother, if truth may be told. We were sons of a wine merchant in Dorth, an honest man who tried to bring us up as sober as he was. In spite of all his warnings, my brother liked the wine too well. It broke our darling mother's heart. Always in trouble for that weakness, poor Scorth left home in flight from the primarch's law before he had ever come of age."

Thorg was boiling now, shooting savage glances at Lady Kye and then at us.

"Years of pain had passed," Scorth's limpid voice went on, "before we heard a word of my unlucky brother. Here at Dragonrock by then, he was training unicorns and inventing his felonious schemes. I never saw him again, but a few years ago he passed through Dorth in flight from angry creditors and the primarch's police. He wanted money to pay his debts and save his miserable life, and our good father borrowed it for him.''

Scorth's tiny hands spread wider, a gesture of tragic regret.

''Too much money, because he'd gulled our father with a map on an old scrap of hopper-hide and a wild tale of gold in the Wind River desert. Took the money and vanished, with his promise to return with wealthy backers for an expedition to find the gold. He left the map for security.

''That visit killed our dear parents, because he never returned nor paid a penny back. The creditors harassed them until they poisoned a bottle of wine and died together. All they left me was that hopper-hide map. Drawn, so my brother had sworn, by Nuradoon's companion. They'd found gold, in the tale he told. Nuradoon was after dragons. The companion came back to make his map, and Nuradoon stayed to die there, so near the gold they never found.

''My poor brother! Penniless forever, born without a conscience, but skilled with tongue and pen. I'd listened to his tale, and I let his map lure me here. Spent all I had for an outfit to follow the trail to Wind River—and found gold enough, if the blessed Three had sent me wind or rain to refine it from the sand. More than gold, I found a holy miracle.'' He gestured at me. ''Nuradoon himself! Awakened to save . . .''

He paused to watch an officer who came rushing to the bailiff. They murmured together, staring at Scorth.

''I knew him.'' He was bowing deeply, almost as if to worship me. ''From the sigil on his helmet—''

''Sire, we know him better!'' The bailiff banged the floor and yelled at Thorg. ''But not for any reborn Nuradoon. He's your fugitive nephew.''

''The traitor's son?'' Thorg surged to his feet. ''How can that be?''

''He's reported missing from his place of exile on Little River. Trackers have traced his trail into the wilderness, toward Wind River. We have identified him now from police descriptions and the traitor's handwriting on a document he carried.''

"Your sacred miracle!" Thorg jeered Lady Kye and shouted at the bailiff. "Hold them for the hangman!"

Back in the same bare cell, we sat huddled on the same hard stone bench, hungry and hopeless. The light through the high window-slit dimmed and grew pink. I sat wondering forlornly what might happen to my mother, till the wicket clanged open. The guards pushed a slab of hard bread through it, and a gourd of water. It slammed shut. Half-heeled boots clacked away. We shared the water and the bread and waited again in red-hued gloom until I must have slept.

"Shhhh!" I felt a hand on my shoulder, heard the whisper and a rustle of cloth, caught a faint new odor in the stagnant air, a sweetness like the white snowbuds I remembered from springtime on Little River. "No sound."

Stiff with cold and blind in the dark, still half-asleep, I heard Scorth breathing beside me, and his startled grunt when he wakened. Leaning off the bench to fumble for my boots, I felt silent hands tugging me toward the door.

Who are you? Where were we going?

I dared not ask. Our silent guide allowed us a moment to pick up our boots and rushed us through midnight corridors where all I heard was the shuffle of our bare feet. I stumbled against a stair. Hands caught me, turned me toward the top, led us along another corridor, abruptly stopped us. Something hummed, something clicked. The floor moved. A light came on. We were in a tiny room, Scorth and I, with a slender figure in a black cape and hood.

"So far, safe." I knew Lady Kye's voice, and her face when she turned. "If you want to come with me?"

"With you?" I was stupid with astonishment. "Where?"

"Who knows?"

"We're with you," Scorth told her. "Wherever."

The tiny elevator stopped. The door clicked and opened. Sweet fresh air struck my face. In the lurid glare of the demon's night, we came out on the tower flight stage. I caught a sharp pungency I knew and saw the dark shape of a kneeling unicorn, its ivory horn shining red beneath the moon.

Scorth whistled, a unicorn sound, and the unicorn whickered softly. Its long black head swung around to me, the great golden eyes level with my own, the horn so close, I ducked. It sniffed my clothing and my hair. Its soft muzzle brushed my cheek. Its warm tongue licked across my face. Suddenly I knew it, from the sound of the whicker.

"Sharabok!"

For one crazy moment, I thought my father had ridden him back to rescue us. I knew that couldn't be true, yet the unicorn kept nuzzling me, neighing softly.

"He congratulates you," Scorth told me. "He is pleased that you have grown so well, from a clumsy colt into a fine young stallion."

I stood stroking his dark muzzle, blank astonishment mixed with sad recollections of my father, till Lady Kye touched my arm. "We must hasten."

Sharabok held his wing for a step, and I scrambled into the saddle. Kye came after me, and Scorth followed her. Sharabok lurched to his feet. The red-lit stage swept back around us. Hooves drummed beneath us. The wind grew colder on my face. And we were in the air.

We flew till the red dusk dimmed and shone gray again with our white sun's dawn. Scorth and Sharabok sang to each other in the language I had never learned. The dark landscape showed nothing I knew, but the stars told me we were flying west, toward the wyvern border.

Shivering in the wind, my leather jacket gone, I felt the warmth of Lady Kye against my heart, caught that snowbud sweetness when her soft hair brushed my face. Almost in my arms, she filled me with more emotion than I could cope with. I longed to talk, to ask all about her, to know what she planned for us, but she kept silent, and I found nothing I dared to say.

Flying low, we dropped into the valley of a narrow stream and followed it into rugged mountain country. The faded moon went down. The good sun rose, and I found an odd little cluster of tall black pillars standing in the valley ahead. Brick and masonry chimneys, I saw as we sank toward them, left in the debris where homes had burned. A round tower on the hill above them had been a water tank. The wreckage of a steam engine and its boiler lay rusting among the charred logs where a sawmill had been. Two huge round millstones lay on the bank of the stream beside the ruin of a water wheel.

"Wolf Gap Falls," Scorth said. "Once a trading center for ranchers and miners." He glanced back at me. "I was here with your father on his first hunting trip, back when he was still a boy. We got a bitch wolf that had taken a miner and denned in the hills. The unfortunate miner—" He grimaced and cut himself off. "I'm afraid your uncle has neglected his border defenses."

We circled twice above the ruins and saw nothing alive.

"It happened only a few months ago." He pointed. "Weeds growing in the rubble, but not yet tall. The survivors cleared out—if people did survive."

"Let's stop." Kye gestured at a meadow by the stream, just above the ruins. "We've been a heavy load for Sharabok."

We came down. Scorth unsaddled Sharabok to let him drink and graze. Kye had brought food. I went to the stream with a bucket for water. Scorth found dry wood stacked against a ruined stone fence. We built a fire to brew a pot of blueleaf tea. Kye found bread and hopper cheese and smoked meat in her saddlebags, and even delta oranges.

I was groggy from one long night of jolting over cobbled roads and this last in the dungeon and the saddle. Now, squatting by the fire, warm again and hunger satisfied, I relaxed to an unexpected contentment. The alien moon was down. We had seen no pursuers. Except for those black chimneys, the valley was a charming spot. The Lady Kye was with us, lean and lovely in her flight leathers, daring enough to defy the rider and smiling as if she liked me. At least for a moment, I felt happier than I had ever been.

"Where now?" Scorth finished his tea and looked at Kye. "What's your plan?"

"I have no plan, except to trust Nuradoon." She gave me an enigmatic glance. "I'm sorry I couldn't recover your helmet."

"No matter . . ."

She turned from me to Scorth, her wide eyes appealing, and my moment of euphoria was gone. No longer the great lady, she was suddenly a defenseless girl, terribly vulnerable. I could only shrug and spread my empty hands.

"You know," I said, "I'm not the actual Nuradoon."

She showed no surprise. "I wish we had the helmet."

"If you have no friends to help us . . ." Scorth paused to scan the slopes and cliffs that walled us in, and the empty sky. "Your husband will be hunting us."

"Husband!" She spat the word. "He'll be furious, because I've robbed him." She smiled at Sharabok, cropping grass beside the stream. "Taken even his prize unicorn."

"And yourself." Scorth's yellow eyes narrowed shrewdly. "I'd guess losing you has hurt him more."

"Perhaps." She flushed with anger. "He thought he owned me."

"One moment in this garden of the Three." Scorth gestured at the peaceful hills around us and Sharabok grazing the lush golden-grass along the stream. "But only a moment, unless we get ready for trouble. First of all, we should know one another." His hairless head bent to Kye. "My lady?"

"If you wonder . . ."

She stopped to look hard at me, her green eyes enigmatic.

I nodded, and we waited.

"Wonder how I got to the riding." She made a face, as if at something bitter. "I suppose I've been a fool, but not quite an utter fool. The rider has, or used to have, a better side than you saw back in the castle. I met him years ago, and once I thought I really did admire him.

"If you want the story . . ."

She waited again for us to ask.

"I'm out of the lowlands." She spoke simply but slowly, choosing her words. "Born to trainers." A fleeting smile for Scorth. "Tramp trainers, we called ourselves, grooming and racing mounts for anybody who would hire us. My mother left us before I can remember. I grew up with my father, at stables and tracks all over the lowlands. He loved unicorns and the risks of the race, and never married anybody.

"He taught me the unicorn songs, taught me to ride, taught me to race. That's how I met the rider. . . ." Again she stopped to look straight at me. "Years ago. He was younger then, fond of racing unicorns. I rode against him in a race at Targon. Beat him. Surprised him."

An odd, bittersweet smile.

"He was proud of his skill, proud of his unicorn. Beaten by a child! I think he was angry at first, but he was a different man then." Her eyes were on me, but she smiled at something else. "Different," she repeated. "Not the monster you saw on the rock."

"He fell for me, if you can imagine. Wanted to ride with me again. Gave me gifts. Took me to meet his mother in her Targon palace. Loaned or more likely gave my father money to buy the stable he'd always wanted. Wanted to marry me. The Wolver Rider! After the gypsy life we had led it was all very wonderful. I loved him, or thought I did, but my father said he was too old for me.

"I hadn't seen his darker side." It shadowed her face. "He used to hide it well, but he couldn't bear to lose. He bribed a trainer when we raced again. Got furious when his own mount still wouldn't let him win, because unicorns race fair. When I found what he'd done, I thought I was through with him."

She stared away at nothing, remembering more than she told us.

"My father loved me. I'd always been happy with him, at least when he was winning. But people change." Ruefully she shrugged. "I think owning the stable changed him. He raced too hard, drank too much, bet too much. We quarreled when he bet and lost a stallion Rider Thorg had given me. A roan named Starwind. I left to ride for Ebur ni Rellion. Perhaps you've heard of the Rellions?''

"Who hasn't?'' Scorth grinned at recollections of his own. ''I was a trainer for his father once, Count Nardo ni Rellion.''

''An old family.'' Wistfully her voice had fallen. ''Proud of all their history and tradition. They owned a great palace in Targon and a unicorn ranch in the hills north of the city. I won races for Ebur, and soon realized I'd never loved Lord Thorg.

''Ebur . . .''

She shook her head and stared away at the black chimneys standing where the town had been. It seemed a long time before she looked back at me.

''He was tall as you. Handsome as Lord Thorg. I thought the Three had smiled when he asked me to marry him. His family liked me. His mother planned a big wedding in the old family palace. I lived a few days in paradise—'' She caught her breath, with a tiny shiver. ''Till that last race . . .''

She stopped for a moment, recovering herself.

''I was riding for Ebur. A filly named Storm Bird. My father had entered Intrepid, a fine sorrel I'd trained for him. Because of that, I begged him to scratch. Unicorns do get attached to their trainers. He'd never wanted my advice, and he rode in spite of me. Perhaps he should have won.''

She shook her head, a shadow of pain in her eyes.

''Intrepid had a better record. Almost to the finish, my father led the pack, but Intrepid liked me too well to beat me. My father had gambled, of course. Bet more than he owned. After the race—''

She had to stop and gulp for her voice.

''After the race, my father came storming back to Ebur's paddock, drunk and desperate, claiming we'd somehow bribed Intrepid to lose. He was looking for me. Ebur got in his way. He pulled a gun. Killed Ebur and then himself.''

Her lips quivering, she sat for a time staring past those black chimneys into the empty sky.

''That's who I am.'' She caught a long breath and turned back to me. ''And how I came to marry Thorg. I was left with nobody. Nothing. There was no money. Only a mountain of debt. When Thorg still wanted me . . .'' Her shrug was half a shiver. ''I remembered the better side I used to know. I guess I was like my father, too quick to take a chance. Anyhow . . .''

She stopped a long time, frowning blankly at the ruined engine on the hill.

"We rode from Targon to the riding three days ago. Thorg got drunk and nasty on the way, and I realized how I'd blundered. I told him I was leaving. He got uglier. That night he tried to rape me. I broke a lamp on his head.''

That explained the bandage, and I felt a flash of admiration.

"He was too drunk by then to know what hit him.'' She drew a long, unsteady breath and made a sad little pout, scolding herself. "Anyhow, that's the man I married. You see the fool I was, but that's enough about myself.'' She looked at me. "Your turn, Nuradoon.''

Ironic amusement flashed in her green eyes. In spite of it, my heart thudded faster. Was I falling in love? With my uncle's wife? Trembling with something close to panic, I had to look away from her. Nuradoon's name had become a painful joke. I was nobody, with no right to think of loving her or anybody. Nor was this the time or place to think of love, not here on the wyvern border, in hiding from the angry rider. The feeling was madness, yet I couldn't help it.

"True . . .'' Even when I found nerve to look back at her, my voice quivered unsteadily. "It's true that I'm his nephew. My father was exiled to a farm on Little River. I've been living with my mother there. My father—I don't know if he's alive—''

"Or a prisoner on Demon's Island,'' Scorth finished for me, and spoke of himself. "I used to ride for him, and I met your own unlucky father when he was training Zeldar and Sharabok for the Rellions—''

Far up the mountain slope, we heard a banshee howl.

"Listen!'' He crouched and tipped his head. "They're watching for the wolves and the wyvern. Maybe for the mages. They'll be telling where we are.''

We finished the blueleaf tea. While Scorth cleaned and packed the breakfast gear, we talked of what to do.

"We'll have to move before we're overtaken." He looked at Lady Kye. "Where are we bound?"

"Nowhere." She shrugged. "I can't go home, because I have no home. Not with my father dead and his creditors fighting for all he didn't own. As for Thorg, he'll have the primarch's police on my trail."

"So, Lady Rider—"

"Forget the title." Wryly she shook her head. "I'm through with the rider. Call me Kye."

"So?" Scorth squinted inquiringly at me and back at her. "We're still in flight from your jealous husband—" He stopped to listen when the banshee howled again, or perhaps another banshee, far up the valley. "So what?"

"This Dragonshield." She looked at me. "What, exactly, is it?"

"All I know—all anybody knows—is what the legends say. They call it magic. My father had no faith in magic; to him it was just a family emblem. As for myself, I've seen more than I like to believe. I just don't know."

"If it was magic?" Her gaze grew sharper. "What did it do?"

"The first Nuradoon is said to have used it to drive the demons off the world. The ninth Nuradoon carried it in his conquest of the riding. My father thought Thorg still has it—"

"He did." She nodded. "Or half of it."

"Half?" I stared at her. "Half of the Dragonshield?"

"I brought it with me."

The banshee had howled again, and she turned as if to search the hills around us for it. I saw her neat body stiffen in the flight leathers, and her neat fists clench. Her face was white with anger when she looked back at me.

"Last night—last night Thorg showed it to me." A stifled violence shook her voice. "Laughing at the notion that it could be any sort of weapon, magic or not. He was drunk again. Ugly because I'd tried to contradict his orders about those prisoners. Threatened to hang me for a Realist heretic."

She tossed her head, with a bleak little grin.

"I told him I'd kill him if he touched me. He didn't touch me.

He's a coward, but he kept bragging about how he and Slarn threw your father out and split the Shield between them. He took me in his strong room to show me his half. I suppose neither trusted the other to keep it all, no matter what it is, so they smashed it.''

"The Dragonshield? They couldn't!''

"They did.'' Her small, hard smile surprised me. "Thorg's a brute. Gave me a dreadful time last night, till the liquor knocked him. I stole his strong room keys, and here it is.''

She dug unto the leather saddlebags for something wrapped in a fine white scarf. A little leather pouch, closed with a drawstring. She pulled it open. Old green velvet lined it, with a small round hollow to fit the Shield. Leaning to look, I saw a broken shard of something like slick black glass.

23

The Canons of Xath

Lyrane paid the innkeeper for a bottle of brandy and a room upstairs. In the room, she filled two little glasses and offered one to Argoth.

"Banshee venom!" he snarled. "It kills the soul."

Laughing, she pushed it toward him. "You drank enough of Kallenayo's beer."

"She-demon!" He knocked it out of her hand. "Tempting me to burn in hell forever."

His voice already thick, he crouched away from her as warily as a hunter facing a wounded wolf.

"You hate women." She stared at him, perplexed at his outburst and still driven to probe and test him as a curious human specimen and a challenge to her femininity. "Why?"

"Hate?" His voice was loud and flat, charged with too much feeling. "Hatred is forbidden." Wide-eyed, he watched her gather up the fragments of the shattered glass. "But you are not to touch me."

"Why not?" Deliberately she tantalized him. "I know you like me. You always liked me."

"I fear you." His voice grew hoarse, and she knew the fear was real. "Women are evil sisters of the rebel demons, sent to lure good men to damnation."

"You believe that?" Lips tight, he made no answer. "Who taught you?"

"The mages of Xath."

She dropped the shards into the wastebasket and turned back to smile at him, her open hands spread wide. He swayed farther away, staring fixedly.

"Mages!" She teased him with the word. "What are they?"

"Holy men." He glowered sullenly. "They watch the sky and wait to warn the world of Xath's return. They've watched a thousand years. But let me warn you, woman! Tonight we saw the sign they wait for."

"So you do believe?" she mocked him. "You think Xath actually inhabits Kallenayo's companion star? You think his demons will really descend again when it reaches perihelion?"

"I believe what I know." His slurred words had a savage force. "What we saw in the telescope was no Realist illusion, but indeed the eternal serpent's mouth, opening to let Xath and his hosts descend through the gates of paradise to judge the sins of men and end our round of time.

"Lyrane . . ." His voice softened suddenly, as if to some unspoken appeal. "Before you die . . ."

Something stopped the trembling words. His jaw sagged slowly open, fine teeth shining. She wondered again. Did he intend to become a mage himself? Would he have to shave his scalp and dye it crimson, file his teeth and dye them black, tattoo his face into a mask of horror? For a shivery instant she saw him grinning at her, a human demon, and the sense of danger in him gave her an intoxicating thrill.

"With the world about to end," she asked him, "don't you want to see a woman?"

Shrinking away, he made no answer.

Smiling silently, watching his hungry stare, she dropped her jacket, shed her kirtle and shorts. Naked, she picked up the candle and displayed herself before him, slowly turning as she held it to light her parted lips, her hardened nipples, her pubic hair.

"Were-bitch!" Breathing fast, he backed toward the bed. "Xath will strike—"

His hoarse voice failed.

"Will he?"

Smiling, she set the candle back on the stand and moved toward him, arms open.

"Back!" He crouched as if she held a weapon. "Will you kill my soul?"

"I think your soul can stand it." She breathed into his rigid face. "I'll be very gentle."

His fists knotted and quivered and fell. She heard the sharp catch of his breath, a stifled groan. Pushing him back across the bed, her arms tight around him, she felt his body quiver, heard a strange outcry before he clutched her to him.

The candle was out when she woke. In the faint glow from the window, she saw that he was gone. Steam fire engines were still hissing and wheezing around the smoking foundations of the observatory when she reached the campus.

"Arson," a student told her. "Somebody poured petroleum under Kallenayo's telescope. They've found the empty can. He's wild about it."

24

Demon Swarm

"Your noble uncles!" Scorth gave me a yellow-eyed leer. "Not a spark of trust between them. Old Nanda watched their squabble over the loot after they'd sent your father into exile. Thorg demanded Dragonrock and the riding. Slarn got a fortune to match, all the lands the old rider had owned down in the lowlands and the family palaces in Targon.

"They laughed at any magic in the Shield. Thorg claimed it as the hereditary badge of head of the Vars. The guarantee of his place as the Wolver Rider and owner of Dragonrock. Slarn had ambitions for his own career in the lowlands—I think he hoped to become the next primarch.

"Now we know their solution."

"They split the Shield," Kye whispered. "Thorg laughed and mocked its magic when he showed it to me. A hard nut to crack, he said. They used a fire axe."

She put the fragment in my hand. What I felt may have been my own imagination, because I knew how much the Shield had meant to so many Vars, but I thought it seemed cold and strange, somehow heavier than it really was. I thought I felt something like the electric tingle I remembered from the moment just before a lightning strike long ago, when a thunderstorm overtook my mother and me on the village trail. It had left me deaf and dazzled, my skin still prickling.

Bending now to look, I saw that the fragment came from something shaped like a lens. Almost as wide as my palm, it was slick black glass, or something like glass. No light came through even when I held it toward the sun.

It had broken jaggedly. Clutching it against my heart, I tried to quench a spasm of hatred for Thorg and Slarn for what they had done, and groped for some better understanding of the Shield. Myths and magic aside, had it ever been anything a Realist like my father might understand? Who had made it? Why? How had it come to the Vars? I thought I might never know, and thought I would never forgive my uncles.

Kye slid the fragment back into its worn leather pouch and replaced it in the saddlebag. We were squatting around the fire again, turning over hopeless plans to stay alive and recover that missing section of the Shield, when I heard Sharabok trumpet. He stood for a moment in the meadow with his ears pricked at the sky and then came running toward us, bugling.

"Unicorns." Scorth interpreted for me. "Men on unicorns, flying up the valley."

He ran to climb on Sharabok and ride him bareback into an iron oak grove above us. I threw dirt on the fire and dragged the saddle into the shadow of the nearest standing chimney. Kye brought the saddlebags. Scorth came back to help us pull weeds to scatter over them. We hid beside a fire-scarred foundation wall, peering over it to watch the sky.

They came following the stream from the lower valley, three men in black. Long rifles sheathed, they dipped and slowed to sweep the ruins with binoculars. I held my breath till the leader shouted an order and they climbed to go on.

"Thank the Three!" Kye reached for my hand. "I thought—"

Her voice stopped. A banshee was howling, loud and near. The men wheeled and came back, low over the naked chimneys and the charred ruin of the mill. The banshee howled again, so close I thought it had followed Scorth and Sharabok into the trees. Kye's hand quivered and tightened in mine, and I heard the faint murmur of her prayer for the Powers to save us.

With none of her faith in the Three, I could only lie there trembling beneath my screen of weeds, watching the riders when I could. They circled twice. One of them fired a bullet that glanced off a chimney near us and whined away toward the hills. At last they climbed again, over the iron oaks and on up the stream. We lay there, silent, till they were gone into the westward sky.

"The Powers kept us!" Kye sat up beside me, smiling. "We can trust them!"

"So we must." Scorth gave me a quick sardonic shrug. "And trust ourselves."

Sharabok ambled back out of the iron oaks, grazing peacefully.

"We'd better go," I said. "Anywhere we can."

"Not today." Kye shook her head. "Sharabok must rest and graze."

"Where?" Scorth squinted at me. "Back to visit your uncle again? Down to Targon, to call on your uncle Slarn? Or on to the archimage in Quar, to beg for a tour of Demon's Island?"

With no answer, I could only wish again I had been the real Nuradoon.

"At least for now," Kye spoke as if to cheer me, "we're alive."

The banshee's howling had ceased. Sharabok drank again and cropped the sweetgrass. The searchers did not return. For me it became a dreamlike afternoon. Yesterday Scorth and I had been prisoners, Kye sitting with her husband above us on the rock, the prison cell waiting and maybe the noose. Today we were free, relaxed and together.

Tomorrow?

Perhaps to escape our dread of that, we talked again of who we were. Kye spoke of the mother she didn't remember, told us more of growing up with her father and his unicorns on the ranch near Targon.

"I—I loved him." I saw her tears. "He loved his unicorns, and loved the thrill of winning. Losing killed him—"

She stopped herself abruptly, fine white teeth sunk into her quivering lip, staring blankly at the stark black chimneys. It was half a minute before she caught an uneasy breath and looked back at us.

"Sorry," she murmured. "No use remembering, but he killed the man I loved. Took all I ever had. The ranch, the unicorns, my place in the world. I was left—left to Thorg."

Hearing the bitterness of that, I longed to comfort her, but what had I to offer? When she looked at Scorth, he told her simply that he had trained unicorns and ridden unicorns.

"What else?"

"I've survived," he said, and turned to me.

I told them what I remembered about my father and our life on the Little River farm, spoke of my mother and our trading trips to the village and that terrible night on the snow-covered square when the mage killed Bastard.

One by one, we went down to bathe in the icy stream. We had no towels, but the sun dried and warmed us. Lying on the saddle blanket, I slept and dreamed that we were back in the great hall at Dragonrock. The lame mage had thrown his staff at me. It changed in the air to a great black snake. I thought it would kill me, the way it killed Bastard, till Kye handed me the Shield.

She and Scorth had fitted its jagged fragments together and made it whole again. No longer black, it shone with a soft white light that tossed the snake back toward the rock. The mage shrieked and fell to his knees, but Thorg stood up, bellowing for the aid of Xath till the snake had wrapped around him.

"Zorn?"

Kye's voice woke me. Sitting up on the saddle blanket, I found her and Scorth already stirring to build a fire and make another meal. Shaken by the dread and wonder of the dream, I made them wait while I told about it.

"So?" Scorth listened with a skeptical grunt. "You're a Mystic in your sleep?"

"Not exactly that," I told them. "I guess I'm too much my father to believe in actual magic. I know the dream was just a dream, but I want to get that other fragment back. Perhaps we can really put the parts together."

Nobody needed to remind me that Slarn had taken his fragment to far-off Targon, where people said he had stolen his aging mother's place as the primarch's favorite lover. I knew no way to force him to surrender anything he had, yet the dream had left a purpose in me, if I could persuade her and Scorth to share it.

Kye had brought a bag of suncorn for Sharabok. He came whickering when she called him and licked it out of the nosebag and went back to graze again. I found firewood. Scorth made another pot of blueleaf tea, and we allowed ourselves a little more of the bread and hopper cheese.

The sun was down by then, the dusk soon dyed crimson. We spread the saddle blanket for a bed and took turns standing watch. The red moon was high when Scorth woke me, his hand on my shoulder. Kye lay asleep beside me, and she had spread her cape to cover us both.

"The demons!" Scorth pointed into the red-washed sky, his voice a rusty whisper. "They—they're here."

The moon was swollen huger than it had ever been, so near I felt its radiant heat on my face. It looked like a boiling kettle of blood-red fire. Dark patches floated on it; crimson plumes and streamers burned around the rim. Its leering face looked dreadful enough, but I saw no demons.

"Yonder!"

He pointed again, and I saw a scarlet spark crossing the sky beyond the old water tank on the hill. A meteor, I thought at first, but it was slower than any meteor. And it moved strangely, twisting oddly back and forth across the red-flooded sky.

Searching? Searching for us? None of us asked, but I heard the dread in Kye's silence when she sat up beside us, and felt it in her tight fingers when she caught my arm.

"Lie down!" Scorth gasped. "Lie still. . . ."

I heard Sharabok's hooves. He came running out of the red dark, hooting in terror. Scorth sang out and ran to make him crouch with us behind the foundation wall. We all lay motionless, watching the thing come and listening to the banshees. They howled as if to greet it, first a single voice far up the valley, then one on the cliffs above us and another on the opposite slope, soon a fearful chorus.

It dived as it neared us, veering right and left to follow the curves of the stream. The core of it was a hot red point that swelled into a tiny globe, burning and dimming and burning again, pulsing like a beating heart. Hot bright lines trailed behind, red fire flowing down them like shining blood. As it came overhead I heard a crackling hiss that kept time with the beat of that heart.

I caught Kye's hand. We clung together, afraid even to whisper, until at last it moved on, pausing over the wreckage on the hill before it climbed away into the east. Gasping for air, I turned my head and found Scorth sunk into a frozen huddle, wide eyes fixed on the western sky. I looked and saw a swarm of red sparks there, already brighter than the stars.

A dozen or more, globes like the first when they came close enough for me to make them out, they were all tied together with thin bright filaments. They pulsed in unison, dimming and fading together. Their hissing rose and fell with the same slow beat, and it swelled as they neared us until it roared like driving rain, louder than the banshees.

We lay there a long time, dazed and shuddering, while they circled and settled over the ruin of the murdered town. Once they hung so near, we covered our heads with Kye's black cape, afraid they might see our eyes, but at last they lifted and flew on—all save one.

It left the little swarm to stay behind, hovering over the wrecked engine and boiler where the sawmill had burned. We watched its thin scarlet tentacles picking up bits of metal, turning them as if to inspect them, dropping them again. It left the engine, floating closer, crackling louder.

I felt a tingle on my skin as it neared us, the same tingle I remembered from that close lighting strike on the village trail. Kye's hand had stiffened in mine. She pointed silently, and I saw pale blue fire dancing over the weeds and broken foundation stones around us.

Almost above us, the thing stopped in the air. My heart stopped with it. My whole body tingled, and I saw blue fire washing Kye's hair. I thought it had discovered us, but it climbed abruptly and flew on to overtake the swarm. We crouched there, watching over the foundation wall, till the banshees were silent and that shining swarm had finally vanished, far down the valley. Kye sat up and pulled her cape around her.

"Those things." She looked at me, her voice a quivery whisper. "Are they alive?"

I could only shrug. They had moved with seeming purpose, but was that life? If they had purpose, what could it be? Were they creatures of the scarlet moon? Answers were hard for me to imagine. They had seemed truly alien, too strange to fit any scheme of things I knew.

She looked at Scorth, her eyes still dark with dread.

"Are they demons?"

"What are demons?" He wiped at the red-shining sweat on his hairless skull. Still shaking, he turned to me with a half-malicious leer. "If you're really half a Realist, what do you say?"

Though the glowing things were gone, the scarlet moon still blazed at the zenith. Somewhere a banshee howled again. Searching the thick red shadows of the burned chimneys and the iron oak grove, I found no room for the Realist faith that human reason could finally explain everything.

"The Realist was my father," I said. "My mother was the Mystic. I don't know enough to be either one." I was simply glad the flying lights had gone, glad to be alive and here with him and Kye. "You said you'd been an acolyte. What would the mages say?"

"I was an acolyte." He sat a moment blinking at me dazedly. "A season in hell. What the lectors taught us was a worship of death." His voice changed, as if he were recalling some ritual chant. "The red moon is the serpent's burning mouth, through which Xath will return from his timeless paradise to terminate our cycle. The mages are his chosen slaves. Their reward is to learn the futility of life and to rejoice at the end of everything."

"Do you believe—"

Kye stopped with a sharp little gasp when she heard the wolf. Deeper and hoarser than a banshee's cry, its wild howl had an edge of desperate agony that sent a chill down my spine. Far off at first, it came from somewhere up the valley, where the demons had passed. It grew louder as we listened, till I reached for Kye's hand again.

"There!" Hoarsely rasping, Scorth pointed with a trembling finger. "And a demon—a demon riding it."

I saw the demon first, the bright red core of throbbing fire. It flew close above the wolf. Its tentacles, those thin filaments of hot red light, had dropped to wrap the tortured animal in a web of fire. Running desperately, the wolf darted out of the iron oaks where Scorth had hidden Sharabok and came on almost directly toward us.

"Freeze!" Scorth whispered. "Freeze!"

We crouched lower behind the broken wall. Afraid to raise my head, yet afraid not to look, I caught Kye's cold hand and watched the wolf. Not a hundred yards from us, it stopped and stood still, black head lifted toward the scarlet moon, jaws spread wide and eyes glaring crimson as the demon's red-beating heart. Its howling chilled me to the bone.

"It's hurting!" Kye breathed. "Dreadfully!"

In a moment it came on. Kye whispered the names of the Three. My breath stopped till I saw it veer around the broken walls where we had tried to hide, dashing on toward the ruined waterwheel beside the stream. There its howling ceased. Strangely, it scurried around the charred timbers and the millstones, sniffing and pawing as if searching. I never knew what it found, if anything, but at last the demon let it go.

Whimpering, it staggered blindly away from the wreckage and stopped to gaze around it and up at the red moon as if the demon had left it blinded. After a moment, it blundered to the bank and toppled off it into the water.

The demon lingered over the wreckage, picking up bits of rusted metal with those red-glowing tentacles, holding them close to its red-burning heart for a moment, and tossing them aside as if they were not what it wanted. We lay there, hardly breathing, until it dropped the last of them and climbed fast to vanish in the blood-colored night.

We waited a long time there under the red moon's glare, all of us silent and trembling, alert for anything else. We heard no more from the wolf. No banshee howled. No more scarlet sparks came down. At last we dared to sit up and speak.

"I thought—" My throat was still dry. "I thought they had us."

"We have the Shield." Kye looked at me. "Did it protect us?"

That shard of broken glass? I wanted to laugh, but the demons had killed the Realist in me. The world had grown too strange and dreadful to be understood, too full of riddles I knew no way to solve. When I turned to Scorth, he merely shrugged.

The moon had sunk low by then, long black shadow fingers creeping from the chimneys and the trees. Too jittery to sleep again, we huddled close together, watching the shadows and watching the sky, uneasily wondering what day might bring.

"Where can we go?" Kye whispered the question, half to herself. "Where can we hide?"

"The farm?" I looked at Scorth. "The farm where I grew up? The police used to watch it, but I imagine the demons have them busy somewhere else by now. I'd like to know what has happened to my mother."

"A long flight." He shook his head, scowling through the scarlet dawn. "We must think of feed for Sharabok."

"We'd planted a suncorn field before I left," I told him. "It should be ripe by now."

"Why not?" He waited for Kye to nod. "Let's go."

The white sun was soon up to warm and cheer us. Sharabok came whickering to Kye, and she poured the last of her suncorn into his nosebag. Scorth built another tiny fire. Kye searched her saddlebags again, for bread and cheese and a delta orange for each of us. Walking down to the stream for water, I found the wolf's body.

It lay on the gravel in shallow water, grotesquely twisted from its last agony. Its mouth gaped open, black fangs shining and glazed eyes staring at the sky. Most of the hair was burned from its hide, and the body had the sharp reek of burning hair mixed with its werewolf stink.

A female, her belly big with unborn pups. I felt a sudden stab of pity for her, and a wave of vast relief that she had not attacked us.

"Okay, Nuradoon!"

Scorth called me when he had Sharabok saddled and kneeling.

"Let Thorg and Xath beware!" He spoke to Kye. Perhaps his one-sided grin was meant to cheer her, perhaps it was meant to be sardonic. "We're the warriors of the Mystic Three, the deathless Nuradoon and his good companions, on our way to fix the broken Shield and defeat the dragons and drive the demons off the world!"

Silent, she had an odd little smile for me.

"Why not?"

I managed to mutter the words, but all I felt was his irony. The black mage and his serpent staff, the wolves and the banshees, Thorg on the Dragonrock: They were shocks I had somehow endured, but the demons had shattered my world. My Realist father had tried to comfort me with his hope that they would never return, not in my time. Now they were here, more dreadful than the serpent staff, too dreadful to fit into any Realist scheme of things.

Yet I tried to keep that old terror to myself as Sharabok lifted with us, away from the burned chimneys and the burned wolf and the wrecked machines that had somehow seemed to interest the demon. I was longing for my father, wishing I had been the tough-minded Realist he might have made me.

My mother had tried hard enough to share her Mystic faith. I had never understood the strength she said it gave her. What had her tearful prayers before the corn and the rose and the apple done to save the riding for my father, or even to save Bastard from the mage's changing staff?

Kye's faith seemed as strong as hers, and just as hopeless. I ached to defend her, but I would never be an immortal Nuradoon. Neither Realist nor Mystic, I had neither faith nor weapon. My own magic shield was only a bit of broken glass. The memories of that screaming wolf and the foul stink of its burnt hair were cankers in my mind. When she turned once to ask how I felt, the best I could manage was a feeble shrug.

We sat silent in the saddle. Even Scorth and Sharabok seldom sang. Kye rode close in front of me, her hair sweet with that snowbud scent when it brushed my face. Alive and warm against me, she was precious and vulnerable. I knew I loved her, and wished forlornly that I had been the living Nuradoon, with the right to tell her so.

We kept low at first, following the stream west and south toward the distant Dragon Mountains. The valley became a narrow, high-walled canyon where white water raced from fall to rapid and rapid to fall. We climbed into the clouds when we heard a banshee howling, and flew forever in icy fog. Lost in it, shivering, I recalled my boyhood joy in that first flight with my father and longed again for his strength and his laughter and his own easy faith in science and himself.

We came down on a cold high mesa scattered with volcanic rocks and patched with snow in the shadows. The high peaks, still far west of us, rose white with eternal snow. There was nothing for Sharabok to graze, but he drank from a rivulet of snowmelt. We went on when he had rested, south and finally east over mountains I began to remember.

The upper Little River ran white and high from snow still thawing. The lower valley looked lush and peaceful when we could see it. I made out the red roofs of the village, and we saw no unicorns. Perhaps the police were gone. Perhaps the demons had not come here. I found the dark coal seams in the cliffs above the exile farm and dared to hope we might find my mother safe.

Kye felt my eagerness and asked for more about her. I pointed out the trail beside the river where we had led the donkey on our trading trips to the village, told her about how she had urged me to see the Dragonshield when I thought I should stay with her.

"She came from Targon," I said. "She could have known your father there—"

My voice dried up.

We had come in view of the farm. The river ran fast and white beneath the golden strip of ripe suncorn. The rough rock walls of the little house still stood, but the grass thatch was gone and the charred rafters had fallen into the empty rooms.

25

Speaker to Xath

Back in holy Quar, Argoth killed his hair, dyed his scalp, filed and dyed his teeth, and endured his first tattoos. Wearing only a rag about his loins, he crawled on his hands and bleeding knees into the great temple hall and knelt before the archimage.

"Holy master . . ." Abjectly he beat his red-dyed head against the hard stone floor. "Holy master, I beg forgiveness for my monstrous sin against the laws of Xath."

"Child, what is your sin?"

"Most grievous, master. I forgot myself. I broke my oath."

"In what way, my son?"

"I coupled like a filthy beast."

"Come to me, son." The thin old voice grew cold. "How could you forget what you have sworn to Xath?"

Trembling, he raised his eyes to the stern-faced man on the crimson throne. The archimage was old and skeleton-lean, his brown leather face crosshatched with livid crimson scars, the bones almost as bare as his crimson skull. Dead alive, Argoth thought, yet the fires of Xath burned hot in the deep-sunk eyes that followed him across the black-tiled floor.

"The woman tempted me, Sire. She destroyed my soul."

"You sadden me, son." The archimage brushed his black cassock with the sign of fire. "You know that penance must be done."

"I am doing penance, Sire. I sleep on a bed of rough stones. I whip my errant body until it bleeds and wash the scars with salt. I drink the piss of beasts.''

"My dear son, that is not enough." Regretfully the archimage shook his crimson skull. "Not for the enormity you have confessed."

"Father, I know—" The archimage rapped the side of the red throne with his snake-eyed mace and gestured for him to raise his voice. "I do seek atonement. What penalty do you require?''

"Not I, my child. You know the laws of Xath.''

"I know the law of purity." He whispered it hoarsely. *"When an organ of the body offends, it shall be sacrificed by fire."* He lifted his head and found a quivery voice. "I have prayed for mercy, prayed for the cleansing of my foul soul, but I still bear the evil organs of the beast. I—I have prepared myself for sacrifice—''

"Not yet, my boy." He saw the archimage smiling, black teeth shining like tiny arrowpoints of polished jet. "You may stand.''

"Stand, Sire?" He blinked in unbelief. "Did I hear?''

"Stand, my son." The archimage gestured with the serpent mace. "Xath is merciful.''

"He will spare me?" He stared. "When my soul is dead?''

"Rise," the archimage commanded. "Hear the will of Xath. Perhaps your dying soul can be revived.''

"I praise him!" Bruised knees trembling, he swayed to his feet. "I praise him forever.''

"You have also served him." The archimage glanced at the iron-bound record book on the lectern beside his throne. "You have reported the blasphemies of those hell-born fools in Targon. You have destroyed the insidious instrument their leader had constructed to support their infidelities. In the Circle of the Cycles, we have weighed your service. In the holy name of Xath we have ordained the atonement that should heal your wounded soul." The archimage paused, red skull bent, keen black eyes regarding him. "If you are truly contrite.''

"I am contrite, my father." He stabbed at his heart as if his quivering hand held the dagger of abnegation. "If I can save my soul, tell me how!''

"If you dare look into the burning face of Xath . . .''

He waited, knees shaking.

"You know the story of Xath's first descent."

"I have read the sacred books."

"We worshiped him then, when he came down through the eternal serpent's mouth. We served him when he asked for service. He rewarded us fairly, revealing all the sacred mysteries recorded in *The Esoterica*. He left us too soon, returning with his shining celestials through the serpent's mouth into paradise. Its great doors closed, and its blazing circle vanished from the sky. His holy voice has been silent for the past thousand years.

"But we remember. We cherish his words and keep his faith alive. We build temples and fanes and chapels in his honor. We sacrifice our treasures and our lives to his eternal fires. We wait and pray for his foretold return. And now, my son, that event is near.

"You have seen his sign!" The archimage pointed with the serpent mace at the high black marble vault as if it had been an actual midnight sky. "The red spark you saw through that forbidden instrument was indeed the burning disk of paradise. Xath will be speaking again, if we have an ear to hear him and a voice to answer. That, my son, will be your path to atonement."

The mace swung down to touch his naked shoulder.

"My path?" He shivered from the touch. "Father, I do not understand."

"We have chosen you," the archimage told him. "You will learn the language of Xath. You will be our ear and our voice when he descends."

26

Man Possessed

It was a sad and lonely homecoming.

We landed in the pasture near the burned house. Sharabok looked spent when I slid off his wing to the ground, dark with sweat, his fine head drooping. Scorth unsaddled him, rubbed him down, and walked him to drink at the river. The old crib was empty, but we let him into the ripened suncorn field. With an eager little whicker, he knelt to feed, husking and shelling the golden ears with his agile tongue, spitting out the cops.

Envious of his contentment, I stood awhile watching him eat before I found the heart to walk down to the little grass-thatched building where my mother had made her pottery. It had not been burned, but I found the wheel overturned, the shelves empty, all her finished work stolen or lying broken on the floor.

Dismally I went on to the roofless rock walls that had been our home. The kitchen floor was littered with fire-blackened pots and pans and shattered pottery. Fallen rafters blocked my way into the other room. Back in the weed-grown yard, I picked up a little object that blurred my eyes with tears of wistful recollection, a tiny pottery disk that had been the wheel my mother had made for the toy wheelbarrow my father finished for my fourth birthday.

Nothing told me what had happened to her. Feeling sick with loss, I walked back to Scorth and Kye. He had shelled a few ears of suncorn, and he was squatting over a tiny fire, heating water for tea and parching the suncorn in a pottery bowl. The roasting grains made a fragrance that woke hunger to wet my mouth till I caught a whiff of bitter smoke and saw our ruined home again. Kye started nervously when she heard my boots on the gravel, as if she had forgotten me.

"Your mother?" She looked at my face and saw the pain. "I'm sorry."

Scorth caught the reek of his charring burning corn and snatched it off the fire. Looking up at me, he shook his head in sympathy.

"Too bad," he muttered. "I'd hoped your mother could hide us. And it looks like the end of the road for us."

The two of them, squatting there with the saddle and the saddlebags and nothing else, looked forlorn as two lost children. Kye's spirit had amazed me, but I saw now that she had reached her limit. My impulse to aid and defend her recalled my odd dream of the Dragonshield whole again, and aglow with magic force.

"End of the road?" My own words surprised me, and I tried to display a faith I couldn't really feel. "Not quite yet! I know the demons have come. It's true we've nowhere to hide. The Shield is broken. But the demons are here, and we'll have to fight—"

"Fight with what?" Scorth squinted at me, yellow eyes sardonic. "Turn that scrap of broken glass into Nuradoon's conquering sword?"

"Remember my dream?" Squatting beside them, I groped again for the faith and wondrous strength I'd felt. "I thought the Shield was whole again, shining with a magic power. Perhaps the actual Shield did have some power—why else was it saved for a thousand years? If we could somehow recover the missing piece, maybe we could really repair it. At least learn more about what it was."

"It's glass," he muttered. "Glass stays broken."

"It was whole in the dream." I turned to Kye, who huddled like some abandoned waif, staring at me sadly. "I never believed in dreams, but my mother did. This one was so real, I can't forget. Let's go on as far as we can. Slarn probably took his fragment to Targon. If we could get there—"

"I know Slarn." Her voice had a bitter force. "A slimy monster! He keeps a harem in his palace and sleeps with the old primarch.

If he has a piece of the Dragonshield, he'll fight like a wolf to keep it.''

"We must try!'' I turned to Scorth. "In spite of my uncle and all the mages—''

"Don't—don't count on me.''

"You can get us there,'' I urged him. "You know Targon. You know Quar, if we have to go there. You were an acolyte.''

"Never again!'' His roasting corn forgotten again, he looked up at me with a look of pathetic appeal on his old-leather face. "I told you why I was there. Searching for your father. But you don't know—you can't imagine—the hell on earth the mages make.''

We waited while he huddled there, shuddered at his memories, till at last he went on.

"They made us slaves of Xath. He's a god of death. That meant purging us of everything human, cleansing us for salvation in his holy fire. I endured it all, till they made us drink a hot red liquor they called the blood of Xath. It burnt my mouth and gave me visions. . . .''

His wizened features worked.

"I vomited most of it, but I still have nightmares I don't want to talk about.'' Mute for a moment, he shivered again and drew a quick breath. "I'm not going back.''

"I'm sorry.'' Kye reached to touch his shoulder. "We didn't know.''

Miserably silent, he bent again to his suncorn.

"It's Slarn,'' I said, "that we have to deal with—''

"The demons are here.'' Harshly bitter, he cut me off. "The mage will be seizing all the world for them and Xath and their peculiar hell.''

"Which means they'll be here.'' I got back to my feet, groping again for what was left of the dream. "Wait for me,'' I told them. "I'm going down to the village.''

"To find help? Something for us to eat?'' Kye looked hopefully at me. "You have friends there?''

"No real friends,'' I had to say. "We were the exiles, always avoided. I may get no help, but I know a woman who ought to know what became of my mother.''

"Can you trust her?" Scorth looked up to mutter at me. "You'll have a price on your head."

"A risk I have to take. If I don't get back, you'll know why."

I crunched a few handfuls of Scorth's roasted suncorn. Kye poured the hot blueleaf tea, and dug into her saddlebag again for a little leather bag that clinked with coins.

"We'll be waiting." She clung to my hand as if she never expected to see me again. "The Three be with you!"

Looking back from the first turn in the trail, I saw them still standing, tiny and lonely, staring after me. A lump in my throat, I wished that I had really been the reborn Nuradoon, or even Ebur ni Rellion. I waved my hand, and saw them wave, and walked on alone.

Weeds had overgrown the path. Once I saw the odd fat footprint of a werewolf, but nothing else to show that anything had followed the trail since my mother and I used to follow it with the donkey. The sun had set and the red moon was rising before I came into the road from the village to the farms along the river and saw yellow-glowing windows ahead.

There were no streetlights. Passing the woodyard and the blacksmith shop in the thickening crimson gloom, I hoped to be taken for a farmer coming home from his work if anybody saw me. The streets were empty until I turned at the Ranko barbershop. Around the corner, toward Mrs. Emok's store, I saw a little knot of people gathering around a red-flaring torch.

Ducking into the next alley, I followed it to the fence Mr. Emok had built around his backyard long ago, when the werewolves had first been seen in the nearby hills. Taller than I, made of sharpened iron oak poles set close together, it looked impossible to climb.

The red moon had risen higher and I saw torchlight flickering out in the street, but Mr. Emok's palisade cast its own shadow across the alley. I ran down it to the yard gate. Meant to keep all intruders out, men as well as wolves, it had sagged since he vanished, and was now ajar enough to let me reach the latch. Inside, I hurried through the shadow of the empty hopper barn and knocked on the back door. When nobody answered, I found a rock and hammered.

At last I heard footsteps and the rattle of a lifted bar. The heavy door creaked open, far enough to let Mrs. Emok see me. An angular, rawboned woman, she wore a shapeless sweater and a grimy hopper-hide apron. A loose wisp of iron gray hair hung across her aging face. Glaring at me with shrewd black eyes under thick black brows, she held a flaring lantern in one hand and gripped a long bush knife in the other.

"Zorn Var!" She hissed my name. "Get off my place!"

"Please!" I begged. "Let me——"

"Murderer!"

"That's not so. I've killed nobody——"

"Except your good mother."

"Is she——" I shrank from the lifted knife. "Is she dead?"

"Dead to us." Her harsh voice sharpened. "Because you broke your rules of exile. Because you ran off and left her to pay...."

"So maybe——" My voice caught. "Maybe my mother's alive?"

"Better if she's dead, since the cops and mages took her."

I'd hoped for better news, and the shock of that rocked me. Speechless for a moment, I stood searching that worn and withered face for sympathy I didn't find.

"Took her?" I echoed. "Where?"

"Where else?" She shrugged with bleak mockery. "Into the burning arms of Xath."

"Please, Mrs. Emok! She urged me to leave her. We'd seen the demon star, and she thought my uncle had a weapon——"

"Which you've stolen?" Her voice turned bleak with accusation. "That's why the mages have been here. And why they'll torture your poor mother now, because they think she conspired with you."

"If we can stop them . . ." I saw her stark disbelief and felt a pang of the doubt that haunted me. "At least we can try. I'm not alone. We have the weapon. I hope it can give some kind of chance, but we're desperate now." I spread my empty hands. "Hiding. Hungry."

"Who isn't desperate?" She tipped her head toward the street and gestured with the knife. "Just listen to the devil worshipers there across the street!"

Voices were rising beyond the palisade, excited yells and then the small shrill chant I remembered from the night Bastard died.

"We'll find a way to fight. . . ."

"You?" She shook her tired old head, blinking at me. "Var's son?"

"We really can." I wished I could believe it. "But not without help. We need information first. Anything you know about my mother. About the police and the mages and the demons and what's happening down in the lowlands."

"If you care about your mother!" Her voice cut like a whip. "She's gone. You hear the mages howling. The demons are already everywhere. That's all I know to say." She backed away, about to close the door. "I don't want you here."

"I have money. I can pay."

"I don't want a traitor's money." She gripped the knife as if to thrust it, but then her hard tone wavered. She lifted the lantern again, peering shrewdly into my face. "For your good mother's sake—let's see your money."

I poured the gold out of Kye's little purse. New gold bells, I saw, minted at Dragonrock and bearing a stern hawk face that must have been the engraver's image of Nuradoon. I held them toward her on my palm. Still gripping the knife, she hung the lantern inside the door and turned a five-bell piece in its light.

"Thorg's Dragonrock mint!" She dropped the coin back on my hand. "Nothing I want. The police and the mages would be asking where I got them. Enough of you!" She waved the knife. "Don't come back."

The door was almost shut.

"Thank you, Mrs. Emok," I called through the slit. "At least for what you've told me." Defeated, I glanced back toward the voices in the street and the flicker of torches on a tree. "If I can get out of your yard—"

"Wait!" Hesitating, she pulled the door wider and paused to scowl at me again. "Perhaps I owe your mother something." She listened to the crowd beyond the palisade, and finally let me in. "Come on to the kitchen."

Still ready with the knife, she made me walk ahead of her through a dark storeroom and its stale stink of long neglect and old decay and Mrs. Emok herself. In the gloomy kitchen, she beckoned me to a chair while she scrabbled through a clutter of half-washed dishes, half-empty jars, and half-spoiled fruit on the table till she found a half-empty bottle of Mr. Alu's apple brandy. She filled two glasses and pushed one across to me.

"I'm sorry for your mother." She tossed off her own drink and shook her head with a moody sigh. "I guess you never knew—she never knew—but she was actually an artist. Truly great. I used to ship her best porcelains down the river all the way to collectors in Dorth and even a shop in Targon. If she hadn't thrown herself away on that Var—"

"They were happy," I protested. "Her heart was broken when my father was taken away."

"A fool if she cared!" Reaching for the bottle again, she checked herself to peer warily at me. "Artists can be fools." Pleased with that judgment, she filled her glass again, took a hearty gulp, and sat squinting at me critically. "I know you can't help the name, but you do have the look of a Var."

"He was always good to me, and she did love him." I looked again for sympathy on her own bleak face. "Do you know what they've done with him?"

"I don't deal with traitors." Her tone was bitterly harsh, but she caught herself. "Not that I'm accusing him or you, but it was your mother I respected."

"If you did, can't you help—"

"I still respect the primarch's law, and I'm no conspirator." She raised a knobby-fingered hand. "Say no more about this weapon, if you claim you have a weapon. I want none of your gold. No part of any plot. Anything I do will be in honor of a worthy artist."

"She would thank you." I waited for her grudging nod. "To make our plans, we need anything you know. First, about schedules of the border patrol."

"They've quit coming."

"News from the lowlands?"

"Nothing good." She made a bitter face. "Captain Kaymath sent the last riverboat back to Dorth without him. He says the world's all in pieces. Gone crazy since the red moon came. If the demons want him, they'll find him here.''

"Do you know what they want? What they are?''

"Ask the mages.'' Her face twitched and hardened. "Three of those blood-drinking devils came up the river on that last boat. Scaring everybody.'' Her head jerked toward the open window. "Chanting and ranting and building a temple to Xath. All to welcome the demons when they come down.''

When I listened again, the uproar in the street seemed louder.

"Bastard was my friend,'' I told her. "I hate the mages. I think perhaps we have a chance to stop them, if we can only stay alive. Could you possibly . . .'' Hopefully, I looked around at her shelves. "Possibly find us anything to eat?''

"For your mother's sake . . .'' She got to her feet, started toward her cupboards, and turned back to me with a black-browed frown. "Don't say where you got it.''

Rummaging, she found a mildewed backpack of Mr. Emok's and filled it with the food she could bring herself to surrender: a long loaf of stale bread and half of another, most of a molded round of hopper cheese, a hard mass of dried figs, a little sack of last year's rocknuts.

"Now get out.'' Suddenly impatient, she interrupted my thanks. "Keep out of sight.''

"I'll certainly try.'' Turning to go, I listened again at the window. The chanting had paused, but I heard a piercing scream. "Let me wait,'' I begged her. "Till the crowd's gone home.''

"I harbor no traitors.'' Grimly she picked up the knife. "Get out of the house, or I'll call the mages. Better keep to the dark. And never mention me.''

She carried the lantern back through the junk room to the door. The red moon looked huger and higher, but the hopper barn still shadowed the yard. The chanting of the mages still rose beyond the palisade. A burst of raucous yelling turned me back toward the house, but the door had already slammed and I heard the bar thudding into place.

Feeling trapped, I peered through the gate into the alley. Mr. Gornal, the old carpenter, was leaning on his cane just outside, his gnarly face lit with the flickering torches in the street. Mr. Keroth, the shoemaker, stood beyond him with a few women and children I didn't know, all staring toward that red flicker.

The barn behind me was doorless and empty, unused since Mr. Emok's time. I retreated into its musty odors of rotted hay and old hopper dung. When my eyes got used to the dark, I found my way up the ladder to the loft. From a little window at the end of it, I could see the mages' new temple.

Built on a great pile of junk in an open space that had been a community garden, it seemed almost a mockery of Xath. Unsawn logs, salvaged planks from old buildings, chairs and tables, wagon beds and fence pickets and sticks of split firewood, all had been roughly stacked to make a wide platform. The temple itself was grimly comic.

Bark still covered the long logs upended to make its pillars, with more raw logs laid across them for a roof. It was empty, except for a huge wooden tub on the floor. Two red-scalped acolytes stood holding torches beside the black-robed mage who stood chanting in front of it.

His words were too far and faint for me to hear, but he might have been the one who murdered Bastard. He stood a long time screeching at the villagers gathered around the platform before he turned to kneel and howl into the vacant temple. My weary legs ached from standing before he stopped and stepped aside to wait for a third black acolyte, who came dragging a young she-goat on a rope.

They tethered the goat in the temple doorway. The mage knelt before her to chant again before he rose to make some silent signal to the acolytes. They ran to seize long-handled dippers and begin bailing some oily red liquid out of the tub, splashing it over the floor and the rough log columns, the whole platform, finally the frightened goat.

When the tub was empty, they ran again to bring the blazing torches to the mage. He raised his grisly black-toothed mask to the scarlet moon, screeched an endless final incantation, and finally tossed the torches into the temple. It exploded into a roaring inferno that drowned the bleating of the goat.

Backing away with his acolytes, the mage paused on the street to kneel again and yowl at the scarlet moon. The villagers stood gazing at him and the temple until the tower of roaring flame had grown so hot that they suddenly turned and ran. Shivering to a shock of my own, I saw a bright red star falling out of the lurid sky.

An actual demon!

I shrank back from the window and tried to look away. The demons the night before had been dreadful enough, diving close around us and riding the screaming wolf, but they had never seemed to see us. If this one had come because the mage had called it down, if the demons and the mages really were in league—

I tried not to think what it meant. Desperately I groped for my father's Realist calm or Scorth's sturdy pragmatism or even the hard comfort Kye and my mother seemed to find in the Mystic Three, but I found none of them. And couldn't stop looking.

The demon dropped toward the blazing temple. Itself a tiny moon, brighter and redder than the vast fire-mottled globe in the sky, it glowed and dimmed, glowed and dimmed with the rhythm I remembered. It slowed in the air to hover a dozen yards above the chanting mage. Its bright, wirelike tentacles reached questingly down toward the mage, toward the flames, toward the watchers, who kept turning back to look as they fled. The tips of the red-throbbing tentacles lifted and curled and shifted as if somehow sensing everything.

One of them touched the chanting mage's skull. Suddenly silenced, he spun to gesture at the retreating villagers. The shining globe left him to dive after them. They shrieked and fled again, all except Mr. Ranko, the barber. He stumbled over a coat somebody had dropped, and fell headlong in a puddle of muddy water.

The demon paused above him. One bright filament stretched down to touch him. His body jerked as if from a galvanic shock, and instantly glowed with the same pale blue fire I had seen around the tortured wolf. Screaming with the same utter agony, he lurched to his feet.

He stood there a moment digging coins out of a leather purse he wore on his belt and tossing them into the air. Those shining arms darted to catch them and recoiled to carry them up to the globe. They vanished into it, and the tentacles spread to reach for more.

Was it hungry? Feeding? The notion seemed absurd, yet that was what I saw. Staring out of that high window, I was clammy with fear, bewildered by too many things beyond my grasp. Feeling weak and cold and ill, I looked back at Mr. Ranko.

Now a pale blue specter, still shrieking as the wolf had, he emptied the purse into the air, tossed it away, and ran after the villagers. They were scattering in frantic panic, but he raced after them with the speed of a specter, and overtook the laggards.

The men he touched staggered and went down as if struck dead. He stopped to rip at them for coins. When those ahead saw what was happening, they began dumping their own pockets as they ran. He scrabbled for the coins in the mud and gravel, flung them up for the demon to catch.

Behind him, the fallen men began reeling to their feet and stumbling out of sight into side streets and alleys. He finally stood alone, far down near his barbershop. Face lifted toward the demon in a red-lit mask of agony, he screamed until at last it released him and lifted away. That ghostly shimmer faded. His body fell like an unstrung puppet.

I drew back from the open window, relieved to see the demon going. The mage and his acolytes had vanished. Though the rough log pillars of the temple had already crumbled into clouds of crimson sparks, yellow flame still washed the mountain of junk where it had stood. Beyond its light, the red moon bathed the empty street. The barber's body lay motionless, hard to see in the shadow of the tall iron oak in front of his shop.

Though the night had not been cold, I found myself shivering, still damp with the sweat of terror. The demon had seared itself into my brain: the pulsing globe, red-glowing tentacles, the pale blue fire that washed the victims. It was hellish, and it made no sense. The greed of the mages was notorious, but an actual gold-eating demon seemed a monstrous joke, with no point that I could see.

Bitterly I longed again for my father's sane Realist universe, and found no refuge anywhere. The demons and their moon were alien to everything human, their laws unknown, their evil beyond any prediction.

Ours was a world of life at war with death. My mother had cherished its living face, neatly symbolized in the seed and the bloom and the fruit on her simple earthen altar. Tonight I had seen the stark face of death, which had to be the eternal victor in that war. Commanded now by the mages of Xath, its armies were the werewolves and the wyvern, the banshees that spied for them, the dragons guarding their secrets in the high mountains west. Sometimes also men like my uncles, and women like the Lady Vlakia. Even the old primarch himself, taxing his people for the gold the mages demanded for the crucibles of Xath.

A red tide of death, as I saw it in my dazed imagination, was rising from the shadows and the darkness to meet the demon's moon. Shivering to a chill of helpless dread, I turned back to the window and again found the flying globe. It was diving straight at me out of the red moonlight, already close, red tentacles grasping for me.

27

The Historic Xath

Creating their deism of terror, the archimages had always denied that any human Xath had ever lived, and burned what skeptics they found. In the aftermath, searchers opening the long-sealed vaults beneath the great temple in Quar found the story of a probable original in a manuscript fragment that had escaped obliteration through an odd accident.

Fortunately for history, it was written on the thin-peeled sheets of whitebark that replaced paper when there was no paper. Fortunately again, the writer had used only one side of each sheet. Thrifty clerks, perhaps never troubling to decipher the barely legible scrawl, had recycled the bark, using the blank pages to record gifts to Xath: the names of donors, amounts of gold or goods, and the degrees of grace granted in return.

The manuscript purported to be a letter written by a half-literate dealer in hopper-hides to his wife, explaining his long absence during what he calls the year of the blood moon. He tells of a man he knew as Xath, or sometimes Xathog the Weasel, who had been a hopper herder on the marshy Dragon delta.

The red dwarf had already appeared when his narrative begins, but the dealer had seen no demons. He was riding across the delta barrens, far from any town, on his annual search for hopper ranchers who might have the hides of slaughtered animals for sale. With his wife sick and debts to pay, he was still concerned with business.

He lost his way on an unfamiliar trail through empty marshlands. Night fell. The moon rose. Wandering on in hope of reaching food and shelter, he saw a distant fire. He turned toward it and found a naked man dancing around a burning hut. The man's body was glowing with a pale blue light, and he was yelling strangely.

"But not drunk," the dealer wrote. "He scared me."

Panicked, his hopper pitched him off. He hid and watched from the brush while the fire burned out and the herder ran away, stumbling blindly over rocks and stumps, stopping again and again to stare and howl at the moon.

The dealer caught his mount next day and rode on to an isolated ranch, where he heard how the herder had burst into the kitchen, still naked, still glowing, still uttering meaningless shrieks. Trying to placate him, the rancher's wife set out a bottle and a glass.

With no apparent interest in them, the shining man stood waving his arms and squalling like a branded hopper, as if trying to speak. When the rancher came in, the man ran toward him. The frightened rancher drew a gun and waved him away. Though the shining man had no visible weapon, he pointed his naked arm at the rancher. Green lightning struck from it. The gun exploded. The rancher fell, knocked out. The man snatched a gold ring off the rancher's mangled finger and darted out of the room.

When the dealer reached a river trading post a few days later, he heard that the man had invaded a schoolroom there. The teacher sent the children out and stayed to face him. The weather had turned bitter. Still naked and shining, he was moaning with cold. Yet he had slapped away a coat the teacher offered, seized a book, and made signs that he wanted to learn to read.

He kept the teacher there two days and nights, without food or water for either of them. In that time, the teacher said, he had read several books and also began learning to speak, though never with any human feeling or intonation. On the third day he collapsed and fell, learning to drink only when the teacher held a glass of water to his lips. Afterward, he sometimes ate and drank voraciously, wolfing down whatever he was offered, yet never seeking food.

The dealer seems to have been in no hurry to get home. With the demons already creating disorder in the larger towns, he had no market for his hides or money for his wife. However uneducated, he had intelligence and curiosity. Consumed with wonder, he joined the followers of the shining man.

A small group at first, perplexed and terrified but yet fascinated, they fed him, tried to teach him, and obeyed or tried to obey the commands they could understand. He seemed to worship fire, burning building after building, screeching nonsense sounds at the flames and dancing close around them. He seemed to worship the scarlet moon. Feverishly active when it was in the sky, he was dull and slow, sometimes seeming almost dead, when it was down and he had no fire.

He wanted gold, though not for any reason they ever understood. He seized gold coins and jewels when he saw them and made his followers collect them. All he ever did with them was to throw them into blazing buildings. Strangely, the metal appeared to burn, rising in brilliant sparks toward the moon.

He neglected his body. His hair and beard grew long. Shivering through winter nights, he never clothed himself or let his followers cover him. Eating too little and too seldom, he grew skeleton-thin. Never washing or bathing, he was covered with open sores. His odor became unbearable.

Weakening as the red moon shrank in the sky, he told his followers that he would have to leave, and taught them what to do after he was gone. The dealer quoted phrases that parallel passages in *The Esoterica*, which must have had more literate authors.

The dealer stayed with him to the end. Leading a few more followers, fearful men and women who obeyed like slaves, he led them upriver from the delta, burning the towns they entered. His murderous lightning bolts had a longer range than guns, and most of the terrified inhabitants fled ahead of him.

Moving toward Targon, he never reached it. One rainy night, after a long march across empty grassland that offered no buildings to burn, his demonic energies failed. His blue glow faded. He fell and lay shivering in the mud, whimpering pitifully but unable to speak or stand.

His followers were afraid to touch or cover him, but they found fuel for a fire beside him and watched him through the rest of the night. Before dawn he was dead. They buried him there, and piled rough stones into a cairn to mark the grave.

Though the dealer's account ended with that act, marginal notes in another hand speculated that the great temple of Xath was built on that spot, its dome centered over the grave. In any case, the dealer left the only known eyewitness account of any human Xath.

28

Rebel Unicorns

The demon globe was already close. Afraid to move, I stood there at the barn window, staring at the dark splotches that floated over its throbbing scarlet brightness like island continents on a tiny world of liquid fire. New tentacles were sprouting from them, and one darted at my face.

Perhaps I cried out. I don't remember, but it never touched me. Its incandescent tip hesitated, drew back, and stabbed again toward my pocket. I knew then that it had sensed the gold coins Kye had given me.

Frozen for an instant, I broke free, snatched the little purse out of my pocket, and tossed it through the window. Three tentacles converged to meet it. Moving with a terrible swift dexterity, they seized it, ripped it apart, caught the spilled coins, and slid back with them into the red-blazing ball.

For another dreadful moment, it hung motionless. Those dark shapeless patches looked like crusted scars. I wondered if demons could suffer disease, and my dazed imagination turned them into the features of a malignant sneering face. The nearest brightened at the center and suddenly extruded another burning tentacle, thrusting at my head.

I tried to back away, but my body failed. The red-hot tip came in inches of my nose and paused there, wavering searchingly. The heat of it stung me, like the radiation of incandescent iron. My skin prickled. I felt a tingling and then a numbing chill beneath my un-shaven beard. A pale blue glow washed my uplifted hands, and I heard a dry crackling like the sound of something burning.

For a hideous instant I thought I had been taken, like Mr. Ranko or that screaming she-wolf. But perhaps I had nothing else it wanted. Suddenly the filament slid away and retracted into the globe. The tingling and the numbness gone, I caught a gasping breath and stumbled away from the window.

The thing had vanished when I glanced back. Weak and gasping, I staggered to a pile of moldy hay in a dark corner of the loft and dropped behind it. I lay there a long time, afraid to move or look again, or even to hope for any weapon against the demons. Why should such a creature fear a shard of the shattered Dragonshield?

Feeling calmer at last, I got to my feet and stumbled back to the window. The pink-hazed sky was starless and empty, the great crimson moon now near the zenith. The sacrificial temple had burned down to glowing embers, and I saw nobody left on the red-lit streets.

Nerve and strength came slowly back. I clambered down the lad-der when I felt able, recovered the backpack, and peered again through the cracks in the palisade. The dark-shadowed alley looked empty. I let myself out into a gusty north wind. Hunched against it, I pushed uneasily back to the vacant street and hurried along it till I saw the dropped coat that had tripped Mr. Ranko.

I picked it up and tried it on. It was homespun, sturdily made and only a little large. I buttoned it, and shuddered again when I came to the shadow of the old iron oak that lay thick and black in front of his shop. Mr. Ranko was gone, but I caught the same faint foul taint that had hung over the wolf's seared carcass. The windows behind the shop were lit; his wife and his son must have carried him or his body inside. I held my breath against the stench and hurried on.

A fine fragrance of roasting meat met when I came back up the trail to the farm. The red moon was down, a sane golden sun just rising.

Scorth sat watching a joint propped over his neat little cook fire. Kye had knelt to pile hot embers over a few ears of green corn roasting in the shuck.

She cried out when she heard me, and I saw the glint of tears in her eyes when she ran to hug me. Scorth met me with a cheery hail and a tasty bite cooked on a pointed stick. He had found hoppers grazing in the suncorn field, he said, and ridden Sharabok to chase a young calf off a cliff.

They listened very soberly when I told them how my mother had been taken, and how the mage had flung that mock temple together and burned it to call his demon down.

"It found me," I finished. "Even where I was hiding in Mrs. Emok's barn. What it wanted was the coins in that purse. I don't know why. It swallowed them and left me."

"Thank the Three!" Kye breathed. "I prayed for you." Hopefully, she added, "I have another purse."

"We won't need money." Scorth bent again to turn his spit. "We can hunt for food and hide in the wilderness."

"Hiding from the demons?" I asked him. "When they're watching from the sky?"

"What else?"

"The Dragonshield," Kye whispered. "If we could get it and mend it—"

"Can we?"

I couldn't help a shudder. The shrieks of the demon-ridden wolf and the demon-ridden barber were seared into my memory, too dreadful to forget. How two bits of broken glass might help us against all the powers of Xath, I couldn't imagine. Yet I remembered the odd cold tingle of that small black fragment when I had it in my hand, and recalled my odd dream of the Shield and its magic.

"Maybe." I was nodding, almost in spite of myself. "I think we have to try."

"We'll fly to the Rellion ranch." Kye's firm tone surprised me. "That's near Targon. Perhaps Ebur's father will help us. Most of the family hates me since the tragedy, but he was trying to forgive me."

"The demons . . ." Scorth shook his head, scowling at her. "They'll be there."

"Everywhere." She shrugged. "The ranch is miles from Targon, out in barren hill country. We can't take Sharabok into the city, and the ranch should be as safe for him as anywhere. There should be feed for him in the barns."

All of us starving, we made a feast on the roast and green corn while we planned the flight. It would be long, but Scorth said he knew a spot where we could stop to rest and water Sharabok. Most of the way we would be over settled country, and we decided to make the try at night.

I slept a little that morning, lying on the saddle blanket on the floor of the pottery building and haunted by dreams of the demon's red-hot tentacles reaching into my face. We left Sharabok free to graze in the suncorn field and spent the afternoon shelling ripe corn to carry for him.

We took off at sunset, climbing so high that I shivered even in my homespun coat. The lights beneath us were all blacked out, and the lurid moonlight washed out the stars, turning the world into a dim crimson shadowland that had an eerie beauty.

It was all new to me, though now and then Kye or Scorth pointed to the red-glinting tracery of a lake or river they knew. Near midnight we came to a narrow clearing in the forest west of Dorth. A rest stop the smugglers used, Scorth said, when they were trading gold from the highland mines for untaxed guns and luxury goods from the lowlands. He must have been a smuggler once, though he didn't say so.

We fed Sharabok the suncorn and found water for him in a little pond fed by a pipe from a spring somewhere above us. Kneeling for us to mount again, he swayed abruptly to his feet and stood listening, bright horn high and small ears intently tipped. After a moment he raised his head to trumpet into the scarlet gloom.

I heard the answer, another unicorn calling from far off in the sky. Sharabok swung his head to neigh at us. Scorth shrugged at Kye and sang an answer. Lifting his great head to listen again, he bolted down the strip without us and climbed fast into the moon-drenched sky.

I watched until he vanished. Listening again for a unicorn song, what I heard was an eerie, far-off note I thought was a banshee's howl. Left standing there with Scorth and Kye on the narrow red-lit strip, I felt a bewildered dread. Sharabok had left us too suddenly, too far from any world I knew. The great trees around us crowded too close, their shadows too thick and dark.

"What's this?" I looked uneasily at Scorth. "Will he come back?"

"I hope." He shrugged. "It'll be hell if he doesn't."

"Don't you trust him?"

"We don't own him." Kye turned to search the moon-red sky, and turned slowly back to me. "Unicorns are never owned. My father used to call them symbiotes. Our two races need and serve each other. We feed them and care for foaling mares. They carry us on our races and our errands. We join against the wyvern and the wolves that raid our towns and catch their foals."

She turned to listen at the silent sky.

"We enjoy each other," Scorth said. "To understand them, you need to know their music and their epic songs. Their history's in them. Longer than ours, filled with terrible wars fought to save themselves from the wyvern and the wolves before we humans were here. Great tales of tragic love and danger and death that make you wish you'd been born a unicorn."

We listened and watched the sky.

"He loves us," Scorth murmured hopefully. "Whatever's happening, he won't want to leave us."

Not quite so hopeful, I stood wondering. A child on the farm, I had loved Sharabok, feared him, never understood him. My father had let me ride with him only that one unforgettable time when he showed me Dragonrock. He'd been taken away before I could learn any songs.

Kye and Scorth seemed more relaxed than I. They watched and listened and spoke of unicorns.

"As much as my father rode them," she was saying, "he never got to know them. I told you how he lost that last race because he didn't realize that Intrepid liked me too well to beat me."

"They're different from us." Scorth nodded and turned to listen again, a hand cupped to his ear. "And not just because they can fly. They're as smart as we are, but only their own unicorn way. Even with no tools or writing, they have their own literature, their own philosophy, even a science of their own. They didn't need us to tell them when the demon moon was due to rise again."

I shrank from the cold night wind, trying to imagine the unicorn world. Our wait had begun to seem forever, and my unease had festered. If one unicorn's whim had killed Kye's father and her lover, couldn't another's leave us stranded here?

Far off, a unicorn bugled.

"I knew," Kye breathed. "He does love us."

We fell silent, waiting till we found his great black wings in the red sky above us. He didn't land, but wheeled low over our heads, singing. Scorth answered, and then Kye. Her voice astonished me, powerful and pure, her haunting notes as strange to me as Sharabok's. He answered her and climbed back into the crimson gloom.

Anxiously I looked at her.

"Sharabok has met friends," she said. "A little herd of unicorns from Targon. One mare is the sister of my father's Intrepid. They're flying on to the north coast. Sharabok wants to join them."

"Leaving us?"

"Don't panic!" Scorth mocked me. "He's asking for more about their plans. I think he'll take us on as far as he can. He knows he can't come with us into Targon."

"Can you ask him to wait at the ranch?" I was still at the edge of panic. "Whatever happens, we'll need him again."

"I asked." Unhappily Scorth shook his head. "But the unicorns have never liked the mages, and he says the demons have been attacking unicorns in the air to get the metals their riders carry. Can you blame him if he wants to get away?"

Sharabok climbed away from us. I heard him bugle to the others, and hear their distant answers. I lost him in the moonlight and stood wondering again till I heard the thud of hooves, far down the dark strip. Scorth ran to meet him. Waiting close beside me, Kye was hard to see in the red gloom, but I caught the snowbud fragrance of her hair.

"He'll take us to the ranch," she whispered. "But then we're on our own. We must trust the Three!"

I had never kissed a woman, but suddenly, without meaning to, I had her in my arms. I heard her breath catch. Her body stiffened and swayed against me. I felt her trembling, her mouth hot on mine. She clung for a moment, and thrust me abruptly away.

"Remember!" she gasped. "Remember what I am. Remember Ebur. Remember Thorg." Her voice grew sharp as a blade. "The rider's wife—no whore!"

"I—I didn't mean—" I was stammering, confused and hurt and angry at myself. "I didn't mean that. I'm terribly sorry."

Facing me, she caught both my arms to hold me back.

"But I—I love you!" My throat was tight and aching. "I can't help it."

"If you do, I'm sorry for us both." I saw the pain on her pink-lit face. "I wish—"

Her voice shook and paused and fell.

"I wish we were in a better world." Her whisper was almost too faint for me to hear. "A world without the demons. One where I was free. And you were all that Ebur was. Really the heroic Nuradoon, awakened to rescue an innocent maiden from her evil captor's castle!"

She tried to laugh, perhaps at herself and not at me, but what I heard was more like a sob.

"But we're who we are." Her face had lifted to me, desperate in the crimson dimness, and her quick voice had a ring of hard finality. "Our world is what it is. The mages seem stronger than the Three. Fate's a monstrous trickster, and we're the victims of a dreadful joke. Your Dragonshield is shattered. The man I loved is dead, and I'm your uncle's wife."

"Forget him!" I tried not to think of Ebur. "He's the monster. Far off in the riding. What do you owe him?"

"The debt is not to your wonderful uncle. What we owe is to

ourselves and the Three. I was married in a sacred chapel. I made a vow I have to keep. Outlaws or not, we're still ourselves.''

Her hands tightened, trembling on my arms.

"Promise me, Zorn! Promise on your honor as a Var. Help me do what I believe is right, for both our sakes.''

Tears in my eyes, I had to promise.

Sharabok knelt. We climbed into the saddle. He rocked off his knees and raced with us down the strip and soared with us back into the red-drenched sky. Above the whisper of his wings, I heard faint unicorn calls, far off in the north. He turned his splendid head to trumpet his farewell to them.

We flew on east. The forest was a field of darkness under us, with no light or other sign of humankind. Feeling lost in its immensity, I sat in the saddle with Kye's warm flesh tormentingly against me, almost in my arms. Yearning for her in spite of that promise, I wished forlornly again that I had been the actual Nuradoon.

Sharabok and Scorth sang to each other, and she interpreted for me.

"He wants to take us with him to the far north coast. He knows an abandoned fishing camp. He thinks the demons will never come there, because there will be no gold to draw them. We can fish for food, he says, and he will bring us home when they are gone.''

"Thank him," I said. "But tell him—did you tell him how much we need him?''

"We've told him what we hope to do," she said. "But the unicorns have their own memory of the demons when the red planet passed before. They pitied us then for all the suffering the demons caused, and he knows nothing of any weapon of ours that drove them away. He thinks Nuradoon and the Dragonshield are only dreams that came to heal our wounded hearts. He begs us to forgive him for leaving us, and hopes we'll understand.''

The huge moon sank as we flew on. The wind bit deeper through my homespun coat. Kye was warm and exciting against me, yet she seemed too far off for me to reach, filled as I was with impossible desires and dreads too vast for words.

At last we saw scattered lights far beneath. Lanterns, perhaps, carried by refugees from the demons? Sharabok hooted, and Kye pointed at a murky red glare on the horizon ahead.

"Targon," she murmured. "Burning."

We veered away from it, into the north. The moon went down in the red-hazed west, and its scarlet twilight faded into pale gray dawn. Far off, we made out the towers of Targon. I had never seen a city, and the size of it awed me. Kye pointed out the old cathedral with its three silver spires, and the Institute where my parents had met, rows of plain brown blocks around a green quadrangle. Dragon River ran past it, grown so wide here that it amazed me.

"Green River." Kye pointed. "Flowing into the Dragon. And that's the citadel on the bluff between them. The primarch's palace, and Slarn's, are there behind the citadel wall."

I found the citadel, the ancient fortress complex on the narrow ridge between the rivers. The towered wall crossed it from river to river. One more barrier barring our way to the missing fragment of the Shield, if Slarn had really brought it here.

The long slopes outside the wall were a forested park, with white-walled villas scattered along broad avenues. Targon lay below, tree-lined streets spreading forever from the three great stone bridges that tied the city together, lost in the south under dark blue smoke.

"Burning." Kye pointed to another thick black pillar rising over the riverbanks in the east. "Docks and warehouses where the freight boats land."

"Bonfires!" Scorth muttered. "Set to welcome the demons."

Sharabok took us north around the western fringes of the city. At last, in bright golden sunlight, he glided down into a shallow valley between barren hills around it and came down to a long flight strip beside a huge barn. He knelt, and we slid to the ground. Waiting for Scorth to unbuckle the saddle, he whickered softly and turned his splendid head to sniff our faces, the shining horn high above our heads.

"His farewell," Kye whispered. "He's sad to be leaving."

"Say good-bye for me," I told her. "Tell him I'm just as sad."

She trilled, and he nickered softly. Gently his black velvet muzzle brushed my face. He swung from me to nuzzle her and then Scorth, lurched off his knees, and stood a moment with his great golden eyes fixed upon us before he turned away. His hooves pounded down the strip. With an ache in my throat, I watched his head lift, his great wings unfold. He wheeled back low, trumpeting as he passed overhead. We waved and he was gone, climbing over treeless hills into the north.

29

The Sentinel Tower

The tallest structure in Quar and perhaps the oldest, the tower known as the Staff of Xath was a lean finger of black granite pointing into the sky behind the crimson-domed temple in the heart of old Quar. Climbing the wide stair to the portal, Argoth trembled with a mix of fear and expectation.

The hidden dungeons beneath him were said to be a place of punishment from which few returned. Yet, searching himself for recent sins, he found no certainty of damnation. His most monstrous offense was his coupling with the she-demon at the Institute, but the archimage had already offered him his chance at atonement. Perhaps he had really been the primarch's bastard son, but surely his unknown mother's secret evil could not overtake him now.

He hardly dared for anything good, yet his mission to Targon had come out rather well. He had brought the archimage a full report of the riotous iniquities of the Institute. He had burned the Realist telescope. His unexpected reward had been this new mission to meet and deal with the celestials. Could that be already beginning? The messenger told him nothing, and he felt his heart racing with emotions gone perilously far beyond any decent restraint.

At the top of the vast granite steps, he found the portal closed, the tall public entrance sealed with twin slabs of heavy iron deeply pitted from long centuries of rust. As he approached, however, a narrow doorway opened between them.

Red-skulled guards challenged him inside and called a strange official who demanded passwords, wanted facts he had not been told about his business with Tower Master Strull, and escorted him at last into a silent electric elevator. Beyond a vast antechamber on the top levels of the tower, he found the master seated between two huge windows that looked far down across the dome's vast red curve to the crooked streets of the most ancient quarter of Quar and the fortress walls that followed the Dragon's long sweep around the city.

Master Strull himself was younger than Argoth had expected, and surprisingly heavy. His naked crimson skull had an oily shine, and the ritual tattoos had given his smooth cheeks a permanent sardonic grin. More odd, the great room had no scent of sanctity. The air, instead, had a faint fragrance of some incense rare in Quar. The massive desk was polished inkwood, bare of everything except a glistening crystal bowl of ripe delta fruits and a full carafe of some amber liquor with the look of sweet delta wine.

Uncertain what to expect, he fell to his knees.

"Stand." An abrupt command. Pale cold eyes peered through the stiff blue mask to study him. "You are Lector Eighty-Nine?"

"Now a demimage, sir. The archimage has raised me."

"Why?"

"For service, sir." Back on his feet, he bowed and wondered again why he had been summoned here. "Service to Xath."

"What was your service?"

"An errand in Targon, sir. An errand for the archimage."

"I was told something of it. I wish to know more." The master gestured at the crystal bowl. "Would you like something while we talk? A honey-apple? Or perhaps an island peach? These are fresh from the delta."

"Thank you, sir, but I must not."

Such indulgences were seldom allowed, and he had trained himself not to desire them. The rich odors of the bowl did set his mouth to watering, but his sins at the Institute had been damning enough. He stood waiting while the master eyed him, eating the shining purple grapes one by one.

"As you will." The master licked his lips. "Perhaps the archimage told you of his sudden strange concern that our cycle may be closing."

"We spoke of that." The master's irreverent manner puzzled him. "I believe, sir, that his expectations have good reason."

"What reason?" The pale eyes narrowed. "Here in the tower, we are sentinels for signs of change. We see none."

"I've seen them, sir. Signs too unmistakable to be ignored, which I reported to the archimage."

"Unmistakable?" Strull gestured at the patterns of red tile roofs that spread from river to river so far beneath. "Do you see celestials in the streets?"

"Not yet, sir." He watched the master belch and reach for another grape. "But I expect them."

"Really?"

"I've been in Targon, sir. At the orders of the archimage, to learn what I could about the activities of the infidels and find how we might deal with their abominations."

"So I understood." Grinning, the blue mask became horrific. "But here in Quar don't we perhaps owe the infidels a debt? But for their inevitable transgressions, our cycle might never end. Xath might have no cause to return. Our own tithes and taxes might dwindle and cease."

"Sir!" The master's irreverent frivolity offended him. "Have you seen their rampant wickedness?"

"I see sins enough." The master reached for a yellow peach, squeezed it critically, and tossed it back to the bowl. "Simply looking from my windows."

"Have you seen Targon?" His voice quivered. "A sink of vile iniquity! There in the service of the archimage, I enrolled at the Institute and found it reeking with every manner of evil. Even the so-called Mystics, harmless as they may seem, are blasphemous skeptics. They call our faith a tissue of error, and offer correction from their own vain illusions. Let them beg their feeble Three to save them when the Lord Xath descends!"

"I've heard too much of what happens at the Institute." The master cocked his crimson crown aside, his blue-scarred grin grown even more sardonic. "Are you sure you didn't allow yourself to be corrupted?"

"I was tempted, sir." He shuddered. "Beyond control. I sinned. But I've confessed. The gracious archimage has allowed me to seek atonement."

"Your soul is safer here in Quar."

"Sir! I was there on my appointed mission. A mission against the Realists. Perhaps you don't understand the extent of their obscene perfidies. They deny the divinity of Xath. They steal our ancient secrets to claim as inventions of their own. They imagine a godless cosmos of their own, ruled by laws they hope to discover and use for their own monstrous ends. They must burn!"

"So shall we all." The master made the sign of salvation, reached for another purple grape, and wiped pink fingers on his cowl. "But not at once. Not until Xath returns to cleanse us all for paradise."

"He is returning, sir."

"No doubt." The master shrugged. "When he must close our cycle of time, an event beyond foretelling."

"Sir, it has been foretold!" He unclenched his fists and tried to calm his tone. "He's on his way. I saw his sign. Saw his herald star, visible as a faint red point in a telescope built at the Institute by a Realist astronomer. If you are not informed, these Realist scientists perceive his paradise as a red dwarf star. A small companion to our own sun, it is due to reach perihelion in less than a year."

"Are you certain?" The master's hairless brows were blue-dyed scars. They lifted skeptically. "Perhaps you don't know that we here in the tower are the appointed sentries of Xath. Our sacred duty is to watch the sky for his signal star. We have not observed it."

"Sir, I have. I risked my soul to learn the Realist theories. I inspected their instruments. I reviewed the records of their experiments and observations."

"Which perhaps you accepted?" The pale eyes widened. "You came back a Realist yourself?"

"Sir, I feel secure in my faith in Xath and happy in my duty to the archimage. The Realists remain blind to eternity, but I respect their mathematics. Checking their orbital computations, I found them correct. Our cycle has closed. Our millennium has come."

"Brother, I fear for you." The master's stiff mask twisted into a comic parody of reproof. "I fear that you have alarmed the archimage for nothing. A graver danger to your soul than any misdeed you may have done in Targon."

"Sir—" Argoth swallowed hard. "I know what I saw. The foretold star of paradise. Xath himself, returning now! The archimage is anxious to receive him with due respect and ceremony. He has chosen me to meet him as our speaker. And his own, if he should speak."

The master leaned to push the bowl of fruit aside.

"You have misinformed the archimage." He stiffened, scowling through that mask of dark-dyed scars. "We are appointed to be the heralds of his coming. We have watched and waited for a thousand years. Here are the records of our faithful vigilance."

Impatiently he gestured at the books around them, walls of heavy volumes bound in old black hopper-hide, stamped in gold with dates that ran down across the centuries. The incense in the air failed to cover their scent of dry decay.

"We have seen no signal of his return," he said. "We see no signal now. Further, brother . . ." His stiff grimace grew demoniac. "I suspect that the cycle now closing will prove to be your own brief career in the service of Xath."

The Puppet Kye

The paddocks were empty, and nothing grazed the rocky hills beyond them. Dragging Sharabok's saddle into the huge barn, we found bales of hay and bags of suncorn stacked in the loft, but the unicorns were gone.

"So?" Scorth shrugged inquiringly at Kye. "What next, with Sharabok gone and Targon still forty miles away?"

She stood gazing moodily off into the barren hills. I saw her tears, and it took her a moment to recover herself.

"The headquarters building." She turned to point at a neat white two-story house on a knoll just south of us. "The foreman and the servants have the downstairs rooms. Ebur . . ." Her voice died for a moment, and it was unsteady when she went on, "Ebur and I were going to live here till he could build a new place for us in town."

I felt her sadness, and a shock of jealous pain.

"If we meet your people," Scorth was asking, "what can we expect?"

"Ebur's dead." Her voice was flat and dull. "A dreadful blow. They all blamed me. His mother always disliked me. Only a trainer's daughter, I wasn't good enough for her son. His sister made an ugly scene. Said I'd seduced and murdered him, scheming for his estate."

She shrugged, shaking her head at the house.

"I hate to ask them for anything."

"We must," Scorth said. "If anybody's here."

He led the way up a wide gravel path toward the door and stopped when it swung open to let the sun catch a rifle barrel. A man came out on the stoop. Tall and gaunt, his long hair white as his spotless suit, he made a figure of stern authority. Squinting against the morning sun, he merely glanced at us and peered toward the strip as if expecting someone else.

"Sir!" Kye called. "Count Rellion!"

"Lady Kye!" He recoiled in astonishment. "I thought you were off in Wolver Riding."

"I've left Rider Thorg." She nodded at us. "I'm here with two friends. Scorth is a unicorn trainer; he once worked for Ebur. Zorn is the son of Rendahl ir Var."

He nodded absently, looking past us.

"We're here on a desperate errand," she told him. "Worn-out now, from riding all night. We need a chance to rest." Her voice fell appealingly. "For Ebur's sake."

He hardly seemed to listen.

"Have you seen my wife?" he asked her. "My family?"

"Nobody." She shook her head. "We just landed."

"They were to follow me from town." His voice grew ragged, sharp and high. "Two days ago. They never got there."

"Sir, our errand is in Targon." Scorth stepped toward him. "Can you tell us the situation there?"

"It's hell!" He was suddenly trembling, his hollowed eyes gone wild. "Hell, since the red moon came. The mages have called their demons down. With fire and terror and death." He shook his head, hoarsely repeating, "Fire and terror and death!"

"No matter." Kye shrugged. "We're on our way to fight them."

"Ebur's lovely bride . . ." He whispered the words as if to himself and then stepped a little back to shake his head at her. "Fighting demons? How?"

"We have a talisman," she said. "Or part of a talisman. The Dragonshield."

"You dabble in magic?"

"What else is left?"

"Nothing." Hopelessly he spread his lean old hands. "Nothing but fire and terror and death."

"There's still magic. Mystic magic, for those who can believe. We're following a legend that the Dragonshield saved us from the demons and their creatures a thousand years ago. We hope it can save us again."

He had turned to peer again at the strip and the empty road. She waited till his vacant eyes came back to her.

"It belonged to the Vars," she told him. "When Thorg and Slarn took the riding from Zorn's father, they broke it in two pieces. We have Thorg's. Slarn has the other, probably somewhere in Targon. We must recover it."

"You'll never get it. Nor get close to Slarn." Standing above us on the stoop, he shook his gaunt white head as if in judgment on us. "Not through the mobs and the crazy mages. And those—those demons!"

Something close to hysteria shrilled in his voice.

"Demons!" He stared off again at the strip and turned back to Kye in desperate appeal. "I never believed the old terror tales, but what else are they? Diving like vultures out of the sky to possess whoever they strike."

"But you escaped?" Scorth asked him. "How?"

"Luck," he muttered. "I had got out of the city three days ago. We were flying to our north country lodge. I came in the steam cart to have the unicorns ready. The family was to follow in the freight cart with luggage. I've waited . . ."

He bit his thin blue lips.

"They never came." I saw tears in his haggard eyes. "A crazy time! The unicorns panicked when one of them was killed in the air. I kept begging and bribing them to wait, but last night at sundown they all deserted me, and the trainers with them. Even the foreman, a coward I thought I could trust."

"Sir?" I had been just listening, but I stepped to Kye's side. "You came out in a steam cart? Can you drive us to the city?"

"Targon?" He shook his head, blinking as if he hardly saw me. "I'm waiting for my family."

"We have money," Kye begged him. "We'll buy your cart."

"What's money now?" He waved it away. "We'll need it when

my wife comes. With the unicorns gone, we'll be driving both carts to the lodge.''

"If she doesn't come—"

Scorth stopped himself, but Rellion had already turned away, stumbling back into the house.

Kye called after him, "May we come in?"

"If you like." He turned back, nodding dully. "You know the place. Do as you like."

Kye knew the place, and we made ourselves at home. The house was built around a long central hall, two stories high. Twin stairways framed a huge fireplace at one end. Scorth stopped to frown at an antique sword hanging over the mantel.

"An heirloom." Kye paused beside him, speaking very softly. "It has been in the family forever. Ebur's great-great-grandfather carried it against the wolves in the riding. The count—" Her voice caught. "The count had given it to Ebur."

"Look at this!" Scorth reached to take it off the wall and show us the pommel. "The Var sigil!"

I saw the unicorn's head outlined in silver inlay, the eyes in gold. Grinning, he put it in my hand.

"Your own sword, Nuradoon!"

I had never held a sword, but I slid the heavy steel blade out of its dusty hopper-hide sheath. Gripping it awkwardly, I turned away from the smoke-black walls of the great fireplace, wishing for an instant that I really was the mythic hero, miraculously reborn, lifting it to defend Kye and defeat the demons.

But I wasn't Nuradoon. The old weapon felt cold and strange in my hand. After a moment I returned it to Scorth, and watched him hang it back where it had been. Kye shrugged at me, with a sad little smile that made me think she understood what I felt.

"Maybe good against wolves." Nothing was funny, but I tried to laugh. "But demons?"

The servants were gone, but I knew kitchens from helping my mother back on the farm. We found the pantry still well supplied, and Scorth was skilled at nearly everything. He flipped pancakes while I made ham and eggs.

Kye found Rellion upstairs, sitting on the edge of an unmade bed, holding an empty glass for a drink he had forgotten to make. He mumbled that he wasn't hungry, but he hadn't eaten since the servants left, and our breakfast gave him a sudden appetite.

Before it was done, he had agreed to let us drive him back to Targon next morning, if his wife and children had not arrived. I had him draw us a map of Targon, plotting a route over the Green River bridge, through the gate in the citadel wall, and over the hill to Slarn's palace compound.

"You'll never get there!" His moment of hope was gone. "You're on an idiot errand. I've seen the demons and what they do. Our best chance is to hide. To wait for them to go away—if they ever do."

Breakfast over, he offered to stand guard while we rested. Scorth carried a chair out to the front stoop for him, and he sat there with his rifle most of the day, watching for his family.

We found the steam cart parked behind the house. Ebur had taught Kye to drive. Scorth knew how to grease it, and we refilled the fuel tank from a yellow-painted drum in the barn. When that was done, we went to bed in the rooms the servants had vacated and slept through the middle of the day.

Hungry when we woke, we set the table again. Scorth put a hopper roast on the spit. Night had fallen when I went out to call Rellion to dinner. The crimson moon was already high. I shuddered, staring at it. The splotches on its sullen face were always changing. Tonight they made a diseased and dreadful leer, scarred with bleeding lesions.

I felt glad to get back inside, to the comfort of bright light and the odors of the roast and the hot bread Scorth had baked. He had opened a bottle of Rellion's brandy and we lifted our glasses to Kye when she came down the stair. She managed a pale little smile.

Rellion was passing his plate to Scorth for a slice of the roast when I saw a flicker of red across his snowy hair. He gasped and froze, pointing stiffly at the window. No glass had broken, but the demon was somehow already inside.

It was a ball of red fire, brighter than the moon, the size of a child's fist. Darker patches marked it, with tentacles like red-hot wires sprouting from them. Its dry insect hum rose and fell with the slow pulse of it radiance. As it floated closer, I felt a prickling on my skin, as if the fine hair had tried to rise.

We all sat motionless for one stunned moment. Rellion was at the head of the table, Kye at his right. He had leaned the rifle against the wall behind him. I heard his chair scrape on the floor. Turning from the demon, I saw him on his feet, the gun raised.

"Better not!" Kye rose, reaching to stop him. "You can't—"

The gun roared. Something like a flash of green lightning dazzled me. I heard Rellion's chair crash to the floor. When I could see again, I found the unharmed globe floating over the table. Rellion had fallen backward. Kye and Scorth were on their feet, stumbling away.

I stood rigid, staring at the demon. Its glowing filaments were picking up forks and spoons, lifting them close as if for inspection. Tossing them away, one by one, it reached suddenly for Kye.

She wore no rings, but a little gold locket on a gold chain hung around her neck. With a sob of terror, she snatched it off and tossed it toward the throbbing globe. Those questing filaments caught it deftly. Blinding light flashed. I heard a sharp explosion, nearly as loud as Rellion's gunshot. Something stung my eyes. I was suddenly coughing to a strange hot reek.

The demon had floated closer to Kye. She stood rigid, her green eyes fixed and staring at me. Her mouth opened as if to scream, but I heard no sound. The pulsing tentacles probed her, touching her hair, her arms, her face. They slowly closed to embrace her.

Scorth snatched the brandy bottle and lifted it to throw. Another green flash dazzled me, but I heard the bottle fall and shatter on the floor. He slumped back into his chair. I had started toward her, running around Rellion and his fallen chair, when light blinded me again.

The next I knew, I lay sprawled beside them. My whole body felt numb and useless. For a moment I couldn't move, and then I had to grasp at the table to drag myself up. Blinking and rubbing at my eyes, I searched for the demon. I couldn't find it, but Kye still stood frozen, distended eyes fixed on the spot where I had been, her face a stiff white mask of terror.

"Kye!" I tried to call her name, my voice only a whispery croak. "Kye—"

I saw no sign that she had heard. Her eyes were blinking oddly, like a doll's eyes. Her open mouth closed. Clumsily and very slowly at first, moving like a mechanical doll, she turned away from us and walked out of the room and across the hall toward the front door.

Trying to follow, I stumbled and nearly fell. The flash had left me stiff and aching, numb to the bone, shivering as if from bitter cold. I had to catch the table again to get my balance before I could shuffle after her to the front door.

When I found her, she was already far ahead of me on the gravel path down to the strip, running in an awkward, stiff-jointed way. The crimson moon was huge and high, and I found a new shadow on its lurid face, a unicorn in black silhouette, gliding down over the barn.

The unicorn was Sharabok. Black wings folding, he touched the strip and came running to where Kye waited, tiny and alone in the red moon-flood. Silently he knelt and dropped his wing to lift her. In a moment he was racing back down the strip. His great wings spread. I watched them climb, small and black against the leering moon.

31

The Voice of the Celestials

Meeting the archimage again, Argoth informed him of Tower Master Strull's skepticism about the herald star. With no visible surprise, the archimage told him that Master Strull would be retiring to a private villa in the suburbs of Quar. He himself was to learn the language of the celestials and prepare himself to welcome Xath.

The assistant signal master, a mage almost as old and darkly scarred as the withered archimage himself, came down from the tower to brief him on the history and facilities of the sentry tower. Its construction had begun almost immediately after the departure of the celestials at the end of the previous cycle, and contact through it had been continued until long after the signal star had disappeared. The assistant master took him in the tower elevator to the top landing. From there they climbed a narrow stair to a door that had a triple lock.

"Welcome, sir, to this sacred place." The old man paused to catch his breath before he turned the keys. "If you become the new tower master, you will be the seventh since my first appointment as custodian. I have never sought promotion, nor inquired why they came or why they were removed, but you will find that I have been faithful to my sacred duty.

"This most holy shrine has been preserved without violation of any kind. You will find everything just as it was left when communication ceased." His ancient frame erect with pride, he twisted the last key and leaned to push at the heavy door. "The roof has never been allowed to leak. The floors have been cleaned. Dust has been kept from the instruments and the records. Time has touched nothing."

The sanctum occupied two floors. Rooms on the lower were walled with high shelves of notebooks and journals. Rust-stiffened file cabinets held transcripts of messages and replies. Time, in fact, had touched them roughly. Brittle pages sometimes crumbled when Argoth tried to turn them, and many were unreadable where ink had faded or words had slipped out of the language.

Time had been no kinder to the floor above. Knowledge had disappeared, along with the skills of ancient technicians and engineers. Electron tubes were dead, terminals eaten by corrosion, batteries decayed to lumps of black ruin, telescope mounts stiff with rust, mirrors gone dark, manuals missing, instruments impossible even to name.

"Sire," he reported to the archimage, "our link to the celestials has been lost. The equipment is beyond repair. Records are gone or impossible to understand."

"For some, perhaps." The archimage smiled sternly through his scars. "We expect success from you."

"Thank you, Sire." He bowed, needing time to recover himself. "I'll find the help I can. We'll do our utmost in the service of Xath and Your Supremacy. But we must start anew, as if we knew nothing. The celestials will arrive as strangers to us."

Starting over, he gathered the lectors who had taught him math and electronics. He reviewed his own notes from the courses he had taken at the Institute and recruited technicians who had managed radio contact among the itinerant mages all across the land. He explained the task and set them to work.

They read what they could of the records, guessed at the rest, studied illicit Realist monographs and engineering texts, rebuilt damaged equipment, reinvented what they could not rebuild. He was beaming his own signals into Capricorn before the restored telescopes could pick up the herald star.

Long delayed, the first replies contained garbled repetitions from his own messages, but nothing else he could understand. A lector searching the moldering files came to him with fragments of a notebook kept by a linguist on the original contact team.

"We are testing the limits of communication," the ancient scholar had written. "We can talk to unicorns, but only because of the experience we share. Though we may walk and unicorns can fly, we inhabit the same world. Like ourselves, they are born from male and female. They live as we do, love, age, and die. We drink the same water and breathe the same air. We enjoy the same sun, see the same rainbow, hear the same thunder.

"But what can we share with the celestials?

"So far as our instruments can determine at this great distance, the herald star has no planets, which means that the celestials inhabit no world in any way like our own. Their nature is beyond speculation. A Mystic philosopher suggests that they are beings of pure spirit, without mass or form. How can we hope for any common needs or interests that might make any useful contact possible?"

"That may be," he told the impassive lector. "Yet we know that useful contact was made. The celestials came. Though why they did and what they are is still uncertain, we have evidence enough that they enjoyed fire and consumed gold. In return for our services, our worship, and our gold, they gave us *The Esoterica* and all the lore we learn in our mysteries. They gave us Xath. I have no idea what they may desire on this fresh occasion, but the archimage expects us to do our utmost to satisfy them. If we please them, we may expect a renewed cycle of time for our world and new favor in the eyes of Xath."

His own more explicit expectations, he kept to himself.

32

Targon

Rellion and Scorth stumbled after me out of the house. We stood together, stunned and silent, on the front stoop, watching Sharabok's black-winged silhouette, Kye already nearly too small to see. Climbing across the moon's baleful disk, they vanished in the red-hazed sky.

"Why did it take her?" Scorth whispered. "What will happen to her now?"

I was afraid to imagine.

She hadn't been screaming; I found a shred of comfort in that. The red-glowing tendrils had vanished before they seemed to burn her the way they had burned the tortured wolf and the village barber.

"She was lovely." Rellion shook his head, murmuring to himself. "She should have been my daughter." Still our eyes were on the empty sky, until he turned abruptly to ask, "Where can it take her?"

I couldn't guess, or forget that last dreadful image. Her green eyes fixed on me, her mouth yawning open for the scream that never came, her face frozen into a bloodless mask of pleading and terror. Nor could I shake off my own haunting sense of guilt and shame. Starting toward her, hoping somehow to reach and help her, I had to run around Rellion and his fallen chair where they lay on the floor. Had she thought I was running away?

At last, when we saw no more unicorns and no more demons, we went back inside. We were all shaken, Scorth still dazed and speechless, Rellion hobbling on a bruised knee. I felt stiff and clumsy from whatever force had knocked me down.

Scorth found a broom and swept up fragments of the brandy bottle. Rellion told me where to find another and limped to pick up his overturned chair. We sat back at the table. He poured the brandy. Scorth sliced the rest of the roast, but our appetites were gone.

"My wife will never come." Muttering moodily, Rellion abruptly pushed his glass away. "I was a fool to hope so long."

"Then let us drive you into Targon," I urged him. "We're on our way there. We can help you search—"

"No use." Helplessly he shook his haggard head. "The demons have got them by now."

"Our piece of the Shield." Scorth looked at me. "Did Kye take it?"

She had ridden away in only the slacks and sweater she had worn down to dinner. We found her saddlebag left in the room, the black fragment of the Shield still in its worn hopper leather pouch. Her little purse of gold bells was still there, and her flight leathers hung in the closet. I shivered when I thought how chilled she would be, flying at night without them. Wherever the demon was taking her.

"Forget the gold," Scorth told me. "Demon bait. But if Slarn really has the other half of the Shield . . ."

His voice faded into doubt.

"You call it a shield?" Rellion muttered bitterly. "A scrap of broken glass?"

"The legend says it's magic," I told him. "I never believed in magic, but the Vars have treasured it forever. We don't know why. It may have no Mystic power, but perhaps—just perhaps—it does. So let's get on to Targon. Get that other fragment. Mend the Shield if we can."

The brandy restored Rellion's shattered nerve. With the third glass, he agreed that we would set out next morning in the steam cart. When Scorth showed him the sigil on the sword over the mantel, he handed the old weapon to me.

"If you're a Var . . ." His old voice quivered. "It would have been Ebur's, but he'll never need it now. Take it. Carry it with your magic Dragonshield."

I had never used a sword, but I buckled the brittle old scabbard to my belt.

"The mythic hero!" Scorth's voice was thick with the brandy, and the squint of his yellow eyes seemed more than half sardonic. "Nuradoon or not, you've got to play the game. Now you've got to fight the demons and the mages."

I shook my head uneasily.

"Here's how." He came swaying to draw the blade and show me how to grip the hilt. "Swing it like a brush knife."

It felt awkward when I swung it, and I slid it back in the sheath. Even half-tipsy, I was neither Nuradoon nor swordsman. Still stiff and aching from the demon's dazzling strikes, I found little faith in myself. But perhaps . . .

"Thank you, sir!" I told Rellion. "I'll do what I can."

Scorth woke me next morning from a dismal dream where I was surrounded with howling wolves, all slashing at me with bright black fangs. I was swinging the Nuradoon sword, trying to hold them off, but it kept turning to a useless scrap of thick black glass.

He had our breakfast ready, and a basket filled with food and wine for the road. We left Kye's gold, but I took the old sword and the scrap of the Shield, hung in its pouch on a cord around my neck.

Steam power had never reached our village, and the cart was itself almost a magic machine to me. Scorth lit the boiler and had me work a fan till the pressure came up. He was the driver. Rellion came limping to climb in the front seat with him. Iron wheels crunching the gravel, we jolted down the road toward Targon.

Grief and dread for Kye hung like a monstrous shadow over me, but I heard Scorth humming a unicorn melody, seeming so cheery that I growled a command for him to shut up.

"Nuradoon!" He turned back from the wheel with a grin of reproof. "Wake up and play the game. Brooding won't help us. If Kye ever needed your heroic spirit, it's now."

"Sorry," I muttered. "I'll try to play the game."

I did, but it was a hard game to play.

The gravel road was empty at first, winding through rolling grassland, and the cart rocked along faster than a donkey could run. I watched the sky for demons and listened to Scorth asking Rellion about Targon and the river bridges and how we might find our way to Slarn's palace.

We came out of the hills into parklike woodland. A hunting preserve, Rellion said, that belonged to the primarch. I saw a little herd of spotted hoppers grazing in the distance, but nobody was hunting today. The scene seemed unbelievably peaceful, and the demons began to seem like a hideous nightmare, too dreadful to be real.

Yet I knew how real they were, and our shard of the Shield seemed an absurd defense against them. Brooding again, in spite of Scorth's injunction, I fingered the pommel of Nuradoon's sword. Or had he ever existed? More likely, I thought, the legend had been invented to hearten such hopeless refugees as we were.

Yet I had to wonder again at the odd coincidence that his helmet should fall into my hands, and now the sword with his sigil. My mother used to say that the Three had power to guide coincidence, and I remembered her hurt when my father laughed at her Mystic belief. Sitting now in the back of the rocking cart, I longed for the faith I had never found. Nothing erased that dreadful image of the demon seizing Kye.

Down beyond the forest and the hopper herds, we turned in to a wider road through a landscape golden with ripe suncorn. White silos and huge green barns and tall windmills surrounded scattered dwellings that must once have looked like islets of prosperity.

No longer. Black patches scarred the bright landscape where buildings had burned. Tall pillars of blue smoke rose here and there, and a dark blue cloud hung over Targon in the south, still twenty miles away. The road was suddenly crowded with farmers in flight. Rellion spoke to a group of them who were clearing the road where a steam truck had overturned with a load of crated apples.

"The demons, sir," one man said. "Those damned demons of Xath. They want gold and love fire and turn men mad. No stopping them, sir, the holy Three forgive me. And nowhere to go."

We jolted around the wreckage and soon found the road beyond clogged with refugees from Targon. Whole families in flight, most of them on foot. Men sometimes pushing handcarts or barrows piled with household goods, women with babies, frightened children crying. Men on hoppers leaping along the roadside ditches. Men on foot yelling curses at men in steam carts who honked air horns and tried to claim the pavement. They were a river of fear flowing against us.

Searching faces, Rellion kept making Scorth slow the cart. Once he jumped out and ran after a gaunt old woman staggering under a cloth-wrapped bundle. When he had seen her up close, he came back to us, sobbing. She hadn't been his wife.

In the middle of the afternoon, Scorth opened his basket and handed out the lunch he had brought, thick sandwiches of hopper ham and a bottle of red wine. Angry glances followed us as the cart panted on.

"You're crazy, don't you know?" Rellion turned in the front seat to mutter at me. "You can say your name is Var, but who'll believe you're the reborn Nuradoon?" He turned to Scorth. "A rusty sword and a bit of broken glass! If you two were smart, you'd get out of the cart and go back the way you came."

"Could be you're right." I saw Scorth's unruffled shrug. "Maybe you're wrong."

The crowds grew thicker and the bitter smoke denser, until Rellion had him turn off the main highway to look for side roads. They were sometimes just as jammed, sometimes dead ends. We ran out of water for the boiler, and I stayed with Rellion to guard the cart while Scorth walked to fill our jugs at a crossroads fountain.

Night had fallen and the red moon was high before we met the flood of fugitives pouring over the Green River bridge. They clogged the pavements and finally forced us off the road. The cart stalled in a muddy ditch, the wheels spinning uselessly. Scorth stopped the engine and vented a blast of steam.

Sadly I recalled the magic wonderland the city had seemed when I glimpsed it from Sharabok's back. The mansions on parklike lawns, the primarch's towered citadel, the triple spires of the old cathedral, all bathed in a luminous haze. They were gone now, lost in the biting smoke, and the whole sky was crimson.

A heavy man in police uniform was suddenly beside the cart.

"Sorry, sir." He thrust a gun into Scorth's face. "We need your cart."

I started to draw the old sword, and slid it back into the scabbard when I saw half a dozen men in uniform converging on us, most of them in police uniform.

"Get out!" the officer shouted. "Now!"

"I know you." Rellion glared at him. "What's your duty here?"

"The same as yours," he snarled. "To save my neck."

"If you've forgotten who you are . . ." Rellion looked back at me. "Stand up, Nuradoon! Draw your magic sword."

Trembling, I did.

"Look at this man!" Rellion gestured at me, his voice pealing into the crimson dark. "More than a man! He's Nuradoon—"

"What do we care?"

"You had better care!" His voice rang louder. "If you fear the demons. He's Nuradoon ir Var! You should know him from legend. He's more than human. The mythic defender of our world. He died a thousand years ago, wounded in the victory that drove the demons off our world. He woke once, seven hundred years ago, to drive the dragons and the wyvern out of Wolver Riding. Here he is, returned to fight again!''

''Hopperwash!'' the gunman snarled. ''Out of the cart.''

''Hear me!'' Rellion shouted at the mob beyond him. ''Hear the eternal Nuradoon! He has died a dozen times, but he lives forever in the shelter of his magic Dragonshield. He saved us from the demons a thousand years ago. The holy Three have now revived him once again, to save our world from the demons of Xath.''

He swung to me. ''Speak, Nuradoon!''

My knees were shaking and dust choked my throat, but Scorth was tugging at my sleeve.

''Speak!'' he whispered. ''They'll believe. They must, because they're mad with panic. Mad for magic. Mad for hope.''

''Follow—follow me!'' My voice was a rusty rasp, but I slid the old sword out of its sheath and waved it high. ''Follow my sword! The magic Demonkiller!''

I saw the gunman shake his head, stepping back uncertainly.

''Deserter!'' Rellion swung the rifle at him. ''Get back to your duty!''

He raised his pistol, but looked uneasily at the others muttering around him.

''Follow Nuradoon!'' Scorth was holding up my arm. ''Follow to the citadel! Kill the demons there! They've possessed the primarch. They've enslaved Slarn ir Var. We must take the citadel!''

''To the citadel!'' I swung the sword high, as if to cut a swath of hopper grass. ''Follow Demonkiller! Take the citadel!''

''Push us!'' Rellion stood erect in the cart, shouting at the gunman. ''In the name of the Three, push us out of the ditch.''

The gunman growled at his men, who stood shaking their heads.

''Are you cowards?'' Rellion demanded. ''Stinking slaves of the mages? Or will you give us a push? For the holy Three? For the mythic Nuradoon? For the world! Against the demons!''

One of them shrugged and waded into the ditch. The others followed. Scorth crouched over the wheel. The boiler fire roared. Steam hissed. The spinning wheels lifted fountains of mud. The cart lurched and slid, but we were suddenly back on the pavement.

''Gentlemen, thank you!'' Clutching at the windscreen to keep his balance, Rellion bowed at our mud-spattered pushers. "The Three reward you!"

The leader spat into the mud, and another shook his grimy fist. Scorth leaned over the wheel, driving on into the tide of refugees.

"Speak, Nuradoon!" Rellion called to me. "Make them clear the road."

He slumped back into his seat.

"Make way!" Standing in the cart, I held the old sword pointed toward the citadel and tried to find a hero's voice. "We come to fight the demons with a magic sword. With magic of the sacred Three. Let us at them!"

My hoarse-voiced words worked no magic, but Scorth kept the cart's steam whistle blasting. Scowling, sometimes cursing us with the wrath of Xath, people moved aside to let us reach the bridge. A stalled transport stopped us on the middle of it. An angry man tried to pull Scorth out of the cart. I slashed at him with the sword. He cowered back, and we were finally in Targon.

Here between the rivers we were in an old section of the city, many of the homes built like forts in an age when people still feared raiding werewolves. Guarded with towers and massive stone walls, they were generally two stories high, often with parapets edging flat rooftops.

The red-lit streets were nearly empty; most people had either fled or barricaded themselves inside. Once we met a black-robed mage and his acolytes leading a crowd of converts howling hymns in praise of Almighty Xath.

"Human demons!" Rellion muttered. "Looking for anything to burn."

Scorth was turning us in to a side street, out of their path, when I heard a rattle of gunshots. Running people screamed and fell. Two or three got up and hobbled after the parade. One man lay still, apparently dead. A woman sat up, hands over a bleeding wound in her abdomen, whimpering for help. The mage marched on, howling louder.

Midnight had come, the huge moon burning straight overhead, before Rellion lifted his hand in a voiceless command for Scorth to stop the cart. Sagged back in the seat, he stared without a word at the fire-scarred ruin of a home. The roof had fallen in. Black windows gaped. Smoke like crimson mist rose above the broken walls.

Silent and desolate, Rellion simply sat there.

Nobody was near. After a moment I got out of the cart and walked to the door. A charred log had served as a battering ram. A mountain of fallen debris blocked the doorway. Broken roof tiles, fallen masonry, a tangle of shapeless ruin. I walked back to meet Rellion's sick stare.

"Nobody," I told him. "No sign of anyone alive."

He sat motionless, as if he hadn't heard, staring blindly past me at the ruin.

"Maybe they're safe," I tried to cheer him. "Maybe with friends. Maybe out of the city—"

"No." The life was gone from his eyes. "They're dead."

Scorth was climbing out of the cart.

"Wait!" Stiffly, slowly, as if every move took all his will, Rellion climbed out and turned to look back at me. "Take the vehicle."

"But, sir," Scorth began, "what will you—"

"Take it, Nuradoon." At first I thought he meant to be ironic, but his bleak half smile looked dead serious. "All is lost unless you really are the eternal Nuradoon. Play out your destiny! Recover that piece of glass. Mend your magic Dragonshield. Fight the demons any way you can."

33

The Celestial Code

In answer to their signals, Argoth and his team received only garbled echoes, mixed with clicks and hisses and high-pitched shrieks
that made no sense to anybody, until the old assistant master of the
sentinel tower brought him another brittle scrap of that ancient linguist's journal with a few phrases circled in red.

. . . she says . . . she believes . . . she insists . . .

"His notes on the first successful transmissions to the celestials," the master said. "Notice the pronouns. The original team
seems to have used females on the microphones. We have consulted
a Realist linguist in Targon, who suggests that the problem may be
our male voices."

"Female voices?" He shook his head. "Why?"

"We asked him why." The old man shrugged. "He says he
can't say why, because he doesn't know the celestials. But why not
try a woman?"

He objected to the blasphemy of a woman in the holy city. Un-
willing to risk his soul again, or the souls of his staff, he made the
staff try a hundred other experiments with pitch and pace and mod-
ulation.

Still they heard the same shrieks and screams, until at last he
called the Institute to ask for a female radio technician. She came
overnight on a fast riverboat. At the dock to meet her, he thought he

had nerved himself against the risk, but the she-devil stunned him when he saw her.

"Mr. Ayth! The priest of Xath!" Her voice was poisoned honey, sweeter than the wind chimes in the doorway to his cell. "Remember me?"

"I remember," he told her stiffly. "Here my name is Demimage Eighty-Nine."

She was Lyrane, in a bright red dress that covered too little of her creamy female skin. Her bright gold hair was a beacon of Hell, and her voice and her scent brought back all the horror of that dreadful night when she got him drunk and lured him far beyond the brink of hell. She was still evil incarnate, mocking him and mocking his name with the same fiendish malice shining in her eyes. Snared again, he couldn't look away.

"I'm so delighted, Mr. Nine." A siren's song. "I'd hoped it would be you."

He flinched from the deadly touch of her hand, but he couldn't help listening. She had just completed her degrees in electronics and math, but she had never even dared to dream of a job here in the forbidden city. Overjoyed that he had sent for her, she was eager to know about her work.

He kept his answers short. On the drive to the tower, he put her in the curtained space at the back of the cart, where he couldn't see or hear her Hell-born allure. Prudently he had arranged to arrive while all the faithful were at their morning devotions. Evicting the old assistant master, he installed her in an isolated private cell on the top floor and had her meals brought there.

Sharing his own terrors, three staff members begged for other duties, but some were soon so happy at work with her that he began to fear for them. Surprisingly, the celestials responded to her calls almost at once. Hardly a month had passed before she came knocking impatiently at his office door.

"Mr. Nine, we're talking!"

Still wickedly naked.

She had refused to wear the decent black vestments he had provided, on the flimsy pretext that they were stiff and itchy. Clad now in something transparently pink and scanty, she was flushed with elation.

"Talking? You're learning their language?"

"Breaking their code."

He had dropped his eyes, but she made him look at her again before she went on.

"They're different."

Of course they were, but he refused to say so.

"Narkelo believes, in fact, that we should be saying *it.*" Perhaps to increase his torment, she had assumed the superior tone of a mage lecturing a backward acolyte. "His analysis of the code and the fragmentary ancient records has led him to suspect that they are, in fact, a single organism, all its parts in direct organic contact. If that's true, they wouldn't need a language. Probably they lack even the concept of language."

Narkelo was the Realist linguist the staff had been consulting. He wanted no advice from any Realist infidel, but he held himself silent.

"The code must have been invented on that first visitation." Her deliberate manner tantalized him. "It seems to lack actual words. The symbols are single-valued as integers. The system seems to reflect an entirely alien way of thought—or maybe something almost too different to be called intelligence at all—but I believe it will be adequate."

"So what do they want?"

"There's no word for *want.*" Her smile seemed maliciously smug. "Nor for *if* or *when* or *because.* The signals seem more like mathematical equations, but with none of the new Realist symbolic logic. When we get them solved, I think the answers will be statements of what we'll have to do."

34

Lord Slarn

"Sir, we can't leave you here," Scorth protested. "Not alone and now at night, with demons haunting the city—"

"You must." Rellion made an effort to draw his sagging shoulders straight and turned his glazed eyes to me. His voice was flat and harsh, with no irony I could hear. "It's your magic, Nuradoon. Your duty now."

"You'll have nobody—"

"Nobody. Nobody." He nodded lifelessly. "I am alone. My wife is surely dead, unless the demons seized her. Perhaps my daughter too. In this mad world, I have no way to know. Yet my place is here." He turned from us to stare blankly again at the scorched and toppled ruin that had been his home. "I have nowhere else."

"If you must." Scorth shrugged. "Thank you for the cart."

He seemed not to hear.

I shook his cold, unresponsive hand. We climbed back into the cart. Scorth fired the boiler. Steam roared. We rolled away, iron tires clattering. Though hundreds or thousands must have still been hiding behind their walls, the red-lit streets lay silent and empty. The city seemed eerily dead. Rellion was but a dim gray ghost when I looked back for him.

I had the rough map he had made for me, and Scorth had been here. Now on the tongue of land between the Dragon and the Green, we drove southwest along narrowing streets that climbed the ridge toward the citadel. Crossing the old city, we wound through narrow ways between fortresslike compounds, and came at last into an open park beneath the looming wall of the old citadel itself.

"Pastureland." Scorth gestured. "For the primarch's unicorns."

The citadel had looked forbidding when I glimpsed it from Sharabok, but now the great gate was open, heavy timbers and thick steel plates crumpled aside as if an angry dragon had gone through.

"A battle, I imagine." Scorth nodded at the wreckage. "Between the mages and the primarch's guard. The primarch never loved Xath, or gave the mages the gold they were always demanding. They know more about high explosives than they ever taught anybody else. I suppose they won the battle."

He drove us through.

Somewhere ahead, I saw yellow flame billowing beneath a great cloud of smoke. Nearer, we met the mages. A score of red-skulled men in black. "They're a hundred yards off," he whispered. "Yelling their hymns to Xath and heading back to the gate. They've got our dear primarch, but I don't think they're after us."

Not so sure, I stood up to see. Grinning in the crimson shadows, he was pointing at a paunchy, long-haired man, bald and barefoot, limping under the demon's tiny scarlet globe. Behind them came a line of creaking wagons pulled by teams of men and women moving as mechanically as the puppet Kye.

"The primarch's gold, I imagine," Scorth murmured. "The private hoard his taxers have been sweating out of all the world these last forty years. Looted now to feed the demons."

We watched till they were gone through the demolished gate.

"Now," I told him, "perhaps we have a chance."

"If . . ."

He shook his hairless head, as red as the mages' in that scarlet light. Though he said no more, my own ifs ran on. If that missing fragment of the Shield was really somewhere in his palace. If we could get inside, get possession of it, get out again. If, in fact, the broken Shield could somehow be repaired. If any actual magic had ever been, and if any actual Nuradoon had ever used it against the wyvern and the werewolves and the demons. Too many ifs. I tried not to dwell on them now.

Scorth fired the boiler and pulled us back to the road. We drove on across a wide open space.

"Parade ground." I saw his sardonic shrug. "For the primarch's heroic defenders."

Ahead of us, the smoky flames towered taller.

"The palace," he muttered. "His final sacrifice to Xath. Not very willing, I'd imagine."

I spread our map to the red moonlight. Rellion had drawn a rough rectangle for the primarch's palace and a smaller square for Slarn's, farther on toward the tip of the ridge between the rivers and just above the bank of the Dragon.

The road led us on toward the inferno, so near that I had to shield my face from its blistering heat. The palace had been enormous. Most of it still stood, but flame wrapped it everywhere. Roofs and columns and walls came crashing down, exploding into towers of flying embers.

"Quite a banquet!" Scorth gestured. "For our celestial friends."

I held my hand over my face to look again. What I saw was a little swarm of bright red sparks dancing in the flames, diving and soaring through the heart of the holocaust.

"We're near enough," I told him.

He was already turning in to a side road that took us through another broad strip of wooded parkland and down the slopes toward Dragon River. Beyond a stand of old iron oaks a mile or two farther, we met a second group of marching mages, another bellowing mob behind them. Scorth drove off the road again, and pointed to a tongue of fire licking into the scarlet sky above the trees ahead.

"Slarn's place." He shrugged unhappily. "I'm afraid we're late."

We watched the mob through the screening brush. Only three mages and half a dozen acolytes, leading perhaps a score of men and women shrieking their ritual worship of Xath. Stiff-limbed puppets dragged a creaking wagon at the rear.

"Plunder," he muttered. "Likely including Slarn's piece of the Shield."

Yet we drove on again when they had passed. The long night was almost gone, the blood-hued moon low and huge in the west. Except for the mobs, the shadow-clotted land looked ominously empty. Some must have joined the mages to escape; others must have concealed themselves however they could.

Slarn's palace had been a small-scale copy of the primarch's, still big enough to be impressive. There was no wind, and a great smoky flame climbed straight into the red-stained sky from the tall-columned portico. Scorth stopped the cart, with an uneasy gesture at the blaze. I saw three bright red points diving and climbing, bathing in the flames.

"So, Nuradoon?" He looked hard at me. "What do you say?"

I shivered. The only humans moving in that silent red-lit world, we were surely tempting targets if the demons wanted us. But the game of Nuradoon was the only game I knew.

"We've come too far to quit," I told him. "Let's have a look behind the palace."

We backed the cart and jolted onto a road that took us along the river cliffs. Gaps in a fringe of stunted trees gave me glimpses of the Dragon. Wide and black, it flowed far below us, a wide track of it shimmering red under the sinking moon.

Beyond the palace, Scorth stopped the cart at the end of a broad open space that must have been a flight strip for unicorns. He turned to squint uneasily at the lurid inferno consuming the front of the building and the three crimson sparks swimming in it.

"Now, Nuradoon?" His sardonic tone challenged me. "What next?"

Why not run, if the demons would let us run? Race back through the gate, if they let us reach the gate? Hide, if we could find a place to hide? Wait till they were gone, if they would really be returning to their red moon before its strange orbit carried it away for another thousand years?

Why not?

He didn't ask, but I read the question in his yellow eyes and heard it in my own heart. I shuddered, and my answer was a long time coming.

"We'll go inside." I felt insane. "There's no wind. The walls are stone. We should have a little time."

"For what?"

"To look," I said. "If Slarn had a strong room, it would have been toward the rear of the building, maybe underground. His scrap of the Shield must have been in it. The looters were after gold. They'd have tossed that sliver of glass, even if they found it."

"If!" His leathery face twisted into a rueful grin. "If! But let's go!"

With a wary glance at the darting sparks, he drove us close to the rear entrance. I had climbed out, but he was still at the wheel when two heavy men came shouting out of the building.

"The cart!" The leader waved a pistol. "We commandeer the cart!"

I faced him, empty-handed. The old sword had seemed ridiculous against demons. Finding it uncomfortable to wear, I had left it in the cart, but Scorth stopped the gunmen with a great blast of steam.

I found voice to ask, "By what authority?"

"The primarch's sanction, sir. Granted to Lord Slarn." Growling at me, he nodded at the door and leveled the gun. "Out of his way!"

I saw Slarn. A small, plump man in a tight crimson jacket and thin black silk trousers with the look of a sleeping garment. His long yellow hair was curled in ringlets. He looked stooped and somewhat wrinkled, but the paint on his mouth and the green around his eyes made his age hard to tell. He stood a moment peering fearfully out of the building and came scuttling toward us.

"Lord—Lord Slarn?" The title stuck in my throat, but I stepped into his path. "You're my uncle. I'm your brother Rendahl's son."

He stopped for an instant. Blinking through the green, his murky eyes were set close together. They narrowed, weighing me, before he gestured angrily for me to move aside.

"Rendahl! Traitor!" He spat the words and yelled at Scorth, "You! Out of the cart!"

I stood where I was, and he glared at me.

"The Dragonshield?" The name seemed to startle him, perhaps to frighten him. He stepped back, blinking at me. I caught a gust of his body musk. "You have a piece of it?"

"Why?" He whispered. "Why?"

"We'll trade the cart for it."

"If you want it—" He laughed, a sudden shrill explosion. "No matter. You're late. The mages beat you to it."

"They took it?"

"It's what they came for." That savage amusement was gone. I saw terror in his eyes, until they narrowed again with shrewd calculation. "The other fragment? You still have it?"

"We do." And I added desperately, "Our only chance against the demons, if there's any way it can be repaired."

"An idiot chance!" Scornfully he tossed his golden curls. "If you think the thing was ever magic. And the mages—"

"They know—" Cold dismay had taken my voice.

"They do. They were asking after you."

He glanced fearfully back at the flames crackling through the roof tiles and brushed abruptly past me. His men were dragging Scorth out of the cart. They all climbed in. Steam wheezed and roared. The cart lurched around and clattered toward the trees at the end of the strip.

Scorth caught my arm to pull me back into the shadow of the building. When he pointed, I saw one of those crimson sparks darting out of the flames and swelling as it neared us into a tiny crimson globe.

Sitting with the driver, Slarn had twisted to watch it. I saw him lean to snatch at the wheel. The cart swerved into the stone curb at the edge of the strip and flipped over. It was lost in a cloud of red-lit steam. When that lifted, I saw it turned on its side, all three men spilled out.

The two guards were scrambling to their feet, but Slarn lay flat on the pavement. The two bent over him for a moment, trying to lift him. One glanced up at the demon. It was already close, its bright red filaments stretching to grasp him. He shrieked. The men dropped him and ran.

The demon stayed to hover low over him. A pale blue glow washed him. The bright tentacles wrapped him. Stiffly, jerkily, his body moved. Clumsily clutching at the side of the overturned cart, it tried to stand. One leg failed, and it fell again.

The demon left it sprawled and still, darting to overtake the guards. One by one, they glowed and fell when the bright filaments brushed them. For a moment they seemed lifeless. Then, moving like unoiled machines, they lurched upright and reeled back to the cart. With no apparent effort, they lifted the side of it and rolled it back to its wheels.

With as little care as if Slarn had been a bag of grain, one of them picked him up and tumbled him into the rear. The other got under the wheel. The boiler fire roared. Steam snorted. I heard something rattle. More steam exploded, but the cart failed to move.

The red globe dived to it and vanished under the hood. A hot blue light flashed and vanished. The rattle stopped. The engine chuffed. The cart rolled down the strip and turned back the way we had come. Scorth and I were left standing there behind the burning palace. Peering over the roof, I saw the two remaining demons still wheeling through the blaze.

35

The Blade of Bar

"The female presents us with a difficult dilemma." Argoth had come to bow again before the red-robed archimage, who had asked for constant reports on the celestials. "Her mere presence here in Quar is an intolerable desecration of the holy precincts."

Pausing to study the archimage's scarred and fleshless features, he saw no expression of distaste or approval or anything else. He went on uncomfortably, still always afraid those shrewd old eyes might read his desire for his own turn in that tall-backed seat of power.

"In spite of all precautions," he confessed, "I have been unable to keep our most inviolate mysteries from her. Though I have reminded the mages of how they risk their souls by working with her, they seem bewitched. I fear that they have told her things she should never have known, which she in turn has doubtless revealed to the celestials."

When the archimage's blue-seamed mask stayed blank as stone, he felt impelled to expand on a topic he had always cautiously avoided.

"You must have considered such difficulties, Sire? All those problems in the interpretation of our sacred records? Apparent contradiction even in *The Esoterica*. Seeming incongruities which seem to have been overlooked, with no attempt at reconciliation?"

That hard old mask showed neither agreement nor dissent.

"Sire, if you ask for my solution—" the archimage had not asked, but he ventured a reckless hint "—I see only one."

"Perhaps." At last, very slightly, the red skull nodded. "Perhaps the female should be silenced when her work here is done. But are you ready to dispense with her now?"

"Not quite yet." The admission hurt. "I have three lectors training to imitate her voice, and a technician attempting electronic duplication. Unfortunately, however, the celestials still seem deaf to everything except her voice. At least for the present, all our contacts come through her."

"I see." The bare skull tipped again. "And what have you to report?"

"Remember, Sire, we're still forced to trust the woman." He shrugged in apology. "What most disturbs me is what she says the celestials are telling her about their earlier visitations. They dispute our ancient records. Shockingly!"

He shifted on his feet, calling himself a fool for expecting any visible response. The whole discipline of the mages, as he himself had learned through pain enough, was designed to suppress all feeling except adoration of Xath.

"Yes?" The archimage's voice had the faintest edge. "Our sacred history?"

"They challenge it, Sire. Challenge all we believe." He muttered it bitterly. "Our first message was a greeting to Xath. The celestials didn't understand. We tried to explain that he had been the divine leader who brought them here. The god who assumed the shape of a man to teach us the required rituals of worship with pain and fire and gifts of gold."

"Interesting." At last that bleak face showed a flicker of response. "Have they found another leader?"

"Sire, the celestials deny that any Xath ever existed among them, or that they ever required worshipers here. They seem to recall us as savage animals, living on a level with the wyvern and the wolves. They claim they got no welcome from us. Instead they met bitter resistance from a barbarian named Bar. Or possibly Var— they have trouble with human phonemes.

"The problem, Sire, is that they're apprehensive now of meeting Vars again."

"Apprehensive?" Very slightly, the naked skull lifted. "They needn't be. The traitor Var is safe on Paradise Island, building temples we'll burn for them. The brother in Wolver Riding has been manageable enough. As for Slarn . . ."

The lean-boned shoulders rose and fell beneath the crimson robe. Chilled with the sweat of his own apprehension, he nerved himself to go on.

"Unfortunately, Sire, there's another Var. The traitor's son, who claims descent from one Nuradoon ir Var, the warrior who is said to have made those difficulties the celestials remember. He is carrying what he calls a magic shield, or a fragment of it, that he says the savage used against them. They were concerned when they heard about it, because it seems that this savage defeated their best efforts to control or kill him."

"They are concerned?" The old man's blue and hairless brows had risen. "The celestials?"

Unhappily, he nodded.

"It seems, Sire, that he threatened to destroy them all if they ever dared to return. The woman says they're afraid of him and this ridiculous talisman. If you can believe it!" He shook his head. "She says they take him very seriously."

"Mere superstition!" The dry voice had lifted slightly. "Have her tell them that."

"Sire, she says there's no way they'd ever understand superstition. Their minds don't work with half-truth or probability. Statements to them are true or false, with nothing in between."

"Then tell them the tales of Var and his weapon are false. Inform them that our own records say nothing about this mythic warrior."

"Sadly, Sire, that itself would be false." He spread his empty hands. "Our researchers have found a fragment of a diary kept by a man who signs himself Barni Bar. Most of it is missing, and the rest is in a dialect now hard to read, but the writer seems to have been a son of this early Var. A member of the outlaw band, he writes of 'the blade of Bar' and his father's threat to use it against the celestials—'demons' as he calls them.

"If you wonder, Sire . . ." He had seen a skeptical flicker in the pale old eyes, but he caught his breath to blunder on. "I make no case for any magic except our own, but the celestials themselves are blind to all uncertainty. They demand that we find and destroy this fugitive Var and every fragment of his broken shield."

36

Dragon River

We hid inside the palace doorway till hot smoke began to burn our eyes.

"Time to try . . ."

Coughing, Scorth stumbled outside. We ran along the wall, keeping close and hoping the smoke would hide us from the demons overhead. We huddled at the corner, with no cover to get us across the road, till something crashed. Peering around it, I saw an exploding cloud of embers and roiling flame. The heat bit my face, and I crouched back till smoke rolled low overhead.

Trusting that to cover us, we ran across the road into the fringe of trees and brush along the brink of the cliff. The building was already far gone when we looked back through the undergrowth. Hungry tongues of flame were thrusting out of every opening. The smoke shifted, and I found a high crimson spark bathing in the blaze.

"Two!" Scorth pointed, whispering. "Another! Three again!"

We shrank lower, almost afraid to breathe, till the roof of the rear wing fell. A gust of searing wind hailed hot embers over us. Slapping at them, Scorth crawled on all fours to look off the brink.

"A trail." He beckoned me to follow. "Down to the river."

The cliff was high and steep, but he had found a narrow footpath down it. The river was wide here, with a long curve around the citadel hill that sent the main current to cut against the farther bank. The water was low now in late summer, and we had reached a narrow sandbar. The moon was half-down, a great scarlet dome with a broad track of scarlet fire glittering on black water under it.

We were trapped there. A hundred yards above us and below, the current came back against the cliff. The river looked far too wide for us to swim. Afraid to risk Targon again, with the mages and the demons everywhere, we huddled against the cliff in a shallow cave where high water had undercut a limestone ledge. Crimson dusk faded at last into gray daylight. The moon was gone, and white sunlight broke through the smoke.

"Nuradoon, the Three are smiling on you." Sitting back against the limestone, Scorth regarded me with a cryptic squint. His lopsided grin was half-malicious, but his tone seemed oddly solemn. "I know how they keep knocking you around. Maybe just to test your mettle? What do you think?"

I didn't know what to think. Except that we were trapped there on the sandbar, with nothing to eat and nowhere to go.

"They've done things for you," he went on as if he were serious. "They let the demons take Lady Kye and Lord Slarn when they might have taken you. Now they've saved us from fire and got us safe off the rock. If we wait, perhaps they'll keep on smiling."

We waited. The rains of cinders stopped. The smoke finally thinned. Scorth kept grinning hopefully, till we saw three black-winged carrion bats flying down the river. He kept uneasily silent till they passed us and vanished behind the cliffs.

"Creatures of Xath." His fingers flickered in a sign of the Three. "Omens against us."

We watched the empty river. The vital artery of all the land till the first rails were laid, it had carried people and freight from the delta ports up to Targon and Dorth and even beyond. Not today. We saw no ships.

After the smoke cleared, Scorth climbed back up the cliffs for a glimpse of the city. Slarn's palace was still smoldering, he said.

Denser smoke rose from the arsenal and the barracks farther down the peninsula. But no demons were near enough to see, nor any live thing moving.

"Forget ghosts and bats," he muttered. "We must trust the Three."

With nothing better to do than talk, I asked what he believed.

"Nothing, really." His shrug was a rueful small apology. "Because I was never sure of anything. In a time like this, who knows the truth? Or if there's any truth worth knowing? Fear of the carrion bats is fear of death, and I do fear death. Your good mother begged me to put my faith in the Three, because she said the life of the seed and the leaf and the fruit is also our own."

I thanked him for that spark of hope, and we kept on waiting. He found a handful of parched suncorn in his pocket. I chewed the golden grains till they grew sweet in my mouth. They left me emptier than ever, but he grinned at my impatience, stretched out on the sand, and fell asleep with a promptness I envied. He woke in the middle of the afternoon, and said my turn had come.

The next I knew, he had shaken me awake from a distressing dream of Kye. A blue-glowing ghost, still ruled by the demon, she was haunting me, begging me to use the Shield and set her free. I longed to help her, but it was somehow lost in the river. Diving for it, all I found was mud.

"Thank the Three!" he was whispering. "I think they've sent us something."

The moon had risen high. When he pointed, I saw a blot of darkness on its crimson shimmer. Far up the river, it grew larger as we watched. Something low and long, with no real shape I could make out.

"A gift of the Three," he said. "Something big enough to carry us, I think. If it comes in reach."

Little River had been too fast and narrow to offer pools my mother considered safe for swimming, but my father had taken me to bathe in them sometimes in the summer when the water was low, and he had taught me how to stay afloat.

We stripped and wrapped our boots in our clothing. When Scorth said the time had come, we waded off the sandbar and plunged into the current, pushing our bundles. As if fate were really with us, we reached the shadow before I was exhausted.

"A raft." Panting, he climbed on it. "Logs for the sawmills down the river."

He leaned to pull me after him. In the red moonlight, I made out a score of heavy logs that had rough timbers nailed across them to make a deck. A scrap of canvas made a tent at one end. A few long poles and a steering oar were stacked at the other. Nobody was aboard.

Dripping and shivering, we wrapped ourselves in blankets we found in the tent and squatted on the deck, watching the moon's red shine on the dark water and the slow creep of the darker banks. As we passed the tip of the peninsula, Scorth nodded at the ancient walls above us.

"Remember, Nuradoon?" Still he seemed half serious, half the sardonic cynic. "Remember the siege a thousand years ago, when you held the old fortress against the demons and the wyvern and the wolves, and finally ran them off the planet?"

"I don't." I'd grown a little impatient with his prodding. "Or remember any such siege in the legend."

"No matter." He shrugged, squinting oddly at me in the crimson gloom. "We're living our own legend now."

Not sure of that, I said no more.

We drifted past the docks and warehouses along the riverbank, all deserted. Fires too far off to see flickered under a distant cloud of smoke. We saw few lights. Though thousands of people must have been left in the city, they feared lights that might draw the demons. Beyond the citadel hill, the banks were far and low, and soon we saw no lights at all. The raft made no sound. I felt no wind. The red-lit world seemed dead. A long time silent, Scorth spoke abruptly.

"You know, Nuradoon, you didn't really need that old helmet or the sword." He seemed more serious, as if his doubts were fading.

"Not against the demons. Sending the raft, I think the Three have proved they have a future for you."

"Maybe," I said. "In any case, we must do whatever we can."

"I need a nap." Yawning, he got to his feet. "Wake me if you think we're drifting into the bank."

I promised to stay awake, and he crawled into the tent.

Squatting there, watching the great red moon sinking slowly toward the creeping banks, I saw no demons, no river craft, not even a drifting log. Scorth crawled out of the tent before moonset, and let me sleep. Good odors woke me to bright daylight. He had spread our wet clothing on the deck to dry and discovered a slab of hopper bacon and a little bag of suncorn meal the crew of the raft had left behind.

"I found a man's hat and a woman's shoes," he said. "They left in a hurry. Cut a rope to free their skiff, because they had no time for the knot."

He had a tiny cook fire going on a pile of dirt ringed with stones, a flat scrap of steel for a griddle. The bacon was frying, and little balls of sunmeal dough sizzling in the grease. He gave me a ripe tomato, and I caught the rich fragrance of a golden delta melon he had broken open.

"Our friends must have been ashore before they panicked," he said. "Robbing somebody's garden."

He served the bacon and bread on pointed sticks. Ravenous, we filled ourselves. When the steel plate was scraped clean, he leaned off the deck to scoop up a gourd of water and came back with one for me.

"Zorn, I've been thinking. . . ." He squatted again, shaking his naked head. "We're on our way to Quar, but I don't like our prospects when we get there. The mages will surely be ready to defend their piece of the Shield."

He squinted expectantly into my face, but all he found was uneasy uncertainty. If fate had cast me in the role of Nuradoon, where was any script or director?

"Perhaps—" his hopeful mood had changed "—we could forget Nuradoon."

"You mean—"

"Look at where we are." Frowning, he nodded at the dense

green tangle of bayonet brush on the creeping bank. "The mages picked a lonely spot for Quar. It stands on an isolated ridge, here in the delta jungle that runs a hundred miles and more along the river. Maybe no paradise, but safer for us than the holy city."

Shrewdly his yellow eyes narrowed.

"Want to go ashore? Live if we can and hope the demons go away."

For a moment I could only shake my head, because that last dreadful image of Kye had seized me again. Her green eyes wide in terror, the rictus of agony on her face, the scream she couldn't utter. Shame shook me again, with the fear that she'd thought I was running away.

"No!" I whispered when I could. "You said we'd trust the Three."

Stiffly, he was grinning. "I needed to be sure."

For three more days, we floated on. Here in the delta, the river was wider and slower. Our world was flat black water and the low green jungle on the barely moving bank. One day we set up a pole for a mast and stretched the tent for a sail, but the wind blew against us.

The melons were gone. We shared the last ripe tomato. Scorth found a fishline the missing crew had used, and we broiled his catch with a scrap of the bacon. On hot afternoons we dived off the raft till I felt a wave of angry shame that we could do nothing better. We took turns sleeping. With nothing else to do on my long night watches, I lived my life again.

In waking dreams as real as the raft, I was back in the grass-roofed house my father built on Little River. I heard him laugh again, the happy giant with black coal dust in his wild ruddy beard. Fondly I recalled the unicorn scent in his worn flight leathers when he carried me to see Dragonrock. He might have been a better Nura-doon.

I heard my mother's quick soft voice again, praying at her tiny shrine with the faith I had never found. I trudged with her again on our donkey trips to trade her pottery to Mrs. Emok. I shuddered, caught again in the helpless horror of that night on the snow-covered square when we saw the black mage throw his serpent staff at Bastard.

Hot tears filled my eyes again when I recalled how she found me afterward shivering above the high water and called my father to help her comfort me with their talk of Realists and Mystics and the problem of evil. A problem I'd never solved. Xath was its symbol. The mages were pure evil. My uncles Thorg and Slarn had been evil men.

What of the demons? Pacing the dark deck beneath their lurid moon, I had time enough to ponder. They had been horribly cruel to that screaming wolf, and the barber in the village, and to Kye. Did that make them evil?

It was a question with no answer, I thought, till we knew them better. Things more fire than flesh, what were they? How did they live on their red-burning world? Why did they come here? For gold? Did they eat it? Did they require it, the way we required food and water? Would that make them evil, or merely strange?

Yet, "evil" or merely our rivals in the struggle to stay alive, they had created Xath and the mages, brought fire and terror and death. They were our enemy. Even if we survived this attack, their moon's long orbit would bring them back, and bring them back again. They had to be destroyed.

But how?

Three long days of nothing, three silent nights beneath the demons' moon. We passed no towns or landings, saw neither ships nor demons. This lower delta hadn't changed, I thought, since the first people came up from the sea, if that was how they had come. I could almost imagine that Scorth and I had been left alone on the planet, with nothing to live for or die for.

Late on the third night, I was on watch, pacing the planks but expecting no trouble. The moon had sunk low behind us, its broad face a dull and sullen red, fringed with exploding plumes of brighter fire. With no wind to ruffle it, the river reached black and flat to banks almost too far to see.

Very slightly, the deck tipped.

I yelled for Scorth and grabbed a pole to push us back. It sank deep into bottomless mud. He came running to push with another pole, but the mass of the raft was too much for us. It plowed ahead till deep mud stopped it. Aground, we were still there when the sun came up to show the river as broad as a lake all around us. It was green and stagnant here. A gust of hot wind off the nearest jungle fringe had a thin, sweet taint of death and decay.

"We're out of the channel." Scorth made a dismal face. "On the wrong side of the river. Here till the water rises. Which will be when the spring floods come."

"So?" I stared at him. "What now?"

"Ask the Three!" He gestured at the shore. "Nothing here on our side but bayonet scrub and swamps full of vipers. The Quar shore? Too far for us to swim."

With a fatalist's stiff face for misfortune, he fried the last of the bacon for breakfast. We split the last suncorn cake, washed down with mud-flavored water. Myself no stoic, I felt as desperate as if the demons already had me. That afternoon, however, he touched my arm and pointed to a tiny puff of white steam, far down the channel.

37

The Broken Blade

Speaking for the celestials—though she still called them demons—
the woman had demanded the artifact. He brought it to her at the
office she had claimed from the old tower master.

"Mr. Nine!" She came to meet him at the door, smiling her
witch's painted smile and calling his number as if it were a joke.
"Something for us?"

She shrugged with a wider smile when he refused to touch the
red-nailed hand she offered, never seeming offended to see that he
hated her as a curse on holy Quar. She had bewitched half of the
contact team, luring them toward damnation with her unholy per-
fumes and all the tempting flesh she kept exposing.

Half the staff already corrupted, she had her slaves risking their
souls to shop for her in the infidel markets, searching out the forbidden fruits and vegetables she preferred to honest lectory fare. He
would dispose of her when he could, but that must wait until he had
some better link with the demons.

Celestials—he bit his lip, correcting himself. He hated her word
because it recalled too much of his own ugly childhood, when they
had been demons to the infidel villagers and the hopper herder's
widow.

"Here."

Her smooth female arm obscenely naked under the outrageous
embroidered blouse, she was reaching for the odd glass fragment.

He dropped it on her desk to avoid her hell-tainted touch and tried not to see her tantalizing smile.

"A gift to the celestials," he said. "We believe it may be part of the artifact they asked for. 'The blade of Bar' mentioned in the archives."

"Only this?" She inspected it with a frown of disbelief. "A chip of broken glass?"

"We recovered it in Targon, from the strong room of Lord Slarn ir Var. He swears under severe interrogation that it is a piece of what he called 'the Dragonshield.' He testifies it has been handed down among the Vars for many generations. The staff believes it may even have come from the diarist who called himself Barni Bar."

Watching her study it again, unable to look away from the glowing skin beneath that filmy blouse or to hold his breath against her soul-snaring scent, he couldn't help a shattering recollection of that dreadful night when she poisoned him with alcohol and lured him to couple with her.

"If that's true—" she paused to frown disturbingly "—I suppose Xath will want to see it."

She had begun calling her familiar by that sacred name. Out of blasphemous malice, he thought, toward him and his faith. The celestials had no names and needed none, so the staff experts believed, because they were not separate beings, but all of them units or cells of a single entity.

"Don't!" he gasped. "Wait—"

Not waiting, she turned to tap a golden gong on her desk. The celestial was instantly with them in the room. He heard the dry buzz, caught the sharp scent, felt the terrifying tingle on his skin, before he found it over his head. A tiny ball of dull red fire spiked with squirming worms that glowed brighter red.

Shuddering, he retreated toward the door.

"You'd better wait." She gestured to stop him, grinning at his apprehension. "Xath may have instructions. I won't let him hurt you."

Her easy way with them made her nearly as awesome as they were. Awkward circumstance had made her their agent, perhaps even their ally. Acting in their name, she ruled him as surely as she ruled all her spellbound slaves.

He crouched back toward the wall, listening while she spoke to it in the language the creatures never seemed to understand from anybody else. A vexing puzzle, not yet solved by the desperate effort of all the team.

The staff linguists had invented symbols of their own for the odd sounds she used. They had produced a grammar and a dictionary. He had made her give him lessons and tried to speak, though only through the radio—so near as this, the creatures gave him goose-flesh. Yet they still ignored every voice but hers. She shrugged and smiled when he asked her why.

It floated closer as they talked. Sometimes he thought he had caught a word he knew, but there were sounds that seemed more like animal grunts, and whistles like birdcalls. Sounds nobody else had learned to imitate, not well enough for the celestials. No matter, he thought; he would even the score when the red moon was gone.

Or might the celestials decide to stay?

"Who knows?" She'd shrugged when he asked, with the same teasing smile. "Xath doesn't say."

Responding to her now, the celestial produced clicks and chirps and round bell tones, not at all like any sound she had made, yet he saw her nodding as if she understood. Glancing at him with obvious pleasure in his frustration, she offered it the black shard on her open palm. A glowing tendril stretched to lift it, turn it slowly as if for inspection, place it very gently back on her hand.

Its speech chimed again.

"A question," she said. "Xath asks how the artifact was broken."

"We have the story from the two Var brothers." The globe moved closer as if to listen, and he couldn't help a shudder. "The traitor's younger brothers, who had seized the artifact when they exiled him. Though they swear the object never had any magic in it, neither trusted the other with it. They've confessed that they split it with an axe."

"Their misfortune." The creature floated away from him, pealing as if it had understood. She turned to frown at him. "He wants to see the other piece."

"We don't have it." He shrank toward the door as far as he dared. "It was last reported in the hands of the exile's son."

The globe rang again.

"Instructions." She used a tone of crisp command. "You will find this fugitive man and the remainder of the artifact. Get them to us here with no delay."

Admiral Nuradoon

That wisp of distant smoke rose slowly higher. When at last we could see the ship beneath it, we built a larger fire, piled damp wood on it, and waved canvas from the tent to make puffs of smoke. The ship steamed on, as if to pass far away.

"They must have seen us," Scorth insisted. "It's just that they have to stay in the channel."

We kept puffing smoke until at last it slowed. A steam launch put off toward us, but stopped two hundred yards across the green-scummed water. Three men in it passed a hand glass back and forth, staring at us. We beckoned and shouted desperately, though I thought they were too far to hear.

"Afraid," Scorth muttered. "Afraid we're possessed."

They moved closer at last, but stopped again twenty yards away.

"We're aground," Scorth shouted. "Without food."

A man at the bow yelled through a megaphone, "Who are you?"

"Honest men. Refugees from Targon."

He turned to speak with the other two before he called again, "Refugees? From what?"

"The demons. They're burning the city. We were lucky to get away."

"Identify yourselves."

We yelled our names.

"Var, you say?" He looked at his companions. "From Little River?"

"The son of Rendahl ir Var, once the Wolver Rider."

Seeming startled, he scanned the raft, shook his head, and talked again to the other men.

"Can you prove it?"

"We got away with nothing—" Scorth caught himself and frowned a silent question at me. "Sir, we do have one relic from the Vars. Half the Dragonshield, if you've heard of that. The magic shield of the great Nuradoon."

They conferred again, and looked back at us.

"Stand by. We'll take you off."

All three inspected us sharply as we scrambled aboard, but they seemed oddly silent.

"The river's been empty," Scorth commented. "We've seen no shipping."

That got no answer.

I recognized the little river ship before I could read the fading lettering on the bow. *Lady of Dorth.* Captain Kalon Thrack stood waiting as we climbed aboard. Weathered like the boat, he was still solidly erect, his thick brown arms bare in the humid heat and splashed with the dragon tattoos I recalled.

"Captain Thrack!" He gave me a puzzled scowl. "I knew you once," I told him. "Remember the delta orange you gave me, when I came with my mother—"

"That skinny little kid!" His face lit, and he turned to the men who had brought us off the boat. "The admiral's son."

"My father?" Wondering what that meant, I blurted the question. "Do you know anything about him?"

"I know your father."

"He's alive?"

He nodded, grinning at me. "Very much alive."

"My mother?"

"No word." The grin became a solemn shrug. "He has tried to learn, but she was removed from the exile farm."

"Where is he?"

"A surprise for you." His shrewd old eyes studied me again. "Perhaps a shock, if you really are a Var. I want to know what's going on upriver. But all that will have to wait. I have messages to send.''

''The potter's son?''

We were standing on the deck. I heard a voice I remembered and turned to see a woman coming out of the captain's cabin.

''Miss Penra!''

Now the captain's wife, she still had the well-filled figure that had captured Bastard's hopeless devotion, though her fair skin had begun to wither and brown beneath the river sun. Her head still had the tilt of arrogance that used to carry her past him without a glance.

When I spoke of him, she took us into the cabin to offer us a glass of wine while she dug into a battered trunk. She found a letter she wanted to show me, a single wrinkled page smudged with his dark fingerprints along the edge and marked with red where she had corrected the grammar and spelling.

''It touched me.'' Her voice had softened. ''I wanted to return it and try to tell . . .'' She shook her head. ''I never—never—'' Her lips quivered, and I saw the glint of a tear. ''I've always been sorry.''

Looking away from me, she took a big gulp of her wine and put the letter back in the trunk without letting me read it.

Giving us no more news of my father, Captain Thrack moved somebody to vacate a top-deck cabin for us. The steward found clean clothes that fit us well enough and brought a basket of fresh fruit, with hard bread and hopper cheese. Looking out at the jungle-clotted banks, I saw that we had turned to steam back down the river.

Miss Penra knocked at our cabin door.

"Kalon can see you now," she told me. "If you want to hear the admiral's—your father's story."

We found the captain waiting in their cabin. As massive and deliberate as a bull hopper leading his harem, he waved us to be seated, opened a bottle of brandy, and waited for her to pour careful shots.

"So you were his trainer?" His wary eyes measured Scorth, and he nodded in cautious approval. "He asked me to look for news of you."

"We'll see him?"

"When we reach Quar." He turned. "Your father asked for me," he said, "when he learned that I used to trade on Little River. He was anxious to hear of your mother and you."

"How is he?" I tried to hurry him. "Tell us everything."

"Lad, his story will make you proud."

He paused with that to sip his brandy, scanning me as searchingly as he had Scorth. His deep-set eyes had a permanent squint from staring over sunlit water, and I saw more feeling in them than I heard in his gravel voice.

"You know how he was taken from the exile farm?"

"I—I was there." Emotion choked me. "The unicorn police took him away on a little yellow mare. He looked back to wave at us. That's all—all we ever knew."

"The way of the mages." Impassive, he nodded again. "The primarch let the damned mages have him, on a blasphemy charge his brothers trumped up. He was sent to Paradise Island."

"Demon's Island." Scorth spoke when he paused. "I was there. Lost my hair on the way." He touched his naked scalp. "Got near enough to hear about him, though I never saw him. Nearly lost my life before I got away."

"Your father was a slave there." Thrack turned to me. "In the convict camps, building wooden temples to be burned to welcome the demons. A bad time for him, but they never broke him. Escape, punishment that nearly killed him, but always another escape. After the last, waiting to burn, he organized one more attempt.

"Claimed to be the original Nuradoon ir Var . . ."

Scorth gave me an odd look, but said nothing.

"The convicts and the mages knew he was a Var, and knew what his brothers had done. Enough of them wanted to believe him. They were the ones who'd never wanted to roast in a burning temple on their way to paradise. The rising of the red moon was our sign to strike. Ours, lad . . ."

His slow smile for me was ferocious as a bull hopper's snarl.

"I'd never worshiped Xath. When his rebels came to seize *Lady,* I swore my oath to him. And that's his story." He gestured for Miss Penra to refill our glasses. "To Admiral Nuradoon!" he boomed like a hopper bull in rut. "Killer of demons! Savior of the world!"

I gulped and almost strangled.

"Where—" I asked again when I could speak. "Where's my father now?"

"We left him at Quar with his little fleet. The archimage still holds the temple and the signal tower, but most of the city has surrendered. The steam trains have stopped and the telegraph's dead. He sent me up the river for news of Targon. Which now I have from you."

He emptied his glass and wiped his lips with the back of his hand.

"I've turned us back to take it to him."

Feeling dazed and a little stupid, I sat staring at him and his wife and Scorth. My father was Admiral Nuradoon! He'd beaten the demons! Or could I believe it? Thrack had been too brief. I remembered the screaming wolf and the howling barber and those red sparks swimming over the burning palaces, remembered the mages and their serpent staves. How could any man defeat them? Even my father?

"Lad, I see you wondering." Thrack turned his savage grin on me. "Do you doubt me?"

Uneasily, I nodded.

"The mages aided us," he said. "When they took over the Targon Institute, they sent Realist scientists and engineers to the island, where they heard about your father and his plots. What they brought was their own theory of what the demons are. A sort of life, your father says, made of fire and magnetism instead of flesh and blood. But only one creature, he thinks, because those fireballs are only the cells of its body, all linked together with radio instead of nerves and muscles. Radio, that's the secret.

"We can jam the radio."

"And kill the demons?"

"Not quite." Regretfully he shook his gnarly head. "To kill them, he says, you'd have to hit them at home on their own red moon. But the radio beam did blow up the fireballs at close range. Drove the rest out of range. And panicked the mages. Now we've got the archimage under siege in Quar."

His hard feature set.

"Battles still to fight. We've got the primarch still to go."

We told him how we'd seen the old primarch, barefoot and half-naked, limping away from his burning palace under the demon that ruled him.

"Just the mages, then." The captain nodded in grim satisfaction. "The mages and their demons. They know the whole world hates them. We can't stop their serpent sticks, which don't seem to work by radio. But they run when we blow their demons up. We're winning the war!"

He pushed the bottle at us.

"Once more, to Admiral Nuradoon! And then I must call him again."

Scorth and I were the only passengers. Or prisoners, it seemed to me. The demons had left the captain wary of uncertainty, and he seemed unsure of us. At his command, we had to stay near our cabin. The steward brought our meals on a tray and kept us off the lower decks, where we might have talked to others on the crew. When I begged to let us see the captain again, he was always busy on the bridge or in the signal room or resting in his cabin.

All that night we steamed down the river. Under the gigantic moon, Scorth and I paced our empty deck, watching the crimson glitter of our bow wave and sometimes searching the red-drenched sky, still in fear of more demons there.

"I still can't believe," I muttered to him once. "It's all too sudden."

"Maybe sudden to us," he admitted reasonably. "Not quite so quick, I think, for your father and his friends. It took them years and lives and unexpected luck. And the blessing of the Three."

He tried to sleep in the berth above me, but I kept him awake till the great moon was overhead, making him repeat all he had told me about his time as an acolyte in Quar and his desperate venture to rescue my father from Demon's Island.

Half-awake long after he was snoring, I lay remembering my father, holding the sack again for the coal he dug above our house, and riding with him on Sharabok to see Dragonrock and jump the wolf into the water, and trying not to sob as I watched the police taking him away on the little yellow mare.

Leaning on the rail next morning, we watched Quar loom out of the river mist. Like Targon, the holy city had grown from a hilltop fortress nestled in a river bend. The dark cliffs and the dark walls climbed sheer from the water. The red temple dome rose like a second moon above them, and the tower behind it was a long black finger pointing into the haunted sky.

The channel carried us toward the farther bank around the bend, so that we passed them a mile away. We left the channel farther below and waited for a steam launch that brought a pilot to guide us through the craft anchored in the shallows. Miss Penra came to stand with us on the deck as we came in toward the dock.

"There!" She pointed. "The admiral! And some woman with him."

My father!

I found him in a moment, striding around a mountain of casks and crates piled up on the deck. Still the same bright-bearded giant alive so long in my recollection, unbowed by all his years on the prison island. The woman hurried after him—

My mother!

Small beside him, still in the same brown homespun she had worn on the morning I left her on the farm and the same sunbonnet she used to wear on the trail to the village. Tears of joy had filmed my eyes. I tried to call, but an aching lump had closed my throat.

"No!" I heard Scorth gasp. "No!"

I wiped at my eyes and saw the way they walked. Awkwardly, unnaturally, the way the demon had made Kye walk. Like mechanical toys. Like puppets.

39

Disposition

Danger had always lured her. Even as a tiny child she had loved to terrify her mother, climbing high on the mine works or leaning over a shaft to look down into its mysterious bottomless blackness. Obsessed with the risks the hunters took, riding across the wyvern border, she had begun slipping away with them as soon as they would take her on their unicorns, loving the dives to spear a snarling, black-fanged wolf.

She knew the danger all around her here in Quar, and played her games against the mages and the demons with the same high excitement. Argoth feared her, and despised himself when he had to yield. Any of them, she knew, would kill her if or when they could. She was winning, however, so long as the demons spoke only to her.

"It's just that they know me," she told Argoth when he kept pressing for her secret. And she added, more to tantalize than inform him, "Though I don't think they generally bother to tell people apart. Of course, they have noticed the difference between women and men. Xath asked me once why he sees no children here in Quar. Maybe that's my secret."

She enjoyed his perplexity.

"They know women bear children. To their way of thinking, maybe that makes them see us as somehow like their star, their mother world. Men must be more like the eruptions that keep bursting out of it. Things that move and burn and vanish without creating anything.''

''Absurd!'' he exploded. ''Realist nonsense!''

Yet she saw his eyes narrow under the hairless blue scars, searching her.

''Call it what you like.'' She grinned happily, pleased with herself. ''But they do talk to me.''

If the mages offered exhilarating menace, the demons were a sharper risk, the sort she had relished since the day she landed with the black-bearded werewolf hunter in that high mountain valley beyond the border, and heard the banshee howling while he was introducing her to sex.

Her heart beat faster that morning in the high tower office she had made the mages give her, when she heard the buzz above her in the room and felt the electric prickle and caught the ozone bite. The red fireball was suddenly over her desk, floating a yard from her tingling nose.

''Discontinue disposition!'' The level of its pealing signal almost hurt her ears. ''Discontinue disposition!''

She had no idea what that meant. Translation was still a matter of guess and intuition, spiked with high excitement. Plotting to replace her, the mages were at work on a computer translator program, but she had helped them no more than she had to.

''Discontinue disposition?'' She repeated the symbols in her own code, with the interrogative sign. ''Amplify context.''

She didn't say *please*. She knew no symbol for it and doubted that the demons had any sense for human courtesy.

''Disposition is disposition.'' The answer was a quick and emphatic repetition. ''Discontinue now.''

''Mr. Nine!'' She called Argoth on the interphone. ''Xath is here with orders for you.''

Perhaps this red-throbbing globe was the one she had always seen. Perhaps it wasn't. It didn't matter. She sometimes wondered if the creatures could tell themselves apart, or if it would matter if they did. Identical or not, she called all of them Xath because it vexed him.

"Orders for what?"

"You'll hear."

The demon rambled around the room, hovering first to inspect the interphone, which Argoth had installed to keep her safely isolated. It examined her paperweight, a gold-veined quartz crystal she had brought back from her last flight beyond the border. Its bright tendrils began tapping the computer keys.

Unlisted flashed across the screen, then *disposition* and its synonyms. She smiled to herself. The demons wanted single-valued positive symbols. Synonyms and even negatives often baffled them. Luckily, she thought, for her.

It left the computer, floating on to open a file drawer and pull a folder out. Watching its tentacles rippling deftly through the contents, she made the label out. *Xath, records of.* It was learning to read, though prudently she had given it very little help.

"What now?"

Argoth was at the door uneasily peering.

"Mr. Nine!" she called. "Come on in. No need to be nervous. Xath has another job for us, but he never wants to hurt us. Not so long as we do as we're told."

He crept inside, watching as the demon closed the folder, replaced it carefully where it belonged in the file, and came floating to meet him, ringing like a chorus of bells.

"The command is to 'discontinue disposition,'" she interpreted. "Whatever that means."

He backed against the wall, cringing from it. His throat worked. "Maybe . . ." He licked his thin blue lips. "I don't know what it means, but we've had reports of trouble on the convict island."

"He seems impatient," she told him. "He wants action."

Sinking toward them, the demon paused as if to listen.

"A convict revolt." He gripped the back of a chair, knuckles white. "Led by an escapee who claims to be the deposed Wolver Rider. He seems to have convinced his followers that he has magic powers handed down from some old folk hero. An absurd pretender, but cunning enough to take advantage of the moment. Mass escapes have been reported, and the rebels are still defiant of the officials trying to put them down.

"But now—"

The demon interrupted him, booming impatiently.

"Xath knows all that," she said. "He's repeating his command. 'Discontinue disposition.' "

"Unfortunately—" he shrugged away from the glowing tendrils spreading toward him "—that's all we know. Some kind of radio interference has stopped radio contact with the island, and even the shipping en route there.

"Tell the celestial—"

It rang like a gong.

"Xath is telling you." She smiled at his startled gasp. "He says 'discontinue disposition.' He wants you to discontinue the rebel Nuradoon."

40

Cold Dark Place

"Zorn!" My mother darted toward me across the dock, screaming my name. "My son—"

My father seized her arm and jerked her back.

"Rennie!" She struggled to escape. "Please! Please—"

They were still twenty yards from the riverboat. The gray sunbonnet hid her face, but I heard agony in her voice. Standing there at the rail, I felt dazed and sick, uncertain of everything.

I had seen no demons. The man on the dock indeed had the shape of my father, the copper-bearded giant of my boyhood recollection. The woman was certainly my mother. But what of Admiral Nuradoon, who had led his little fleet up the river to defeat the mages and chase the demons off the world?

The rigid figure on the dock, my mother pleading at its feet, might have been no living man, but instead a statue of Xath. Afraid to understand, or even to try, I could only stand there, staring at the dock. Scorth caught my elbow, gasping something I didn't hear. Miss Penra had run back to her cabin. On the bridge, the pilot and Captain Thrack were calling orders to the deck hands tossing ropes to tie us up.

"Captain! Captain Thrack!" My mother broke free and darted toward us, desperately screaming. "Help—"

She tripped over something I couldn't see and sprawled to the planks. My father jerked into action. Stalking after her like some mechanical giant, he moved with a terrible clumsy power. He snatched her arm before she could rise, hauled her back to his side.

"Rennie!" She sobbed his name again. "Can't you see—"

Something choked her.

I shook Scorth's hand off my elbow. Crewmen stood ready to run the gangplank out, but I didn't wait. When the dock looked close enough, I climbed on the rail and jumped. It was nearly too far; I sprawled to hands and knees. Looking up, I found my father towering over me, tall and terrible.

As a child I had feared him. I had been small and he was large. He had been the Wolver Rider; he would be so forever, at least to my mother and me. He had known everything. He had sung the unicorn language and ridden Sharabok over the forbidden wilderness where the werewolves hunted. Yet never really terrible. I recalled him laughing and always kind.

This dreadful giant wasn't laughing now. Behind the tangled beard, his face was white and stiff and hard. His eyes were nothing I knew. They looked colder than the winter ice on Little River. Even his voice was strange.

"I am Admiral Nuradoon ir Var." Dull and rough and flat, it might have been a hopper bull trying to speak. "And you . . ." He seemed to shudder, those dreadful eyes blinking as if his vision had blurred. His grasp had relaxed, and my mother tried to break away. He dragged her abruptly back and shouted hoarsely at me, "Your name is Zorn. You are kin. You are therefore a Var."

The bonnet had slipped. I found my mother's face, framed in the thin gray hair that fell loose around it, uncombed and dirty now. Her face was drawn and pinched as if from long starvation, dark with grime and cut deep with lines of pain. Tears had cut pale streaks down it.

"Dear Zorn!" She reached to help me rise. "Thank the Three!"

Why? What had the Mystic Three ever done for her? Scrambling back to my feet, I had time to frame that bitter question before she could catch my hand. Wasted to tendon and bone, it was filthy as her face and cold as ice, yet its strength seemed more terrible than my father's frozen face.

"Mother!" I tried to hug her. "Can I—how can I help—"

He seized her again, and I felt that dreadful strength run out of her. She quivered and went limp, hanging like a rag doll on his arm. Her face twitched, and I heard a faint whimper, a sound like the whine of a hungry hopper cub.

"Artifact?" My father's inhuman eyes glared at me, and he mouthed the question strangely. "Broken artifact called Dragonshield? My son possesses missing section, now required. Give!" He held out his hand. Grimy as my mother's, it was scarred with deep scratches, streaked black with dried blood. "Give—"

Behind me, Captain Thrack was shouting. The ship's whistle bellowed. My father rocked back as if dazed by the blast. Free, my mother stumbled away from him.

"Keep it!" she gasped. "Use—"

Something took her voice. She crumpled to the dock. I bent to help her, and she shrank from my hand. Some kind of seizure shook her lean-fleshed body and let it collapse again. She twisted and lifted her head, turning her pain-stained face to me.

"No!" She was wheezing for her breath, and I could hardly hear her words. "Don't touch me! Save the Shield! Run—"

A shudder stopped her.

Captain Thrack was bellowing orders from the bridge. The pilot had fled; I saw him already far down the dock and running hard. Men were swinging axes to cut the mooring cables. The gangplank was lifting. Scorth leaned toward me over the rail, yelling something lost in the clang of the ship's bell and the roar of steam. The stern wheel was already spinning, the ship pulling out.

I ran desperately, with no time to look back. The lifting gangplank was already a yard away from the dock, but I jumped for it. Scorth ran out, reaching to help. Sprawling on the end of the plank, I caught his hand and staggered with him to the deck.

"What happened?" he whispered. "What's wrong with the rider?"

I didn't know.

"I think I do." Dismally he shrugged. "I think the demons have got Admiral Nuradoon."

Panting, I clung weakly to the rail, staring back at my father. He stood where I had left him, motionless as stone. My mother was pulling herself to her feet. Arms spread, she stood a moment pleading with him. He ignored her. She reached for his arm. As if stricken

by the touch, she fell again and lay struggling on the dock, tossed
with convulsions.

Shame and pity sickened me. Shame because I had been so helpless, because I had run away. Even though she'd told me to run,
even though I knew nothing else to do. I looked at Scorth for any
crumb of comfort. He made a bitter grimace and spread his little
hands.

Even with no pilot now aboard, the captain took us back through the
ships anchored in the harbor shallows, steaming faster than we had
come. As long as I could see my father, he stood where he had been,
rigid as marble. My mother's convulsions slowed and ceased. She
crawled away from him on hands and knees and sank back against a
crate of delta oranges. I didn't see her move again.

We were halfway back to the main channel when something
clanged against the hull. I heard a glancing bullet whistling away.

"Take cover!" the steward yelled. "We're under fire."

We retreated to our cabin, but Captain Thrack was still on the
bridge when I looked back, ignoring a rattle of gunfire from the vessel we were passing.

"Only merchant craft," Scorth said. "Armed with whatever
weapons the rebels captured from the guards on the island, now in
the hands of the mages. The primarch did have three or four river
gunboats. All probably docked at Targon. I imagine the archimage
will be sending them after us."

A few more bullets whined around us, but the anchored ships
were soon behind. When we came back on deck the docks were lost
behind a bend in the river, and the temple dome had dwindled to a
small red moon setting in the jungle.

When the steward came with a tray of fruit and hopper cheese for
lunch, we asked what he knew. He shrugged. We asked to see the
captain, but he was busy now in the signal room. Drinking redthorn
brandy, the steward said, because he was hearing nothing good.

In the humid heat of an endless afternoon, we steamed on down through the delta toward the sea. The river widened to a brackish lake, green with patches of floating weed. The sky was a milky gray, thunderheads climbing far off in the east, toward Demon's Island. Watching for demons, for unicorns or wyvern, for anything at all, we saw nothing moving except a flight of carrion bats circling over a bloated carcass.

Below the lake the channel divided, branches like the fingers of a hand spreading among low jungle islands. Most of them were muddy and shallow, unsafe for navigation, and the captain stayed on the bridge with a little telescope, searching out the channel markers on the shore. Still he had no time for us, but late in the afternoon we found Miss Penra walking the deck and asked her what was happening.

"Who knows?" She shrugged unhappily. "The captain has been talking to the island. His people say we're beaten, but they can't tell us how. They've all received orders to surrender to the archimage. Orders purporting to come from Admiral Nuradoon, but transmitted in the clear, not in his secret code."

With no more patience for us than she used to have for Bastard, she turned to hurry on.

"My father," I called after her. "What changed him? So dreadfully?"

Reluctantly she paused.

"It makes you wonder." She stood a moment blinking somberly at me, teeth sunk into her lip. "I used to trust the Mystics and the Three, but after Bastard . . ." I saw her shiver. "After this—you've got to wonder."

"Have you any idea what went wrong?"

"The captain has a theory," she said. "He's getting bad news from our people in Quar and the few ships we have left on the river. He thinks the demons are learning to block our radio beam. The one that was knocking them out. He thinks they've taken your father. He's afraid they'll take us before we get back to the island."

"Is the island safe?"

"So far." She glanced uneasily back across the lake. "So far."

She left us with that, but we stayed on deck, watching for demons, watching the swordbrush jungle, watching our good white sun go down. Ahead of us, the dusky horizon turned pink and rose, glowing redder till the demon moon came up.

The heat that night was a suffocating blanket. I sweated under it, and images of terror haunted my dreams. I saw Bastard again, crushed to blood and shapeless pulp in the black snake's coils. Saw Kye again, as she had stood in Rellion's dining room, her body washed in ghostly blue, her mouth fixed in that silent scream, her imploring eyes fixed on me. And my father transformed again into an inhuman demon-god, my mother crawling abjectly to his feet.

Once I woke and walked outside, seeking a breath of cooler air and escape from that clinging dread. We were steaming fast down a narrow channel. Captain Thrack was on the bridge, staring as fixedly ahead as if his own brawn pushed the ship. The red moon stood high, grown more gigantic every night. Glittering under it, the slow current looked black and thick as clotting blood.

The merciless heat still sucked at me like a vampire, and that dread came with me back to my berth. Trying to sleep on my clammy sheets, I dreamed I'd found Kye. We were riding Sharabok, climbing to escape that life-sapping heat, flying toward the demon's moon.

I held her in my arms, small and vulnerable and dear to me, even no longer herself. Her body felt strangely stiff, and cold as ice. She was shivering, moaning with pain.

"It hurts." The words she breathed were hard to hear. "Hurts so much." Accusingly her tearstained face looked up to me. "Why did you run? Why didn't you help?"

"I wasn't running, really." I fumbled for excuses, and knew she wouldn't believe. "Rellion and his chair had fallen in my way. I had to run around them."

She was gone from my arms before I could finish. Sharabok was gone. Yet somehow I was still flying through the bloodred moonlight. It lit all the land beneath me. I could trace every twist and bend of Dragon River, pick out the dark cities along it, even see

Demon's Island in the dark ocean beyond the delta. I watched them dwindle, till all I could see was a dim red disk, smaller than the moon.

Still! I climbed, and the red moon grew. Its leering, dark-splotched face changed suddenly to Kye's, still rigid with terror but now crusted with dreadful scabs and scars. She hated me because I'd failed to save her, yet I kept on climbing. I had to reach her, to comfort her, to make her believe I hadn't really run away.

Near enough at last, I spread my arms for her and saw that she was no longer Kye. I was reaching for the moon as I knew it really was, the red dwarf star, the globe of dull red fire that had grown from the faint red fleck I had first seen in my father's little telescope.

Changing again, it was no longer just the star. It was my own mother, too, reaching her own incandescent arms to take me. I loved her tenderly because she had created me, because she loved me, because she had always suckled me with the hot red milk of her fire.

Yet, since I had grown so large, that milk was no longer enough. A long famine had left me weakened and sometimes ill. Now she had found help for me, a feast spread over the frozen planet we were passing. Flying down to see it, I had come back to thank her for the abundance she had found for me and the multitudes of slaves she had busy there, swarming to prepare the savory yellow meat that would rekindle my own failing fire.

I clung a long time to her, reaching all around her, sucking up the healing energies that burned in the exploding jets of her incandescent milk. I praised her for her everlasting beauty, praised her for her boundless power, blessed her for her unending love. Yet I could not stay.

I had to hasten back, because that passing world would so soon be gone. I tore myself out of her embrace and lifted again through killing darkness toward that cold carcass of a planet we were passing. I felt warmed a little by the pathetic sparks of fire that flashed and died ahead of me, signals of devotion from my waiting slaves.

And I felt chilled again when I saw a darker shadow spread far across that dead world's darkness. Its shape was too dim for me to see. I wanted to run from it, as I had run from my father on the dock at Quar.

But I knew it intended to pursue and devour me.

Something mauled me.

Anger blazing in me, I tried to fight it off and found myself too stiff and cold to move. Trapped in nightmare, bound and frozen, I lay helpless in some cold, dark place. The gift of flight was gone, all my senses dead.

Something roared at me, shapeless and dreadful in the dark. It dragged at this strange and clumsy body that was not my own. My glowing heart had gone cold with dread. My nimble limbs had stiffened. I was heavy, blind, lost in bewilderment.

"The captain!" The thunder had no meaning. "Trouble for us."

I fought that frozen prison body, fought to wake its feeble senses. I found the tight wrappings that bound it, the cold pad under it, the narrow walls around it. I found the monster's head bellowing close above me, a dim brown moon.

Remembering, I began to understand.

I had fallen on the frozen surface of this passing planet. Trapped by the feeble creatures that infested it, I was locked somehow in the pitiful body. It was floating in a tiny box on a stream of liquid water. I needed light, needed heat, needed the nourishing metal my slaves had promised.

The creature around me meant no harm. Perhaps it even wanted to help, but it could do no good. Without understanding, it had brought me no yellow metal, kindled no fire to renew my life. It was merely dragging at this useless husk.

"Zorn? Are you okay?"

Struggling, I broke the body's frozen stiffness, sat it up on the edge of the pad. Reality dimmed, and nightmare possessed me. The body had been owned by a creature named Zorn. Fragments of his mind still haunted me. The little monster howling at me was a slave named Scorth, a rider of unicorns. The box was a boat floating on Dragon River.

Something thundered at the door.

"Open!" A roaring voice. "Open now!"

Scorth opened the door, and I made that prison body stand. Clumsy in it, I lumbered after Scorth. My beloved mother world had vanished. The alien sun had risen, the cold white star that held this dead world in orbit. Too far off to thaw the frozen lavas, it did reveal uncanny strangeness all around me. The deck of the floating boat, the liquid water flowing over the solid world-crust—even the puny little Zorn-thing that had become my prison.

That frigid dimness shut me in. The ship was all alone on the flat black water, the riverbanks only far-off shadows, but we were not alone on the deck. The Zorn-body trembled, cringing back from the monster that came stalking toward it.

Zorn had known the body as a Captain Thrack, who ruled the boat, but it had turned strange to him. Its heavy shape was nude to the middle. It shone with a blue but heatless fire. Its face was a rigid mask beneath that glow, and it growled like a rutting hopper bull.

"Artifact?"

The angry sound perplexed me, but the creature Zorn understood. It pulled its wrappings open to find a small object suspended from the body. The Thrack-thing tore it away and ripped it open. Blinking at a broken scrap of something black inside, it roared again.

"Dragonshield?"

41

The Artifact

"Here it is."

Argoth showed her a black glass lens shape, not quite so wide as the palm of her hand. Frowning at it, she asked what it was.

"Ask the celestials." He shrugged unhappily. "The staff believes it's the artifact they've been demanding."

"The 'blade of Bar'?"

"If you want to believe."

"I thought the object had been broken."

"It was."

Standing over her desk, he leaned so close, she had to breathe his odor, the odor of his unwashed body mixed with the vile reek of the sacred weeds the mages wove into the thorn shirts they wore as punishment for wanting comfort. Even now, as long as she had known him, she couldn't help recoiling from the stiff death mask of his face: the fleshless, blue-scarred features, the black, sharp-filed teeth, the deep-sunk eyes, the naked crimson skull.

"Two pieces," he said. "We recovered one from Rider Thorg, out in Wolver Riding. The other was recently found on a wandering vagrant. We've repaired it, as you see." Frowning at it, he shook that appalling head. "Rather, it has repaired itself."

He held it closer, and she drew farther from his odor. Mages were forbidden to bathe.

"A lens?"

"It's opaque." He shook that bloodred skull. "Even to X rays. It isn't glass. Not any kind of glass we know. Diamond can't scratch it. It has fine wires threaded through it. The broken ends were visible at the fracture, like flecks of gold and silver. When we fitted the fragments together—" he scowled at it uneasily "—something happened. Something nobody understands. The wires shone—you could see them under the surface. Perhaps those broken ends fused themselves together. The break healed itself. The fracture has disappeared."

"What's it good for?"

"Show it to your friends." A baffled shrug. "Half the staff think it's magic. Perhaps your friends can explain it."

He tried to hand it to her.

"Give it to Xath." She waved it away. "He'll want it from you."

"I've other errands." He laid it on her desk. "I've told you all I know."

"Better stay." She reached for the signal button. "Xath will want to know how you fixed it. All about it."

"You can tell him—"

"The demons aren't malicious." She grinned, amused at his anxiety. "They have damaged a few people, generally because they didn't understand us, but they're learning now. They can transfer themselves out of their own energy systems, into our nerves and brains. That needn't hurt you. Not so long as you do what they want."

Perhaps that was true, but he had never been sure exactly what they wanted. Now, in fact, since all the sacred history of their earlier visitations had come into question and old dogmas had been shattered, he felt lost, no longer certain what he was bound to believe.

Endure, he told himself. *Endure till they are gone with their passing star, leaving us alone in another cycle of Xath. He could deal freely with the woman then. And let the archimage look out for his high-backed chair!*

Or might some of them stay?

He tried not to dwell on that unpleasant question.

Unwillingly he picked up the vexing object and watched her ring her signal bell. Waiting near the door, he hated her impudence to him and her reckless blasphemy and the lure of the naked flesh she loved exposing. He heard the hissing crackle, caught the sting of ozone in his nostrils and felt it in his eyes. The celestial came from nowhere, its bright little globe suddenly drifting just above her soft-curled, pale gold hair.

Startled in spite of himself, he backed toward the wall and stood sweating, holding the cursed artifact on his outstretched palm, silently imploring almighty Xath to burn both the woman and the object.

"Mended." The sounds she clicked and whistled and trilled were most of them nonsense, but he caught occasional words. "Weapon . . . archives . . . blade of Bar."

The celestial volleyed pings and peals, paused to listen at her, and finally floated toward him, reaching with glowing tentacles for the artifact. In spite of himself, he shuddered and shrank away.

"Steady." She was almost laughing. "Hand it over."

He held it higher, cringing from the tingle on his hand when the burning tendrils wrapped it and lifted it delicately away. Breathing again, he watched them turn it for inspection beneath the crimson globe and finally drop it in her hand.

"He's disappointed and annoyed." Her amusement was gone. "As you know, they've been hoping to find and dispose of the magic weapon that hurried them off the planet when they were here before, but he seems to understand this object no better than we do. He doesn't see how it could be any sort of weapon.

"He wants to know what it is."

"I've given you the lab report." Impatiently he gestured at the artifact. "Still a mystery to all of us. Harder than diamond, lens-shaped but opaque to light, metal wires embedded—"

The metallic ping cut him off.

"He's aware of all that." Her tone grew sharper. "He wants to know its purpose."

"I told you." Miserably he spread his sweaty hands. "We've no idea."

She chirped and twittered again, and nodded very gravely to the celestial's unmusical chime.

"He dislikes ambiguities." A woman and an admitted infidel,

with no right here in the sacred city, she spoke with an archimage's commanding tone. Boiling within, he could only listen. "He resents the discrepancies in our history of the object. Which is it? The so-called Dragonshield? Or the Blade of Bar?"

"Two names," he said. "One from our archives, the other from popular legend. Tell him they likely refer to the same—"

The quick *plink* interrupted him.

"Listen, Mr. Nine." She might have been a head lector, mildly reproving a forgetful acolyte. "If you want to keep your job, you'd better learn to understand the demons. They don't like probabilities and uncertainties. They want facts. Black or white, nothing gray."

"Can't you tell them we have no facts about this object?"

She waited for the demon's ping.

"Just imagine, Mr. Nine." Insidiously appealing, she warmed her hateful voice. "Just imagine you really were the demon you look. Your people are here to look for gold. Their vital processes require it. They don't have much longer here on the planet, and they're in deep trouble.

"Those madmen on Paradise Island have killed a number of them. That mischief is being stopped, but they fear a greater danger now. More frightening, because they know so little about it. They came back here trusting us to respect the treaty of friendship they made with us a thousand years ago."

The small red globe had sunk closer, listening. He heard it click, saw it dip and lift as if to nod.

"Exactly." She cooed to it, and turned again to him. "They've kept their word," she said. "They gave you Xath. They taught you the science to make your black magic. Now they expect action from you."

Emphatically the celestial clanged.

"He wants answers," she said. "He wants them now."

"After a thousand years . . ." He tried to swallow his frustration. "With the facts forgotten? The records lost or gone to dust? What does he expect—"

The demon pealed impatiently.

"Tell it we'll try," he added hastily. "Tell it we'll do all we can."

"He doesn't want promises." Gently she chided him. "He doesn't want questions. He does want that weapon discovered and destroyed." She shook her head, with a slow, sardonic smile. "If you want to stay out of his sacred fire, you'll get that done."

42

Awakening

Escaping to my mother from that fearful world of ice and darkness, I felt well content for a time, restored to health by the golden plenty my slaves had provided and happy in her shining arms, filled again with her luminous milk.

But only for a time, before the Zorn-thing's alien brain awoke to break my peace. It drew me away from my mother, back into dark and chilling space. I saw her again through its unseeing eyes: a cooling star red with seas of glowing magma, splotched with darker islands where the lavas had cooled, erupting plumes of incandescent gas. I fought that invading monster, struggling to regain myself, till a harsh sound jolted me.

Sound? Here in empty space?

Bewildered, I opened my eyes to dreadful blackness. Blind at first, I had to grope for the monster's senses to discover that I lay on a narrow pad in a suffocating box. That grating squeal stabbed again. Light flooded in, and dazing recollection.

The box was our cabin on the *Lady of Dorth.*

"Zorn?" Scorth was at the creaking door, peering cautiously at me. "You awake?"

"Scor—"

My tongue was stiff, and the sound I made was a mewing bark. I fought for breath, for life itself. Laboring to move, I sat that dead body up on the edge of the berth.

"Zorn?" Scorth had stopped in the doorway, yellow eyes staring. "Do you know me?"

I managed a stiff little nod and tried to grin.

"Thank the holy Three!" He edged farther into the cabin. "I thought the demons had you."

"They did." Words began to come. "But I think they've let me go."

"They've still got Captain Thrack." He glanced uneasily behind him. "He wants you."

Still groggy from the nightmare, trying to shake off the sensations of the demon I had been, I could only sit there till I saw Miss Penra behind him in the doorway. Her right eye was bruised and swelling, her cheek smeared with drying blood.

"Mr. Var! Come on out." She tried to be as commanding as she must have been in the schoolroom, but her voice shook. "It wants you now."

"Better obey." Scorth beckoned. "He got rough with her."

My lifeless muscles failed me when I tried to stand. I toppled back across the berth. He pulled me up and steadied me out to the red-lit deck. My mother world—I tried to shrug off that haunting memory—the demon moon stood high above the funnel. Captain Thrack came lurching toward me, clumsy as I felt, his body washed in ghostly blue.

"Nuradoon?"

I recognized the name, but nothing else in his inhuman gobble. He stood glaring at me, his eyes unblinking and strangely glazed. When I made no answer, he turned to Miss Penra, bawling at her like a branded hopper bull. She came limping after him across the desk, one foot bare and the ankle swollen.

"It wants to know what you are," she said. "Nuradoon? The man who tried to make trouble on its last visit? Or just another man-thing? Called Zorn ir Var."

"Zorn." My own voice was still a rusty croak. "Zorn Var."

The captain growled at her again.

"It wants true facts." Trembling, she interpreted the mouthings I couldn't understand. "Mr. Scorth says you are in fact Nuradoon the Ninth, the legendary hero. He says you went into the Wind River desert as a modern man, and came out wearing Nuradoon's helmet. You had found it with his bones, and found his sleeping spirit, which awakened in you to make war on the celestials—that's its name for the demons.''

She crouched farther from him, listening to his snarl.

"It wants the truth," she whimpered. "Who are you? Are you in fact that eternal warrior? Did you wake to drive the celestials back into the sky?''

Anxious and perplexed, I looked at Scorth.

"That's what I told him." He shrugged. "What can we lose?''

What, I wondered, could we gain? I saw nothing likely. Still a stranger in my own body, I was swaying on stiff and quivering legs, my mind still clogged with shreds of the demon that had owned me but somehow let me go. I saw the captain reaching a dragon-wrapped arm to seize me again.

"I did sleep in the desert." I searched for anything the creature in him might believe. "I found a skeleton and a helmet. The helmet was marked with the sigil of Nuradoon ir Var. I am told it has a magic power.''

My voice was better, and the captain dropped his arm and growled at Miss Penra.

"What is that power?" she whispered. "How can it harm the celestials?''

"I don't know—''

The captain's hoarse bark cut me off.

"Why do you fight the celestials?''

"I fear them," I said. "I hate the mages of Xath. They are evil men—''

The captain bellowed at me.

"The weapon you had?" Miss Penra quavered.

I spread my hands. "I have no weap—''

Bellowing, the captain thrust his fist at me and snarled ferociously at her.

"The Dragon-thing?" Her voice rose accusingly. "What was its magic? How could it harm celestials?''

"All I know is that old legend." Helpless, I shook my head. "Nobody knows anything more. Not even if there ever was any kind of weapon. Too many centuries have gone. The facts are all forgotten.''

The captain stood a moment glowering at me with those glassy eyes. He lurched abruptly at me, stopped himself, and grunted at Miss Penra.

"Answers unsatisfactory," she said. "It wants truth."

"I can't remember," I said, "because I never knew."

The captain's glowing body stiffened. Hot as the morning was, it quivered as if to a sudden chill, snorted, and reeled clumsily away. Miss Penra stood shaking her head, hands spread imploringly, till it turned to growl again at her. Sobbing, she limped quickly after it.

"An awkward fix." Scorth gave me an apologetic shrug. "But we can't deny we had that scrap of black glass."

Feeling drained of all energy, as if life itself had been sucked out of me, I stood there with Scorth for a time, leaning on the rail and sweating under the red moon's glare. When a bend brought us near the swordbrush bank, I saw that we were steaming upriver, fast. The wind of our motion relieved the heat a little, but overwhelming exhaustion drove me back to the ovenlike cabin.

I woke abruptly, with a comforting sense of life restored, the breathless heat no longer quite so oppressive. Scorth was snoring peacefully in his berth across the cabin. A dull red beam still shone through the porthole, but my demon had left me. I was myself again.

Rejoicing in that odd sense of liberation, I walked out on deck, and the wind of our motion felt gratefully cool. Except for the chuffing of the engine and the muffled splash of the wheel, the ship was silent. The night was clear and still, the black water mirror-slick. Low in the west, the red moon was no longer so hot, and now it seemed safely far away, half its fearful mystery gone.

We were steaming back to the mages and demons of Quar, but I knew nothing to do about them now. Back in my berth, I slept and woke again to the white light of our own sun shining through the port when I heard the steward knocking at the door with our breakfast tray. I asked him what was happening. He answered with a sullen shrug; I saw that he had a bandaged arm and one sleeve torn off his tunic.

Uneasily we ate the fruit and hard bread and stale hopper cheese. The captain was still on the bridge when we ventured out of the cabin, standing rigid as if carved from wood. We saw nothing of his wife. Silent at their work, the crewmen avoided us. We could only wait.

Before noon, the red temple dome rose over the riverbank ahead, the thin black tower beside it. Two gunboats were anchored now among the traders in the shallows. They ignored us. The pilot who came out to guide us through them was a red-skulled mage, who spoke only to the wheelman. He brought us to the docks, and I saw another black-robed mage at the wheel of the steam cart waiting on the pier.

"A woman!" Scorth jogged my arm. "Here in Quar!"

Leaning on the rail, uneasily waiting, we watched the pilot's signals, the captain barking orders, the cowed crewmen tossing their mooring ropes and running the gangplank out.

"Mr. Var!" The woman startled me, shouting our names. "Mr. Scorth."

She ran from the cart, waving to welcome us.

"What next?" Scorth shrugged at me. "Let's go."

The crewman stood aside to let us off the boat, and she came smiling to meet us at the foot of the gangplank. A lean, athletic young woman in revealing white shorts and a lacy white blouse. Her hair bright gold, and her blue eyes shining, she had the men staring as if they had never seen a woman.

"I'm Lyrane." She shook my hand, her grasp warm and firm. "Your hostess here." She paused to glance at Scorth and look sharply back at me. "So you're Zorn? The son of Admiral Nuradoon?"

"My father?" I asked. "Do you know anything about him? And my mother?" She frowned as if the question troubled her, and I added, "I saw them together on the dock."

"I've seen them."

"You have? Where—how are they?"

"A frightful ordeal." Suddenly very sober, she seemed sympathetic. "You must have been dreadfully worried, but I've done what I could. They're safe. Recovering."

"Can we see them?"

"Later. You've no time now." She didn't say why or give me time to ask. "They're under care at the Grugarn Lectory. I suppose we can drop Mr. Scorth there on our way."

"If you know . . ." I stared at her, still bewildered and wondering what we might expect. "I'd like to ask about someone else. A woman I saw the demons take, on Count Rellion's ranch."

"The unicorn trainer?" She waited for my nod. "She was asking about you."

"Is she—was she hurt?"

"She was well enough." She glanced at Scorth and keenly back at me, as if trying to guess how much Kye meant to me. "At least when I saw her. The celestials brought her in for interrogation."

"Interrogation—"

The remembered terror of her seizure took my voice: the throbbing glow and hiss of the demon's scarlet heart, its bright tentacles reaching for Kye, the pale fire that bathed her, her mouth yawning in that soundless scream.

"Is she still . . ." I whispered, "still possessed?"

"Oh, no. They had to release her before she could talk." She paused, still searching me. "They were asking about that black glass artifact, or the piece of it she said she'd given you. Turned out she knew nothing."

"So where is she now?"

"Riding unicorns." Her momentary half smile had mischief in it, as if my concern amused her. "The archimage is touring the country to supervise the gold collectors. They picked up a unicorn to carry him, and she's his trainer."

The Lady Kye, riding for the mages?

That was hard for me to imagine. Scorth stood looking at me and then at this woman who seemed so strangely at ease here among them and the demons, shaking his naked head. Uncertain what to expect of her, I could only shrug.

She had beckoned to the black-robed man in the cart. He brought it panting and wheezing to us, and she nodded for Scorth to sit in front with him. He frowned doubtfully at me, shrugged, and climbed in reluctantly. She opened the back door and waved me into the rear compartment. The cart took us off the wharf, jolting up a cobbled street between rows of warehouses.

Bewildered and uneasy with her, I sat tense and well away.

"You look shocked." She was laughing at me. "To find a woman among the mages."

"I suppose I am."

"They needed me."

She didn't explain.

Ignorant of women, I had no idea what to make of her. The flower scent she wore filled the small compartment. Her body rocked against me when the coach rounded a corner.

"Sorry."

Muttering that stupid apology, I tried to draw farther away. She laughed again. Her eyes met and held my gaze. They were an intense violet blue, the pupils slowly darkening in a way that took my breath.

"Nice to know you, Mr. Zorn!" Abruptly she caught her breath and turned away. "Welcome to the sacred city."

The coach was rattling along a narrow street between rows of shops with merchandise displayed outside: food, clothing, tools, pottery that might have come from my mother's wheel. Drying laundry fluttered on the balconies, and half-naked children scrambled aside and stood staring at the cart.

"Infidels." She gestured at them.

"You work for the mages?" I couldn't help the question.

"A matter of relative ethics." She glanced again at the driver's compartment and dropped her voice, but her tone was still casual. "I don't have to love the mages or the demons, but I've begun to understand them. I try to make the best of the odd accident that brought me here. Sometimes I can limit needless harm."

I nodded uncertainly, puzzled more than ever.

"Sometimes I like it," she added. "A risky game, playing them against each other, but that's the sort of thing I've always loved. So far I've been lucky."

Beyond the street of infidels, we had turned in to a wider avenue through fortlike stone houses set far apart behind tall wrought-iron fences.

"Residential." She gestured. "Homes of the senior mages who've escaped their dormitory cells. They must enjoy their privacy."

The coach slowed, turning off the avenue toward a red chapel dome that rose behind a gray stone wall. We stopped outside a barred gate where two bare-skulled acolytes with tall black staves stood guard.

"The lectory." She opened the compartment door. "I must arrange for Mr. Scorth."

"Can't we stop?" I asked her. "If my father and mother are here."

"No time for that." Still she didn't explain. "Later, perhaps, if the archimage allows it."

She walked to the gate.

"I don't like her." Scorth leaned to look back into the compartment, his tawny eyes apprehensive. "Take care of yourself."

The guards challenged her, serpent staves lifted. I couldn't hear what they said, but they scowled at her and scowled at the coach and finally opened the gate, standing aside when she beckoned to Scorth. With an uneasy shrug, he walked through, leaving me uncertain when or if I might see him again.

"An ex-acolyte?" Back in the coach, she frowned at me. "Or how'd he lose his hair?"

I said I didn't know, and asked, "What now?"

"The tower."

I waited silently, but she said no more until we had turned in to another wide avenue that sloped steeply upward. She pointed, and I saw the narrow black column that climbed high above the temple's vast crimson dome.

"The citadel," she said. "Built on a dead volcanic plug and the ridge the glaciers left against it. The river cuts close to make a natural strongpoint."

"I saw it from the river."

"Not that I'm a geologist." She shrugged. "But my father manages a mine out on the wyvern border. I read his books, and I used to ride with him to inspect new prospects."

She turned from me to open the little window in the partition and call something to the mage at the wheel. We climbed the knob to circle the temple square and park in a courtyard beside the tower. She got out again to speak to the guards outside the massive doors before she beckoned me after her.

The guards looked hard at me and waved us on. A silent elevator took us fast to the top landing. I followed her up a narrow stair to her office, a big room with an enormous window that looked down across the docks and the river bend. It had a thin, dusty reek from the moldered documents that cluttered her desk and packed the shelves all around the wall.

She nodded at a chair and tapped a signal bell on her desk. My breath caught when I heard the dry electric hiss and felt the ozone bite. My skin tingled, and the small red globe was throbbing a yard above my head.

"My celestial contact." She was smiling as if in pleasure at my shock. "I call him Xath. He has questions for you."

43

Demon Killer

Waiting for him on the dock when the riverboat came in, she liked
what she saw: a lean, tall man in faded misfits. He looked worn as
his clothing, bronze hair gone shaggy and redder beard long un-
shaven, but he was younger than the mages, with none of their
scarred and pain-drawn austerity.

The actual Nuradoon?

Striding down the gangplank to meet her, he looked as bold as
the werewolf hunter who had flown her across the wyvern border
and taught her how to love. He paused for an instant on the dock, as
if eyeing her with the caution of a hunter stalking a crippled wolf.

After her long exile here among the black-toothed mages and the
silent acolytes, she was happy to meet another unbeliever, a man
who looked still open to emotion. She saw the flash of puzzled admiration in his eyes, and his grasp was warm and strong when he
took her offered hand.

She sensed the wary challenge in him, and a hint of diversion she
might enjoy. She was relieved to be rid of the unicorn trainer. His
hairless scalp betrayed some aborted service to Xath. Half-demo-
nized, perhaps, before he got away. She didn't like his piercing
stare.

In the tower office with her guest, she signaled for Xath and
watched him start and flinch from the red-throbbing demon when it

exploded into the air just above his head. Recovering, he caught his breath and turned angrily to her.

"Harmless," she told him. "So long as you cooperate."

"What does it want from me?"

"Call him Xath," she said. "What he wants is answers. First of all, he wants you to confirm what we've been told: that you are in fact Zorn ir Var, the former rider's oldest son?"

"Just Zorn Var," he said. "The 'ir' is a family title, conferred by the father. Not for me to use until I prove my right—"

The demon pealed impatiently.

"Xath doesn't care for such quibbles. His people are sexless. They don't understand human families. Not that it matters. What he wants is information about the weapon you had with you on the riverboat."

"Weapon?" He shook his head. "I had no weapon."

"An odd piece of broken glass. I believe you had it under your shirt."

"Oh! You mean the fragment of the Dragonshield?"

The demon clicked.

"He wants all you know about it."

"Nothing, really." He spread his open hands. "It seems to have been handed down among the Vars for generations. There's a family legend that an ancestor, a warrior named Nuradoon ir Var, carried it on his campaign against the demons—"

Sharply the red globe pinged.

"We've heard all that," she said. "And repaired the artifact."

She bent across her desk to pick it up. A thick black lens shape. He bent to study it, rubbed his fingers over it, and looked sharply back at her when he found no sign of any break.

"Xath sees what it is. He wants to know what it does."

"Maybe nothing—"

The demon clinked.

"Xath expects additional information." She reached for the artifact and laid it back on her desk. "Come across the hall." She gestured toward an inner door. "We'll find more comfort there."

He followed her into a high-walled room with huge windows looking down across the well-kept lawns and shrubs of the temple square. She beckoned him toward a half circle of big hopper leather chairs around a small table. The demon stayed with him, hissing softly just above his head.

"You'll get used to him." She made a fleeting face at it. "All he wants is honest answers." She gestured at a bar across the room. "What would you like? Apple brandy? Perhaps a dry delta wine?"

"Thanks." He eyed her alertly. "Not now."

"Have you tried redthorn tea?"

He shook his head.

"I hadn't," she said, "not till I got here. I'm from the highlands, and it grows in the delta marshes. I think you'll like it."

She filled two glasses from a steaming urn and came to sit with him at the table. Uneasily he tried the tea. Its crimson hue was a little too much the color of blood, but it had a pleasant, bittersweet tang.

"The tower master's suite." She nodded at the room around them. "A senior in the service, not very happy when they moved him out to make a place for me."

The demon was clicking and chiming again, too near his ear.

"Listen." He set his tea aside. "You're wasting time. I know nothing of any historic Nuradoon, if there ever was a Nuradoon." He glanced up at the buzzing globe and heard it ping as if speaking to him. "I'm no historian," he told it. "No magician. Just a student potter off a little farm on Little River. There's nothing I know—"

It clanged to stop him.

"Really?" She leaned across the table, a glint of malice in her eyes. "He says you have stated that you were this immortal Nuradoon."

"That was a lie."

"Your mistake." She was more amused than angry. "The celestials are honest. They don't expect false statements, or understand them."

He nodded, with an uneasy glance at the demon. "If you'll let me explain—"

The demon plinked and pealed.

"I'll explain." She looked up to click her tongue at it. "They feel injured because we've disappointed them. You saw the shelves and files of old documents in my office across the hall. They're records of those long-ago encounters. Neglected for centuries, and most of them now hard or impossible to read.

"Among other matters, they recorded an agreement with the celestials. The main point was that they would train their human friends in science they hadn't known, and the friends promised to have a lot of gold accumulated to give them when they came back. The mages have remembered a lot of the science—which is their magic. But the rest of the treaty . . ."

Her bare shoulders lifted to a small sardonic shrug, and she sipped her tea with a sharp sidewise glance at him.

"Not that the gold is any great problem. The celestials seized the temple hoards, and now they're collecting on their own. What troubles them is a letter we've found in the files. It's addressed to a woman named Norlanya, who seems to have been my own predecessor. A translator for the celestials."

The demon dropped closer. Listening, he thought.

"It's from her brother, who's fallen out with her and joined the resistance group under Nuradoon ir Bar—he spells it with a *B*. She's still an agent of the demons; she helped negotiate the treaty. He calls her a traitor to the world. Begs her to join Nuradoon.

"He admits that they'd been losing the war. Taking refuge now in the high mountains west. Yet he promises her that Nuradoon will win in the end, with a weapon he calls 'the demon killer.' She must have told the demons nothing about it. We found no reference to it anywhere else in the file.

"But here it is."

She opened a folder on the table to show him two yellowed pages sealed between transparent sheets. The edges had crumbled raggedly, and the corner of one was missing. The script looked strange and the ink had dimmed. Peering at it, he found no words he was sure of.

Brother and sister, a thousand years ago . . .

"Interesting—"

The demon clanged, impatiently, he thought. He gave the ancient pages back to her.

"But what has it got to do with me?"

"Can't you guess?" She looked up to trill something to the demon. "The staff doubts, of course, that any such weapon ever existed. The message was probably a desperate bluff. But the demons want certainty. If any weapon does exist, Xath wants it discovered and destroyed. He requires your help.''

"I can't—"

An imperative clang interrupted him.

"You're the last resort.'' She shook her head, with a small ironic smile. "Everybody else who ever saw the artifact or knew anything about it has been interrogated. Your father and mother, since the mages have them now. The two brothers who broke it. The wife who stole it. Nobody knows anything. Nobody except this Mr. Scorth. He still swears that you're the original Nuradoon.''

"Tell them we were bluffing.''

"Bluffing is something they don't understand.''

"Tell them I know nothing—''

The demon rang, an imperative gong too close to his ear.

"Xath believes Mr. Scorth. He knows you came with him out of the desert, carrying the old helmet and claiming you were Nuradoon. He knows you've been threatening the celestials. He knows you claimed that the artifact—the Dragonshield—would be your magic weapon. And he believes you.''

"Nobody else did.''

The demon pealed again.

"The demons don't lie,'' she said. "They can't. All of them are organs of a single creature, they never had anybody to deceive.''

"I know nothing—''

"Better remember something.'' She smiled as if in secret amusement. "He says you will remain here as my guest until you reveal the secret power of the Dragonshield.''

44

The Silent Mage

A prisoner in the tower, I kept asking Lyrane about my father and mother, about Kye, about Scorth, begging for news of anything at all.

"Whatever you want from Xath, you'll have to earn it." She always answered with the same enigmatic smile. "You can ask for anything you want when Nuradoon's weapon has been discovered and destroyed."

"I don't think he had a weapon . . ."

"Perhaps he didn't." She would shrug as if the Dragonshield didn't matter, not to her. "But you know how Xath feels about uncertainties. You'll be here until the entire truth has been established beyond any question at all."

Seeing no hope of learning any truth about the Shield or Nuradoon, I used to dream of escape, with never any plan that looked possible. The tower was tall. The city of Xath surrounded it. My tiny cell had no window. A mage with a deadly serpent staff stood guard at the elevator door. With the demons everywhere, I knew nowhere to go, even if I did get out.

In many ways, she tried to make my life there endurable. Showing me a little room back at the end of the hall behind her office, she asked if it would do. It was small and bare enough; the mages were taught to scorn luxury. Yet it had a narrow bed, a hard stool and a wooden shelf for a table, even its own bathroom. To me, in comparison to the pallet on the kitchen floor where I had slept while I was a child, it was almost luxurious. She found new clothing for me, boots that fit, a comb, a bar of soap. No razor was allowed, but an acolyte came to shave me. When I wanted exercise, she let me walk the hall.

Ordering our meals, she demanded delicacies from the infidel markets instead of the meager fare of the lectories. The acolyte who cooked and served them had learned his skills as an apprentice chef in the archimage's kitchen. Commonly he brought my trays to the shelf in my cell, but sometimes during an interrogation he spread the meal for both of us in her living room, where the huge window gave me a tantalizing glimpse of the world outside.

The interrogations were harder to endure. The demon always with us, the inquisitions went on hour after hour, day after day, never with any reason or result that I could see. Often in the office, sometimes in her living room, the little crimson globe hummed and whirred above my head, stinging my eyes with its ozone, pinging and clinking and pealing and crackling its signals for her translation.

Suffering through the sessions, I sometimes wondered at her own apparent patience with the demon's insane pursuit of a hopeless truth. The ceaseless repetition of aimless question and meaningless response must have been tedious, yet she never seemed bored. Sometimes I even suspected that she was inventing more questions than the demon did, relieving her own boredom by making me squirm.

From the beginning, they should have known how little the centuries had left for me or any human to know about that first invasion of the demons. They had pored over those scraps of lost history crumbling in the tower files. The had grilled people who knew far more than I did. And they had, of course, studied the artifact itself as they repaired it, exposing it to every test the mages and the demons themselves could devise.

Yet they pressed relentlessly on, probing through all the years of my recollection. They demanded more than I recalled about life with my father and mother and our early years on the farm. They wanted the rules of the solitary games I used to invent for myself and the plans of the little mud Dragonrocks I used to build on the riverbank. They asked for every moment of our donkey trips to trade my mother's pottery in the village, every meeting with every person I had known there.

Bastard seemed to fascinate the demon.

The mages had discovered his finger-marked letter in Miss Penra's trunk. They had questioned her about it, and the demon seemed insanely curious. Who had he been? How had he died? What was the meaning of his name? Why had he wanted to watch Miss Penra walking by the smithy? Why had she always ignored him? Why had he felt the pain expressed in the letter? Why had she never replied, yet saved the letter?

That led them to matters of sex. We humans must have been as incomprehensible to the demons as they were to us. All of them elements of a single sexless entity, they were perplexed by our individual differences and bewildered by our conflicts and emotions. They carried the inquisition far beyond anything related to the Dragonshield or Nuradoon.

I began to feel that I was only a specimen human, impaled under a merciless lens. Once, alone with Lyrane when the acolyte left our lunch trays on her desk, I asked her what made the demons so inquisitive.

"Xath doesn't say." She shrugged. "He never says."

"Have they changed?" I asked her. "Since that last invasion. If they just took the gold then, and carried it away. What's the difference now?"

"They're learning." We were in her big office chamber, and she paused to frown at the tall shelves of black-bound volumes. "They killed the first people and animals they tried to use. Burned or electrocuted them, trying to operate them like meat machines. Getting inside us now, using our own brains and nerves instead of their own energy systems, they get more out of us and do less damage."

She seemed untroubled, but that sent a shudder through me.

"Why do they want to use us at all?"

"Xath never says."

"Do you think . . ." Chilled with the notion, I stopped to search her face. "Do they mean to take over? To stay here when their star moves on?"

"Why would they—" She cut off her question, to give me another sober look. "As a matter of fact, they have considered a permanent presence." She frowned. "I don't know what they'll decide."

I sat staring at her, our lunch forgotten.

"Aren't you human?" Her eyes widened, as if my own shock surprised her. "How far can you go, helping them enslave our world?"

"Zorn, please!" Her voice fell as if my words had hurt. "I'm no monster!"

"If you play demon, you are demon."

"You don't know them." Her tone turned urgent. "They aren't evil, certainly not for the sake of evil. All they want is to stay alive. In any case, they can't possess many of us, or any for long. Not even if they do decide to stay. That's because they were born in the plumes of hot gas and plasma that erupt from their star. Our planet's too dark and cold for them. That's why they love to bathe in fire.

"The most they're considering is leaving a little colony here to prepare for the next passage of their star. A hardship for any who stay. Fatal, I think, unless they spend most of their time out in space, flying closer to our own sun and dropping only now and then to deal with their contacts—"

"Traitors," I muttered. "Their agents will make themselves tyrants. As bad as the demons!"

"Really, my dear!" From anybody else, her soft-voiced protest might have showed affection, but I saw the ironic gleam in her eyes. "They're simple creatures. They didn't know how to lie or cheat. Not till the mages gave them lessons. That's why they need human agents. I'm trying to negotiate payment for what they are taking. Payment in science we can use. I don't feel evil, and I'm doing my best to keep them from causing accidental harm."

"Spreading panic? Burning cities?"

"Accidents have happened because we didn't understand each other." She spread her red-nailed hands. "But most of the harm has been done by the mages, out of their false notion that the creatures want to be worshiped. The sort of thing I'm working to prevent.''

She looked so earnestly innocent that I wanted to believe her, yet the images of Bastard's death and Kye's stifled scream and my father's blind inhuman stare clung like burrs in my mind.

"I understand them," I told her bitterly. "Too well! And I think I understand why they're so bent on finding the weapon. If it does exist, or ever did, it could be a threat to any that stay behind. And you! Working for them, you're another monster!''

"They want to be sure." Resentment had flushed her fair skin, but she was nodding thoughtfully. "They do like certainty.''

Lyrane was not beautiful, not as I had imagined beauty. Larger than Kye, she was athletic rather than dainty. Deliberately, I think, she painted and dressed and perfumed herself to tantalize the mages and torment me. Her allure began to haunt my dreams.

I hated her. However blameless she might feel herself to be, she was the willing agent of the demons, the archimage's tool and now the mistress of the mages. Though her manner to me remained outwardly gracious, I sensed an unfeeling detachment in her probing, as if she saw me as the demon seemed to, a human specimen under study.

The endless interrogation kept shifting from my parents and Bastard and Miss Penra, back to my own emotions and experience. The demon already knew something about human anatomy and the mechanics of reproduction, but they kept pressing me to tell how I had felt and behaved with every woman I had known or seen since I was a child.

Mrs. Emok? I said she had dressed and behaved and spoken just like the village farmers did. My own mother? I had loved her dearly; I still did. The village girls? Some of them had looked pretty, but I had been the exile's son, as coldly avoided as Bastard was. Kye? I'd liked her, maybe loved her, though she had been too deep in grief for her father and her own dead lover to care much for anybody else.

"Xath wants to know what you feel for me."

We were sitting by the desk in her office. The demon hung buzzing above us, its ozone burning my nostrils, that dull red glow pulsing like blood from its small round heart down through its wirelike tendrils. It clicked and ticked and plinked, but I had no way to tell whether the questions really came from it, or if she was inventing them.

I said she was attractive.

How did she attract?

She turned to pose for me, sitting straighter in her chair, slightly smiling, a mocking challenge in her eyes. Looking at the sheen of her bright gold hair, the ivory smoothness of her bare arms, the generous breasts under that sheer blouse, I said she was a woman.

Why was I attracted to a woman?

I said I was a man.

Could I explain that attraction?

Poets had written about it, I said, but I was not a poet.

The demon pealed and Lyrane smirked.

Did I wish to engage in sex with her?

Shaken with confused emotion, with dread of the demon and fury at her and an irrational burst of hot desire, I stammered something incoherent.

The demon pinged.

Why was my face changing color?

I squirmed and clenched my fists, wishing I had some way to smash it. Grinning at me, she trilled and whistled to it. It clicked and ticked and tocked.

Had I ever engaged in the sex act with a woman?

"Not—" Suddenly I couldn't breathe. "Not yet—"

Lyrane laughed.

My heart pounding, hardly aware of what I was doing, I dragged her out of her chair and kissed her red-painted lips. Her nails raked my cheek, but I scarcely felt them. She spat and fought my arms. Amazed at my own sudden joy in rebellion against their ceaseless probing, I snatched her closer, delighting in her hot breath on my face, the hot ripple of her straining muscles, the racing throb of her heart against mine.

I hardly heard the demon's warning roar. Ducking away from the burning tentacles, I pushed her back across the desk, stifling her cries with my mouth on hers. She twisted against me, clawing at my back, but I held her till the tentacles hauled me away.

Fighting free of me, she screamed for it to let me go. It held me, plinking and clinking till she gasped a signal that made it click and vanish. She stood a moment staring at me then, violet eyes wide and darkening. I had torn the blouse off one splendid breast. It was streaked with blood from my face, and I saw the nipple hardening.

"Nuradoon—" I heard an odd catch in her voice. "If you are a man, prove it!"

She moved a little toward me, arms opening. I swept her up and carried her through the open door into the hall. The mage stopped me there, gaping for an instant before he yelled and ran toward us, lifting his black serpent staff.

She twisted in my arms, calling a terse command in her code with the demons. That halted him. I carried her on into her great living room. Shock overtook me there. Appalled by my own mad lust, I stopped and let her down. Beginning to mutter some confused apology, I saw her tearing off what was left of her blood-spotted blouse, sliding out of her skirt. Naked, she stood a moment before me, turning slowly to show her white magnificence.

"If you've never had a woman . . ." I heard no mockery in her soft laugh now. "Here among the mages and the demons, it's too long since I've had a man."

She drew me into her bed and taught me more about sex than I had ever imagined.

Late that night I lay awake and alone again on my own narrow cot, too full of her to sleep. She was seared into me. The hot perfection of her white flesh and her lithe feline power under it, the fragrance of her breath, the tastes of her thrusting tongue and passionate body, a kind of joy that I had never known.

Was I in love?

Or bewitched?

I felt torn between realities. I was still her prisoner, the black-cowled guard with a black serpent staff glaring at me from his station at the elevator when she sent me back to my own tiny cell. Still teasingly secretive, she had told me nothing of my parents or Scorth or Kye. She was still the mistress of the mages and the queen of the demons, still delighting in her strange game with them.

And yet—

The lock on my door clicked softly. A hinge creaked faintly. A hooded mage stood in the open doorway. A silent silhouette against the light beyond, he carried no serpent staff. His face invisible, he lifted a warning finger and beckoned me to go with him.

I pulled my clothing on and followed him out to the elevator. The tower was strangely silent, no guards in sight. The little cage dropped us fast. We found no guards on duty below, none in the anteroom, none at the tower entrance.

Outside, under the moon's hot glare, the mage gestured for silence and beckoned again. I followed again through the tower's crimson shadow to the wide courtyard beyond and heard the soft whicker of a kneeling unicorn.

"Praise the Three!" I recognized the voice of Scorth, and Sharabok's whicker. "They're flying with us tonight!"

45

The Secret of the Shield

Sharabok bent his folded wing. I climbed into the saddle, Scorth into the trainer's seat. He sang a soft command. Sharabok lurched and lifted, ran back through the shadow of the tower, spread his wings to clear a hedge. We pounded down a moonlit avenue, soared out of the sleeping city.

I called against the rushing wind, "Did you see my father? My mother and Kye?"

"Nobody." I saw a dismal shrug. "Nothing."

"But Lyrane promised us—"

"Your lady friend?" He twisted in the seat to glance back at me, his face still hidden under the loose black cowl. "Her promises!"

"Do you know where my father is?"

"Yonder."

He turned to gesture at a long, dark building with a high wall around it, already far below and slipping back behind us.

"The Grugarn Lectory. Once, in fact, it was a lectory, a training school for initiate acolytes. A special prison now, for special enemies of Xath. Your good parents are probably really there, but I was locked in a solitary cell till your girlfriend got me out."

He muttered the "girlfriend" with ironic emphasis and leaned again to croon to Sharabok. Soon over the river, we flew west low above it, into the dark-mottled heart of the sinking moon. With no visible joy in our freedom, he sank into a mute black huddle.

Murmuring sometimes to Sharabok, he said nothing more to me till we had come down in the red-dyed dawn on a long sandbar. Sharabok unsaddled, he peered from his black cowl at me.

"What did you do to your woman?"

"No more than she wanted. Not that she's mine."

Still filled with too much emotion, that was all I wanted to say.

"Enough, I guess." His eyes were invisible, but I could imagine his squint of knowing calculation. "Enough to make her get me out of prison, get Sharabok saddled and ready, and clear the guards out of our way. If you'll forgive me, I can't help wondering why."

"I don't know why."

"You don't?" A skeptical snort. "Or why she gave us the Dragonshield?"

That took my breath. "You have the Shield?"

Silently he dug it out of a saddlebag, tied as it had been in the same worn leather pouch.

"Hold it up," he told me. "Look through it at the moon."

Its slick black curve seemed opaque as ever. When I tried to study it in the crimson dusk, it looked unchanged: a thick little lens shape of something like black glass, opaque as a slab of iron. I frowned at him.

"Try again. Longer."

I held it to my eye a full minute, and still saw nothing.

"Keep looking."

I kept it lifted toward the moon.

"Enough," he said at last. "Look again."

I found it covered now with fine red lines glowing through the black. A map of the continent. Sharply accurate, it showed the long bends of Dragon River, the Green and the Little, even the broken track of dry Wind River. There were white-shining points for Targon and Dorth, blue-gray shadings for the highlands, brighter blues for the Black Rock and Wolf's Head ranges, brighter color still for the higher Dragons.

"Odd." The cowl moved to his shaking head. "Sunlight brings nothing out. It takes the red moon, which must mean it was made to be ready when the demons returned. Do you see that small green star?"

I found the bright green point close to the far west coast, glowing against the deeper blues of the highest Dragons. He was staring from under the hood when I looked back at him.

"We're to follow the map," he said. "If you think you can trust your lady friend—"

"I don't," I told him. "She's with the demons and the mages."

"She seems to trust you." The cowl lifted and fell to his shrug. "She says they've found evidence of some lost weapon that Nuradoon never used."

"If he had it—" I shivered from all I recalled of my time in the tower "—why didn't he hit them then?"

"Who knows?" Again the cowl shrugged. "But your girl says the demons are convinced that it still exists. They think the map was made to guide people to it. They want us to search."

"Why us?"

"Your girl says they tried and never got there. The spot's high in the central Dragons. Wyvern and actual dragons are said to den in the peaks around it. Altitude too high for unicorns. A few explorers have tried on foot and found the going no better for men. Most of them never got back."

"If the demons and mages and explorers couldn't reach it, how can we?"

"I asked your girl." With a sardonic grunt, he turned to peer back down the dark river the way we had come. "She says the demons know you claimed to be the true Nuradoon. If the Shield's yours, if its magic's real, they think it can get you there."

"What do you believe?"

He shrugged. I couldn't see his shadowed face.

"You must have got close to that indicated point," I pressed him. "You and my father, chasing the wyvern queen. What do you think of the odds?"

"Not good." The irony gone, his voice had slowed and fallen. "We had gone as far as Sharabok and Zeldar could take us. I saw the queen fly into a gap in the higher summits beyond the glacier. Ahead of me on Zeldar, your father tried to follow. And something—something hit us."

I waited while he turned to look at the dark-scarred dome of the half-set moon.

"Something." His shoulders lifted under the cowl. "Something more than altitude and cold. Your father and Zeldar were higher. Closer to it. It hit them harder. Knocked them down.''

"You felt it?"

"Terror," he muttered. "If you can imagine a jolt of sheer terror. A paralyzing jolt, with no cause I could see. It must have struck from somewhere ahead. Out of those peaks where the wyvern had gone."

"If it happened to my father—" wondering, I frowned into his hooded face "—he never spoke about it."

"Not to me." The cowl shrugged again. "Not to your mother. Maybe he didn't remember—he was out of his head for days, you know, with the fever the wolf bite gave him. I don't think he was sure afterward, just what he'd felt and what he'd dreamed. You can't imagine . . ."

He cocked his hooded head to look into my face, perhaps to see what I thought of him.

"A shock of sheer fear, as hard and sudden as a lightning bolt. Something I never understood." He seemed to shudder. "We'd lived in danger, your good father and I. We knew how to deal with anything we could see. But that! It could freeze a man to ice . . ."

His voice fell to a whisper, almost as if he were speaking to himself.

"I don't like remembering." He paused uncomfortably. "Not that I was ever a daring man, or wanted to be. I've always looked to saving my own hide. But I knew your father's courage, and I saw it broken there. I saw panic in the way he was leaning to turn Zeldar back before they fell.

"Once . . ." He shook his head and caught a long breath, muttering now. "Once I tried to get the opinion of a Realist doctor. All I got was a narrow-eyed stare. I think he took me for a coward, inventing excuses for abandoning your father.

"We did try to reach them when we got able to move. Sharabok and I. But that—that something stopped us again. Call it anything. Call it magic, if you want."

"I've seen dark magic," I told him. "A mage throwing his serpent staff."

"It happened." He seemed faintly grateful. "I don't know how."

"A weapon, maybe? If there is a weapon." Wondering, I stared past him into the crimson glitter on the black river. "Something put there to guard the pass?"

"And the wyvern's den?" Again he seemed sardonic. "A nest of dragons? Would they have weapons?"

"What else?"

"That's what your girl and her devils want to know." He paused to peer from under the hood. "If you're Nuradoon enough to find out for them. She seemed to think you'd take the chance."

Still not sure what I felt about her, I tried not to care. In the balance against everything else, my tangled feelings were nothing at all, yet she haunted me. Staring again at the bloodred river, I wondered again at the strange game she played with the mages and the demons, hated her again, longed for her in spite of myself.

"I don't trust her," I said. "I have no reason to trust her."

"So?" His grin grew sardonic. "Want to give it up? Turn back? Throw the Shield away?"

I shook my head.

"So!" He shrugged as if pleased. "That's that."

I dragged the saddle into the mudbrush thicket above the bar. He walked Sharabok down to the edge of the water and let him kneel to drink. When Scorth took off the hood, I saw that his head was dyed red as a mage's. He waded out to scrub his scalp and bent to drink from his cupped hands. Leading Sharabok farther up the bank, he left him to browse in a stand of silver cedar. We spread the saddle blankets at the edge of the thicket and slept till Sharabok woke us, singing.

"Somebody following." Scorth sat up to peer into the lifting river mists. "Your girl and her demons? Maybe watching to see where we're going or what happens to us. We'd better hide till night."

We dragged our blankets out of sight and watched through the brush till we saw a black unicorn flying up the middle of the river with two riders. Could one of them be Lyrane? Or Kye, perhaps, if the demons were still using her?

Flying low but keeping to the middle of the river, they were too far off to let us make them out. The unicorn kept turning its head to search the banks, neighing and neighing again. Calling, I thought. Sharabok kept silent.

"Your lady friend?" Whispering, Scorth squinted uneasily at me. "Still a riddle to me. A woman here in the holy city, where women are poison. What's her power to do all she's done?"

My emotions ebbing, I felt readier to talk about her now.

"The mages hate her," I said, "but the demons don't talk to men. She's the link. I doubt that the mages trust her. Maybe not the demons either. A dangerous game, but she seems to love it."

"And love you?"

"I don't think so."

The unicorn flew on out of sight up the river. When it seemed safely gone, Scorth found food for us in the saddlebags and suncorn to fill Sharabok's nosebag. He carried that into the thickets. I made a little fire to heat greenthorn tea. We filled ourselves with bread and ham and dried fruit, and watched the river.

In the middle of the afternoon Sharabok neighed another warning. Hiding in the thicket, we watched two more unicorns coming up the river. They were flying low and wide apart to let the riders search both banks with binoculars. When the nearest passed, we saw that its solitary rider was a mage in black.

Scorth whispered, "What do you think?"

I could only shake my head.

They went on upriver. When we could relax again, Scorth explored the saddlebags. There was another meal for us, he said, but nothing else for Sharabok. We made hot tea and he doled out a little more bread and hopper ham. We took turns on watch till the sun went down and gray dusk thickened into another bloodred dawn.

The slick curve of the Shield had gone blank again when I looked at it, but the map came back when I held it up to the climbing moon. Scorth called Sharabok out of the cedars, and we flew west again high above a dark and empty-seeming world. Twice we saw fires blazing in the clusters of distant lights that must have been villages. The mages had burned them, I thought, to welcome their guests.

Near midnight, the moon enormous at the zenith and looking close enough to touch, we left the red-glinting river and circled north of Targon and Dorth toward the scarp. We landed in the highlands at moonset, on a deserted strip Scorth said smugglers had cut.

Unsaddling, we heard banshees howling in the forest around us. Watching us, perhaps, for the werewolves and the mages or even the demons? We had no way to know. There was good water in an icy stream that ran by the strip. With no suncorn left, Sharabok could only graze the summer weeds.

"He has to eat," Scorth said. "For energy to fly."

We took turns watching and sleeping through another everlasting day. Sharabok whickered once to warn us when he sensed another unicorn, stood for a moment with his ears tipped to listen, and trotted into the iron oaks out of sight. We hid until he sang to tell Scorth that the searchers had gone on.

I slept once more while Scorth watched. He woke me from a frightful dream. Lyrane was singing to me in the unicorn language, trying to lure me back to the tower. I ran from her, following the Shield toward that green star. It had risen now, burning in the moon-red sky. She overtook me, her nude body streaked with my blood. My own mad lust drove me to take her in my arms. She changed when I touched her, changed into a shaggy she-wolf, ripping at me with red-stained claws, snarling and slashing with bright black fangs.

I thanked Scorth for shaking me and walked down to the stream for a drink. The sun was still high, but I didn't try to sleep again.

Sharabok whickered hungrily when the sun was setting, but we had nothing for him. With a lift of his horn that seemed philosophic, he knelt for the saddle. The map appeared again when I held the Shield to moonlight, but the scale had changed.

Dorth and Targon had vanished, with all the east half of the continent. The west half was enlarged, and a line of fine white points had appeared. They ran on west from where we were, marking out a trail across the highlands and into the foothills of the Dragons and up through the higher valleys toward that green star, brighter now.

We flew all night, though Sharabok was tiring. The moon climbed again behind us, blazed huge and hot and red above us, sank ahead. The rugged landscape lifted under us, sloping up toward the Dragons. The air grew colder. With no flight leathers, I shivered in the saddle, though the moon's radiation saved us from frostbite.

We came down at moonset to let Sharabok drink and rest and graze. He found pools of meltwater, but the rising sun showed only naked boulders and scattered clumps of a wiry thornbrush he couldn't eat. After a few hours we went on again by daylight, flying low over rocks and ice toward the snow-crowned Dragons.

The map dimmed and changed again, to show only the lower ranges we still must cross and the lofty summits that cradled the green marker. The line of tiny white dots still traced a path for us to follow.

Sharabok had to labor in the thinner air here. We came down twice to let him drink and rest. Water enough had trickled down from the snows, but ice and rocks grew nothing he could graze. I heard banshees wailing the last time we lifted, and saw Scorth shudder.

Noon had passed when we landed at the mouth of a canyon with sheer black walls and a mountain of blue glacier ice at its head. A thin stream of white meltwater came foaming down it, but Sharabok made no move to drink when Scorth pulled the saddle off. He stood trembling instead, breathing hard, his bright horn sagging toward the barren rocks.

"So here we are." Scorth gave me his most innocent baby smile. "What now, Nuradoon?"

I'd never felt less like the real Nuradoon, whoever he had been. Reeling with hunger and exhaustion, and shrinking from the bitter wind, I wanted no more than a hot shower and hot food and a bed.

"We have to play the game." I tried to grin. "Sharabok doesn't look able to take us home."

"Or anywhere." He squinted up the canyon at that towering glacier wall. "We're afoot. With rocks and ice against us, and bluffs too high to climb."

I slid the Shield out of its pouch and found our route ahead magnified again. Brighter now, the white dots traced a way around the canyon, across the ice field above it and through a narrow pass in the snowcapped summits ahead, finally into a circular valley with the green star burning at its center.

Scorth studied it.

"Your father and I got right about there." He pointed at the glacier above us. "I saw the wyvern queen not far ahead of him. She had disappeared into the pass before Zeldar was knocked down. Your father had got back off the ice and down into the valley behind us before your mother and I picked him up.

"So?" Doubtfully he frowned at me. "What do you think?"

We were both shaking with cold, teeth chattering. The air burned my nostrils when I gasped it in, yet I saw no choice. With very little hope, I had to play Nuradoon.

"I think we've outrun the mages," I told him. "I can't imagine them here."

"Can we go on?" He blinked at me, miserably uncertain. "Afoot? With next to no food? Without mountain gear? Already frozen?"

"I think we have to try."

We cut the saddle blankets to make them into coats belted with straps we cut from the saddle, cut the smaller saddlebags into caps with holes for our faces, made mittens of the empty sacks that had held the bread and ham. With the remaining scraps of those in our pockets, we started climbing a boulder slide, searching for the white-dotted trail.

Sharabok lifted his head to whicker after us. Scorth turned to sing something to him, and he neighed a forlorn farewell. I heard banshees howling as we climbed. The boulders were huge blocks of fallen stone, most of them impossible to climb. Gravel slid as we tried for ways around them. The slope went up forever, and the moon was rising before we reached the canyon rim.

Looking back in its crimson dawn, I found Sharabok alone and tiny far below. He had wandered a little from where we left him, looking for grass he would never find, but I thought he had seen me when he raised his head as if for a neigh I didn't hear.

Shivering in the wind, we ate a few more morsels of our bread and ham. Rolled together in a hollow for the warmth we got from each other, we tried to rest. Bathed in the unicorn pungency that clung in the blankets, I slept a little and shuddered again through that nightmare dream of the naked and alluring Lyrane who became a savage she-wolf when I touched her.

The bloated moon was high. We sucked at bits of ice to moisten our dry tongues, and again we climbed. Scorth said the moon now warmed us better than the sun, but I felt no difference. All the rest of that savage crimson night we climbed and slid and climbed again across the slippery ridges and crevasses of the glacier toward that far mountain gap.

I had learned to ignore the banshees, but once when we had stopped for breath, Scorth jogged my elbow and pointed into the lurid sky. The moon's glare had drowned the stars, and I saw nothing except its dark-pocked disk till he pointed to a dim black shadow floating over the peaks. Great black wings that soared and circled and finally dived to pass slowly low above us.

"A wyvern," he whispered. "The wyvern queen."

We battled on. My makeshift mittens were worn-out and gone by then, and my numb hands bled and stuck when I fell and had to grab at the ice. The queen followed us, shrieking like some fiend out of Xath's inferno. The moon was setting before we got off the ice.

A dreadful chorus of werewolves waited for us on the rocks, howling louder than the wyvern. Bruised from all our falls and groggy with fatigue and cold, I crouched away from their black-shining fangs and the bellow of the diving wyvern.

"Now, Nuradoon!" I saw Scorth's hopeless shrug, heard a sardonic mockery rasping in his whisper. "Time, I think, to try the magic of your shield!"

I fumbled with dead fingers for the pouch beneath my shirt, pulled the drawstring with my teeth, and nearly dropped the slick black lens before I could flash it toward the wolves. As if struck by some magic force I had never imagined, they yelped and whimpered and cowered away.

"The holy Three!" Crouching from the wind, Scorth blinked unbelievingly. "Praise the sacred Three!"

Slinking only a few yards back, the wolves turned on us, baying again, black fangs grinning. They kept us company as we staggered into the narrow gap between the snowcapped cliffs, wary of the Shield but snapping and snarling as close as they dared.

A few hundred yards off the ice, we huddled away from them in a narrow hollow under a cliff, too far spent to go farther. We chewed the last of our bread and ham, tried to suck at chips of ice that burned our mouths, and took turns trying to rest and flashing the Shield at our black-grinning company.

I dozed again through the returning nightmare, always more vivid and dreadful. Laughing at my terror, Lyrane drew me back into her bed. Her arms were around me, her hot mouth on mine again before her teeth became the bitch wolf's fangs and her red talons tore at my flesh.

Mercifully Scorth woke me again, and we limped on into the gorge with our snarling crew. White sunlight was burning now on the high snows above us, but pitiless night still filled the gorge. The sheer black cliffs were alive with echoes of the wailing wolves.

We saw no more of the wyvern queen, and midway into the pass something began happening to the wolves. They still growled around us, but none ran ahead. Crouching farther from the Shield, they dropped away one by one till we came out alone into the open.

The sun was gone again by then. The rising moon had flooded the vast flat plain ahead, though we were still in frigid shadow. The map in the Shield lit when I held it to the crimson sky. The bright-dotted trail ended where we stood, and the star at the center of that great valley had changed. It was now the green-glowing image of a windowless tower, topped with a needle-sharp spire.

"The wyvern tower." He seized my arm, hoarsely whispering. "There's a legend about it that old Nanda remembered hearing when she was a child. A fortress against the demons, that Nuradoon built. The first Nuradoon. The demons never took it, and he lived there till he died, after they'd gone. It's abandoned to the wyvern now, if you want to believe the yarn.''

"The Shield was made to show the way there.'' Uncertain what to believe, I stared at the map and stared at him. "But only when the demon moon is in the sky. If there is a weapon, it could be there in the tower.''

"Or it couldn't.'' Grimly he shook his head at me. "Still a long way to go, for the shape we're in.''

That sheer-walled gorge must have been cut by grinding ice when a glacier filled that great bowl, but we found no ice in it now. Limping out into the open, we found ourselves in a vast volcanic caldera, ringed with black cliffs that towered toward slopes of blinding snow. The floor itself was nearly free of snow, but scattered with odd black cinder piles that looked like the mounds of giant moles.

Climbing farther up a little cinder hill in the mouth of the gorge, we found the tower. Black and solitary, it was still miles away across the crater floor, pointing its spire into the bloodred sky. Not far from its foot, I saw something move.

And terror struck me.

46

The Dragon Pack

More agony than merely fear, that wave of terror possessed me totally. I might have screamed if it had left me able. All I wanted was to get away, to run, to hide, to cover myself, yet I had lost the will to move. Paralyzed, conscious of nothing else, I slid back down that cinder mound.

And out of the terror.

For a time, that was all I knew or needed to know. Faintly I recall the gritty feel of the cinders under me, somehow warm, a bed that let me relax. I remember hearing Scorth's anxious outcry, too faint and far away to matter. I remember fleeting dreams, when I thought I was a child again.

I saw my father's sun-streaked beard and heard his booming laugh and felt the iron strength of his great hand when he leaned off Sharabok to haul me into his arms for that ride over Dragonrock. I heard my mother's hurt voice when she snatched me back from the bank of the white-foaming river before I could jump. I saw Bastard again, standing stubborn against the red-skulled mage, and watched that black serpent staff squeeze his life out.

Later, Scorth was bending over me, calling my name and calling me Nuradoon, his cold fingers lifting my eyelids to see if I was alive. I tried to wink and lay there, caring only that the terror had gone. It had left me drained and aching. I needed to rest, needed the warmth of the cinders. I was alive again. I slept.

Later again, he woke me. He helped when I tried to move, helped me slide farther down the mound. I sat there a long time, still weak and sick, gasping the icy air, staring at him and staring up at the sheer black canyon walls and the narrow strip of indigo sky, trying to get back into myself.

More cautious than I, he had escaped with only a jolt.

"Keep your head down," he warned me, when he thought I was able to understand. "What hit us was what hit your father and me. It killed Zeldar. I think some kind of radiation that came from the eyes of the dragon."

"Dragon?" I felt a vague astonishment. "What dragon?"

"You didn't see it?"

"Something . . ." I stared at him stupidly, trying to remember. "Something was moving near that tower. You call it a dragon?"

"What else?" He shrugged. "The legends speak of dragons, and this is their country." He nodded at a long ridge of boulders fallen on the edge of the mound. "I've been looking out between the rocks. I've never seen a dragon, but it looked big enough. It has the shape of a worm. Or perhaps a caterpillar. Bright and round and black, larger than you ever tried to imagine, crawling on legs so short and thick, they're more like claws. Jaws as wide as its head. Two big bulges that look like eyes. At least till they open. Only to narrow slits, but purple fire shines out of them then. That's what hit us, that purple light."

He stopped to scowl at me.

"Do dragons fly?"

I didn't know.

"It does have wings." He had lost his saddlebag cap, and his hairless scalp was still faintly stained with the crimson dye. He shook his head now, yellow eyes narrowed. "Or organs shaped like wings. But not, I think, for flight. It's too big to fly."

I felt too slow and dull to wonder.

"Reflectors, maybe?" he added. "They seemed to be lifting above the eyes and cupping toward us before I ducked behind the cinders. Maybe to focus the radiation on us."

I simply sat there, my mind as numb as my body, not yet recovered enough to be amazed at dragons or anything else. He stood a moment frowning at me, and clambered back over the boulders to peep out again.

"I was looking for a way across the crater." He turned to frown uncertainly at me. "If you're able to go on."

"We must." I sat kneading my dead hands. "The Shield was guiding us toward the tower. We might find the weapon there. If we can get past the dragon."

"You can." His squinted grin seemed warily cynical. "If you're really Nuradoon."

Though our hoax was his own invention, he had made those jabs at me till they had begun to seem more than merely ironic. I wondered if he was really aiming them at himself because he was still afraid to believe the old hero's spirit had really been reborn in me.

Life seeped slowly back to wake my dazed brain and relax my stiffened muscles. I stretched my arms and legs, stood up when I could, and limped off the cinder pile to join him.

"Careful," he said, "if you want to look. The thing's behaving like a watchdog. It has turned away from us now to follow something in the sky. Something I haven't found. Keep low. Duck if it turns back toward us."

I raised my head enough to see the nearest cinder heaps.

"The mounds are warm," I said. "Is the old volcano still alive?"

"Could be." A doubtful shrug. "Though the tower must have stood where it is the last thousand years. I see a lot I don't understand. The mounds, and those farther hills." He nodded at them. "Or are they pyramids?"

Uneasily I raised my head for a better view. Too far off for my eyes to measure, they looked immense. Too large, I thought, for anything artificial, yet too cleanly shaped for any sort of natural formation.

"A riddle to me." He scowled at them again. "Some of them

shine like precious metal. They all stand in line. Are the dragons here to guard them?''

The dragon's head was still lifted away from us, and I risked a longer look. The line of pyramids ran straight toward the tower. The closest and smallest had the yellow gleam of new gold. The next, somewhat taller, was silver-gray. Another, even larger, had the greenish brown of weathered copper. The next, an actual mountain, had the darker brown of rusted iron.

''Giants, do you think?'' He stood blinking at me. ''Mining these mountains? What do you think?''

I still felt too heavy and dull to think, yet I tried to fan a spark of improbable hope. If Nuradoon's mythic weapon did exist and if he had left it here in the tower, if the mere threat of its use had been enough to drive the demons off the planet, I knew we had to reach it.

If we could.

Trapped there in the mouth of the gorge, I still felt weak and vaguely sick from shock, giddy from hunger and thirst. Dragons, pyramids, the wyvern tower: they seemed more dream than real. When I heard the clink of falling water drops, I was slow to believe my ears.

''Thank the holy Three!''

I heard Scorth's hoarse whisper and saw him stumbling around the rock pile. He found tiny pools on the rocks where water had trickled down from ice or snow the sun had thawed on the cliffs above. We knelt to lick enough to wet our throats, and he climbed back to peer again between the boulders.

''Yonder!'' He ducked back, with a gesture at the sky. ''That's what the dragon was watching.''

A great black-winged wyvern, when I found it soaring over the white summits beyond the tower. We huddled lower behind the rock pile, watching. Gliding lower, it made a slow circle of the crater rim. Approaching us, it went out of sight beyond the cliffs and appeared again when it came overhead.

''Riders!'' he breathed. ''Did you see?''

''Who could tame a wyvern?''

''The mages did,'' he said. ''I don't know how they do it, but one has been seen riding a wyck, flying back out of the wilderness to lead the raiding werewolves.''

We crouched lower, afraid to move.

"This is a female." He shaded his eyes to look. "The same queen, I think, that your father and I chased into the Dragons back before you were born."

She passed almost over our heads. Doll-sized on her black immensity, two riders sat in a boxlike saddle secured on her back with some kind of cinch or straps I couldn't make out. Both wore brown flight leathers, but one was cowled in black. I saw the glint of sun on glass as they turned away from us to scan the line of pyramids, but I couldn't make their faces out.

We saw the wyvern well enough. She had a kind of majesty from the clean-lined power of her body, and she was all deadliness. Her talons, long and cruel and black, curled now and drawn behind her in flight. Her fangs, shining black and curved to kill, grinning from out of monstrous jaws wide enough to swallow a unicorn foal. Her eyes, green and strange when the great head swung to search the gorge where we lay.

I held my breath, and she didn't see us.

"The eternal Three!" I heard Scorth catch his breath when she had vanished above the northward cliffs. "Still with us."

"Are they predators?" I asked him. "What is there large enough for them to prey on?"

"Sea creatures," he said. "Sailing up the west coast, the old explorers found no place for a settlement. Only a thin strip of rainless desert between the mountains and the sea. Nothing grows there, but sea creatures come to calve and breed on the beaches. Some of them gigantic, but not fierce enough to keep the wyvern off their calves.

"The explorers saw the wyvern diving to snatch them up. Fighting one another for hunting territory. And perhaps for mates and denning spaces in the high Dragons. That's probably what the fangs and claws were evolved for. Wyvern against wyvern!"

We followed the queen and her riders around the great caldera and around again, spiraling lower and finally toward the tower. At last they dropped out of sight somewhere near it. Scorth raised his head for a better look.

"The dragon's moving again," he said. "Turning back toward the tower." He blinked inquiringly at me. "Your chance to play Nuradoon—if you want the risk."

I didn't. What I really wanted was no more than comfort and food and a drink of good water, but I clambered unsteadily to my feet.

"Nobody's coming with a hot lunch for us." I tried to grin, tried to play the part. "We can't go back. Nuradoon or not, we've got to push ahead."

We climbed the cinder pile. From the top, I had a better view of the tower. Black from all the centuries of weathering, narrow and round and tapered, it had no openings I could see. The dragon was crawling back toward it, a lumbering dark worm shape almost as large as it was. I couldn't find the wyvern. Hidden, perhaps, beyond a cinder hill.

Naked to the dragon's killing eye if it discovered us, we slid down the mound and tried to run for the nearest shelter we saw ahead, a narrow valley between the cinder ridges. A dozen steps and we had to stop, panting hard in the thin and bitter air. A little breath recovered, we stumbled into the cover of the hill and worked our way around it to that gold pyramid.

"Actual gold!"

Three times as tall as we were, it was built of massive rectangular blocks laid in precisely regular courses. Unfinished, the outside layer climbed hardly halfway to the peak. Scorth found his knife and scratched a few yellow flakes from one great block.

"Real gold!—thousands of tons!" He blinked in astonishment. "To bribe the demons?"

I thought not. Owning it, the demons would never need to keep the mages scrabbling to squeeze coins and jewelry from all their converts to Xath. The pyramids, however, were not our problem now. When our breath had slowed, we limped on toward another cinder mound that might hide us on our way to the next pyramid, the huge pile of dark-tarnished silver.

The going was hard. Weak and worn and cold as we were, every slope became a daunting mountain. Each pyramid was larger than the last, farther away and farther around. Sometimes we had to crawl on hands and knees to keep out of view in the gaps between them. Always I had to fight the yearning just to lie there and rest.

The trek took forever. The heatless sun dragged across the sky. The moon's lurid dome lifted over the peaks behind us. Our shifting shadows became scarlet monsters, and the moon had cleared the peaks behind us before we had to leave the cover of the iron pyramid. The tower was still a long mile ahead across the red-lit cinder plain, tall and black and strange, pointing like a warning finger into the blood-colored sky.

"What is it?" Staring, Scorth shaded his eyes against the burning moon. "A ship?"

Impossible, I thought. A friend of my father's at the Institute had dreamed of airships, but his little models had never flown. As far as I knew, the demons had come from their red moon with no ships at all. The tower was smoothed and curved as if for flight, but it loomed so huge and high that I couldn't imagine any force lifting it.

Yet what else?

With nothing more to shield us, we stopped behind the last ledge of huge, dark-rusted ingots to recover breath and nerve. I was asleep, dreaming I lay again on my pallet on the kitchen floor, waiting for Father to kindle the cooking fire for breakfast, when Scorth groaned and rose.

"Now, Nuradoon?"

Too used up to wonder whether he meant to mock me or himself, I reeled back to my feet. We limped on, out into the open. Before we had gone a dozen yards, a raucous bellow froze me. When I found life enough to turn my head, I saw the wyvern queen diving out of the scarlet gloom above the iron pyramid.

With no cover, we could only stand where we were. Enormous eyes glaring down, she swept low over us. Seen close, she was monstrous as the demons pictured in my old book of legends, her long body scaled like a snake's, her featherless wings slick black leather. Her eyes were a livid yellow-green, lidded with thick black shields that shaped them like stubby arrows.

I thought she had already seen us. Perhaps she had, because her cruel black talons had hooked and spread as if to snatch us up. But the black wings spread to lift her. With a grace that seemed impossible for anything so large, she rose and slowed and perched like a bird on the tower, great black talons gripping two thick fins projecting from the spire.

The saddle box was gone from her back.

"Our friendly mages?" Scorth breathed. "What became of them?"

We stood there, afraid to move and understanding nothing. Shifting on her perch, she shrieked again and bent her armored head to stare down across the cinder fields. She would certainly see us if we tried to go on. I looked uncertainly at Scorth—and forgot about her.

I felt the cinders quiver under us. Looking at Scorth, I saw the dread on his grimy baby face and saw him pointing at the ridge beyond the pyramid. The dragon was coming over it. Still far away, gleaming dully under the moon. Clumsy as it seemed on the heavy claws that were also its multiple legs, it came fast.

The great jaws yawned open, the gigantic teeth glinting like polished metal. Perhaps the wyvern had been screaming to set it upon us. I don't think it had sensed us, however, because it wasn't coming directly at us. Trying to balance the risk of running for cover against the risk of standing still, I stared at Scorth and saw him pointing again across the cinder slopes.

I saw nothing, but I heard a strange, unceasing boom that seemed to come from somewhere under us. The ground shook, and that booming roar swelled louder. Deeper than the rumble of summer thunder, it became a kind of moan and sank to something deeper than sound.

An earthquake?

A new eruption of the old volcano?

Too much was happening. Weak and reeling, far beyond exhaustion, I didn't want to care. Yet I had to care. Beyond the approaching dragon, I saw a cinder cloud climbing, a new mound building. The ground heaved up. A monstrous black shape heaved out of it.

Another giant black worm, and not the last. Behind it, the whole ridge was suddenly alive. A score of black plumes erupted into the crimson moonlight. Dark, gigantic worms exploded from the cinders. A phalanx of dragons, they all came at us, steel teeth gleaming red as blood.

"Freeze!" Scorth rasped. "Maybe they won't see us."

I stood fast, trying to hope, knowing I had no time for hope. The whole world shook to that subsonic vibration. The voices of the dragons, speaking through their native stone? Ahead of the dragon pack, a new mound grew. Another huge black worm crawled out and stopped on top of it, twisting its monstrous head as if uncertain where to go.

The wyvern's shriek cut through the thunderous rumble under us. The dragon slid off its mound, slithering toward the tower. Turning on her perch, she flapped her great black wings and bellowed again.

Scorth caught my arm and stood a moment peering at me wordlessly, the look on his grimy blue baby face a queer mix of wonder and terror. Gasping for breath, he gulped and finally found his voice.

"Your great moment, Nuradoon!"

I stood there, stunned for a moment, gazing at the moon's blood-colored gleam on those great steel teeth, dully wondering what he meant. He hauled again at my arm, and I fumbled clumsily under my saddle-blanket coat for the Shield. Before my numb fingers found it, the dragon had stopped. Its armored eyes came open. I had time to see the widening slits of purple fire.

And then, for the second time, I felt that deadly sledge of something worse than terror.

47

Nuradoon

Scorth had snatched my arm when he saw the monster's eyes begin to open. We went down together in the little hollow where we stood. That paralyzing radiation only touched us, but the cinder beds still quaked and moaned beneath us. I heard the wyvern's evil shriek, heard Scorth's frantic gasp:

"If you are really Nuradoon . . ."

I heard him. I knew what he meant. I saw the Shield still clutched in my frozen hand. The crimson-lined map was gone. An image of the tower filled the whole face of it, glowing brightly green. I tried to raise it, but my arm was dead.

"Nuradoon . . . " His breathless whisper became a prayer. "Nuradoon!"

Fighting that paralysis, I listened to the wyvern shrieking, listened to the cinders grating under the crawling dragon, listened to the muffled thunder of their voices underground—if that groaning thunder really was the dragons speaking. And I bent all my will to move that dead arm.

It tingled. It jerked, almost with a life of its own. Slowly it lifted.

I flashed the Shield toward the dragon phalanx—and heard a breathless stillness. The grating of the cinders stopped, and the roaring under us. The quaking ceased. The wyvern screamed once more, and even it was still.

"The Three!" Scorth whispered. "They love you, Nuradoon!"

I breathed again, and tried to stand. The loose cinders shifted underfoot, but he caught my arm to steady me and I kept the Shield shining toward the dragons. They all had halted where they were. Those purple-glaring eyes had closed. The wyvern queen had vanished from her perch on the tower.

I just stood there. Groggy from hunger and the fatigue of all our sleepless treks, I had to wonder what was real. The red-lit plain, the snow-crowned summits around it, the tower and the wyvern and the frozen dragons, the great metal pyramids behind us; for a moment they were all fantastic illusion.

Yet the numbing cold was real, the bite of the wind on my stiffened face, the dry rasp in my throat when I breathed. Scorth's hand was real, shivering on my arm. His startled gasp was real.

Turning, I saw the foremost dragon moving again, coming at us. "Stop it!" he begged me. "Stop it if you can."

Stiffly, only half-alive, I forced my tingling arm higher and turned the Shield as if it had been a signal light. The dragon came grinding on. But more slowly, I thought, those dreadful eyes still veiled.

"Nuradoon!"

I heard Scorth's hoarse appeal, but I knew I would never be any kind of Nuradoon. Any magic working here had been in the Shield, not in me. With nothing more I knew to do, I was still too faint from shock to do anything at all. We could only stand and watch the dragon until it had come so near that I felt the heat of its armored head and coughed from its burnt-sulphur stink.

What Realist, I wondered, could ever hope to understand it?

A monstrous riddle, its black enormous bulk filled half the scarlet sky. Its steel teeth shone red in the moonlight. Bright and bare, they had no lips to cover them. They were made, I imagined, to eat their way through solid rock, but why? What sort of worm could inhabit living stone?

Scorth was dragging at my arm again, but at last the dragon stopped, only a few yards away. Its eyes were still shut—if those blazing slits were eyes of any kind—but I felt that it was surveying us. It rumbled suddenly, a strange deep, solemn sound, very faint at first, that rose to drumming thunder and slowly died away.

I heard the wyvern shriek, somewhere out of sight.

"Holy Three!" Scorth was whispering. "Preserve us!"

I saw two thin gray tentacles sliding out of its armor from behind its head. Reaching toward us, they paused above us long enough for me to see that each ended in a cluster of delicate spiral coils. These wavered above as if somehow sensing us, and then picked us up.

My heart thudding hard, I could only stand there while that tentacle slid around my body beneath my arms. Strange as the black snake that crushed Bastard, they were quick but very gentle. Lifting us over the dragon's head, they set us on its back and held us there while it lurched into motion, carrying us on toward the tower.

The dragon's back was dark and slick, comfortably warm. It was careful with us, moving at an easy rocking gait. The tower loomed huge as we neared it, taller than the tower in Quar we had fled. We found the wyvern queen perched on a cinder mound just beyond it. She flapped her great black wings and shrieked as we came near, and the thunder of the dragons shook the ground again.

I saw the saddle box lying on the cinders as we came around the tower, and two human figures standing near it. One was the black-cowled mage, gripping his tall black serpent staff, but both were bundled against the cold in bulky brown flight leathers. I didn't recognize them until the dragon had set us gently down before them and backed away.

Argoth and Lyrane.

"Nuradoon!" Her voice had the eager lilt I could never forget. "We've been waiting."

Rosy with cold, her fair face had lit as if she liked me. I felt my heart thumping. With the fur parka pushed off her loose golden hair and her violet eyes innocently wide, she looked more the unspoiled schoolgirl than the willing consort of mages and demons. I hated her and wondered at her and longed to take her in my arms.

"Mr. Scorth." She smiled and bowed to introduce him. "Master mage Eighty-Nine. The next archimage, if our errand here succeeds."

Half-hidden under the cowl, Argoth's lean features stayed frozen into that blue-tattooed mask of sorrow and pain and ferocity that had frightened me whenever I saw him.

"Don't speak of that." A harsh, impatient rasp. "Nuradoon . . ." He paused, mad eyes probing me as if in search of more than he saw. "We have a task for you. A task in the service of the celestials."

"Before we talk about it—" I had to stop for nerve and breath "—I want the truth about my parents. Are they still in prison?"

"Guests, Mr. Nuradoon. They're guests of Xath. Do your work for us if you care about them, and they'll be free to leave the lectory."

The dragon had set us down on an uneven slope. The cinders slid under me, and his black, sharp-filed teeth grinned through his hideous blue tattoos as I staggered and waved my arms to get my balance back.

"We're starved." Frowning at the saddle box, Scorth turned hopefully to Lyrane. "If you have anything to eat."

"Later," Argoth snarled. "When your work is done—"

"Look at them." She shook her head in sympathy for Scorth, clumsily belted in his saddle-blanket coat, his naked scalp blistered red, his lips cracked and swollen. "They must have something now. I'll speak to Xath."

She looked up into the red-washed sky, clicking and singing the code she used with the demons. I heard the clink and ping and whistle, and saw the tiny globe pulsing red above us.

"Xath's unhappy," she said. "He lives in fire. He doesn't like this miserable cold. No more than I do." She trilled to it. "I've told him our errand must wait."

Scorth followed her to the saddle box.

"Errand?" I asked Argoth. "What do you want from us?"

"You will open a door."

In sudden luxury, we sat on the padded benches in the saddle box with blankets over our shivering knees. The demon floated low above us, its alien energies pulsing like blood through the spray of wiry tentacles. It buzzed and hummed and rattled while Lyrane dug into a compartment in the side of the box.

"We came to serve," Argoth muttered at her. "Not to picnic. The celestials don't countenance delay."

"They've waited a thousand years for Nuradoon." I heard a hint of mockery in her voice, perhaps for him, perhaps for me. She must have been uncertain what to think about the Nuradoon myth; I know she relished her own risky game. "They'll wait a few minutes more."

"They'll be angry."

"They're honest." Her tone reproved him. "They promised to keep us safe so long as we aid them. Keep our bargain, and we can trust them."

I asked uneasily, "What's the bargain?"

She let Argoth answer.

"The celestials want that weapon." His cold eyes probed me. "We suspect that it was left in the tower. If it was, you will secure it for us."

"So that's why you released us?" I asked Lyrane. "So you could follow us here?"

She shrugged and dug into her hamper for a bottle of water. It was nearly too cold to drink, but we gulped it eagerly.

"You're here," I said. "Why wait for us?"

"One slight problem." She was slicing bread and hard hopper cheese, but she paused to give Argoth an ironic glance. "The door is locked. We had no key."

"Neither do I." The bread and cheese had my saliva flowing. "I've always told you I know nothing at all about any weapon. I was never here before."

"Nuradoon was."

She and Argoth sat facing us across the saddle box. The black staff on a rack beside him, he held himself stiffly straight, eyes like wet black pebbles staring from under the cowl. She hummed and droned and whistled to the demon, listened to its humming and droning and whistling low overhead, and finally spoke to us.

"You may dislike the mages, but they aren't fools." I thought her half smile for Argoth seemed ambiguous. "They've just discovered a manuscript, or fragments of it, that dates from the last visitation. It records the interrogation of a man who had brought an ultimatum from the leader of the resistance group holed up here in these mountains.

"Remember?" Her glance at me was half inquiry, half ironic challenge. "Were you that leader?"

My mouth full of bread and cheese, I shook my head. Argoth growled something I didn't understand. The demon clicked and thumped.

"The leader's name is missing from the manuscript," she said. "But he must have been Nuradoon. If there was a Nuradoon." She paused to watch for my reaction. "He seems to have died under torture before he revealed the nature of the weapon, but he did describe the tower and drew a rough map of its location."

Under Argoth's forbidding scowl, she passed us an ice-cold bottle of golden delta wine.

"He had brought the celestials a warning to get off the planet and stay off. It contains the threat that they will be destroyed if they return. And it promises that the tower can be defended against all attacks."

I thought I saw a flicker of malice in her glance at Argoth, as if his glowering hostility amused her.

"There's no description of any defenses, but they've been successful enough. All through the centuries, occasional explorers have tried to get here. Mages after the weapon. Others after fabulous treasure the dragons were said to be guarding. Nobody got here—nobody who ever came back.

"Not till she could bring us here."

She nodded at the wyvern queen perched on her cinder mound.

"So the demons and the mages weren't treason enough for you?" I shook my head at her, as bitterly bewildered as I always had been. "You're playing your funny games with the wyvern and the werewolves too?"

"Please!" Her fair face flushed. "You don't know the truth. If the queen looks frightening, it's because you don't know her story."

"So?" Scorth muttered. "What's her story?"

"An unlucky wyck." She nodded again at the wyvern queen. "Caught in a storm before she'd learned to fly. Blown away from the mountain den, down into the highlands. A wolf hunter found her hurt and dying. He shot hoppers to feed her, trained her like a unicorn, rode her back over the mountains far enough to see the tower. He has made flights for the mages—"

"To raid the riding!" Scorth whispered. "Hunting men!"

He had been offering me the wine, but he had stiffened, yellow stare fixed on Lyrane. I sat lost in my own bitter recollections of the ragged blue scar of the wolf bite on my father's arm, of his exile from Dragonrock to the Little River farm, of my last glimpse of him and my mother on the river dock at Quar.

"Hunting men!" He turned to glare at Argoth. "You and your demons!"

Argoth shrugged, no change on his hooded face.

"Don't blame her." Lyrane gestured at the ungainly creature blinking those uncanny purple eyes at us from her perch on the cinder mound, and it shrieked as if in response. "She's stayed loyal. The trainer who saved her let her hunt and mate with her own kind, but she always came back to him, and more recently to his son.

"Blame the mages, if you like. They've been playing games of their own with the wolves and the wyvern, trying for any way to get here—the dragons don't mind the wyvern, I guess because they've always been denning in the peaks. Not that it ever did the mages any good. They've always failed to get into the tower or discover any sort of weapon."

The demon beeped impatiently, floating off toward the tower.

"Your task, Nuradoon." Argoth reached for his serpent staff. "Get to it."

I stood up unsteadily. Already giddy with hunger and exhaustion, I felt light-headed from the wine. Giddy enough to feel a moment of pity for all the privation and pain written on Argoth's stark face. Even my dread of the demon had faded; buzzing and clicking at me, it seemed only an annoying pest. Lyrane was radiant in the red moonlight, a dream of loveliness. I could almost believe that I really was the reborn hero.

"Ready, Nuradoon?" A bright expectancy shining in her eyes, she nodded toward the tower. "There's the door."

It stood on a knob of dead lava jutting out of the cinders. Walking with me toward it, Scorth stopped to squint at its base: an array of massive black metal rods, thicker than the body of a man, that supported it on enormous flanges half-buried in broken stone.

"It really is a ship?" Staring at those enormous rods and flanges, he turned to Argoth. "Did it bring the dragons?"

The demon drummed, and Argoth's serpent staff waved me toward a broad ramp that ran down from the bottom of it. Uneasily, no longer with any sense that I might ever be Nuradoon, I walked up the ramp to a deep recess in the wall. Lyrane came behind me with a little pocket light. She shone it to help me find the door.

I saw a black seam around it, but no hinges, no visible lock, no knob or handle, no possible way to open it. If the mages had really been here with chisels and drills and high explosive, they had left no mark I could see. Baffled, I turned to spread my hands at Argoth.

"Get it open."

"I have no key."

The demon clinked overhead, and I saw Argoth shudder.

"The celestials want it open," he gritted at me. "They don't care how."

"If I can't—"

"Your misfortune." His serpent staff thumped the cinders. "The misfortune of your parents in the Grugarn Lectory."

"You can do it." Lyrane smiled at me, blue eyes bright, her low-voiced words half an eager wish, half a mocking taunt. "If you are Nuradoon."

"You are." Scorth lifted his voice with a certainty I had never heard. "You've proved it. Getting here alive."

Unsure of anything, I felt under my shirt for the Dragonshield. It had dimmed, but the tower's green image shone again when I held it toward the moon. I walked back up the ramp and flashed it at the door.

Beyond the dark metal, something thudded like a distant hammer. Faintly something clanked and groaned. Flakes of rust flew from the seam around the door. The groan grew louder, rising to a whine. A massive slab of old metal slowly lifted. I saw darkness behind it, and caught a cold breath of strangeness.

I stepped back from it, trembling.

"So you are!" Lyrane was beside me, so close I felt the warmth of her breath. "You really are!" Her voice had fallen to a whisper, and I saw her pupils darken. "I wanted you to be, and never quite believed."

Urgently the demon pealed.

"Come!" She caught my arm. "Let's go in!"

"No!" Argoth's staff crunched hard into the cinders. "This can be another trap. Var will enter it alone." He thrust the staff toward me. "We'll wait for your return. The celestials are judging you. "Understand?"

The demon clinked, and I said I understood.

Lyrane gave me her pocket light, and Argoth rapped brittle orders at me.

"Explore the building. Keep alert. Careful what you touch and where you step. Note and remember everything you can. Don't delay. When you come back—"

"He's Nuradoon," Lyrane warned him, with an odd glance at me. "He'll have the weapon."

"We have his parents." He waved the black staff at Scorth. "And his friend."

At the top of the ramp, I looked back for a moment. Scorth shrugged and made his baby smile. Argoth glared sternly out of the black cowl. Lyrane waved her hand as if to say farewell. The wyvern queen raised her wings and shrieked again.

I caught my breath and walked into the tower.

48

The Pilot

The little pocket light found nothing beyond the door. Heart thumping, I walked into darkness, into still, cold air and a faint dry scent like the scent of my father's books when they had lain a long time unopened on their shelf against the bedroom wall. Something hummed behind me, and the dropping door sliced off the scarlet moonlight and silenced a startled warning from Scorth.

Still no Nuradoon, I stood there a long time, listening, stabbing that feeble beam around me, waiting for anything to happen, waiting for my rapid breath to slow, waiting for more courage than I found. I heard no sound, saw nothing but the dark.

Feeling trapped and helpless, I fumbled for the Shield and found the tower image gone. The whole face of it now shone green. Wondering what that might mean, I nursed the faith I had begun to find in its unknown powers and kept on searching the soundless dark.

As my eyes adjusted, I began to make out the walls around me, the smooth white walls of a narrow corridor that led away toward the center of the ship. They grew easier to see, until I realized that they had begun to glow with their own soft white radiance.

They grew slowly brighter, and I stood searching myself for resolution to go on. Must I wait for the daring of Nuradoon? Strange as the tower seemed, no harm had touched me. Perhaps my dreads were all imagination. Even a rat, I scolded myself, would scurry to explore any trap that caught him.

With no more need of the pocket light, I caught my breath and walked down the corridor. A door at the end slid silently open to let me into a small round room with no other opening. Flashing the Shield's green glow at the walls, I stood there waiting, my heart still thumping.

Nothing happened, until at last I heard a voice, so small and strange I wasn't sure at first that it had been a voice at all. It spoke a single syllable, the accent so odd that I didn't understand until it was repeated.

"Deck?"

"Deck?" I echoed. "Deck?"

"Which deck, sir, do you wish?"

The words came again before I felt sure they were words at all. I stood quite alone in the empty room, the smooth curve of its glowing wall bare of anything. I wished for Lyrane, even for Argoth and the demon. Anything I could understand.

"Top." At last I found an answer. "Top deck."

The door behind me closed. I felt no motion, but when it opened I was high in the ship, if this really was a ship. From the outside, I had seen no openings in its dark shell of long-weathered metal, but now the walls of this big round room seemed more transparent than glass.

Glancing out, I felt a moment of escape from perplexity, back into a world at least half familiar: the huge moon riding high, spilling its crimson light over the cinder mounds now far below; the wyvern queen, tiny as a songbird on her tiny hill. Even the saddle box. Scorth and Argoth and Lyrane were too near the entrance for me to see.

The voice had not spoken again. The stillness seemed somehow more than silence, the air colder than cold, as if the ghosts of things unknown were watching. Or had I grown too much like my mother, sharing all her Mystic dread of powers greater than her holy Three? My father, I thought, with his Realist faith in himself and the power of human understanding, would have done better here.

I stood there longing for him the way he had seemed when I was a child, the unbreakable spirit in his booming laugh and the iron strength of his great body. If the Shield had made me like him— It hadn't. I was jittery, breathing too fast, chilled with my own anxious sweat.

Trying to shuck off that unease, I turned to explore the room. The floor was a wide circle, most of it empty. A few desklike objects were spaced against that transparent wall. Some of them were topped with arrays of knobs and buttons that began to glow and wink with color when I came near them. I decided not to touch them.

"I wonder—"

I must have spoken aloud, because that inquiring voice startled me with another odd-sounding utterance.

"Service?" The strange accent baffled me until it spoke again. "Service, sir?"

"I'm looking for information." The voice had come from nowhere, as if the walls had spoken. "Where . . ." Shivering, I gulped to smooth my voice. "Why can't I see you?"

"No crew or passengers are now aboard, sir."

"So who is speaking?"

"Pilot, sir."

"Where are you?"

"Reference and control programs are stored in computers standing near you, sir."

"Is this—" I had to catch my breath. "Is this a ship?"

"Wavecraft *Far Ranger,* sir."

My old book, *The Legend of the Land,* had spoken of a wooden vessel that brought the first people up Dragon River from the sea, but not of wavecraft.

"Where . . ." I stopped to wonder at the colored lights winking on those boxlike shapes against the wall. "Where did you come from?"

"From Planet Earth."

Planet Earth? I'd never heard of any Planet Earth. Overcome with too much that was new and totally bewildering, I needed the comfort of something I knew. Breathing hard, I turned to look out again across the cinder fields. Strange as they were, I found a kind of comfort in a solitary dragon crawling toward the rust-red iron pyramid and the distant red-washed snows rising into the red-washed sky. My sense of realty a little restored, I turned back to discover whatever I could from the empty ship and the bodiless voice.

"How long was the voyage from Earth?"

"Duration of flight unknown, sir."

Searching those arrays of winking shapes and colors, I found no dials, no pointers or arrows or numerals or anything else I knew. "Don't you have clocks?"

"We are equipped with excellent chronometers, sir, but they are useless in wave flight. Wave speed is the velocity of light, which reduces time to zero. Chronometers stop."

The words had come too fast for me to make them out, and most of them were new. When I said I didn't understand, the voice repeated them, syllable by patient syllable, still no more familiar, still meaningless to me. I shook my head and tried to ask for something I might understand.

"When did you get here?"

"Landfall took place two thousand seventy-one Earth years ago, the equivalent of two thousand forty-four local years."

Time enough, I thought, for the ship to be forgotten.

"Can you go back?" I asked. "Back to this Planet Earth?"

"Impossible, sir. With time suspended in wave flight, no internal mechanism can measure distance traveled or stop the ship. Any trip continues until wave conversion is reversed, which happens only though encounter with an adequately powerful external gravity field. Our own reconversion for the landing here was initiated by close passage near this sun."

I stood there, blinking at the glowing walls, searching for any clear meaning in words I had not heard before.

"In any case," the voice was adding, "Earth can no longer resemble the planet we left. Our selected flight direction was toward a distant galactic cluster, which may or may not be the one in which we are now. Hundreds of millions of years must have passed on Earth since we left it. Possibly several billion."

Millions of years! Billions! Ages beyond imagination. The notion staggered me, stranger than the dragons or the ship or the voice itself. Understanding nothing, I had to look out again, at the red-lit ring of peaks around us. Mountains grown, perhaps, while the ship had been on its way. Shivering a little at that, I tried to collect myself for another question.

"Are other people still alive? On Earth or anywhere?"

"Impossible to say, sir. One hundred wavecraft were launched, ours among the last. They scattered in many directions, all toward remote galaxies, because we wished our seed to scatter and endure. Times in flight and distances made must have differed greatly. In this galaxy, in this era, we are no doubt quite alone."

Staring out at the snakes of crimson flame crawling over the dark-scarred face of the demons' moon, I shivered again and found a bright black worm digging its way into the cinders.

"Did you bring the dragons?"

"We brought no dragons, sir. Passengers and crew were members of your own race, the original settlers of this planet. We brought the seed of useful plants and frozen embryos of a few domestic animals, but no dragons were aboard. Though the mythologies of Earth made reference to dragons, no such actual creatures were known to exist there."

"They're here," I said. "These big metal-skinned monsters that appear to live underground all around the ship. They seemed about to attack us, until I showed them this."

I displayed the green-glowing Shield.

"Those drilling units are not known to us as dragons," the voice said. "They are cybers. Self-replicating cyberlife miners. They were released here to extract and refine metals useful to the colonists. The object you carry is a command token. It controls them."

Groping through a kind of daze in search of anything I might understand, I asked the voice to repeat and walked back to that transparent wall. Far across the red-lit cinders, one of the cybers broke out of a black ridge and lumbered toward the golden pyramid.

"The demons came for gold." Baffled by too many riddles, I turned back to face the empty walls. "They have their mages scouring the land for bits of gold. With a mountain of it here, why didn't anybody know?"

"The site was chosen for security," the voice said. "It is a natural fortress, and the cybers were programmed to repel enemies."

"Yet you tolerate the wyvern?"

"The creatures called wyvern and werewolves are natural predators. The colonists named them for the mythological creatures they happened to resemble. They are harmless to the ship. The only actual foes come from a red dwarf star. The colonists called them demons.''

"We came to search for some defense against them," I said. "We were guided by the token and the legend of a warrior named Nuradoon."

"We find no record of the name Nuradoon," the voice said. "You are the first in a thousand years, since the dwarf's last passage. Another soldier came at that time, also asking for a weapon. His name was Nur."

Nur? And Nuradoon? Were they the same? Had that mythic hero been real, and really reborn in me? Impossible. For all I felt, I was still the lonely farm boy from Little River who had dreamed of unicorns and the Dragonshield and grown up to be a potter.

Yet—

"This warrior Nur?" I whispered. "Did you give him a weapon?"

"We had none," the voice said. "We had left the tools and arts of war back on Earth, because too much war had wasted it. A mistake, perhaps, because even the native predators had been a peril to the colonists, even before the demons descended to sweep them near extinction.

"We gave the defenders the aid we could, and shared useful data from our memory banks when the star had carried the demons away. Through the next thousand years, they were able to begin the recovery of their crippled culture, reclaiming the delta and spreading new settlements up the Dragon before the dwarf and the demons came back with a second age of terror. Another thousand years have gone. This raid is the third."

"So we're helpless?" I muttered when it paused. "Condemned to be crushed back forever, every thousand years?"

"Not so," it said. "Have you forgotten? We warned the soldier Nur of this invasion, but also informed him that it would be the last."

"The last?" I stood blinking into the emptiness, wanting something real, something human, to confirm what I had heard. "How— how can that be?"

"Look into the token."

The face of the Shield was black again when I lifted it. A white dot shone near one edge. A thin green line ran straight across the other. They were linked by three dotted red ellipses.

"The white point represents the sun." The voice spoke with a quiet precision I took for certainty. "The green line is the path of a passing star, one so massive that it cannot shine. The ellipses show orbits of the dwarf, which have allowed it to make three close approaches. Fortunately, it follows the invisible star. After this passage, it will be taken too far to return."

49

Aftermath

The voice and the shifting glow of the walls guided me off the ship. A flash of the Shield opened the outside door. Back in the red glare of the sinking moon and the sulfur-tainted cold of the great caldera, I heard the demon peal and saw it in the air before me, floating over Lyrane.

"Nuradoon!" Her face lit with what I thought was actual joy. "I was praying for you."

Scorth had fallen asleep in the saddle box, but our voices woke him. He stumbled to join us, rubbing at his bleary eyes and still groggy with fatigue. Argoth came back from the hill where the wyvern perched.

"The weapon?" His haggard eyes searched me from under the cowl. "Did you get it?"

"There is no weapon," I said. "There never was."

The demon dived at Lyrane, ringing sharply. She flinched as if it had tried to strike her. Scorth shivered, blinking in sleepy dismay.

"I warned you!" Argoth grinned through his monstrous mask. "I always warned you!"

"We need no weapon," I told him. "I was told of something better. Your demons and their moon will never return."

"You lie!" Hooded eyes glaring, he hammered the cinders with his staff and swung on Lyrane. "Xath is no coward, to be terrified by your pretending Nuradoons."

"Perhaps he can recognize the truth." I flashed the Shield at the beeping demon. "Let him look at this."

He whirled back at me, as if to swing his staff. Lyrane caught his arm.

"Nuradoon . . ." She breathed the name, and I thought she was utterly bewitching. "What have you found?"

"The tower is the ship that brought us here. The human colony. The crew gave us the Shield as our key to the science and the history of our civilization, stored in computers aboard. It holds a star map that shows why the red star won't come back—"

The demon dived at me, shrieking.

"Our sun." I held the Shield toward it, pointing. "The green line is the path of an invisible star passing by. The red lines show the dwarf's shifting orbit around the black star. After this passage, it will be too far to return—"

Xath darted at Argoth before I could finish, flashing and howling till Argoth had to back away, hands lifted to shield his face.

"Xath is furious." Lyrane smiled as if his helpless fury amused her. "If you knew this, why wasn't he told?"

"But we didn't—didn't know," he gasped his protests. "All we had was myth and rumor. We've searched desperately for the truth—"

The demon hovered over me, whistling and squealing. Crouching away from it, I felt my skin prickle, felt its ozone sting in my eyes. Red-blazing tentacles snatched the Shield away from me, held it close to its red-pulsing heart for a moment, flung it to the cinders. I heard a brittle pop. A thin sharp reek of ozone lingered in the air, but the demon was gone.

For a long moment we all just stood there. I heard the wyvern's high-pitched bellow. Argoth shouted something. Lyrane laughed. Scorth blinked at me, lemon eyes wide. Shivering in the icy air, I stared at Lyrane.

"Well, Mr. Nine!" Her soft laugh mocked Argoth. "I think we've said good-bye to your demon friends!"

I watched his hideous, dark-scarred mask quiver and dissolve into tears.

"Too bad for you." She shook her head in mock regret. "Because you'll never be an archimage. I'm almost sorry—" She shook her head, looking hard at him. "I know you meant to kill me when you could, but now—"

She turned to grin at me.

Scorth sang in the unicorn language to call the wyvern queen down from her cinder hill and made her lift the saddle box with her fearful black-fanged jaws and long prehensile tongue, and set it on her back. She carried us back to the flight stage at Dragonrock. Scorth slept through most of the flight, but he found bags of suncorn and rode her back into the high Dragons to rescue Sharabok.

In Targon, we found the land without a leader. The old primarch and most of his government had died at the hands of the mages. The archimage had sacrificed himself in a temple burned around him in a ceremonial meant to bring the demons back. The dark magic of the mages disappeared with their departure; the black flames had died on the altars, and the black serpent staves were suddenly only dead wooden sticks.

My parents were still shut up in the Grugarn Lectory, but we found them safe. Free again, my father regained enough of his old rugged fitness to serve through the next two years as acting primarch and organize the election of a ruler to replace him. Refusing to be a candidate, he returned to his old seat on the Dragonrock.

All that happened nearly five years ago. The red dwarf dwindled in the sky and finally disappeared, even from Kallenayo's rebuilt telescope at the Targon observatory. He followed it until it disappeared, and he assures me it is indeed the captive of a massive unseen companion, moving on a path that will take it away forever.

My father and mother live again in Dragonrock castle, though she spends much of her time in her pottery outside the walls. She looks younger now, and happier. They often fly together on Falcon Child and Rellion Pride, the sorrel stallion the Lady Kye has given him.

At breakfast with them on a recent visit, I heard their old debate resumed, as amiably as ever. He reminded her that the Realist science of the ship had brought people to the world and promised now that the demons could never trouble us again.

"No great danger, even if they could come back, because we've learned to trust ourselves." And he added, with a teasing grin at her. "Realist science over Mystic superstition!"

"Rennie!" she protested. "Please—"

Ignoring her, he reached across the table to offer me his dark-tanned hand, the scar of the wolf bite still winding up his forearm. He did look fit to trust. Though the years had left gray in his hair, his thick beard was still streaked with color and he sat very straight.

"Thanks to you!" He was beaming through the fiery beard. "For proving one more time that human brains and guts and muscle can always beat the dark. My son, I'm proud of you!"

"I'm no kind of hero." Uncomfortable, I had to shake my head. "No matter what anybody did, it was all sheer luck, bad and good. Blind chance that the black hole brought the red dwarf here and dragged it away again—"

"Blind chance?" My mother's lips quivered with emotion, and I saw her dab at her eyes with a napkin. "Your Realist science may rule the universe, but it was the holy Three who put us here and see to our survival."

She smiled at me, wet eyes shining.

"Who else arranged the orbits of the demon star?"

Scorth wants to build a railroad, with tunnels under the highest passes, to let us haul out the metals the dragons have piled up for us in those great pyramids. The wyvern queen could bring out gold to pay for it, but my father says it has to wait until the land is better recovered from the mages and the demons.

Lyrane and I have spent most of the summers back aboard the

ship, when decent weather lets Scorth fly us there. Listening to Pilot's lectures and studying records and machines, we're learning all we can of the science and civilization the colonists brought from Earth. We bring our notes and copies back to Targon, where she has set up what she calls the Nuradoon Library.

She is filling it with historic manuscripts salvaged from the archives of the mages as well as our records from the ship. She named it for me, because she says I'm the actual Nuradoon, the man who finally banished the demons and began the world's recovery. More honor than I ever asked for, but this narrative was written in my office in the building.

If there's any honor, it should go to her. Though I once took her for a traitor to our race, she always did what she could to shield us from the demons and ease the demands of the mages. And it was she, of course, who put the Shield in my hands and let me reach the ship.

At least she is winning an unexpected distinction as an academic scholar. Her encounters with the demons seem to have sharpened a real linguistic gift. In our studies of the old archives and the ship's computer records, she finds meanings in the jargon of the ancient mages and the languages of the old Earthmen that confuse the rest of us. She has become such an authority on the invasion that I like to call her the demon queen.

I've seen the Lady Kye in Targon. She's now the Countess Kye, since she discovered that Count Rellion's will left the family title and estates to her. She spends her life breeding and training and racing unicorns. I told her once that time would surely heal her wounds.

"I'll never marry again." She was blunt about it. "Your Uncle Thorg was more than enough for me."

For now, at least, she seems content with her unicorns.

Adjustment has been harder for the mages. Branded forever with their red skulls and black teeth and snarling tattoos, they can't go into hiding, even despised and hated as they are. Many still live in their old lectories, feeding themselves from garden plots and little farms on the lands they had claimed for Xath. A few still work as carpenters and craftsmen, building homes instead of sacrificial fanes.

Argoth found a woman he believes to be his mother, sick and starving in the slums of Targon. He moved her into a country villa vacated by an uncowled master mage. Said to be ungrateful, she spends the money he gives her on the schemes of rogue ex-mages who promise to recover the magic of Xath and use it to restore the fortune and beauty she once enjoyed.

Retiring soon, my father has arranged for me to replace him on the Dragon seat. He has begun renovating the old Var palace in Targon, but my mother wants a simpler life. She is having a small country home built on the Little River farm. She wants Lyrane to marry me and become the new Lady Rider, but Lyrane says she isn't ready. She enjoys her independence, but we are good companions.

Scorth has taught her to ride Black Dragon, the fine black stallion Argoth gave her when he closed the old temple stables. She sings to unicorns instead of demons now. My father has given me Sharabok, who somehow seems to understand my own halting signals. Our best times are those when we ride together into the high wilderness beyond the wyvern border. Our favorite spot is a narrow valley below the snow, where hot springs keep a deep pool warm enough so we can strip and swim.

On fine summer days, the unicorns unsaddled and grazing on the lush sweetgrass, we spread the blankets for our lunch and finish a bottle of delta wine. Always dazzling when she comes nude and dripping from the steaming water, pink with the mountain chill, she seems lovelier when we have found wolf tracks in the sand around the pool, loveliest when a werewolf's eerie howl makes her hold me harder and cry out with joy.

One of the true pioneers of science fiction, Jack Williamson started writing the same year that the first SF magazine, *Amazing Stories,* appeared. Since 1926 he has written some of SF's acknowledged classics—*The Humanoids, The Legion of Space,* and *Seetee Ship,* to name a few. His work has always been on the leading edge of scientific extrapolation; his concepts of robots and antimatter remain fascinating decades after their original publication. Along the way, he wrote an SF comic strip, *Beyond Mars,* and after earning his Ph.D. in English literature at the age of fifty, taught one of the first SF courses in a university curriculum. In 1976 he was named a Grand Master by the SFWA, only the second writer to be thus honored. A two-time president of that organization, he has continued to be active in it, and his novels continue to demonstrate an agile and questing mind that after more than eighty years is still fresh.